PRAISE FOR

"Patch Work, so aptly entitled, conveys, urgently and movingly, the human capacity to encompass the fundamentals of a life, hitherto not fully lived; indeed, to encompass life itself. It is a story of love, of loss, and, most significantly of regeneration.

As the many glorious flowers and plants in the story unfurl, and the pages rapidly turn, more authentic a personality emerges after many years of drought, and the embers of life gather force and light. Dorothy Judd, in the person of her central character, draws on an adult lifetime of psychotherapeutic understanding to explore the depths of individual development, the poignancy and glory of the lifecycle, the significance of time and renewal.

The pages capture the deep significance of transience itself."

Margot Waddell,
Author, Fellow of the British Psychoanalytical Society and Visiting Lecturer at the Tavistock Clinic.

"Dorothy Judd's stunning prose paints pictures of the interiors of her characters' minds, laying bare their failings and triumphs with razor-sharp acuity. Like a Lucian Freud portrait, her writing has a beautiful honesty."

Rebecca Mascull
Author of The Visitors, Song of the Sea Maid, and The Wild Air

"Dorothy Judd's background as a consultant psychotherapist in the field of dying and bereavement adds rich depth to these powerful themes. The smell and warmth of rural France in the summer are exquisitely evoked as active participants in this mature reflection of conflict and growth at the point of death. Poignant, exciting and ultimately restorative, Patch Work deals with the major issues without sentimentality or cowardice."

Dr Valerie Sinason
PhD MACP Member Institute of Psychoanalysis

DOROTHY JUDD
PATCH WORK

love and loss

A NOVEL

@iamselfpub
www.iamselfpublishing.com

'The foxglove blossom – a third part bud, a third part past, a
third part in full bloom – is a type of the life of this world.'
John Ruskin – *On Art and Life*, 1853

'In dreams begins responsibility.'
- Old Play
Quoted in *Selected Poems*, W. B. Yeats

For my father, Samuel Woolf.

"J", who invited me to travel alongside her journey towards death.

And to little "R", for whom I first went through fire, forever changed.

Dorothy Judd was born in 1944 in apartheid South Africa, and as a child of 11 faced the profound experience of loss and exile when her family emigrated to London. It is not surprising that those early experiences informed and enriched her professional life, first as an art therapist and then as a child, adolescent, adult and marital psychotherapist. In her clinical and research work, disability, loss, transience and bereavement were her key contributions that culminated in her seminal book, *Give Sorrow Words – working with a dying child* (Karnac, 2014 – 3rd Edition.)

And now she explores those preoccupations in the form of a novel.

Dorothy is married to the historian and writer, Denis Judd, and they have four children and six grandchildren.

In 2016, she was longlisted by Cinnamon Press for *Patch Work* in their debut novelists' competition.

AUGUST 19TH, 2003

A screech and a crash tore through the fabric of her dream.

She held her breath.

And listened.

A brief silence was broken by sudden bird calls. Threads of light illuminated the shutters' edges and the clock showed a quarter past six.

It could have been part of a dream. She tried to go back to sleep.

But turning on her back, she lay still, straining to listen. Imagining. *One of the farm vehicles failing to brake or Annette going off early, as she said she would. That steep drop by the* mirabelle *tree. . . . a blurred figure falling? Was that in my dream? A crash through the trees. Yet, no one else was around here for miles.* Her heart drummed high in her throat. Now sleep was impossible.

Like someone drunk, Jane rose. Stumbling to open the shutters, she flung her fleece jacket over her nightdress and pulled on her trainers, cursing that she would lack a phone if Annette had left for the Pyrenees already.

To calm herself, she told herself that it was probably nothing, perhaps one of those wild boars that roamed here – though it sounded like a herd of them.

She unlocked the front door and zipped the key into her pocket while running towards the bend in the little road.

In those few seconds, she smelt the pellucid air and soaked up the freshness after the stifling heat of the previous day, and noticed the yellow-smudged eastern sky. This was what she had escaped to France for – this pure intake of nature.

11

She rounded the bend. *Was this the place from where the noise had come?*

There was the *mirabelle* tree with its orange baubles, but the trunk seemed crooked. A branch low down was broken and bent, its fruit dangling futilely over the drop.

Such silence, innocent calm. *Nothing bad could have happened. Unless, unless someone is dead.*

Peering closer through the dense viridian, she could see a line of branches newly torn, like limbs ripped off by shellfire, leaving the pallid flesh of tree trunks exposed.

Holding onto a sapling to anchor herself, she called, 'Hello, hello.' Hesitant at first, she then became bolder, 'Hell-ooo…?' How Jane longed for someone like a farm worker to appear, rattling along on his tractor.

Oh God, what now? Drive to Ceneyrac and ring the police, perhaps for nothing. What if this undergrowth damage was simply from someone dumping an old sofa over the edge. So very early in the day? Perhaps an ambulance would be more appropriate? She rounded on herself to be more decisive when time could be of the essence.

How she hated that phrase: '*time may be of the essence.*' How it reverberated with what they had told her at the hospital. *Yet, how could a few days make much difference when they'd said it was 'palliative'?*

Jane chose to follow the loop of the road, knowing it wouldn't do any good if she got injured by clambering down the precipice. As she ran downhill, she glimpsed something red, deep in a thicket. This flash of unnatural colour sickened her further. She was determined to find that red thing – tractor, car, harvester, dumped sofa.

She stopped to peer hard into the depths of this jungle. Annette's car was silver. Pausing at a point lower down the steep incline where the ground levelled out, she crossed a corner of a maize field, through the narrow gaps between the straight rows and veered off into the forest. Wiping the perspiration from her upper lip, she prayed for it not to be too bad. Those ripped branches returned to her mind and the screech that had entered her dream before the crashing sounds.

'Hell-ooo, hello! *Je peut vous aider?*' But her voice sounded weak, absorbed by the pine needles and leaf mould underfoot. She tried to ignore the scratches from brambles, painful nettle stings and her ripped nightdress. There was an unexpected further drop nearby, and a sheer rocky area that she could not traverse. It was all much more difficult than she had imagined. She found herself going further away from the red object and this indirect route was no easier than making a beeline for it.

She marvelled at how on earth they ever made detailed maps. Feeling so little and helpless, she could see why rescue teams used helicopters. Almost in tears, she contemplated failure and envisaged the dragging walk back. She would then have to pull on some clothes, before driving to the nearest telephone box, eight winding kilometres away, where she would tell her story and hand it over to others. Why had she not decided that in the first place? The thought that she was driven beyond her capabilities to help someone in mortal danger frightened her. But perhaps there was nothing untoward here, after all.

And now she was wasting time, standing still.

She gave a last call through cupped hands, throwing her voice up to the sky. This action reminded her of Lennie. Whenever he was near water, he became boyish and saw how far he could throw a stone or spit over a bridge to see the blob land far below, always trying to propel himself further. The silence felt more absolute after her shouting. A grating sound, followed by – possibly – a slight thud.

'Ye-es? Who's there?' she called.

Then, unmistakably, a soft growl, like an animal.

'Where are you? Please, please call out! *Repondez, pitié!*' In a panic, she tried to follow the debris of the trees and the patches of ploughed-up forest floor. Leaves and branches whirled fast around her like smeared paint. 'Yes?' she called again, loudly.

13

This time the answer came quite clear. A man's voice said, *'Je suis là, ici! Comment vous voulez que je sache où? Je suis coincé... dans cette putain de voiture. Mon dieu... trouvez...* Please, please find me!'

Now she knew that the person was lower down, in the further drop beyond the rocks. 'I'm coming!' she called, pleased at how optimistic *'J'arrive'* sounded. Clambering over a small hill of earth and a short rockface, she ignored the merciless thistles and found footholds and handholds from outcrops of ferns and grasses, before peering over to see a red car on its side, still and tranquil.

Birds sang as if they accepted this rude start to their day, and they and the undergrowth were already absorbing it. Jane briefly allowed her mind to play a trick with perspective and scale, turning this into an abandoned child's toy.

But reality broke through with panic, not knowing if she could cope, or what she would find.

'I'm coming!' she called again heartily, masking her fear. *Thank goodness he speaks English.*

This must be a dream from which she would wake. She pictured the car going *bumpity-bump bumpity-bump* down the slope like a cartoon, flattening vegetation and landing gently with no harm to the occupant. For the first time, she thought that there might be more than one person. *Children?* The closer to the vehicle she came, the more she felt as if she was watching a film in slow motion, noticing details like a particular yellow heart-shaped leaf on the loamy ground, and the beauty of the red car against the dark green – like the Bishop of Llandaff dahlias she had grown last summer. She registered a scrape on the side of the car, and a large dent in the roof as if it were a piece of sculpture catching the sunlight.

Yet, the vehicle was surprisingly shiny and smart, and the glass of the windows apparently intact. Petrol fumes overwhelmed the green forest smell.

She kept up a commentary with whoever had called out to her, shouting, 'Yes, I'm coming! Won't be long now!' while sliding down the other side of the boulders and pulling her nightdress down for protection. If only she had put on pants before dashing out.

Soon she was by the car, which lay on its side.

Peering down through an open window that faced the small triangle of sky way above the trees, with this strange sideways perspective, she saw a man lying still in the gloom, looking quite comfortable on his side, pressed between the glass and the steering wheel. Perhaps he was not the one who had called out. With a jolt, she realised he could be dead.

'*Monsieur, monsieur, ça va?*' she whispered.

'No...' muttering something that she could not hear. 'What d'you think!'

Glancing at the disorienting sideways space, she noticed strewn clothes, a canvas bag, wine bottle – probably empty – shoes and plastic bags.

She found herself suddenly shouting, 'Anyone else with you?'

'No,' he replied, giving a little laugh. 'It's enough...,' his eyes remaining closed.

She reached in and gently touched his arm, '*Monsieur?*'

The young man – for he seemed to be about thirty – half opened one eye and groaned, '*Ma jambe, ma jambe. Mon dieu, ça devait arriver!*' He rolled his eyes upwards before closing them again.

'Oh, could be worse, much worse,' she found herself uttering. 'Where does it hurt?'

Her talent for being good at 'first aid' in all its varieties, from emotional to physical, sensible and practical, rose to the occasion. As a girl, she had told her mother that she wanted to be a Boy Scout when she grew up, not a Brownie. 'Brownies' with an 'ee' sound on the end seemed so little and helpless.

'Let's see if this door can open,' she said, hoping that her optimism would seep through to the stranger. '*Voila!*' she opened the door skywards, trying to enfold him in her stream of words, English and French. 'These new cars have such solid doors. Thank goodness. Well, then, here we are. *Et voila.*'

Now nothing separated her from this prone thin stranger with his sharp beard and sunken unshaven cheeks, ragged jeans, which might have been torn months or years ago, and rank alcoholic breath. She took his wrist and felt his pulse, though was never sure about her accuracy in this matter. Now following her instincts more, she continued, '*Monsieur, vous êtes-vous cogné la tête? Pourquoi avez-vous l'air sonné?*' She climbed down across the front seat, careful not to fall onto him, and felt his brow as if he were one of her sons. Not surprising, she thought, about a bump on one side of his head and a small gash in his cheek. He was wearing a seatbelt, she noted.

Should I move him or get help?

As if reading her thoughts, he said, 'I'll be fine, *Madame*, I'll be okay. Just my bloody leg – can't feel it.'

'You don't sound too bad!' Jane exclaimed, relieved at his good English.

'And my throat, or my lips,' gesturing down his throat with his mouth open. 'Something down my throat. *Du sang?*' She felt a wave of panic. *Perhaps he isn't alright, after all. The human body is so fragile, so many things that could go wrong.*

She peered into the gloom, as he trustingly opened his mouth, breathing his fetid breath. 'No, can't see anything funny, I don't think. Only a bit swollen – your top lip. Maybe cut a bit inside? But we'll get you checked over. Gosh, you're lucky, could have...'

'Lucky! *C'est déjà pas mal!* I don't think so! *Merde,* you don't know half of it.'

She glanced again at the dishevelled contents of the car and began to wonder what his story was.

'Now then, undo your seatbelt, can you? And how about I go and find someone, perhaps a farmer – try not to let yourself go to sleep – or I'll walk, run, back to get my car and drive to Ceneyrac, where I can ring for an ambulance. Okay? Oh, unless you have a phone?'

'No, definitely not,' he interrupted. 'No ambulance! And no, no phone. I'll be alright. I already decide I'll leave the car here. Too bad about that. People can believe it's been stolen, disappeared. I'll soon recover. Really. No one need ever know.' He made an enormous effort to appear normal, forcing a wry smile. With his glassy eyes wide open, he tried to focus on Jane, despite his disadvantageous position.

She could easily believe that the car would lie here for hundreds of years, rusting and merging with the undergrowth, perhaps never to be discovered in this corner of France. But Jane sensed that she had collided with another's story, one that was complicated and possibly even sinister. She had not come all this way to have to deal with a stranger's drama. She began to wish she had never tried to help him.

'But why? Why, *Monsieur*, why all this rush into... into normality, when you have just had a terrible accident?'

His eyes blurred and closed.

Oh God, he's probably concussed. Of course, I will have to get help. Maybe taking a solitary holiday without Lennie wasn't such a good idea. If he were here, we'd manage somehow.

She heard a small plane overhead. Perhaps somehow the news was out, and people were already searching.

'Well, now, *Monsieur* – what's your name?'

He stumbled as he said, 'Ch...,' breathing deeply, turning 'Ch' into a sigh. 'Pierre, Pierre Baudier.'

'Okay, and I'm Jane. English, as you've gathered. Well, Pierre, I'll go and get help as soon as I can, you just wait here. Any water in your car?'

He interrupted her with a wail of protest, 'No, *Madame*, you must not go, I said already, no need to bring in others.' His lip curled as he spoke, a hunted look in his eyes. She was reassured that there was so much fight in him, but disturbed that he must have something big to hide.

A familiar pain in Jane's left side reared up, her back ached, and now the troublesome vision in her right eye blurred the sight of this frail man.

'Listen, *Monsieur*', abandoning the intimacy of his name, especially when she suspected it was not the real one. 'I am not sure I can deal with this,' she admitted, working it out as she went along. 'I also have to do what I think is best. I know it's… your life, and your car, and your accident, but how can I just ignore your injuries when you land at my feet like this, when you may have serious injuries, and then if you… haemorrhage or something, how do you think I'll feel?'

'*Allez vous faire foutre!* You can go, *Madame* English woman. Yes, bog off. Sorry to be rude, but this is my body. And my accident. This is not the time for me to consider you. You're worse than my mother, God rest her soul! *Merde!*' he cried out, fighting back tears.

Jane withdrew into the shade, breathing hard, also trying not to cry. She was shocked at how much his situation echoed her own, and her need to decide for herself what to do about her cancer and her treatment. Knowing she hadn't really begun to find a sane path for herself, how could she now impose a moral high ground of 'oughts' and 'shoulds' onto a stranger?

Thinking and breathing fast, she decided to cooperate with his wishes for the time being. In her hyper-alert state, she noticed that Pierre had not claimed the car as his own when he'd listed his body and his accident.

She came forward into his line of vision, 'Alright, Pierre, I will help you, as best I can… with your body, even if I don't know what on earth is going on with you.' Her voice trembled but her mouth was set. 'In the way you want, maybe. I realise there's far more here than meets the eye. Okay then, try and see how much you can move.'

He nodded slightly and a tear meandered down the cheek of this truculent man, surprising Jane.

'You live near here, *Madame*?' he asked, barely audibly. 'Somewhere I can… sort myself out?' Although she did not recognise his accent, she thought he talked like an educated young man, despite his rough appearance. 'Won't take long – depends on the leg,' he continued, raising his head slowly, stretching his arms upwards, which was sideways from Jane's perspective. 'Bugger, my neck. Who else lives there with you?'

Knowing she was taking a risk in trusting him, Jane told him she was staying alone for about a week in a rented house nearby. Her own extreme circumstances made her more foolhardy, not less. 'But there's a landlady in the house right next to it,' she added.

As if my own drama isn't dramatic enough.

AUGUST 18TH, 2003

Jane Samuels' mouth turned downwards, even as a child. People used to say to her, "It's not so bad!" or "It may never happen!" or "Cheer up!"

On the day of her arrival at her holiday house, she gave a weak, straight-lipped smile at the irony of choosing this place, called *La Retraite,* and finding that it was right next to a graveyard. Only a strip of harvested wheat as sharp and stubby as a wire brush separated her rented property from the plastered perimeter walls enclosing the plot of bodies that had rested there for anything from a few days to seven hundred years. A derelict chapel anointed by a crooked cross watched over the graves and the little shrine.

Annette du Plesis had shown the newcomer the layout of the cottage.

Why bother, I know this is the toilet, that the bedroom – I'm sure everything I really need to know is in the visitors' book. I haven't come all this way to prop up a lonely French woman with English connections, who insists on speaking old-fashioned English, even though I'd rather converse in French.

Annette gestured out of the bedroom window. 'Sorry about inclement weather! You must be overbowled by the rain. So sorry!' *She seems to think the climate really is her responsibility.* Annette's words spewed out like the rain thundering down at that moment, yet she took the time to enunciate her English so well. 'This is going to be rrestored!' she announced as she pointed at the chapel. 'It's a Templiers chapel, you know.'

'Thank you, thanks, that's fine. Lovely. Yes. I'm sure that's all I need to know... about the cottage. Fine, yes.' Drawing upon her dwindling courage, she added, 'All I really want is somewhere quiet, somewhere to paint and... think.'

'Oh, you are a painteur! What do you make? The landscape?'

'Oh no. Not really, Nanette,' shrugging. 'Perhaps. This and that,' she added, wishing she had never begun to explain. She decided that the less said the better with this woman.

'It's sufficient to have something to do,' the landlady responded wistfully. 'Something...' swallowing her words with a shrug.

Later, Annette would say to her English husband, '*L'anglaise* doesn't look very well. Needs a holiday. You know, her face gets sort of under shadowed when I talk. Anyways, she's not really English, is she? Something a little... Arab about her. Stevern, you're not listening to me.'

But back in the present, she added to Jane, with a half-smile, 'Me, I'm just biting my time, you see,' before adding, from the doorway, 'Oh yes, and if you want to maintain the place cold, cool, close the shutters, particularly in the afternoons.'

Jane nodded with a smile. Her eyes remained remote.

'Well, I must depart, must continue with my cleaning,' the older woman said, as if the visitor was holding her up. 'After all, I'm the hinchpin around here. My husband is away a great deal. But, by the way, it does not really matter, but my name is called *Ann*ette.'

Jane apologised with genuine feeling, taking a step towards the French woman.

Her mistake had touched her own sense of discomfort, even displacement, when people did not remember her name correctly. 'June', 'Jean' or 'Joan', and sometimes 'Samuel' instead of 'Samuels' for her surname. This indicated a carelessness on their part, as if they had no interest in who she might really be.

When she read and loved *Jane Eyre* at the age of sixteen, she had begun a transformation from the 'plain Jane' associations of her name. Although the protagonist was plain, she was so thoughtful and quietly passionate that the scrap-of-a-name, the staid-Jane, developed into a more rounded open sound, the mouth and voice chiming a positive note for Jane Woolf, as she was then. Jane began to believe the meaning of her name fitted her nature: from Janus, the god of gateways who looked both in and out and was, therefore, the god of endings and beginnings. Hence, her birthday month, January, was also derived from this name. Years later, she learnt that 'Jane' did not stem from Janus after all, and worried that she was wearing borrowed garments. But, by then, she had grown into the name and liked it. She wondered whether borrowed things could become one's own, if there was no one demanding them back over time.

Lennie called her 'Janey' even before they married. That had been alright then, and for years and years, but commensurate with a growing sense of her more solid self, that diminution had begun to irritate her.

Surrendering her maiden name of 'Woolf', after years of teasing and misspellings, had been another matter when she married Lennie Samuels. As a young adult, she had, at last, come into a surname that sounded right. This garment fitted well.

Jane noticed how easily Annette was relieved at that moment of warmth from her, the guarded eyes briefly flickering with something more hopeful. She observed the retreating figure's shape, like an upside-down pear: her fulsome torso, narrow hips, and slim legs.

Jane sat on a white limestone plinth that was part of a grave in the small cemetery. It was set amongst the motley graves and cypresses and the blighted, solitary cedar. The parched, gravelly ground was littered with fallen pinecones and empty tiny snail shells.

She narrowed her green-grey eyes in the glare from the overhead sun before rolling up her white cotton trousers, kicking off her sandals, and opening the top buttons of her blouse. Her head rested against the gravestone. The inscription had faded beyond recognition.

The white sun flamed down on her bare arms, face, feet, and on her grey curly hair, scorching her covered thighs. Like someone released from prison, she breathed deeply. She did not need to bother with sun-protection lotion any longer. But then, was it the other way round, was she really adjusting to a life, or what was left of it, inside a prison of a sort?

Lately, Jane had considered all the things that she did which were an integral part of taking care of herself, like cleaning and flossing her teeth, not eating too much chocolate, nor the succulently grilled fat on a lamb chop, or the tastiest part of a roast chicken: the crispy fatty skin. Or bacon fat, driving carefully, being cautious about not falling down stairs, eating organic vegetables, putting on moisturising face cream at night, taking vitamins and minerals of dubious value. She found herself continuing to do the things that might prevent added complications or discomfort to the life she had left, but gradually decided not to bother with the many things designed to boost her wellbeing in ten or twenty years' time, or which carried a vague promise of prolonging life. But then was she self-destructive? Was this precisely the time she should be more careful, more determined to do whatever she could? How hard to find the balance...

Soaking up the heat that almost hurt her arms, she basked in some tranquillity for the first time since setting off on her journey here. She remembered the day of the diagnosis a few weeks ago. Or rather, the recurrence. But no, that wasn't the first shock. She had not felt at ease since she first noticed things that she had tried to ignore, but then came the lump – no, lumps – and strange aches and pressures in her body that refused to be ignored. Their word, 'aggressive', which they used about her breast cancer five years ago, came back to her mind. She saw it as a persistent rat that would not give up, making an inevitable return.

Jane sighed deeply, a sigh with a tremor midway, as if she had been sobbing. Her breaths carried hiccups of distress as a memory of the tension between herself and Lennie darted into her mind, making her chest feel tight.

A cicada started its loud sawing nearby. That and the occasional sweet twitter of a linnet emphasised the silence.

Oh yes, Jane, it's easier to be pessimistic. You know where you are with that. Black and white. Death or life. One excluded, and yet defined the other. But it's the in-between, where the two worlds are both in some balance, that's so hard.

A few years ago, Jane would not have been sure that she wanted this little church to be restored, even if they had done it well in their solid French way, with wide pale grouting and original details lovingly repaired. The preserved large stones protruded from the walls without any obvious reason, like harmless warts, and there would, no doubt, be strong new guttering of galvanised zinc.

For she felt that restoration sometimes masked the passing of time and the inevitably of death. Jane had always admired the way that nature overran whatever lay in its path, adding the patina of lichen or moss, mould or fungus, weeds or ferns, or even a gradual erosion or disease, or a crumbling into dust of what had once been solid – emphasising how small and helpless man's place in the world was when organic processes could hold sway over people's strivings.

But now her illness made these thoughts far more complex. Her overview was challenged by the choices open to her, involving drastic interventions to postpone a premature death. Jane knew she had to use this time to try to understand the bobbing thoughts that sought the surface, like corks.

The more she worked as a psychotherapist, the more she realised how complex everything was – even though she had been doing the work for twenty-five years.

She began to feel exhausted, leeched by the sun, almost dizzy. It was hard to believe that she had only arrived the previous evening. Wiping the perspiration from her lip, she relished the pleasant alternatives of whether to have a sleep or a swim.

She rose, aware of a persistent ache in her left hip, and slipped on her sandals. As she opened the iron gate its latch-clang tolled across the fields and beyond into a vast emptiness.

She promised herself that she would return here one evening when it was cooler.

As Jane swam length after length in the jade-green pool, her naked body moved easily in the welcoming silky water, her breast-stroke hardly causing ripples, her shiny seal head emerging only for breath. The more she swam, the more she felt a joy and a radiance, a connection with something that she dared call sublime.

Now it carried an edge of pain that was almost unbearable. She knew it connected with the loss of Timmy.

When their baby died, Jane had felt something akin to this: an impossible kaleidoscope of a celebration of life intermingled with anguish and loss. Then as now, the mix was far too acute, too jagged to encompass.

Baby Timmy's blond curls, adoring eyes – the whites so clear – his bright smile when she went to him in his cot after a sleep. Until that day, when he hadn't woken… Dried vomit around his mouth. No consolation that it was 'unusual' at that age. That made it worse. Much worse.

Of course, she included him, always, when counting her children, even though he died when he was just thirteen months.

She pulled herself back to her surroundings, noticing that the pool was lined with dark green plastic instead of the regulation turquoise and shaped in an irregular oval, giving it the look of a grotto. Her eyes took in a buddleia and the large brown and cream butterflies that settled on it.

The lumps and bumps beneath the surface – the cancer beneath the skin that had broken out in her skull, in her side, in her hip, probably elsewhere too – and which had been confirmed by the scans, seemed to vanish. She felt sleek and healthy as the flicker of a thought of a miracle danced across her mind.

Looking at the sunlight that shimmered through the leaves at that moment – this world of slivers of silver and gilt, indigos and luxuriant greens of every hue above and below the surface of the pool – her thoughts drifted to all matter being made of connected stuff. She and the water and the leaves and the air were one, and now, if she was diseased, that was the way it was. Sometimes things rotted, and died, sooner than their fellows, so why should she protest if it was the way of the world?

Because she wanted more; more of her time here. Of course she did.

But she also found herself arguing that the length of a life wasn't the only consideration. An ache of sadness in her chest momentarily made her lithe body feel heavy.

She heaved herself out of the pool, as she used to when she was young, and lay face-down on the baking stone slabs. She was not sure if her spinning head and the tilting world were the result of water in her ears, the headiness of the experience, the heat, or the fact she had hardly eaten all day. But she quite enjoyed the sensation.

'Knock knock. You are having a nice relax! Your note, Jane...?'

Jane grabbed her robe and sat up to see Annette carrying a hosepipe, wearing long shorts, a large t-shirt and Scottie dog slippers, which Jane instantly disliked.

'Oh yes, Annette. It's just that I don't seem to have a bathmat.'

'Yes, I come to say you have one, a blue one.'

'Oh. Do I? Can't find it in the cottage, I'm pretty sure. It wasn't with the two towels you put out in the shower room. Have you just put it out – since my note? Is that what you mean?'

'I say you have one, a blue one.'

'Never mind, I'm sure I can manage without one,' Jane muttered.

The landlady walked across to a vegetable patch beyond the garden.

A charge of anger towards Annette (*No, 'Nanette'*) took Jane by surprise. Anger for her meanness, her pettiness. *As if I had stolen it! Why didn't I say something to her instead of being my usual polite self?*

Now Jane's outrage spread to the way the woman kept rushing out when it rained, turning all Jane's garden furniture upside down, making the place look wrecked.

Ha, and the brochure says 'private'. Just because she says, 'Knock knock' when she comes round to see me, she seems to feel she has perfect liberty to barge in whenever.

Jane thought of sharing these thoughts with Lennie.

She returned to the cottage, needing to put music on to calm herself.

The higher notes of a Schubert piano sonata rang out, loosely knitted to the rumble of the lower ones, while she neatly placed the CDs she had brought into a niche in the thick walls. But Annette was still under her skin, threatening to ruin her retreat. The Schubert sounded too definite now, too hurried, too certain, too loud. She turned it off.

The soft shush of rain, almost one continuous tone, began to soothe her. It sent shivers down her back at the luxury of all this time, time to reflect, to do nothing if she so wished, to please only herself – as long as she avoided Annette. She couldn't get a signal on her mobile phone, even if she wanted to call home.

Ochre, yellow and pale cream leaves drifted down from the huge lime tree that crowned the garden, although it was only August. Looking through the French doors at the abundant seeds waiting to drop beneath their gracefully splaying pods, she thought how probably not even one seed would be allowed to fulfil its destiny here, in this cultivated place, unless it floated elsewhere on the wind. Was that what she had done? Floated away from her home territory in order to… She hardly dared think 'take root' or 'grow'.

She remembered the baby that Alice and Jack were about to have back in England and thought of his head engaged and his body furled into its tight space, waiting to be unleashed. They knew – well, almost certainly – that it was another boy. 'Theo', she mused aloud, turning over the name that his parents had ready and waiting for him, like a receiving blanket. Strong and clear. She wondered what he would look like. She imagined him all pink, like the illustrations in books about how babies grow in the womb, with doll-like features, eyes closed.

She did not feel that 'another' boy was a negative description. On the contrary, she saw it as being triply blessed: for Alice and Jack to have Tom and Will, and now Theo, three fine sons, and for her to have three grandsons, all hopefully healthy and bright and lively, with their own personalities waiting to unfold. After all, she and Lennie had had three sons, including their firstborn Timmy, as well as Alice.

But what if this was a girl after all? What would they call her? She allowed herself to think how lovely a girl would be, but then challenged her thoughts: *Why should a mixed brood be better?*

A sharp pain stabbed her side. She did not know if it was the cancer. Or a deep hurt at the loss of all that sharing, of a future of more grandchildren. And of seeing the two she already knew and loved more than she ever thought possible, grow up into big boys before it would be remotely conceivable to leave them.

The sun came out and birds began to call more urgently for having abated. Jane stepped outside. She narrowed her eyes at the intensity of the saturated colours of the geraniums and the terracotta tiles. Pulling down a sopping bough of the laden fig tree, she reached a fat golden one in a favoured position, like the biggest and greediest puppy in a litter. It broke off the branch easily, which did not swing up fully as she released it. She tore the flesh open and tasted the textured ambrosial insides. And ate the soft skin too, with an inner smile. And thought of Lennie.

She wished he could taste this too, that she could share it with him; but not share everything here, for she knew she had to be alone. Alone with her news, her fate, to rail or cry or rejoice even, without consideration for anyone else, least of all Lennie, who suffered, even panicked, when she was hurt or off-colour or cross, so that she lost the right to her own feelings.

She knew that few things could be truly shared. People overlapped occasionally, felt similarly, but rarely the same. She had learnt with the pain of disillusionment, that everyone was fundamentally alone. Like stars in the wide firmament, we may be seen sometimes, recognised, but real connections are fleeting.

Changing sandals for trainers, she decided to stride out while the sun shone – to follow the path behind the cottage, and look for the lake she had seen signposted – like a child who was allowed to follow her impulses, not weighed down with others' needs. With her linen jacket around her waist, she locked the front door and stepped out into the warm washed afternoon.

The road shimmered, the breeze-swept maize clattered like rain on a tin roof, a hawk wheeled above with the quiet determination of its species. She was glad to be away from Annette.

Passing an oak tree, she plucked a small cluster of tender green acorns. Jane had always admired acorns – the way the cups fitted so perfectly, evoking memories of her father making little people out of them with pins: the cups becoming hats, or pipes. Discarding the leaves, she looked at her particular bunch of three, in gradations of size, from large down to very small. How like tiny boys' penises peeping out of the foreskin. She had seen plenty of those in her years as a mother and a grandmother of boys. She put them in her pocket.

She picked one of the delicate pale pink and white convolvuli twining on the verge, its small trumpet trembling in the almost imperceptible breeze. She thought that if she was looking for omens, this could signify that Alice would have a girl after all. She placed it in the other pocket of her jacket, to press later.

A heavily laden *mirabelle* tree, its fruit like bright orange lights, added to her sense of nature's abundance. She reached across a steep drop, pulled a branch towards her and grabbed a few of the ripe fruits before it sprang back. A greedier or more reckless person might have risked the precipice and gathered more, but she contented herself with a handful as she walked on, tasting the sweet-sour flesh and spitting out the pips.

How blessed she felt. Her life was rich; well, rich in recent years. Again, the irony of it – to reach a point of relative happiness, and then...

She shook her head at this pain, this sense of tragedy: a lump-in-the-throat tragedy for her, and for Lennie, and the children, and grandchildren... her sister Ruth, and Harriet, and her patients.

Kicking a stone in the road, she marched on faster, now feeling an exhausted hatred for the world. How could she love all this, when it was like a feast, a table laden with luscious food, teasingly shown to a starving woman who has been told that she can only have a morsel and no more?

But then, she argued, but then, she wouldn't know, wouldn't feel hungry, wouldn't feel deprived, *afterwards*, so why feel bothered that there was a *'Fin'* sign dramatically curtailing everything. *Isn't everything unutterably painful because of its transience, even for those with years and years ahead?* Jane didn't know any more, she had never felt lonelier in her life. Yet she had chosen to be alone here. She wished she could cry.

She remembered how she cried, went to pieces, after the recent hospital visit. The thought of all that treatment, that whole rigmarole again, bloody doctors and nurses doing their job. Some doing it very well, but for Christ's sake, she didn't want that. That wasn't the real world, the world of the wind on her face, or sun after rain, the loamy smell of rain on dusty earth, all of this. She breathed deeply. Little Tom… and Will. Now she saw their distinct faces, their translucent eyes, and felt an ache of love for them, for their intense little minds, their silky skin. And with a thought as delicate and tentative, and yet as robust, as the first tappings of a bird beginning to release itself from its shell, she cried for the impending end of her love for the new baby, an ending before a proper beginning.

No. She decided to have chemo, and maybe radiotherapy. She'd have to grab whatever she could of extra time.

She walked with unseeing eyes, the sun a warm balm on her head, uttering a silent prayer to life, to the one thing that she knew in all this mess: her love of life. Her thoughts swung from angry abuse at only realising this now, when it was too late, to gratitude for everything, for life.

She called out an apology to God, wiping her tears with grimy hands, leaving grey smears. By 'God' she meant 'life' – *lichayem,* nature, the way all matter is related, beauty, her parents, and everything that was transient. Yes, she knew she would die sooner rather than later, and of course, she couldn't just say 'so be it', she would rail and bleed with anguish. And drink whatever she could from the fountain of beauty and truth before she went. And then, that's it. The candle goes out.

She was glad she had brought *Don Carlos* with her. This was one of those operas she had known vaguely for years but had kept in reserve, not overplayed and milked, like *Lucia* or *Traviata, Rigoletto*, or *Don Pasquale*. She knew she would need it and come to it quite fresh.

She thought of Lennie again and thanked him for his love, for allowing her to come here. But hell, she retorted, of course, he 'allowed' it. How could he not? She knew that when there's a mighty crisis, he realised what she needed, even though he was having to put aside his needs. Yet, as soon as she returned to London, he would be waiting, like an encroaching tide, to reclaim her and re-establish the status quo. His needs were always paramount. *Is that inevitable or could there perhaps be a change to this balance, now?* She sighed with a deep weariness.

After a clamber up a stony bank populated by spindly weeds with flares of yellow flowers, she arrived at the edge of the lake. The rotting carcass of a fish on the shore compounded her impression that it was stagnant. She turned the fish over with her trainer, expecting it to smell bad. As a brown and orange butterfly lightly twirled in the air, swooping onto one of the yellow sunbursts of weed, she realised that everything, even death, was cyclical. Everything has its season, its moment, and then is replaced by some other rhythm, like spring after winter. So, if she was winter now, there is a spring; of course, there is. There's baby Theo, and Tom, Tom who she couldn't love more than she did, and sturdy Will with his twinkly eyes, who would live on. And gentle, kind Alice, and her good son, Max, and her young son Eddie, with his aspirations. Fresh tears coursed down her cheeks, but they were sweet and not bitter.

She sat on an earthy slope and lay back, unconcerned about what sort of bed she was choosing, and closed her eyes. Her arms felt weightless. Other than a sensation of slight nausea, she felt at peace. The illness was like an irritating noise, a rough edge, through which her thoughts, like connecting threads, ran – the weft and warp that kept her world together, that had splendour in its structure. The evening sun calmed her. She thought of the word 'embalmed'.

Not much further to go before I reach the edge of the world, she thought with a soft smile.

When she surfaced, she wasn't sure if she had slipped in and out of a light sleep. Sitting up and leaning over her bent knees, she swayed slightly with the equilibrium of the place, not knowing how long she had been at the water's edge. 'Watchless,' was a good word, Jane had thought when she'd abandoned her watch that morning – she needed to escape from watching and being watched.

The sun was now lowering, casting the landscape in the particular luminescence that Jane loved. That twilight still time; the suspension between day and night, perfectly suited her present state of mind. Her breathing became lighter. No longer pulled by regret, memory, anticipation, and desire, she stayed in the moment, the world perfectly balanced in its turning circle. Like the fish wrinkling the lake's surface at that moment and the ducks doing what they always do; like the sheep moving along a far track shepherded by a dog and a man, she was doing what she had to do.

The sun dropped behind distant trees. The sheep had disappeared, taking their bleating with them. Where they had been, a car passed on the track. Swallows sashayed over the water. A splash alerted her to a large fish leaping skywards and then disappearing. *Convolvuli* furled up for the night. Flies alighted on the fish carcass nearby.

She shivered slightly and put on her jacket. Enough of this place for today. Soon it would be getting dark.

Beginning to feel hungry, she wished she had put some potatoes in the oven before setting out. It was hard to believe that this was only her second night here, for time was stretching out languorously and her imagination had begun to embrace details and thoughts far more vivid than she could make space for in London.

Back at the little house, a note from Annette – economically using the back of the paper on which she had written to her – had been pushed under Jane's door,

Len has telephone. Please to ring him.

Oh goodness, yes, of course, was Jane's first thought. Then she asked herself why? Why should she when she had told him she wouldn't be in touch unless there was a problem. *Was this just because he was anxious? Perhaps there was a problem with the new baby. Or perhaps he has been born already.* She could not ring Lennie on her mobile, and would have to ask Annette if she could use her phone.

She walked round to the adjoining house and knocked on the open front door.

'Sorry to disturb you…'

'No, that's fine. The message. He didn't sound urgent. There's a call box in Ceneyrac.'

Jane registered Annette's need to protect her own space, while at the same time, she seemed so free to come round into her space with chatter. Jane explained that she had not been able to buy a phonecard, adding that, in this country, all ways of buying one shut down for hours in the middle of each day.

With barely disguised displeasure, Annette gestured towards the phone on a sideboard and replied, 'Alright, use my phone.' Although she walked away to offer some privacy, Jane was sure she was straining to hear from the next room.

'00 44', then leave off the first '0', dialling on, she reminded herself. She pictured Lennie an hour behind her time and heard the answerphone come on with her own ponderous voice. Thinking she must make it sound less cautious, she began to leave a message in as lighthearted a way as she could, wanting Lennie to know she was alright, as alright as anyone in her situation could be. But he lifted the receiver, screening calls as usual.

'Jane? Janey! Oh, so glad you've rung. How're you, darling?'

She told him she was fine, really feeling well, that it was a lovely place, going through a lot, before asking why he had rung.

'Everything's fine this end. No news about the baby yet. No, well, I just wanted to see how you were. That's all. And a minor thing, well, maybe it's minor. Someone called Eve, Eva… Can't remember her surname, left a message on the answerphone for you, wanting you to ring her. A patient? American accent.'

Jane knew who it was, it could wait. Eva contacted her sporadically for consultations. But this reminder of that world of responsibilities was like a burr against her skin that she longed to remove. Jane reassured Lennie that it was alright, she was allowed to take a holiday in August and didn't need to feel responsible in this instance. Jane sensed that Lennie did not know what to make of her firmness these days, something more resolute. Maybe he found her callous.

'I'm glad you're okay then,' he said.

'Oh yes. Hardly any symptoms,' she added, more for his sake than hers. 'Can't really speak long. I'm on the phone of the *Madame* who owns this place. As I said in my earlier message, my bloody mobile doesn't work around here. Do you want me to…' but decided not to offer to ring again. 'I'll be back soon enough, as you know – Tuesday of next week, 26th. If you need to contact me – and, of course, if there's news about the baby – ring me via *Madame,* you know, Annette du Plesis. Okay?'

'Sure, fine.'

'Before we say goodbye, just tell me how you are?' She did want to know and felt guilty for leaving Lennie with his side of her tragedy.

He talked about taking Max out for a meal the night before and meeting his editor for lunch at Bertorelli's. Jane tensed up at the thought that Lennie was going to tell her exactly what he ate, but instead, he went on to mention that he had played golf the day before. And then he talked about speaking to Alice on the phone about the imminent birth, and how cheerful and well she sounded but, of course, she was tired. Tom had told his mother that he thought that the baby would be born by the time he turned eight. Lennie, never sure of any child's age, had checked, 'He's four, isn't he?'

The mention of this grandson conjured up for Jane an image of the child's thick mop of dark hair, his pretty mouth, his radiant eyes. She meant it when she said, 'Thank you for holding the fort, darling.'

'That's fine. Just enjoy yourself – as much as you can. Any time you want to ring me, do.'

'Okay. Thanks. May ring from a call box. Even buying a phonecard isn't easy around here. Depends. Don't tend to go far. Better go. Lots of love. Bye, darling.'

'Thank you, Annette!' she called, hoping to escape without a long conversation. 'I'm leaving ten euros.'

'Oh, I'm sure that's too much,' said Annette, appearing from the kitchen, but not offering change. She told Jane that she would be away for a couple of days from early the next day, visiting her brother in the Pyrenees. Jane smiled and nodded, disappearing through the doorway as soon as politeness allowed.

Like the lake after the big fish had burst through the surface, the tranquillity of Jane's mood was ruffled now, as she opened the fridge and contemplated supper. Looking at the white Bordeaux, her eyes were unable to focus on the delicate label. Her right eye seemed under a dark cloud, as it did from time to time. When she closed it, she could see better. She cursed herself, fearful of having to drive the hire car back to Toulouse next week. Something heavy in her heart seemed to rise to her throat, an unpleasant feeling that she knew was depression.

Jane retired to bed early that night. The warm sounds of cicadas eased her unhappiness. She looked at the chapel in direct view, so perfectly framed, and thought that whoever built this limestone dwelling hundreds of years ago must have planned the position of this window with that little building in mind.

Before closing the solid wooden shutters to keep out the mosquitoes, she paused, arrested by what seemed like a glow of light from the derelict bell tower, with its exposed wooden armature like the bare skeleton of a beached whale. Was the moon playing strange tricks with the light? But yes, when she looked again, it did look like a flickering luminosity within the tumbledown tower, and more weakly, a soft radiance behind one of the lower mullioned windows festooned with ivy. She thought she would see if she could see it again the next night. Or ask Annette what it could be.

AUGUST 19ᵀᴴ, 2003

While the young man slept on the sofa in the living room, Jane allowed herself to gaze at him. He looked so trusting with his hands near his head, palms upwards – so unlike his guarded wakeful state. She noticed his grimy long fingers, his fine cheekbones, his aquiline nose, the way one leg flopped to the side, knee bent, forming a triangle of space. She interrupted her stolen glance at the soft bump to one side of the zip in his thin jeans, to tell herself to stop wasting time and get on with things.

Jane sponged her breasts and arms and face, before dressing hurriedly in a long white skirt and a slate-blue shirt that hid her scratches and bruises.

Gulping down orange juice as perfunctorily as filling her car with petrol – simply to keep going – she glanced again at the interloper's face, which now took on the colour and texture of stale white bread. Shaking her head slightly, she wondered with renewed incredulity at this stranger on her sofa. But here he was. She was reminded of a book the children loved when they were little, *Flap Your Wings*, where a couple of birds find a large egg in their nest, which they feel compelled to incubate, and then care for the baby alligator that emerges. 'If it's in your nest, you feed it!' the father bird intones as they fly around to try to meet its voracious appetite. He would be sure to have gone by the next day at the latest, once he'd rested.

Jane had told Pierre she would close the shutters and lock the door in case the landlady returned sooner than expected and come snooping around, while she went to buy provisions. She felt cross that she acted like an accomplice in some crime, in the house she was legitimately renting.

On the way to Ceneyrac, Jane saw a sign advertising bread with the French penchant for using English words: *Little Pain.* It seemed apt, that's exactly what she had in her side. But, compared with everything else, it seemed insignificant now.

She bought artisan bread, but hesitated over the different varieties of cheese, having no idea what the stranger would like. Should she choose something basic, and inexpensive? She picked out a wedge of the twelve-month-old hard cheese made from ewe's milk, which she had bought the day before, some smoked Gouda with cumin seeds because it was on special offer, as well as pork dried sausage, and bacon and eggs. She could not resist a kilo of fat misshapen tomatoes that would be much tastier than anything in England. And pale lilac garlic, and a few maroon-skinned onions. As if assembling a still life, she added curvaceous yellow peppers. She grabbed some cloudy apple juice, and several bottles of local wine, worrying that the foreigner might be too fond of alcohol. Lastly, she threw a fat slab of Swiss plain chocolate and a smaller one of milk chocolate into her trolley, no longer worried about getting fat.

She felt happy in a strange excited sort of way and remarkably energetic. As an afterthought, she grabbed a large jar of expensive Basque fish soup, and some *rouille* and croutons to go with it.

Driving off, she remembered his request for cigarettes. She cursed. Unused to buying these things, she stopped at a *tabac* in the next road and bought two packets of Craven A, because they reminded her of her parents' cigarettes decades ago. At last, she managed to buy a phonecard.

On the road home, she turned around once more to go to the *pharmacie*. She knew she was not fully functioning, that it was all too much, as she went in to buy disinfectant and crepe bandages, gauze bandages in case, and arnica tablets and cream. She already had plenty of painkillers.

What else did she need? Her composure faltered momentarily, despite the blonde woman behind the counter buttoned up in a starched white overall like a dentist, inspiring confidence in everyone who crossed the threshold into this air-conditioned haven of clinical expertise.

Jane asked, 'Excuse me, but what else would you recommend for someone… in shock? You see, my… my… What's the word, nephew, he had a bad fall yesterday. The doctor did see him, but he may have banged his head.' Quickly, she covered her tracks. 'Of course, he was X-rayed. No problem there. But I just want to help him if possible, to gather his strength.' Jane looked up at the row of white and gentian-blue ancient ceramic jars proclaiming compounds and poultices in Latin script on a high shelf, wondering if their gravitas was genuine or fake.

She left with a large bag containing food supplements, vitamins, a sedative to help him sleep and something herbal to calm his nerves. Perhaps she would use these purchases as much as he. The pharmacist looked satisfied and so did Jane. In a moment of euphoria, she reached for a pack of condoms on the counter, as appealing as sweets at a supermarket checkout, attractive coloured ones, the packet declared – something she had never bought in her entire life – and said as nonchalantly as possible, 'Oh yes, and these too, please.'

She heard the calm reply, '*Madame*,' but did not look into the pharmacist's eyes.

Jane nearly added to the woman, who no doubt had seen it all many times, 'Better safe than sorry,' but fortunately, the phrase in French did not trip off her tongue.

The morning heat hit her. She did not know what she was doing as she climbed into her car, accusing herself of losing her mind, telling herself she was a bloody menopausal married woman, dying of a terminal illness, buying condoms! Commanding herself to chuck them out the window, she pushed them into the glove compartment, tucking them underneath the instruction manual. Her mind was working in crazy ways, she realised – more so these days – as she drove fast along the straight-as-a-die avenue beneath a cathedral of plane trees. Behaving like a sixteen-year-old, she berated herself; just because she was far from home, did that give her permission? Strobes of sunlight broke the trees' dark shadows across her vision.

Wondering if it wasn't only Pierre who was in shock, she slowed down and took the bends more carefully.

She unlocked the front door quietly. Pierre started when she entered, his face betraying terror, but when he realised who it was, he slumped with a '*Pardon*! Only you!' – using the more formal '*vous*', despite both using '*tu*' earlier. And returned to sleep, his mouth soon flopping open to emit soft snores.

After quietly unpacking the shopping, she wrote a note in her imperfect French, also using 'vous'.

17 h.
Servez vous les provisions dans le Frigidaire.
Cigarettes pour vous.
Je depart a promener. Je rentrer vers 19 h.
Jane

She then placed it in the centre of the table, along with the cigarettes and a box of matches. She tiptoed to hide the rest of the wine under the stairs, leaving an opened bottle in the fridge.

Jane put on her large straw hat, for the sun would still be quite strong, and tucked her passport, flight tickets, camera, mobile phone, and purse into a basket, which she locked in the boot of the car. She remembered some cash upstairs in her bedroom, but could not be bothered to fetch that.

Jane felt weary as she set off on a walk. She could see the funny side of taking this break in order to rest.

She did not know which direction to take, except that she needed to put some distance between herself and the stranger, to have time to think. She took the little road towards the nearest hamlet.

As she walked, her observations of the sights around her were like background music, sometimes ways of seeking meaning and clarity for the conversations in her mind with some of the important people in her life. Her mind jumped from one person to another and back again, like photographs in an album randomly placed. With each voice, she heard differing viewpoints about this stranger who had landed at her feet and how he might impact on her own serious situation.

Jane tried to summon her mother, but she had died such a long time ago that all she could usually salvage was a pink round face and a large forehead topped with wispy grey hair. Her mother's depression and ferocious battles of will with Jane had discoloured any tenderness and love, and obscured deeper memories of her mother's face glowing with a light of its own.

The word 'preoccupied' came to her mind now. Yes, how apt, her mother was pre-occupied with Ruth, the first-born, and with Martin, who died at birth, eighteen months later, all before Jane had had a chance.

Jane had learned from an aunt that her mother had returned gifts for the forthcoming baby during her pregnancy with Jane. Martin's blue curtains and room had remained exactly as they were.

When Jane and Lennie's baby, Timmy, had died, they were aware of the awful repetition of Jane's parents' history. How determined she had been not to allow that death to overshadow her subsequent babies. She was grateful that their next baby was a girl, for she was more able to see her as different. But Jane had not known if her depression at the loss of Timmy would, by default, repeat history. She knew that her children – Alice and Max and Eddie – each had their own difficulties, but not this particular one, she felt, of not being wanted in their own right.

Now her eye was taking in straight rows of maize, the top of each plant fanning like lizards' feet. She thought of the other child she had found, now waiting for her back at the cottage.

She turned to Lennie in her mind and imagined him saying, 'Darling, you must do what is best for *you*.' And yet she was sure he would oppose her sheltering someone who could be a criminal and add that it might be dangerous having him in the house. 'Sounds very dodgy to me,' he'd say, and remind her that she must remember her own needs. Yes, he would say that people don't avoid the authorities for no reason and would instruct her to find out more about him as soon as possible. She was convinced that Lennie was only concerned about her for his own reasons, so that she could be restored and come back to him in better shape. He often implied that she was too nice to others at the expense of what she gave to him. Perhaps there was something in that, she acknowledged now. And sighed. But that was a choice she made.

Her mind skirted away from this and on to her father. Although he had died six years earlier, she could see his chiselled face and felt a wave of acceptance from him. He would say she was right to help this stranger – after all, what if she was in dire need, she would be grateful to be taken in by a good Samaritan.

Now her sister Ruth interjected, her dyed-brown curly hair framing her delicate face, saying that Jane was crazy to let a stranger into her house. He could do anything. Yes, just imagine, rob her, even rape her. Although Ruth would not spell out these horrors, her mind would be teeming with them and her demeanour would betray this, her thumb and index finger forever smoothing each other. Ruth was always the nervous one and had carried some of Jane's own fears over the years. Inevitably, this made Jane bolder than she might otherwise have been. She could imagine Ruth adding, 'Anyway, I'm sure he's a criminal. He even looks like one.' How like Lennie Ruth is, she realised for the first time.

She needed to go back to her father, who would emphasise how she must look after herself at this terrible time in her life. Jane could see his wise face, his curly black hair and clear-cut features. She remembered a line she had recently come across in a Don Paterson poem, *"See how the true gift never leaves the giver."*

How she wished to have her old friend Harriet here now, to help her find some clarity. That serious face, with her almost transparent eyes that defied description because they changed so much – dark blue encircling what could range from pale aqua to blue-green. And yet, despite the unpredictability of her eyes, she was one of the most steadfast people Jane knew. Harriet's short neat dark hair somehow fitted her solid presence. Harriet was so supportive, and would always push her own needs to one side, though Jane tried not to lose sight of them. She felt a wave of gratitude as she remembered how recently Harriet had encouraged Jane to paint more.

Now, in Jane's mind, Harriet's presence was similar to her father's. Harriet would say that it was good of Jane to take in this stranger, but she would just have to find the balance between her own need to reflect and gather strength alongside what this 'chap' needed. Yes, thought Jane, that's the word she would use, ten years younger. Jane sensed that if anyone could manage that balance, Harriet could.

Past a field of creamy coloured cows, beyond a walnut orchard, she entered the hamlet of Moulin Vieux, although there was no windmill in sight. There were clear signposts to other places at its one crossroad, as if no one could possibly want to end up here for its own sake. But it did have one lichen-covered washed-out-yellow post box with barely decipherable collection times, and a few grey snails stuck to it like an advertisement for the service it offered. The tiny, unremarkable church with grass growing from every horizontal surface always seemed to be locked. The hamlet looked deserted, despite well-tended pots of geraniums and barns of tractors and harvesters. Jane's glimpse of gardens around the backs of shuttered houses hinted at a hidden life.

Her thoughts returned to Pierre. Perhaps he was waking up, and she ought to get back. Or would it be best to keep out of his way, not get involved, and just encourage him to go as soon as possible? She remembered his hurt leg and possibly damaged neck. Perhaps she should persuade him to take a shower, assess the damage and clean up the wounds on his head. Now she felt anxious about how shocked he might be, and whether the bump on his head was significant.

So she turned around on the same road, unsure if there was a different route that would loop back to her cottage.

Exhaustion weighed her down. Six o'clock now. She knew she had had a stressful day and should be resting more. What would have ensued if she hadn't heard the crash, or had decided to ignore it? Surely, Pierre would have survived somehow without her.

She remembered going through such depths of emotion only yesterday about dying. 'Probably dying', she added. And now she could not really think about anything. She sighed deeply, feeling a pain in her chest. Or was it her heart.

A small thread of a recent thought that had not been allowed to develop, about not having to face old age and all the decrepitude that it could bring, returned to her mind. That thought had given her some relief, to imagine dying while she was relatively able-bodied – well, if you could say that if your body was as riddled with cancer as an old woodworm-infested cupboard. She imagined sharing that thought with Harriet, and in a different way with Adrian, the psychoanalyst she went to occasionally for consultations. She joked with a few friends that Adrian was her guru.

Walking slowly now made her feel more tired. She tried to take an interest in her surroundings, in the neat row upon row of apple and pear trees topped with fine netting like bridal veils. Forcing herself back into a brisk stride, she smiled at how she and Pierre had been thrown into a kind of intimacy only that morning on the climb back to the house.

After getting him out of the car, she had hoisted some of his possessions across her shoulder in his canvas bag, and with her other arm acted as a crutch for him. It was not only his hurt knee and his painful neck, but his dizziness that made him lean on her heavily, in spite of his slight and wiry build. She had tried not to breathe in his smell of stale sweat and rank breath; it seemed that he had not washed for days. There were times when she almost had to drag him, drawing on all her reserves of strength, over boulders or up steep inclines, until they reached the looping steep road.

They had both managed to make light of the situation, as if they were two exhausted revellers after an all-night party. He had joked about finding such a pliable walking stick, and that he never did like Renaults anyway. She had added that the rabbits and birds would turn the wreck into a wonderful chateau, but next time he shouldn't try flying without a parachute. And then jested that she had been out for an early stroll and fancied some company. Jane momentarily worried that he'd see this joke as emanating from real loneliness, so she quickly added with a smile that actually she had come to France for a bit of peace and quiet. He was quick to apologise for the imposition, she to rebuke him for being so polite, as if he had crashed on purpose.

Jane had not been sure how much his profuse sweating was an unhealthy fever and how much of it was to be expected. Perspiration had run down her back. She removed her fleece and tied it around her waist, despite feeling exposed in her thin, cotton nightdress, which revealed her heavy breasts just beneath the floral fabric. I'm old enough to be his mother, she had reminded herself, and was sure that he thought the same.

They had to stop several times to rest, for both their sakes. Jane felt she was pushing herself beyond endurance.

But in their bantering way, the disparate couple made light of the hard, sweltering climb up the steep road, and reached the *mirabelle* tree whose fruit Jane now saw as gaudy. She pointed out to Pierre where the car had damaged part of the tree as it had begun its downhill slalom.

Pierre, who had been swerving in and out of awareness, noticed the solid black tyre tracks towards the steep drop.

'Oh God! Look at those!' he exclaimed as his pale face took on a greenish hue.

Jane recalled again the terrible screech of brakes that had awoken her.

'We're almost back now. My cottage is just around this bend.'

'I think I'll come back later and scrape those marks off the road somehow.'

'Why bother?' she said. 'The only people who pass this way are farmers, or occasionally locals. Look, there are other marks on the road. But, I suppose, they could wonder...'

They had scrambled through a gap in the shrubbery at the back of the cottage by the pool, to avoid going up the front path, and entered the little cottage quietly.

Now, as she began the last half kilometre of her solitary walk back, she imagined a consultation with Adrian.

In her mind, Jane could see his intelligent, sapphire eyes as he sat in his usual corner in that sombre room, with one of his bright ties emblazoned on his chest. He would say little, and she would find herself saying much – sometimes more than she intended.

And then she imagined Adrian saying that she didn't scramble to Pierre's rescue for no reason; that there was something she wanted or needed from this.

'What?' she imagined asking, not knowing. 'Yet, that's why I've come to see you,' she would say feebly.

'Another lost soul?' in his characteristic, slightly amused way of talking, as if enjoying his own ideas.

'Why, am I lost? Well, I suppose I am. But how can a meeting with another lost soul clarify anything? Surely, it will only confuse me further; his issues aren't mine.'

She imagined Adrian looking at her in a friendly way, and giving a little nod. She wanted more of an explanation, but he seemed to be in his own world. Then she imagined him abruptly beginning to talk about how she seemed not to have begun to think about her illness and what that might mean for her. So that when she collided with this stranger, in the wreckage, there was no way that she could know what her own predicament was.

Yes. That's kind of obvious, Jane now thinks. *But why do I need to go and see Adrian to hear all that when I – sort of – know anyway?* Yet she knew that this strange business of psychoanalysis was so often about another's mind simply, and sometimes beautifully, clarifying what one already knew, but could not or dare not know.

'Did you say 'collides' or 'colludes' with the stranger just now?' Jane imagined asking Adrian.

'Quite,' he smiled.

Oh God, he's so bloody elliptical. In her daydream, she looked at her watch and saw that only about fifteen minutes of the precious fifty minutes remained. As usual, she could not bear to be caught out by time with him and had to prepare herself for closure.

She stopped in her walk back and sat on a rock by the quiet road. She wanted to think further about all this before getting too close to the house.

What if she brought the dream she had last night – in fact, before this whole episode – to Adrian, knowing how interesting it was to bring dreams to him. So she revisited it and imagined explaining it to him.

'I'm with lots of… refugees, I think they are; I'm one too, in crowded conditions. There are children too. We're all trying to amuse ourselves by playing games, and so on. It's all very orderly. I'm given cracker biscuits to attach to my arm with Sellotape, to hide them up my sleeve. I see another load of people, with children, arriving in a truck. I realise that their arrival will make things impossibly crowded, and wonder whether we should send them away.'

That was all she could remember.

Jane stood up, and walked onwards, looking at the road without seeing it. She wondered if she should have a quick swim when she returned to the cottage.

She returned to the dream. 'Cracker' was the South African word for firework. Lennie was South African: he used that word, and she had too with the children when they were little. Like some sort of incendiary, almost like a suicide bomb, she speculated. So, what's supposed to be sustenance is really dangerous, and is 'up her sleeve'. Perplexed, she thought the dream was probably about something very dangerous she was participating in, naïvely, and yet... She paused, feeling stuck. But then she managed to think further, about her ambivalence towards letting in more people, more people like her, homeless even, into an already overcrowded place. It was prophetic of what had happened today, of course, where she did let the refugee in, even though she was running out of resources herself. But then....

She stood now, four-squarely, facing a rough, grassy field, holding her elbows firmly below her backpack.

She knocked gently before unlocking the front door and entered the shuttered living room. The young man started, sat up, mumbled, and pulled a rug over himself.

'Alright! Only me! Really, don't be so worried.' She rattled on, 'Slept all this time? Didn't see my note? But why so anxious?' Trying to reassure him, or was it herself, she added, 'Perhaps it's only normal after such a terrible accident.'

He lay back, breathing deeply, and closed his eyes again.

She mustn't let him sleep, she wouldn't know if he was concussed. She wondered if he was just exhausted, for reasons of his own. He could be here forever if she didn't make him wake up, assess the damage, and send him on his way.

She opened the shutters to reveal the fig tree outside. The bright light and a green warmth spilt into the room.

'Okay, Pierre, coffee? A cigarette? I bought you Craven A – is that alright?' as if she was the supplicant.

A little smile crept into the corner of his mouth, 'That will do, thanks. Yes. Coffee, please. A strong one. Must take a leak. Where's the bathroom?' he said, half opening an eye.

'Upstairs, I'm afraid,' indicating the wooden spiral staircase nearby.

'Shit! *Pardon*. Depend, dependable? What's the word? On the leg.'

'You speak French, Pierre. I'll understand. There's enough difficulty, without you struggling with English.'

The decision to stick with his language was easy.

He sat up, swung his legs over the edge of the sofa, and attempted to stand by leaning against the wall. 'Oh Christ! Hell, agony,' screwing up his face. He clutched the back of his neck, 'Pulled a bloody muscle, torn more like, or something, in my neck too.'

Jane did not know what to do. It occurred to her that he could be laying it on thick, to gain both her sympathy and several days in her care. Remembering her refugee dream, where letting in another convoy of the homeless was not necessarily the best thing to do, she hardened herself; her situation was not exactly easy either. She remained silent, her lips firmly sealed, watching him as he limped dramatically towards the stairs. He winced as he took the first step up, using the bannisters as crutches.

Was she causing him more harm by making him go upstairs? The narrow spiral staircase was difficult for anyone to negotiate. No point in being rigid. *Should I let him pee in the shower cubicle, or outside?* 'I'll fetch you something,' she suggested. He nodded.

She brought him a plastic bowl, satisfied with this use of stingy Annette's bowl. She walked outside briefly while he used it. Then returned, emptied it into a drain outside, rinsed it under the garden tap, and left it there.

When she came back in, Pierre was sitting up and pulling a cigarette from the packet. She noted that he had done that quickly enough.

Soon they sat with mugs of coffee while potatoes and onions sizzled in the oven and the last of the evening sun slanted through the open French doors. Beyond a sloping stretch of grass, they could see the pool. Jane, like Pierre, put her bare feet up on the coffee table. Noticing the dirt under his too-long toenails and the ingrained griminess of his feet, the memory of his unwholesome smell that morning left her feeling slightly nauseous.

He gave her a crooked smile as he said, 'You're having quite a nice day then, after all.'

'You're not serious, surely?'

'Why shouldn't I be? You have a great place here. You've been shopping. You have a car... You're quite strong and well... so?'

She realised how completely out of touch he was with her situation, not just all the factors that had made her take this break in France, but what she had put herself through for him. Either he was completely selfish and callous, incapable of gratitude, or he could not bear to think about her because he was overwhelmed by what he was going through, and was still shocked.

She turned to matter-of-fact mode now, to avoid sliding into bonhomie too easily when there were serious matters to attend to. It was not her choice to spend her precious break with this stranger, especially as she liked him less and less. If he had been more perceptive, he might have noticed a tightening of her lips.

'Well, as soon as we've had a bit of a breather, we'd better see how injured you are. Take a look at that leg for a start. And maybe your neck. How about a shower?'

That startled look crossed his face again.

'Don't worry, the shower is off the kitchen, down here. And we will, of course, observe the proprieties.' He gave a little high pitched laugh that seemed to go on several seconds longer than necessary, as if to say that was the least of his worries.

She added, 'For my sake, then. Alright?'

'Yes, *Madame*, as you wish!'

'Not just "as *I* wish". Surely, you too want to get sorted out?' She felt as if she was speaking to her middle child, Max, trying to inject some motivation into him.

'No, I meant about "the proprieties"!' He began to chuckle, again a laugh that went on and on, and then, with an apparent effort, took control, like someone drunk trying to appear sober. Jane wondered if he was hysterical, if the laugh could easily have been a cry.

'Okay, no, I mean yes, really, we'd better, I'd better, see how I...' His sentence petered out. Now he seemed to be humouring her.

She noticed that when he talked, his eyes frequently searched corners of the room, or the space under a cupboard, before returning to the same spot a few seconds later, as if looking for something that sharp perusal would discover.

'And, by the way, if the woman who owns this place, Nanette – I mean Annette – appears, we'll say you're my cousin,' she stated. 'Okay? She's away for a day or two. But it's probably better all-round if she doesn't see you.'

He nodded, surveying her out of the corners of his eyes for the first time.

'And, once we've assessed the physical side, we'll have to think about the practical and all that.'

He gave a little whistle of exhaled breath, on which smoke puffed into her face, and put out his cigarette harshly in an ashtray.

While Pierre was in the shower, having thrown his dirty clothes outside the cubicle onto the kitchen floor, Jane thought that a few glasses of wine and some supper may be a good way, after all, of getting him to talk about himself.

She cautiously placed a clean bath towel over the door handle of the shower room, telling him what she was doing. She planned to ask Annette for a second towel.

After adding some chopped yellow peppers and garlic to the vegetables in the oven, she began to set the table. She enjoyed the ceremony of peeling the plastic from the neck of a bottle of red Buzet, and carefully opening it. She took a large gulp of the dark wine. No, she thought, she wouldn't put music on, though if she was alone, she would have done. He might get the wrong idea. Anyway, he'd probably hate her choice of music. She avoided lighting candles for the same reason.

She closed the shutters and switched on the lamps.

The young man appeared with the white towel wrapped as tight as elastic around his slim hips, his hairy chest glistening with moisture, smelling pleasantly of her expensive Clarins shampoo. She smiled inwardly at the cheek of him. But if anyone needed a tonic, he did. That reminded her of her purchases at the *pharmacie* – the supplements and tablets – and quickly shoved the other impulse-buy back in the glove compartment of her mind.

'Well, a new man!' she exclaimed with genuine pleasure, trying to avoid noticing the bulge of his genitals beneath the towel, his flat abdomen accentuating that area. 'And how is the leg?' The impersonal 'the' again, as if it did not belong to him. *The* cancer, *the* illness, *the* treatment.

He shrugged in a way she always thought of as typically French and said he didn't really know. The knee was very painful, and a bit swollen, but that was all, he added. He pointed out a large bump on the side of his forehead, and mentioned a stinging cut on the top of his head he had not noticed before. But he did not show her his leg. She asked if she should see it.

'Yes, if you want,' he said slumping down on the sofa again.

There he goes again, 'if I want'. What does he think I am? Some freaky sex-starved old lady? It's for his bloody sake. She didn't want him exposing himself while she examined the leg, so she suggested that they should first think about clean clothes for him. He gestured towards his canvas bag. She asked what was in it. He listed, as if accounting to his mother: clean underpants, some dirty stuff, toothbrush, and some papers.

While he lit up another cigarette, she poured a glass of the dark wine for each of them, and then rummaged in his bag. She could not help but notice his identity card, printed with 'Charles Baudier'. At least the surname was authentic. She found grey underpants, which were probably white once, and threw them to him.

'Clean, I hope. Goodness knows what else you should wear while I wash your old clothes. How about I lend you a t-shirt and some baggy pull-on trousers – you're much slimmer than me, of course – but they could be unisex?'

'Fine by me,' his voice conveying a wave of optimism. The smell of roasting vegetables wafted across the room. 'Good dinner!' he added, raising himself to reach for the baguette and tearing off a chunk, scattering crumbs and chewing greedily with his mouth half open.

Before dinner was ready, Jane climbed the staircase slowly, aware of how much her body ached and how much she needed a hot shower. She glanced at the chapel before closing the shutters. There was no glow of light from within this time.

She brushed her hair, applied some dark lipstick, wiped it off again, and brought down a loose black t-shirt and cotton white trousers for Pierre.

'While you slip these on, I'll go and snip some mint.'

When she returned, she thought he looked quite Moroccan in her baggy cotton trousers, with his dark little beard. Or perhaps it was because she was sniffing the sprigs of mint that she associated with couscous. He wore a leather string around his neck with a strange pointed stone attached. She could not help smiling as she asked, 'Where are you from, originally? Your family?'

In a slightly guarded way, he said they were Spanish a long time ago, but now they were French, adding, 'Well, Occitan French.'

'And you?' he asked. 'You're not typically English are you?' She wondered if he was just trying to distract her from himself, yet she was always quite pleased when people said that because, to Jane, being 'typically English' could denote 'ordinary' or 'boring'. On the other hand, she never knew if a reference to her Jewishness was about to emerge and whether the enquirer would be prejudiced.

'Why do you think that?' she asked. "English" can mean lots of things, you know.'

He shrugged as if it was of no consequence. 'Oh, I don't know. Something a little... darker, sort of... like someone from Egypt or Iran, or one of those countries, originally.' He poured himself a second glass of wine without offering her one.

'Interesting you think that! Well, my grandparents all came from Eastern Europe – Poland and Russia – ages ago.' She decided to put her cards on the table. 'They must have come from the Middle East originally – you know, they were Jewish. One of my grandsons says I have "Bible blood".' She wanted Pierre to know that she had grandchildren.

He nodded as if she was simply stating something obvious. Okay, so he's probably not anti-Semitic, she thought – though you never know. She began to feel resentful about all this chit-chat. It wasn't likely to lead to an interesting exchange; Pierre seemed remarkably self-absorbed. She always resented making friends with people she would never see again, when she was overfull with real friends and family for whom she did not have enough time. Especially now.

While they sat at the little round table and ate artisan hazelnut bread and salami, with roasted vegetables dotted with garlic, the silence hung solidly between them. She could hear her own chewing and noticed his crude handling of his knife and fork. He seemed quite relaxed. To make the meal more enjoyable, and to satisfy her curiosity, she broached the subject of what brought him to this part of the world, and where he lived normally.

He glanced at her obliquely, gesturing with a finger that he had a mouthful to chew – but she realised he was gathering his thoughts. He took a gulp of wine and breathed deeply, 'Well, I came to the little graveyard near here...,' but then broke off, saying that he'd rather not go into all that. He slid from being pleasant and relaxed to tense as rapidly as his car had plummeted downhill that morning. 'You don't need to know, and it was never part of the deal, was it?' A bristling silence followed. Then he growled, 'Remember, in the car, my car, you promised you wouldn't push things? Otherwise, I'd have managed somehow on my own.'

Under a wave of unease, she was struck by how resolute he was, how suddenly he not only stopped being pleasant, but seemed unaware of how much she had helped him. He did not feel that he owed her any explanation. She could have said, 'Oh, of course, I understand.' But she did not want to make it easy for him. She thought again that maybe he was still suffering from shock, or perhaps had a personality disorder. *He takes for granted that I have been his rescuer, his nurse, his housekeeper, his cook, possibly his financial support and his chauffeur.* Her newfound grittiness, one of the benefits that her illness brought – like a terminal moraine that a great glacier brings with it, she had joked with Harriet – made her say, albeit politely, 'That's all very well, Pierre. That's fine for you. But what am I to feel about this complete stranger who lands on my doorstep, who might be a criminal for all I know, or... I don't know what. Who wants to sleep here tonight, who I have to hide and deceive my landlady for? Who hasn't a clue about what *I* might be going through these days.' To her surprise, and Pierre's, she began to cry. She tried to fight back the tears, biting her lower lip, swearing silently at herself for being so emotional. He withdrew into a frozen state. All she said was, 'It's not worth it,' gathering her composure, staring at the now black French doors reflecting the kitchen lights and sipped some wine.

They ate in silence for a while, Jane aware of the sounds of their chewing and swallowing.

AUGUST 20TH, 2003

She awoke at dawn aware of his snoring. She looked at his thin, drawn face in the dim light. Like a Christ figure, she thought.

It felt… alright.

She began to question, to ponder on Lennie, and then her thoughts changed direction, to accept that this would be a secret that she took to her grave. Especially as that day may not be that far off. Lennie wouldn't bear it; he – and the children – mustn't be hurt. It was her life, her little life, or what was left of it.

She tried to go back to sleep, but felt an unsettling deep tremor in her womb, a tingle of pleasure, like she had felt years ago. If only he would wake up.

But the poor boy needs to sleep, she thought tenderly, as she would towards one of her sons. This association shocked her, but it did not make her regret what had happened.

Pierre turned in his sleep, giving a muffled cry like a bird in the night.

She thought about last night. The first night of his stay. About how it seemed to begin when she attended to the wound on his scalp.

AUGUST 19ᵀᴴ, 2003

She sat next to him as she dressed the wound on his scalp, overcoming her abhorrence of wounds within hair, pushing aside her memory of a boy at school with a gaping bloody gash on his head that showed through his short hair, of her dog, years later, with a cut in his side, and of their cat, with stitches in her purplish shaved skin after an operation. Shivers ran down her spine. The process of gently bathing the wound gave her a strange sensation that she hardly dared to own, a tremor in her womb. She wanted to kiss him, gently.

Instead, she turned away to put the bandages on the table. He turned to her and began to massage her shoulders, hard, but with consummate skill. How did he know that her tension resided there? How did he know what she needed before she herself realised? She lay on her front, while he proceeded so firmly, his fingers and thumbs seeking knots of tension in her shoulders and kneading them, painfully yet pleasurably. She could have resisted, could easily have felt it was too forceful, too intimate. But she relaxed. And melted, dissolving into molten lava that did not know or care where it would flow. Of course, the wine helped – they were onto their second bottle of good Bordeaux.

She smiled then, more to herself. He may have seen her smile or sensed her mood. He gradually caressed her back more gently, lower down, hands now beneath her t-shirt. How did he know how much she loved having her back stroked, ever since she was a child? She knew she would go with this, with the tingle through her body. The discordant voices in her head would be ignored.

She turned on her side to face him and smiled. He paused, as if unsure how to proceed. She reached out to take his hand. The older woman. He leant down to kiss her. His roughness and passion shocked her; she was more aware of him than of herself, almost fearful of what he was doing. But his flame travelled along her dry veins, invisibly, and met with her own most extreme and needy self, her own fifteen-sixteen-seventeen-year-old self, which had hardly met its equal since.

Now she laughed inwardly with pleasure and excitement. She gave him all that she had deep within her, her raw voluptuous self.

He pulled her from the sofa onto the floor and pressed down onto her, his slim body hard and light. He almost devoured her ears and her neck and her breasts, as if he was starved, while she gave and took his spirit and vigour and strength. Unstoppably, Jane travelled back forty years in the space of a few minutes. She felt she was an ultramarine turbulent ocean and he was a giant seabird that dipped down into her waves, to find what he needed and to fill her up with sweet nectar. Both their bodies were taut, but hers was soft too, and soon she hungrily began to meet what she longed for without having realised how much she hungered. With every pore in her body, she tasted and savoured him, with her tongue and her hands and her cheeks and her insides and her mind, until the waves swelled and broke on the shore, while a soft lapping and swooshing continued to pulse, in a place where the breeze and the sea and the blood were all one temperature.

Through Jane's joy, tears of grief erupted, tears for what she had lost and had now rediscovered, only to lose again. She was shaken into the possibilities of transformation, of a continued existence. Pierre kissed away her tears, not comprehending her turmoil.

These were no longer two ill people who lay there, laughing and crying with relief. The phrase 'just what the doctor ordered' came to her mind, but she felt it would be lost in translation. She thought of sharing the phrase with Lennie, but stopped before the thought was fully formed.

All she said was, 'Your knee wasn't so bad after all!'

She did not think he had seen the scar on her breast in the semi-dark, but did not worry if he had. Perhaps this will drive the cancer away, she dared to think, her breathing briefly quickening.

As he began to fall asleep, she affectionately called herself an idiot for buying those condoms. As if AIDS would matter now. Thoughts of Lennie sent a chill through her.

Jane could not sleep deeply. She wanted to dance, to swim, to run, to roll down grassy slopes, to make the world spin as much as she herself was spinning, to laugh, to sob, to skip, to make love and be made love to, again and again, for the quickening in her veins to become that intense throb.

She sensed that a passion which had been re-ignited would have to work harder than a passion that was born for the first time.

Gradually, over the years the passion that had receded behind propriety and necessity, had been covered over with patches, like layers of callused skin. The resultant garment was quite beautiful in its assemblage of faded fabrics; time's magic had made it a whole of a sort.

Pierre too had been restless in the night, as if he could not fully give himself up to sleep.

AUGUST 20TH, 2003

And now, now she looked at his uncovered naked body, vulnerable and helpless; his penis sleeping too, like a child's soft, plump limb, resting innocently. As she watched, it changed slowly, unfurling like a bud opening, like a speeded up film of the process. She smiled, rarely having witnessed this miracle while its owner slumbered. *Now what?* She wondered what he was dreaming about. Did he sense that she was watching him? Or did he just want to pee? Would he wake up? She longed to touch it, to surprise him by taking it gently in her mouth so that some of its growth would be her doing, whether he was aware of her or not. But she waited.

Her own body began to fill with a power she had not felt, not so fully, for years. She waited, holding her breath.

The sun had fully risen by now. Bright light streamed through the shutters' cracks.

Pierre turned onto his front.

Jane felt cheated. There he was, hiding his prize, his most beautiful possession, keeping it to himself. He clenched his firm buttocks slightly, and then fell into a deeper sleep. Men are lucky, she thought, not for the first time. With amusement, she watched a fly settle on a buttock, walk across the dome, and fly off. She admired the concavity of his lower back, could imagine his spare form being sculpted out of marble – only then would it lose the fuzz of dark hair on some areas.

She wondered whether she should wake him gently, but that would be selfish. His state of arousal probably had nothing to do with her, Jane Samuels, a woman of fifty-five with terminal cancer. She feared that she could get into a maudlin state of self-pity, feel used and bad for what she had done. But then she paused, backtracked, and thought about what she had received. Even if she never saw him again, she felt enriched. She had used him too. She had supped at his fountain of youth and health, and it had revived her own. Rarely had she lived in the moment; hardly since she was a young woman.

Hours later, after Jane had crept out of the room, showered – feeling that her body was quite beautiful in its shapely way – and had coffee. She encountered Annette, who seemed to look at her in a curious way. She told her about her cousin who had stayed the night on the sofa. Then Jane had a swim, and returned to the bedroom with a tray of coffee, *pain au chocolat,* two ripe nectarines, and cigarettes.

'Not a bad hotel, Pierre!'

He smiled without looking at her, pulling a sheet up to his waist, and squinted at the sunlight as she opened the shutters.

'The whole world is up, and you lie here! Well?'

He combed back his short hair with his fingers, and stretched for a cigarette. 'Well? What about it?'

'Well, for one, I know nothing about you. You could be an axe murderer for all I know!'

He laughed and coughed at the same time. She hoped he was spluttering from the cigarette smoke.

He reached out and took her hand.

She pulled back. 'You know I'm old enough to be your mother. And I'm married.' She needed to add, 'Happily married,' even if it was not entirely true. She paused briefly to reflect, and then looked at him for emphasis. 'Children. And grandchildren. Didn't tell you that, or maybe I did?'

'Didn't ask.'

'Just as well,' she replied, ignoring his self-centeredness. Both became silent, enclosed in their own thoughts.

'Who would have thought,' Jane said, more to herself.

'I think you think too much.'

'Hmm, you're right there. Out of the mouths of babes,' she added in English.

'What was that?'

'Nothing.' She took a deep breath.

Here she was, sitting on the edge of her – or their – bed, and the world outside seemed as remote as another country. She thought of the longings she'd had only that morning while he slept. She could now carry on with all that, or stop.

She closed her eyes. He did not appear to notice her reverie, as he drew deeply on his cigarette as if his life depended on it. Her mind teemed with questions. Was she clutching at straws – at a fantasy? Was she pathetic… or was she giving herself something, something like the warm sun, or the pool, a total experience of belonging in the world, in a primeval world where cares didn't exist? Was she really finding her young self, which was there somewhere? She longed to curl up at his side and sleep like a baby. Half-opening her eyes she saw this self-centred boy, and felt she was crazy. Lennie would understand her need to be held now, he would hold her in his arms. And yet, and yet, she felt that if Lennie really understood, she would not be in this bizarre set up with Pierre.

Now it was Pierre's turn to open his eyes. He looked at her, her pained expression, her over-ripe upper arms, and reached out to her.

'I'm sorry, sorry Jane, sorry to have caused you all this trouble.' He stroked her arm with the backs of his fingers, impersonally. 'Sorry. You've been good to me. I'm not good at saying "thank you", but I hope you're alright?'

She heaved her body onto the bed and curled up next to him, like a small child, looping around so that only her head and knees touched him. He put out his cigarette, took a gulp of coffee, and put an arm across her body. His pause for coffee confirmed her isolation.

He gently stroked her soft arms, her cheeks, her back through her nightdress, and she began to feel bathed in his care. She could almost have slept, but he slithered down the bed until he lay at her side, and pressed his tautness against her knees. Such a different feeling now suffused her from the repose she had felt. Like a seedling sensing the advent of a warm spring, she swelled and rose to meet his sunshine.

The confusion of one moment being a child, another a lover, before that a mother. She did not know if she felt rich or crazy.

'Jane, Jane, you know the car, my car?' She liked the way he pronounced her name, with a soft 'J' that sounded intimate, not quite 'Jeanne'. 'Well, can you go and find it, today, go and fetch some papers of mine? I left them in the boot. Oh God, I hope the boot isn't smashed shut, not openable. My passport, for one. And my sketchbook, years of sketches that are my sort of diary, that I can't bear to lose. Please, yes?'

'Pierre, you must be joking!' She sat up and looked at him. 'Don't you remember how hard it was to clamber up from the car, let alone to reach it in the first place? If you were well enough for all that,' smiling at him with a shy glance down towards his covered body, 'maybe *you* can go and get the things! Anyway, most documents are replaceable. The sketchbook, no, but the other things, surely.'

'But Jane...' his voice broke off, forcing himself to stay with the problem. 'But it's also my identity, my... that I don't want...'

All her suspicions surfaced. 'Oh, I see. So you want me to be your partner in crime?' She then threw in, as a tester, 'More than I already have been,' and shook her head, feeling angry with both herself and Pierre. Glancing at his angular face, she considered booting him out, there and then. His cornered look had returned.

'Look, Pierre, if you tell me what's going on, maybe I can help you, maybe I'll understand. I know that everyone can get into scrapes, everyone takes the wrong path at some time in their lives.' She for one was in a big scrape right now.

'Okay, then,' the Frenchman replied. Jane was pulled round from her thoughts by the speed with which he launched into his story, as if he had an urgent need to offload it.

'Well, the car – it's my sister's. Did I tell you that when you found me in it, when I was a little...' he swivelled his index finger towards his temple '...*loco*? No? Must have been more than a little dazed to have left my papers and sketchbook in the back. Anyway, my sister, Giselle, didn't want to lend me the car. I'm not insured to drive it, although she has lent it to me in the past. But it's only hers, I mean, that she can only afford one because my mother, our mother, left her some money when she died, and didn't leave me any. In fact, Maman, or someone, must have left her loads of money, as she seems quite rich, judging by her apartment and her clothes.' His eyes searched into the interstices of the room again, beneath the wardrobe, penetrating the skirting board. He continued, 'So, in a way, I can say I have as much right to that car as Giselle. Or maybe more.'

Now his voice became strained. 'She and I had a row, a big row. I completely lost the plot. It must have been the day before the accident. And then I stole her car keys, and drove and drove, didn't care where, but, like a homing pigeon, ended up here, near here. It felt like I was having a... I think it's called a breakdown. I guess I was drawn to my, our, mother's grave. I slept in that old chapel. Well, didn't sleep – I'd had too much wine that evening. Had nightmares about Giselle and my mother both being dead, not exactly sure what – and very early in the morning I drove off, to go back to Giselle, to sort it out. I remember thinking I was being selfish, childish, Giselle has her troubles too. I'd only gone about a hundred metres, I think I was crying, when I skidded off the road. Can't remember the accident as such, only the absolute silence and stillness afterwards.'

He pulled another cigarette from the packet, his fingers trembling. The match would not connect with the tip as he tried to light it.

Jane had sat still and quiet while he talked, almost holding her breath. Poor boy, she thought, but then she began to doubt whether she believed him, or if she wanted to be involved with all that. What did it matter to her if he wasn't insured, if he and his sister were estranged? The more he talked, the more she sensed a quagmire of disturbance in him and probably in Giselle. Jane's reasons for taking this break pressed in on her and added to her impatience. Now, more than ever, she saw Pierre as a screwed-up kid with something of an orphan about him. She hoped that was not what she had been attracted to. She knew she had to be resolute, more resolute than polite decency would suggest.

'Oh dear, well. At least you've explained something,' she said, trying to sound matter-of-fact. 'Okay. So, if I go and get your stuff, *if* I do, will you promise me one thing in return? Will you promise that you will take yourself back home, or wherever, by the end of today?' A bruised look crossed his face. 'I'll give you a lift to someplace where you can get a bus or a train,' she continued. 'Agen station would be a good idea – there are trains from there to Nice, Toulouse, Bordeaux or Paris. I'll help you to find out about the connections you need. And I'll lend, no, give you some money. 70... 75 euros. I'm not driving all the way to a big town, but I'll take you to Agen. Alright?'

He nodded, silently looking at her. But then, in a tone that Jane perceived as forced jocularity, 'Can't wait to get rid of me, hey? Am I that bad? You didn't seem to think so this morning, or last night!'

'I wish you hadn't said... No, you're right. I'm in a muddle, yes, I am.'

'You certainly are!' he added.

The cruelty she discerned enabled her to maintain her firm stance. 'You see, Pierre, I haven't begun to tell you my story. And I don't think I need to. But I'm not simply a middle-aged bored or lonely woman.' She fought a tremor in her voice which she knew could lead to tears. 'I could be quite melodramatic about my circumstances, but I don't need – or want – to tell you. Except, you see, I have an illness, which is... ' she tried to sound nonchalant, tossing her head to the side, '...serious. But I don't think you're that interested anyway.' She held her breath, wishing she had not risked telling him, risked laying herself open to his reaction.

'Why didn't you tell me before?'

'I didn't want to think about it myself. Or for it to get… in the way. Anyway, I hate admitting that sort of thing.'

'What do you mean? That you get ill?'

'Yes.' She looked down.

'I don't understand.'

'It's true. Admitting illness can feel, for me, like admitting weakness. Ridiculous, in a way, I know.'

'But, well now, I'm sorry, sorry about all that. But you'll be alright in the end, won't you?'

She gave a little shrug.

'There are good doctors these days,' he added, confirming her sense of his limitations. And then he seemed to force himself to say, 'Do you want to tell me more about it?'

'No, not really. Later, maybe.'

'Will you go and find the things, then?' He reached for a nectarine at that moment. It seemed his way of attempting to appear blasé. It struck Jane that they were both caught in attempts to appear nonchalant.

If she had needed any more motivation to make this last gesture – raising her eyebrows at the huge understatement in that word, 'gesture,' as she thought it – his undue haste to extract this favour and his lack of interest in her provided ample reason. She said, 'Okay, but let's shake on your side of the bargain too – about you going on your way sometime today?'

They shook hands across the bed as amicably as two school friends in a pact.

While she dressed, she noticed how he peeled the nectarine gently, allowing the knife to pull the thin skin off, truly what 'peeling' was meant to be, with no cutting involved. Reluctantly, she noticed his tapering long fingers, and thought that men have either stubby fingers, or tapering fingers. Lennie's were stubby.

He did not offer her some of the fruit, as Lennie would.

After eating it, he wiped his hands on the sheet, pulled on the clothes Jane had lent him, and descended the spiral staircase silently. He hardly limped now.

She wondered why he had not asked more about her illness. She knew she did not encourage him, but had wanted him to rise above her inhibitions.

Jane calculated how many more days she would have, after this. Three, or was it four, whole days before travelling back. She felt like crying.

From the window, as she rubbed moisturising cream into her arms, she noticed Pierre, in a break between showers, reaching up to the fig tree and plucking two of the ripest figs. She knew he would not offer her one. They were ripening rapidly day by day, so there would be others.

Downstairs, she noticed a fig and one of Annette's deep pink geraniums on a Provencal plate at the place where she usually sat at the table.

'For you, Jane. You look nice, that colour suits you.' He seemed to really look at her, as if for the first time. 'Pretty', he added, more to himself than to her, still gazing at her.

She smiled and was glad that some glow of the night before had returned, like red in the sky after the sun has set. 'Yes, "magenta" it's called in English, my favourite colour,' she replied, quite shyly.

'I'll have the fig when I return from my hike. Thanks. I'll need it more then! You can see I'm wearing my toughest jeans. If Annette comes snooping around you'll just have to put on a convincing act at being my cousin. Say that my mother is half French or something. But I think Annette is at the market in Ceneyrac this morning, so don't worry too much. Oh yes, I'd love you to do a drawing for me, if you want.' She indicated her own sketchbook. 'It's not private, by the way,' she added, frowning. 'I don't think my sketches are precious, the way some people's are.' She knew he wasn't bothered about her comments.

He stretched out on the sofa with a cigarette as she left.

She remembered that her valuables were still locked in the boot of her car from that first time she had left him alone, before she really got to know him. She thought how paranoid she had been, but decided to leave them there for the time being.

The skid marks on the road were still visible. She glanced over the precipice by the *mirabelle* tree. Already, the torn branches and gashes were less conspicuous, but the leaves of broken branches looked dead. If she had not been looking for signs, she may not have noticed anything. Heavy rain in the night had subdued nature's ebullience. Everything seemed bowed down in the languid light. Now the boles on another large tree looked like diseased breasts.

Noticing for the first time large limestone boulders, she marvelled at Pierre's luck in not hitting one of those on his plunge.

She peered into the forest to see if she could glimpse that patch of red from here, but she could not. It must be more hidden by the wet branches, or perhaps her position was different. She walked briskly to the point lower down where she would leave the road and go through the maize field to the spot.

Her body felt so fit – except for her vision in one eye – as it had that first day when she swam. The phrase 'beating cancer' crept into her mind.

Blanketed by a soft, warm drizzle, she came to a little clearing in the field. Wondering if she had come a different way from before, she was fearful of losing her bearings.

A track in the field had been roughly cleared. Mud was churned up from wide wheels; nettles and brambles had not yet had a chance to reassert themselves. A farmer must have been taking his tractor this way.

Her spirits were lifted by the sun coming out dramatically, as if making up for its absence. Doves purred nearby, and a bee droned stridently. The bright leaves, illuminated, all struggled to reach onwards and upwards. Breathing deeply, she thanked nature and life for all this beauty. Rediscovering her love of forests, the smell of fungus, year upon year of leaf-fall as soft as feathers beneath her feet, she could almost forget that she was on some secret mission. She'd half hoped that nature would already be obscuring the car – such an ugly thing to have landed in the middle of all this.

Resolutely retracing her footsteps of only one day earlier, Jane recognised the rocky outcrop that she had clambered up and over to reach the car. She climbed up and peered over. Birds sang rightfully, imperviously. There was no car, nothing to disturb this place. Perhaps she was in the wrong spot, or nature had been exceedingly effective at hiding the sore. But then the wheel tracks and the flattened area below began to make sense.

She sat for a few minutes on the rock, looking down. Of course, this was the same rock. Those were the tufts of ferns and roots she had grabbed hold of. She was relieved that the car had been removed. Now her collusion would have to stop; there was no possibility of her fetching papers for someone who might be a criminal.

Some of the horror of her first reconnoitre with this place crept back to her now. Questions began to crowd in on her. *But why had the car been removed? So soon? If it was the police, surely they'd have made enquiries by now all around the neighbourhood, especially of Annette and her. There were so few dwellings around here. Or wouldn't they have made forensic tests on the vehicle in situ and the surroundings, and not been so hasty in removing it?* With a wave of panic, she realised that her fingerprints would be on the car door. She debated whether she had anything to hide. Further questions swarmed into her head, as to whether it was criminal not to have reported it straight away, and if she could plead that she was out of her mind, owing to her illness. She told herself firmly that she would ring the police as soon as she got back, even before she went to tell Pierre what had happened. If Annette was there, she would use her phone. And if not, she would creep into the cottage, get her car keys from the hall, and drive to the nearest phone box. She hoped that Pierre would not hear her return. And if he was startled by her quick reappearance and then disappearance, so be it. Things that seem fraught can sometimes be so simple, she realised.

The clamber back, without a semi-crippled man hanging onto her, did not feel as arduous as she had remembered. Of course, he would have to go. She again thought of the previous night, and shrugged. All her life she had been capable of impulsive acts, and even after years of psychoanalysis, she did not know if they were crazy, or a hidden part of her finding a voice.

Out of breath, she turned the bend in the steep road, on the last lap.

Where her car should have been, sitting solidly, its dark green merging with the trees on the grassy verge, was an empty space.

'Lennie, is that you? Thank God. Must talk to you. Okay?

'You're not going to believe all this. Two disappearing cars in one day. A young man crashed nearby. I was helping him, felt sorry for him – but he must have stolen my car. I've already told the police. I don't know if they know of the car that plummeted over the precipice. Oh, they must know…' She gabbled on, 'How could he, how could anyone, be such a crook? Nearly all my money, and tickets, and passport, and credit cards, oh God, yes, and photos of the grandchildren, and I just remembered, my mobile too, all in the boot of the hire car!

'Huh, yes, I suppose the police might catch him,' she continued. 'But meanwhile, I had to confess to Annette that I'd hidden the young man'– but she did not tell Lennie that it was even more complicated, that she had had to tell Annette that the man was not her cousin, after all – 'and I had to use her phone to arrange for another hire car at great expense, and notify my credit card companies, and so on.' Jane knew she was going on too long, keeping Lennie out, not wanting his questions.

'Darling, please can you pay for some of this, for the time being? I mean, I told the car hire place, Hertz, in Toulouse, that you would ring them with your credit card details? The insurance will cover it, I think, but just in the short-term they need a credit card number. I'm so sorry. Never been such an idiot in my life.' She forced herself to slow down. 'Their number from England is – got a pen? – 0033 561 30 00 01. Yes, Hertz.'

'But Janey, really, how could you have left your keys there, and your valuables in the boot – with a stranger? And what do you mean, you were 'hiding' him?'

Jane took a deep breath. 'Yes, I know. Really silly of me. I never for a moment thought that would happen. Please don't…'

There was a brief silence, before she heard Lennie trying to reach her, trying to overcome his incredulity.

'Me? Yes, I'm okay, sort of. Been a hellish sort of holiday though. I know I needed space, and then… all this.'

There was a silence. And then she heard his voice again, reasonably calm, but edged with anxiety, a semitone higher than usual, asking her if she was really alright? Should he fly out to be with her, to take her home? He would cancel his meetings over the next few days. She realised what a huge effort he was making, to rise above his own upset at her behaviour.

Only now did she feel like weeping. Something real, something solid, someone being kind, on this moving ground in this little corner of France.

Bravely, she said that she would be alright. 'No, really darling.' Indeed she meant it, she knew that there was a solid place somewhere inside her that she would eventually find, that did not have to depend on Lennie. 'I may be a day or two delayed in getting back, what with rearranging everything – you know, getting a document instead of my passport. May even manage to relax a little now. Oh yes Lennie, can you cancel my appointment at the hospital – with Dr Greenberg – for the 28th? And see if they can fit me in on the 30th. I know that's a Saturday, but they may see me then, especially as the

Monday is a Bank Holiday. Thanks. The number is on a pink Post-it on the noticeboard by the downstairs phone.

'Oh, and the *baby*! I even forgot to ask. Any news?'

'No, I'd have rung if there was. He's just a few days late. Alice is fine. Spoke to her again last night on the phone. It's you I'm worried about. I didn't understand some of what you were saying, about the police not knowing about the crashed car. You won't get mixed up in anything dodgy, will you?'

'No, 'course not. Can explain later. Can't really use this phone, as you—'

He interrupted, 'But how are you, besides everything else?'

Jane knew she could not make sense of all this with Pierre, did not know if it could ever fit on the same map as her cancer. Or as her husband.

All she said was, 'Yes, you're so right – about "everything else". Love you, darling. Better go. The police are coming round soon to ask questions. I'll let you know my return details and all that. Bye.'

Jane was relieved that Annette was hanging washing on the line, out of earshot. 'Thank you, Annette,' she called. 'I've left some money.' She could not bear to talk more with that busybody now.

She wandered back to her cottage, wishing for the police visit to be over so that she could begin to gather her thoughts.

She noticed the row of tiny hooks inside the front door, where she had always left her car keys. The front door key was still there, at least.

The ripe fig and the deep pink geranium waited on the table, on the Provencal plate. She tipped them into the bin.

In her mind, she handed it all over to the police to puzzle out.

A shiny cerulean blue car stood in her grassy space, instead of the bottle green one. Hertz were as good as their word.

With a smile, she now hid the car key inside a little bureau, in case, knowing she was 'locking the stable door after...' *He'll probably crash my green car, too. It'll serve him right.*

Later, making a pasta sauce from onions, plum tomatoes and fresh basil, she noticed that a bottle of Chablis had disappeared. What a bastard, she thought; he probably justified it as his just reward or something. But she refused to be further shocked at the man's insolence – indeed, criminality.

It would have been easy for Jane to now feel thoroughly used in every way, including their time in bed, or rather, on the floor at first. But, but, she struggled to think, she had wanted it too, hadn't she? Of course she had. Does it have to matter if all this emerged later? Does it change what happened, when that felt so good – even loving in its own way. She remembered the massage he gave her: not knowing now if it was a seducer's tactic, or a real sense of what she needed.

She thought about something that she had not been able to define the second time – the next morning: how he was just him, there, existing, yet involved with her, but not, in fact, making demands on her for anything. She had not known that with anyone before, except perhaps with her first proper boyfriend, Mike Shand, but she could not really remember. Pierre could be so responsive and giving, and yet so much himself. She had felt the opposite of used. This left her all the more confused by what had happened later, and no doubt all those lies about his sister and her car. He probably doesn't have a sister. Her own lies to Lennie stopped her feeling indignant.

Sipping a rich claret on the patio, she watched the sun's rays streaming through the trees and hoped, without bitterness, that Pierre was enjoying her Chablis. She wondered if people have to go through life finding, indeed snatching, moments of beauty, intensity, and somehow managing to keep those separate, walled off, from all their bad experiences. She felt increasingly muddled, for she knew that this reasoning flew in the face of her work, the effort to integrate the bad with the good, even the way that life and death defined each other inexorably.

But there began the seed of an idea, a thought that she had to keep nuggets of beauty separate, separate from the cancer, the lies, the betrayals, the bartering, the hurt, the disappointment, her years of painstakingly patching over her passionate nature. Like the sun coming out after the rain: she didn't keep thinking of the rain and the clouds, but rejoiced in the sun, with its promise, its balm. She didn't dwell on the few decaying figs being eaten by wasps or ants at this moment, but found and devoured the mellifluous ones. If she was rotting, in a way, or so the scans told her – sometimes it was difficult to believe – she must, she really must, contemplate joy, gaze at trembling leaves, now, as much as she could.

She fell asleep that night lulled by great wings that enfolded her, indebted to this strange life that was more sweet than bitter.

AUGUST 21ST, 2003

After tea in bed, she emerged into the bright day with a spring in her step, having decided to walk all the way to Ceneyrac. She knew she could still try to enjoy her retreat. She would stop on the way back with a picnic.

She brought her sketchbook and notebook. Sketching small details in nature always appealed to her. This activity linked her to people – often women – through the centuries, who had taken this interest in cataloguing the minute details in nature's patterning, logic and variety. Now she felt like an explorer setting forth, her sharpened pencils in their case, wearing her large straw hat. She had wondered whether to bring watercolours, but then decided to make notes of the colours and perhaps add them later.

Ignoring a barely discernible *Propriété privée* worn wooden sign, the grain raised in wealds, nailed to a tree, Jane walked into the field it was meant to protect. She wanted to examine the pale-beetroot colour thistles she could see. Their fat tufts were surprisingly soft, so perhaps they weren't thistles after all. Black furry bees with orange bottoms drowsily sated themselves, reminding Jane of a baby at the breast, pumping it, sucking insistently. Elderflower heads hung down laden with glistening black beads like caviar, its red branching stems so like the circulatory system. Jane loved finding the universal patterns of nature, each one adapted to suit the needs of its species, but also clearly part of a supreme logic. She tasted one berry and spat out its bitter juice.

When she opened her scuffed sketchbook to find a clean page, there, like an interloper, was a sketch of how she might have looked twenty or even thirty years ago: her curly unkempt hair, her heart-shaped face, lying in a way that could only be called 'voluptuously' on a soft *chaise-longue* that sagged beneath her wide hips. The figure was draped in something flowing and diaphanous that showed her breasts. It was flattering, and touching too. Like a lepidopterist, Pierre had netted the young Jane and pinned her down, but not killed her in the process. He had observed her eyebrows, her particular earrings, her bold onyx ring, something of her smile. She was not the only one who noticed detail, and recorded it. The style was quite naïve but appealing: fine lines in places, dense detail and cross-hatching in others. She marvelled at his particular use of Matisse-like line and how it conveyed the volume of what he was describing.

The way others see us. Like holding up a mirror, but distorted by their perceptions and desires and fears and prejudices. And imagination, she added. She stared at this young man's vision of woman, of sexuality, and she understood something of what she had felt with him in those two intense exchanges.

And he had left the drawing for her. A parting gift? Or shot? She could have felt pain, or embarrassment, at the beautiful fantasy on the page and how she really was nowadays; at the contrast between breasts with an upward thrust, defying gravity, and those that sag. But she chose to see this simply as his idealisation of her. At the moment, in the face of his betrayal and her illness, she needed that.

He must have done it just before his getaway. Not for the first time, she wondered when he had decided to steal the car, and how calculating he had been. Indeed, perhaps there had not been anything in the boot of his car.

She could not stop now to draw the plants or the bees or the berries, though she sensed that if she could overcome her disquiet by forcing herself to sketch, she might feel better.

She stared at his drawing. Now Pierre's disappearance – the suddenness of it, the betrayal – was like a monstrous slap in the face.

What he really felt about her became her main preoccupation, more than his mysterious motives and criminality. She needed to know if he had simply used her, as he had used her hospitality and her relative strength, had seen her as a means to take himself off on the next part of his journey, and if – the worst of all possible interpretations – he was now mocking her for her readiness to be used, perhaps for her neediness. But why does that matter, she asked herself, if I felt alright at the time, if I enjoyed it, isn't that all that matters? She had betrayed Lennie in a big way. Yet, Pierre, or Charles, or whatever his name was, betrayed her – didn't that equal everything out, wasn't that the law of talion? Her confusion increased.

A helicopter flying to and fro irritated her.

She stuffed the sketchbook into her basket and wondered if she should destroy his drawing.

Tired, Jane turned back towards the cottage. The whole point of this retreat was being wasted, in fact, was proving to be the opposite of beneficial. All she saw ahead now was illness and deterioration. She was no longer sure about her thoughts on that walk to the lake, when it had made sense to clutch at life, more life, more chemo, at whatever cost. All that felt like weeks ago.

Yet again, facing thoughts of death, her mind reached out to little Tom and Will, and the baby about to expand his lungs and breathe real air – or perhaps he had already. She took a deep breath herself. Those are the important things that really matter. Her outward breath became a heavy sigh. But I have no energy, little spirit for them.

She did not know if she would ever again feel so infused with life and optimism as she had when she had lain by Pierre's side, stranger that he was.

Quietly waiting in the shade next to her Hertz replacement, Jane saw a police car: more reassuring than menacing in its white and blue efficiency, with its flash of luminous green – colours more suitable for advertising washing powder or tennis shoes, she thought.

She was sure she had answered enough questions by now – as far as they were concerned. Surely, it's only a stolen vehicle? She felt a pang of fear at her economy with the truth. She had only told the police that the stranger who she had let into her cottage had hurt his leg, how he had recovered on her sofa for two days before stealing her car. She had not mentioned clambering to his rescue, nor the crashed Renault, as she worried that she would be on the wrong side of the law for not reporting it in the first place. If the Renault disappeared, somehow, what has that to do with her, she reasoned. She did not know if she was being stupid. She wished she could discuss all this with Lennie.

Increasingly, she veered towards the assumption that the speedy removal of the car from the forest floor was not the work of the police, since they had not made enquiries of her and Annette, but that it had something to do with Pierre's murky life. She did not want him to be in further trouble by reporting the crash to the police. Remembering his deprived, hunted look, she wanted him to have a chance to break out of whatever torments he was in by promising him some money, his salvaged identity papers and sketchbook, and a lift on his way to wherever. She felt that there could have been a parity to the situation up to that point: invigorated by the contact with him, he too had imbibed some goodness, softness and affection from her. If he had not stolen her car – and her Chablis – she would have felt reasonably hopeful that he had been helped by her.

Two policemen stepped out to meet her, removing their flat-topped hats, apologising for disturbing her again. They were not the officers of the previous day. The younger one was handsome in a dark, Mediterranean way, with a neat moustache. Jane tried to avoid looking at him, yet was drawn to him, for there was a similarity to Pierre that unnerved her. The older one was stout, his blue shirt tightly stretched across his chest. He wiped the perspiration from his brow with a large white handkerchief and smiled, touching the black leather holster of his revolver as routinely as someone might check that their fly was zipped up. Jane felt uneasy and thought, as she had often done before, that she preferred British police because they did not usually carry guns. All these chains and gadgets, pockets, epaulettes, clips and badges made them look like glorified boy scouts.

The older man asked in a deep baritone if she could help them by answering further questions.

'Yes, of course, with pleasure. Do you want to come in?'

She unlocked the door of the cottage and gestured towards the sitting room, which was cool with its thick stone walls and comfortable armchairs. She really needed to sit down herself.

The older man introduced himself as Inspector Lagarde, and his colleague as Officer Bonnet. Lagarde removed a notebook from his back pocket, the folded-over pages kept in place with a rubber band, and removed a ballpoint pen from his breast pocket. Could she answer a few more questions about the young man who she assumed had stolen her car? He added that, of course, they cannot be sure that it was him. 'It could have been someone else.' Jane nodded wearily, thinking how all over the world, the law is so pedantic. She was pleased that normally she didn't have to have much to do with the police.

He wanted to go over what she had already told his colleagues.

'But, Inspector, you know I'm only here for a brief holiday, you know I am a mother and a grandmother, and you know – well, I told your colleagues – I am... seriously ill.' Again, Jane hated telling people about her illness, even after so much practice at it, as if she was publicly announcing her own failings.

'Ah well. You know I only offered the stranger some resting place, so he could travel on. The word "hospice" really means "resting place,"' she continued, 'originally for pilgrims and travellers. Nowadays, we misuse the term if we only think of it as a place for the incurably ill or the dying. That was what I was offering the young man: a resting place – like, what we call a "watering hole" for animals – perhaps because of my own grave illness and my wish to receive similar treatment.' Jane knew that she was being far too discursive, too fanciful, too garrulous, but she intended to show them her eccentric, middle-aged scholarly self, to distract them from any other clues they may pick up. 'Perhaps it was foolhardy of me, but my illness seems to make me act in ways that I would not normally,' she added, looking down at her sandals.

She realised she was now closer to the truth than she wished, in danger of saying too much. The trouble is, when one lies, she thought, it is more difficult to be sure of consistency than if one is strictly truthful. Lifting her gaze to the trees beyond the pool, Lennie came to her mind.

The police officer retraced the steps she had taken. 'Madame, yes, I know my colleague has already interviewed you – I'm sorry – but as you declined coming to the police station to make a statement… Your name, please?'

'This is very tedious.' Years ago, months ago, she would have complied straightforwardly. Now she was more able to say what she felt.

She gave her name, adding, 'Actually, my title is 'Doctor''. His manner changed to one of ingratiating respect, 'Oh you are a *doctor!*'

She explained curtly that she was a Doctor of Philosophy.

He remained obsequious with a hint of flirtatiousness, 'Another time I would like to ask you more about that. But I suppose we must stick to business. Let's begin with your first contact with the man. When was that?'

Jane replied wearily that she had opened the door to a young man on Tuesday, 19th August. '2003', she added, mischievously. Neither man seemed to think that she was being pedantic.

She now decided to be simple, straightforward, and as brief as possible to get all this over with. Nevertheless, she found herself explaining how she could not be absolutely sure of the days of the week when she was away – let alone the date. How she avoided wearing a watch, wanted to get away from calendars, and lived in a fool's paradise of unawareness.

She continued that in a corner of her mind she kept a grip on reality, so that her conscientious self could return to England as planned. And how she then had to face the shock of the contrast when she returned to the frenetic life she normally led. The Inspector had stopped writing and was looking at her in confusion. She was amazing herself at this degree of verbosity.

'He, the young man, looked quite exhausted....' she added, to rescue both herself and the Inspector.

'What time was it?'

Jane came to with a jolt. 'Goodness, I've no idea. Well, let me guess. Don't wear a watch these days, as I said. It was the morning, certainly. I had tea by then, and coffee I think, after getting up quite late. So, perhaps ten o'clock? I had dressed by then, that I do remember.'

'One moment, please, while I catch up,' writing fast. After a minute he continued, 'Can you describe him?'

Jane began to object, again, to the meaninglessness of these questions when she had already answered similar ones the day before, but knew that the men would be satisfied and depart sooner if she complied with their rules.

'Well, he looked exhausted and in some pain, I think; thin, unshaven, small beard, short dark greasy-looking hair.' She glanced at Officer Bonnet, and continued, 'Not very clean, generally, and he smelt... a little unsavoury. You know, of... what's the word in French? When someone has not washed.' She decided not to mention the smell of alcohol on his breath. 'Wore old, torn jeans, you know, like lots of young people these days. It's the fashion, isn't it? Though I always think... ' She managed to stop herself rambling. 'And a checked shirt. Cotton, probably. You know exactly, because I handed over his effects – goodness, isn't that what one says after someone has died? I handed over everything that he had left, afterwards, to the other policeman.'

A shiver of pleasure deep in her womb took her by surprise. She never ceased to marvel at how her body sometimes had a mind of its own. There was something of his that was hers, possibly still alive, inside her, that she had not parted with. How long did they say it lived for? Seventy-two hours she seemed to remember. How long was that? Three days? And if not that, there were the memories, the memories she would never hand over.

The Inspector was busy writing after rechecking that his carbon paper was in place. He did not notice the flush to her throat. With her hand fanning out over her neck, she self-consciously looked at the younger man. He not only literally took a backseat on a hard chair, slightly behind his colleague, but seemed to be an unnecessary silent accessory. She realised he was listening, though, and possibly was very observant. She did not know whether to include him more in her answers. What was he picking up? Had he noticed her blushing? He was the sort of man who had the material to go far in the force, she felt. She determined to bring into focus the details before her, like the old-fashioned use of carbon paper in the year 2003. She resisted offering them coffee or a cold drink, staying with her resolve to be business-like.

She volunteered now, not waiting for the next question: 'Of course, I lent him clean clothes, poor chap. He had so little in his bag. He said he had lost some of his luggage. So I lent him loose white trousers and a black t-shirt, a plain one. You'll want to know that there was no logo on it. I don't see the point of paying more in order to do someone else's advertising. Can't remember the label inside – I bought it in some market in England years ago. I like sleeping in it,' she added, and then wished she had not, for she perceived the younger man frowning slightly. She wondered if she had burst a more romantic bubble he had of her sleeping in sexy lingerie, rather than a washed out shapeless old t-shirt? But then Lennie liked her in it.

Now the younger man seemed to glance at the sheets she had purposely washed, washed on the hottest cycle the machine could manage, and hung on the line in the garden.

'Oh yes, he carried a grey, canvas shoulder bag, as I said to the other guys before.' She felt pleased with the fluency of her French. 'He took that with him, of course, when he fled.'

'What was he wearing on his feet when he arrived, Doctor?'

She paused before replying, trying not to talk too much. 'Oh, I can't be absolutely sure. Old trainers, possibly. Can't visualise them. Don't think it was sandals. And he didn't leave socks behind with his old clothes, did he, and I didn't replace them for him. But you didn't ask me about socks,' she added, smiling.

And so the senior man trawled through the events of that first morning, and then that afternoon, and into the evening. She told him about the young man taking a shower, using her *Clarins* shampoo, her feeding him, even buying him cigarettes – Craven A – and how he slept on the sofa. And still Jane avoided making eye contact with the policemen, even though she felt that it would have been more ordinary to do so.

Now the older one asked at which point she had telephoned her husband in England?

'I can't see why that's relevant. But, if you want to know, I only phoned him when my car was stolen. He and I have an understanding when I'm away, to hardly communicate, except when necessary. We're not part of the mobile phone brigade, joined by an umbilicus!' How do you say it, "*ombilic*"? she added with a smile, now looking at the younger man quite challengingly. He gave an uneasy smile in return.

'And, Doctor, what did you tell him, your husband?'

Again, Jane wondered if she was getting into deep water, for she could not in fact remember exactly what she had told Lennie, nor if she had answered a similar question to the first policeman the day before.

'I told him I needed him to telephone Hertz in Toulouse, to pay some supplement before the insurance was sorted, for the replacement hire car. The bastard Pierre, I mean Charles, took all my credit cards, passport, etc., as you know!'

'We'll get onto that in a moment.'

'Just a minute, Officers, I mean, Inspector, I can't help feeling that you are talking to me as if I have committed some crime. I am trying to help, you know. But there is a limit to my patience. At this rate, I'll have to get myself a lawyer. Fortunately, my insurance fully covers any legal aid I might need.'

Neither man seemed to listen to this.

'Look at that pool, look at the sunshine,' making an effort to sound dreamy, rather than irritated, but felt that all she managed to sound was fake. 'I can think of better things to do with my time than this,' she added, regardless of whether this forcefulness would prolong the questioning.

Eventually, they left, but only after the Inspector read to her everything he had written, all eighteen small pages of it, and she had signed and dated the statement that it was the truth, on little dotted lines at the bottom of each and every page, and he had countersigned each page as the witness. And after they had accepted glasses of water. She expressed relaxed helpfulness, which belied her increasing disquiet, as she said goodbye.

Jane felt thankful that Annette had not been snooping around lately.

Jane swam, but with her swimsuit on this time, unsure if further officers of the law would return.

She would be in England in a few days' time, she registered, her head surfacing after a length underwater. She needed to find solid facts in this moving world that she now inhabited. She pulled her shoulder straps down below her arms, so her breasts floated free. She did not know if she wanted to think of Pierre or not: if she hated him or felt passionate about him. Perhaps it was possible to feel both. At the same time? No, she felt that it was not in her nature to hate someone who thrilled her body.

The water felt like warm milk. She lifted out some dead leaves, contorted into curved and twisted shapes that floated lightly on the surface, their desiccated quality not altered by the element beneath them.

The more she raked over the interview with the policemen, the more anxious she became. She fretted that they would ask the pharmacist what she had bought, and find out about the condoms. What if they found the hire car and the condoms in the glove compartment? What if Pierre told them all about the crash, and about her part in rescuing him? And then, about the sex? She tried to refute her anxieties, telling herself that it only mattered if he was a serious criminal, and if they thought she was an accomplice. 'Crime doesn't pay,' was the cliché that came to mind. Now she worried that they would telephone Lennie. What exactly had she told him? Had she told him about the crash and rescuing the man? Lennie would see no reason not to relay that to them.

Deciding to try out the new hire car, Jane stepped out onto the verge while Annette was trimming the long grass; a task which so clearly arose out of her need to find out what was going on.

'Ah Madame, Jane. Lots of busy-ness here! I hope nothing bad has happened? Do you need my assistance?'

'Oh no, thank you, Annette. Just… just something that the police are worrying about. Nothing, I am sure. But, yes, a young man stole my hire car. I was going to tell you. No great crime, really. Just annoying. So now I must go to the village, to try out this new car.'

Annette appeared deflated at the pace at which Jane drove off.

She drove to the small supermarket in Ceneyrac to buy pork chops. She told herself that her missing – no, stolen – CDs were only things. She could manage without them and replace them later. She also bought a new phonecard at the small *tabac*, grateful for the cash she had left in her bedroom.

Passing the telephone box on her way back, she stopped the car. She went to it without really thinking, following an instinct.

The doors of the booth were stiff and only worked in unison, almost trapping her arm. The heat within the airless space caused a sweat all over her body. Mopping her midriff with the linen of her loose shift, she phoned her own mobile number as if in a dream. Her voice answered with a message, sounding ponderous. She put the receiver down. And dialled again. This time she decided to leave a message in her clearest French, without using Pierre's name, unsure who would have the phone by now. It could be in the hands of the police.

'Hello. This is Jane, the owner of this… the phone, the one that you are listening to. I would really appreciate it if whoever hears this message, whoever has my mobile, could please ring me here. I'm at a callbox, and the number is: 05 65 217899. I repeat, 05 65 217899. It's now 5.25, that's 17.25, on the 21st. I'll wait here until 17.30. You see, there's a number I really need stored on that phone, I need it desperately. You're welcome to the phone. But please just help me by ringing me and I'll tell you which number I need you to look up.' She hesitated. Then, 'Many thanks.'

Jane stepped out of the booth to breathe the cooler air and feel the faint breeze. Early dried leaves shuffled around her feet among cigarette stubs, a grey-with-age netting bridal ribbon tied in a bow, and a deflated dirty balloon that looked like a dead hibiscus. Dogs began to bark insistently through a high wire fence, scrabbling between branches of buddleia. She worried that their noise would override the phone ringing. Not daring to think who would ring her back or what she would say, she was amused at her boldness and ingenuity.

As she waited, she felt sure that if Pierre heard the message he would never ring back for he would be convinced that she was now working for the police.

The iron hands of the simple clock high on the church façade stated 5.29. She waited another minute, then heard the single metallic clang of its bell. And waited another two minutes. As she collected up her basket, she told herself that it was just as well. When making sure she had reclaimed her phonecard, the phone rang. She hurriedly looked around. No one was about. With increased strength she heaved the doors open and grabbed the receiver,

'Yes?'

She heard a man's voice, 'Hello?'

'Yes, it's me, Jane,' she said. She heard what sounded like Pierre, seemingly relaxed, and could imagine him smiling, even welcoming this contact with her. She felt that quiver again in the depths of her body. She astounded herself at how quickly she could forgive him; was it only the day before that she felt him to be a rat of the first order?

'Well, well, what have *you* been up to then? But it's good to hear from you,' she said, deciding not to begin on recriminations and real questions, even though there could be plenty of those, for she would risk losing contact with him altogether. She needed to keep it simple, to see if he felt she was an old fool or if she sensed he valued her by the way he talked to her.

'Are you okay, then?' Jane asked.

'Yes, fine. My leg is much better. Thanks for the loan of your car! I left it for Monsieur Hertz, even though he has plenty more.'

'What a nerve!' she managed to say, truthful yet friendly, enjoying the challenge of this fine balancing act. 'Honestly! But you'll be glad to know that I didn't tell *les flic* about the "accident".'

'Well, I think of you, Jane.' He seemed not to care what she had or had not told the police.

'Me too. I think of you.'

'*Bons souvenirs.*'

'Yes.'

She listened intensely, waiting for the next move from him. There was a silence.

'What are you doing now?' she asked.

'Talking to you,' he replied.

She smiled. And wondered if she should be the one to end the conversation, to not feel rejected.

'It's good to hear from you,' he said warmly. 'But what was the number you wanted from your phone?'

Jane had forgotten about her subterfuge, but quickly rallied: 'Oh yes! A friend of mine, she's very ill, and I must ring her to see how she is. Don't have her number anywhere. She's ex-directory. Please look her up under "Harriet".' Jane spelt the name. 'But I don't think you can while you're on the line to me. I just realised, this is your call to me. It's expensive. I'll ring you back in a few minutes, by which time you can have looked up Harriet's number.'

With that they rang off. Pierre sounded either irritated by her or confused. She could not work it out; his mood seemed to shift from warm to ambivalent. Jane felt guilty at having given Harriet a serious illness.

The church clock struck six when Jane drove back to her cottage. He had not answered her last call to her mobile. She had waited in case for some reason he was going to call her at the phone box. But he did not.

All the confidence she had gained during their telephone contact drained away, like rain on drought-stricken soil. Perhaps it's just as well, she told herself; just as well that he hadn't phoned her back.

She stayed with the 'just as well' thought, and decided that there was now a full stop, and not a comma, after Pierre. Yes, a bold full stop. She wondered what that would feel like. She did not know whether she would have to mourn something, yet another grief, when there were major losses all around – or whether it would feel like a dream, even a wonderful dream, that she knew was part of her.

Clouds had gathered over the sun. Thunder, like heavy furniture being moved in heaven, rumbled. In the far distance, she saw what Will, her grandson, called 'flashlings'. The air-conditioning in the car began to cool her.

By the time she returned to *La Retraite*, water rushed down the deep gutters on both sides of the narrow street, carrying leaves. She knew what fun she could have with Tom and Will if they were here, making boats out of leaves and watching their progress. The air smelt stale, not that rain-on-dusty road smell she loved. *Perhaps it's more about my musty self.*

The shower did not manage to overpower the sun for long. Soon birds re-established themselves with clear calls, the electricity which had failed in her cottage was restored and Annette's cat Sweet William began to prowl among the wet leaves. Jane registered the swishy sound of a car on the little road. The thunder continued to growl in the far distance, like a disgruntled ogre that would not entirely give up. She thought of a story she could make up for Tom and Will. And baby Theo, if he existed, safe and sound. Any day now she really should hear about the baby.

The day had been so fragmented, so unsatisfactory, that she decided to go to bed early. After supper of the chops, which she had grilled, a tomato and basil salad, eaten with the laziest accompaniment – a large packet of oily, savoury crisps – and two glasses of Luberon cold rosé, she climbed up the steep spiral staircase holding firmly onto the handrail, aware of her vulnerability if she should fall while alone. She gave a little laugh at the way she was continuing to preserve her life and perhaps always would. She held on to the William Trevor she had been saving, saving for this precious break, *The Story of Lucy Gault*. So grave, and yet perhaps it was not altogether tragic. The choices people made were so understandable in the book, even if, with hindsight, they were the wrong ones. So far, the book seemed to be all about missed opportunities.

She did not want her life to be like that, and yet perhaps it was. The closer she was to death – adjusting her sentence to 'probable death' – the more she realised that this was not a rehearsal; what others put off to another day or to some amorphous hope for the future, she could not.

Before closing the shutters, she looked at the little chapel opposite, silhouetted against a sky evolving from golden yellow to bruise-blue. Dogs set each other off barking monotonously and one howled, the ogre in the sky had not fully relented but grumbled on, and her unease and disease remained.

August 22ND, 2003

Jane awoke feeling heavy, having slept deeply. The air had resumed its mugginess after the brief respite from the rain.

She swam, and dozed, and ate, and walked as far as the nearest farm. Suspended, in a grey mood that did not match the bright day. She read a recent copy of *The Guardian Review*, which she had brought with her, but even that did not interest her as much as usual.

In the afternoon, she slept to the accompaniment of the drowsy drone of flies, with the shutters closed.

She had had so much sleep, and yet still felt tired. Perhaps this was what 'unwound' meant. It was pleasant, but it felt as if she was in a backwater; if she stayed there much longer she would stagnate. She wondered if she was depressed because she now had to get Pierre into perspective. Did that mean, to see him for the ruthless person he had been, and to allow him to recede?

Everything, all the people in her life, now seemed remote, even the things in the cottage, the fig trees and the walnut tree outside, the sounds of cicadas and birds. It was a slightly eerie feeling she had had before, as if everything was in slow motion.

By the evening, she gave into her lethargy and sensed that her body and mind needed to hibernate. Her symptoms had recurred: the obscure vision in one eye, the aches in her side.

AUGUST 23RD, 2003

Jane awoke feeling more energetic than the day before.

After reading her book on the patio over a coffee, she flicked on the television to try it out, while she washed up. On the news she glanced at an unreal svelte woman in a purple dress. She had neat blonde hair and was standing against a shocking pink background, announcing White House meetings that Jane hardly followed. The Labour Government in Great Britain was still working out the probable suicide of Kelly, forest fires raged in the south near Marseille, fireworks were still banned because of the drought, a storm wrecked boats near Montpelier, there was a high toll of traffic on certain holiday roads, and one serious pile-up near Toulouse was shown on the local news, as well as a mention of the disappearance last week of a young woman, Giselle B..., who worked for a bank in Lyons. The police were not ruling out suspicious circumstances.

She stopped her activities to look at the television and glimpsed a slightly blurred photograph of a young woman in a red dress, followed by a mention of helicopters and heat-seeking equipment being used to sweep rough ground as fears for her grew. She thought she had heard 'Giselle Baudier', but could not be sure. Perhaps she had imagined the surname.

Then motor racing was shown briefly in St Antonin. When the weather forecast appeared in lurid colours of sun symbols dotted over France, Jane changed channels to find a programme called *It's Never Too Late To Learn To Play The Piano*, which seemed to be interviewing people who had taken up pastimes from hang gliding to playing the cello, either late in life or against the odds. With a guffaw she said, 'Sometimes, it really is too late!' and switched it off.

Her mind returned to the shocking possibility that the woman could be Pierre's sister. Perhaps she should buy a local newspaper.

She decided to go across to the chapel before it became too hot to do anything.

Walking along the perimeter of the stubbly field, she thought she noticed the dark figure of a man half-hidden by a tree in a small copse nearby. She looked again and the figure had disappeared. Perhaps her imagination was becoming florid; she could have imagined that name on the television too.

This was her first return to the chapel since she had noticed that strange light emanating from within it that night, before Pierre's crash. She approached the more derelict side of the exposed wooden structures and the image that had struck her from a distance – of the ribs of a beached whale picked dry by gulls and the elements – now returned to her mind. It was half buried by stones. A large stone that had formed part of a wall looked like a sad face lying on its side, or was it like a skull? Weathered dry joists jutted out of crumbling walls, and some stones had turned to dust. Stone and wood seemed to be in centuries-old competition as to who would outlast the other. It was not clear who was winning. Three cypresses propped up a grey cloud. An orange-brown butterfly with black spots and tortoiseshell markings closed up in the wind, and then settled on a dead leaf and rocked from side to side, as if on waves. The silence was punctuated by a cock crowing in the distance.

Roughly daubed black paint on a galvanised metal strip declared *Défense d'Entrer*. Rebellious in the face of safety strictures, she entered, descending four steps into the building that was open to the sky.

Elderberry and buddleia trees grew in the middle. Ivy sprawled almost everywhere, some dead and brown. She noticed how moss could act like cement, keeping crumbling stone walls in place. A cicada began to thrum feebly. The buzzing of bees and flies and the twitter of a tiny bird somewhere high up in the tower contrasted with the heaviness and deadness all around. Inexplicably, there was a pile of sawn timber and broken roof tiles, also in a pile. Green marks on the inside walls, where rain had swept in through the mullioned windows, half obscured faint amateurish decorations of umber stylised hills that someone had once painted on the stucco. There was the ubiquitous recent graffiti, of hearts pierced by arrows, and letters that did not seem to make a word. Some beams hung down perilously. A few nailed floorboards were still in place. Jane noticed a wooden ceiling, or perhaps a floor, above her in a higher area, which she thought may have been a bell tower. She marvelled how some of the stones and carvings could look new, and how the centre of a mullioned window, made as it was of small sections of broken stone piled crookedly one on top of the other, did not topple.

She had always been drawn to old crumbling places and had shared her fantasies of restoring them with Lennie who patiently indulged her – in prospect only – even though it was the last thing he would really want to do. If she had considerable funds, would she want to restore this place as a dwelling, she wondered, and what would it look like? Her own disease gave these musings complicating dimensions. She realised that now she was less inspired by the fantasy of restoration. It flew in the face of a natural crumbling into dust.

A fighter plane burst overhead like a thunderclap, louder than any she had ever heard before. There was nothing to do but freeze, its volume and suddenness too overwhelming even to feel terror. It departed as suddenly as it had arrived, but left Jane with a delayed reaction of disturbance.

Stumbling over gnarled bleached roots, so like bones, to reach a well-preserved small area through a gothic arch, she found the remains of a little fire: stones in a circle around pale grey ash. And a bottle of Evian water and two dark empty bottles of Cahors wine lying on their sides, as well as an empty packet of Gauloises. The fresh and clean labels looked artificial and out of place in this decaying but natural world. A few spots of white paint stood out glaringly on the dusty flagstones. And a flat area, that had been cleared of leaves and debris, was so unblemished that she discerned a foot or a hand had recently swept it, to the length of a person.

Of course, she thought of Pierre. The plane so close overhead had frayed her nerves; now Pierre's crash, the horror of it, came to her mind in a way that she had not imagined before. Looking up at a weathered little wooden shutter by a small window, the iron hook to secure it was still there, she was reminded of a witch's house in a storybook.

Fearful lest that figure by the trees was somewhere, she wanted to leave, to escape from this place that now irritated her as much as the flies settling on her bare arms. She passed an old tin drum amidst ferns in a separate area, and wondered if someone had lived here once, lived here as of right, and not like a hunted animal.

Her eyes were drawn to a white bone in a corner, or what was left of a large long bone, broken across. The shaft filled out to form the knob that would fit in a socket. She was sure it was the femur of a human. How extraordinary that a person's remains would be left lying here. She imagined her sister Ruth saying, 'No! Germs and all that,' but ignored her warning as she lifted the clean dry object to observe its hollowness and admire its strength.

She felt remarkably detached from the fleshed out real person this had once been. Like a find in a glass case in a museum. That she too would become a collection of bones in a cemetery did not upset her, merely underlined what she already knew – that this pattern was as old as life itself, and that dead was dead. Except, a small voice crept into her mind, except if those who were left behind suffered.

She placed the bone down carefully, respectfully, in the corner.

And left this disturbing building by descending a sweep to the lower ground of the outer staircase, whose supports again looked new. Looking up at high arrow slits, she thought about people having to defend this place once.

Crossing through the little graveyard as she left, her eyes were drawn to a grave whose leaning stone had a cypress tree enveloping part of it, so that they became indivisible – a fortunate outcome, for a grave to become part of a living growing tree. She wondered which would outlast the other.

On it, the name 'Baudier' entered her line of vision. She went closer to see a new array of artificial hydrangeas on the grave of Odette Baudier. The inscription on a red and black marble plaque standing on the base read:

> *Maman, mot que l'on dit tout bas*
> *Maman, mot que l'on n'oublie pas.*
> *A ma Maman.*

The last line was in gold, the others freshly painted in white. Jane noticed that the word '*ma*' in the last line was irregular and looked jagged, and that the spacing was different. It covered another word that had been painted over in the same colour as the marble, a dark maroon. She deciphered the underlying word as '*notre*'. A pale cloud of leaves was painted around the words. The dates on the unpolished stone were 1948 – 1996.

Jane remembered Pierre saying something about visiting his mother's grave, and how that had led him to drink and to drive recklessly. So, perhaps his story about his mother leaving everything to his sister was true. She began to pity him. Perhaps he saw her as a surrogate mother. She hoped he did not confuse the passion between them with feelings for a mother.

She peered closer at the inscription, and the care with which it had been repainted in old grooves in the stone, except for the new word, which attempted definition despite conflicting with the engraving. It seemed that a soft cloth had wiped off excess wet paint, leaving faint smears. A tiny insect had been trapped and died in the paint, its legs protruding.

The plastic blue hydrangeas and ferns placed centrally looked more tasteful than the flowers on other graves, which were crude effigies of roses, lilies, carnations, lilac, chrysanthemums, daisies and tulips. Those were in motley collections and mixed seasons, in total disrespect for reality, some made even uglier by gaudy silver edging.

Jane leant against a low sun-warmed wall. The cones on the diseased cedar hung down like witches' claws, while the scratchy sound of a cicada filled her head.

She knew she had not managed to put a bold full stop after Pierre. She did not know if circumstances, or perhaps merely a coincidence, had led her back to him.

That afternoon she lay on a sun lounger in the shade, unable either to doze or really continue with the Chekhov short stories she had begun to read. She identified with the way the characters' yearnings often led to a way forward, even if that was no more than 'hope', but how their lives were so unfulfilled, for any real connections were lived outside of their main relationship, in a secret life. She wondered if this reflection of her life was true of many lives.

By Jane's side were plums with a hazy-mauve blush, which contrasted with the chrome yellow bowl they were in, and almost black Muscat grapes. She luxuriated in the grapes' sweetness, rolled their flesh around in her mouth and realised how fine and smooth the texture of a grape was, like a firm jelly, while a plum, even a ripe sweet one, has a slightly sinewy texture. She scrutinised one grape pip: its bifurcated shape like a scrotum. She wondered if her mind worked in unusual ways.

Leaning back, with the luxury of time, she observed just one leaf moving on this still day: one leaf on the vast walnut tree would twirl and dance, and then stop, and then another, or a whole bunch would move in unison. How precise a gust of wind could be, sometimes no more than a little funnel of movement.

High in the sky, a silver jet's trail, as fine as a spider's thread, had been intersected by another plane's trail. Now a cross was written on the blue.

The voices of children passed unseen along the small road nearby, voices as light as petals fluttering in a breeze, their crystalline freshness carried by the clear air.

How well she deciphered sounds in this place. She could distinguish the low rumble of a high aeroplane from distant thunder, although, at first, she had been unsure. She knew the rattle of dead leaves on the grass, different from Annette's footsteps; the cry of a bird, different from that of a cat; and the tap-tapping was a woodpecker and not a thrush bashing a snail shell on a stone, as she had interpreted the sound in a very English way earlier; the gurgle of water in the pool, different from rain on the patio; the lowing of cows nearby which she had, at the beginning, mistaken for a rare visit from Annette's English husband with his droning voice.

She thought of the telephone contact with Pierre the day before, and how mellow he had sounded. Perhaps he had run out of money, perhaps the 'pay-as-you-go' credit on her phone was used up. What if he had no way of topping it up, for surely they had checked her identity each time she topped it up. Jane considered adding to the credit by buying a voucher, now that her credit card had been stolen. She still had some euros she had kept in her bedroom.

These thoughts troubled her. She accused herself of being crazy, but felt a frisson in her chest as high as her throat, at just the thought of sending Pierre this 'gift' of the maximum 'top-up', knowing that £30 made little difference to her, but might be helpful to him. And then she would know if he wanted to talk with her, if he had really been unable to call her back with Harriet's number because there was no credit, or if he thought her a mad needy old woman.

If she never took this any further, she would never know. The passing of time would bring its own resolution, possibly one of disillusion, but if she contacted him she would know with greater certainty, and would have to face either hurt or… or, she hardly dared to think, some sense that her contact with him was not all misguided.

She tried unsuccessfully to find Adrian in her mind now, to explore what she should do. She imagined him saying, eventually – after she had borne some frustration and not-knowing – that the stranger seemed to give her something, some comfort, which her marriage did not, and asking her why she felt that one ought to get everything from just one relationship? But then she wondered whether he would actually say that, or whether that was that just what she wanted to hear.

The overture of *La Traviata*, that she had played on her first day here, came back to her now and how she had heard the familiar bars in a new way: the beginning evoked the warmth and tenderness of her marriage, the richness and depth of its sexuality, in contrast to the frippery and excitement of the courtesans' life. She felt that the subtitle, *Woman Who Has Lost Her Way*, befitted herself. But she did not want to be like Violetta, who forsakes true love until it is too late, after only a brief period of happiness. The opera's evocation of a struggle for life against terrible odds had always moved her. Now she found the last scene unbearable.

She realised that her illness must be playing a part in her madness, and she needed Adrian to help her to think.

She opened her eyes, to notice dead trailing nasturtiums that Annette had not watered in a pot by the pool. She felt like cutting off the dead stems and leaves in order to give the few green leaves a chance.

Thinking in a confused way of Pierre, she found the name and even the image of Mike Shand repeatedly displaced him. Mike, her first lover in her late teens, several years older. Perhaps he was the same age as Pierre was now. He was a real 'grown up,' on his way to becoming a successful painter.

On sunlit afternoons in Mike's flat in Islington, her passion, like a dammed river, had its release. On the many drives to his place, in her father's borrowed old milky-green Hillman, her body would become suffused with longing, and as glowing as the blood-red light through the drawn unlined curtains of his bedroom. The certainty that he, freshly showered, would be magnificently ready for her beneath his flimsy dressing gown when he opened the front door, was almost unbearable for Jane. Strips of chrome-yellow light where the curtains did not cover the window flooded the room with a high summer intensity.

For the first time in her life, there was no danger of anyone discovering them, no need for secrecy and deception. The only fear was pregnancy, but that always came later, for each time they lived in the present, with the intensity of creatures on a seashore, with only the tides and the sky and the stars at night to accompany them. Like a cat who settles down with suave assurance soon after some terrible fright had caused it to rush away, she behaved with Mike as if all danger had abated forever.

She used to bring two *éclairs* in a chic box from a French *patisserie* with authentic thick coffee icing and strong coffee *crème anglaise* inside the light pastry, which they would eat later, between sips of cold, sweet white wine. She remembered the added dimension to the eating of those *éclairs*, how instead of being a finale they became an interval.

It annoyed her now to conflate Mike, after so many years, with Pierre, Pierre with Mike. Yet she knew why.

AUGUST 22ND, 2003

'Young Woman Disappeared From Bank' was the headline in *Le Petit Bleu*. A smiling blurred picture of his sister stared out at him. Charles Baudier was buying cigarettes in a bar. He went closer to the newspaper. The article described Giselle Baudier, a woman of thirty-five 'with local connections', disappearing after she left work at Credit Lyonnais in Lyon on August 18th, and not having been seen since. It stated that she was last seen wearing a red dress with a frilled neckline. No doubt, the photograph was enlarged from the bank's identity photograph.

'Armagnac, please. Make it a double.' He gulped it down as if it was water. The black and white sign listing the prices of all the drinks became a grey blur. The burning sensation in his gullet and stomach distracted him for a moment, but did not calm him.

He went to the *tabac* over the road, bought a copy of the same newspaper, and climbed into the smart green Citroën waiting outside.

His trembling hands struggled to light his cigarette. The air conditioner would not come on. He rummaged in the glove compartment for an instruction manual and came across a new packet of fruit-flavoured condoms. He pocketed them without much thought.

Charles reread the article. The newspaper asked for anyone who could help the police in their enquiries to come forward. Nothing bad could have happened to Giselle. She was always the lucky one, the favoured one. He wondered whether the crashed Renault had been discovered by now.

Surely, the English woman had told the police all about him, how he had stolen it and driven without insurance.

He remembered talking about Giselle with Jane. 'The English woman', he always called her in his mind, but 'Jane', he said now, aloud, with a soft 'J'. He saw her naked full body before his eyes. With his forehead leaning on the steering wheel and eyes closed, the Armagnac warming him, he mumbled, 'Jane, sorry. You were good. A good person. If only...'

But then, like a bitter aftertaste, feelings of rejection flooded back: when she said she'd give him money to see him on his way, made him promise he'd go. He couldn't blame her, but he became hard then, deciding it was 'each man for himself'. He had been wrong to think things could be different with her, despite her age. Of course, his old way of being tough was better than feeling so hurt, even needy.

Melancholy images of his mother looking at him from a distance hovered before his eyes. She had a look of disappointment on her face, an expression that he knew so well.

He knew he had to change tack, and leave the car somewhere, yet he drove on, hardly seeing where he was driving. *Giselle, Giselle, it can't be, you must be alright, somewhere, maybe hiding like me. Giselle, I'm sorry. Sorry to all the women in my life! Maman, Giselle, and now Jane.* 'Ridiculous!' he exclaimed aloud. Yet his heart felt a surge of maudlin love for all of them, and pain at his cruelty.

Emotions flamed from the brandy, his head swirling. He needed to be careful now, careful he did not crash. But what difference would that make? No great loss to mankind, or womankind either. No Papa, no Papa anywhere, that's for sure, so what kind of a bloke am I? A will-o'-the wisp, a fly-by-night, always looking for something.

'Giselle,' he moaned aloud, before rushing onto, 'If she's... dead I'll never forgive myself. I'll kill myself, for sure, I'd have to. How could I live with her death?' Tears sprang to his eyes. He pulled up on a gravel verge.

Now he thought that he would try to contact Jane one day. He wondered how. Perhaps he would write to her, get her address through the woman whose cottage it was, and tell Jane he was sorry for being a thief and a deceiver, but that he did like her, did think of her. He was not a truly bad person. She had seen something good in him, so perhaps he did not need to tell her that. Yes, she was his guardian angel, his rescuer, and what thanks had he given her? His prick! He gave a little guffaw, and then thought that he should drive on, he may attract attention here in this godforsaken little village of Rousillon. He was lucky to have got this far.

On a wave of resolution to change tracks, he decided to leave the car here. He had enough cash to keep him going for a while. He would find a job, anything, on the railways, the roads, anywhere. As long as he kept his head down.

He put Jane's cash, her mobile phone and charger, and the newspaper in his canvas bag, which still had his razor and underpants in it. He left her camera, passport, plane tickets and credit cards in the glove compartment. He locked the car and posted the key back through a small crack in the open window, not really thinking things through but following his instincts. Mr Hertz will find it, surely.

A sense of relief overcame him.

He knew well how it felt to be a hunted animal. Now, perhaps, he could be the hunter who sought Giselle. No, it can't be something bad, he reassured himself again.

Charles, you must go forward, don't look back over your shoulder the whole time, there must be another way to live. If I fail, I'd kill myself. 'Simple as that,' he said aloud, resenting the tears that sprang to his eyes.

Charles had not accounted for the heat. The tar on the road bubbled up in blisters. Even though the air conditioner hadn't worked, at least there had been a breeze in the car.

Yet, as he stepped out, he began to find some strength within, and felt that his own life-force would somehow see him through. He thought of the first lovemaking with Jane, and the second. He now felt open to whatever came along; he may meet someone, a woman, a young woman, start an honest life with her. Anything is possible, he told himself, echoing his mother's words. He chose not to hitch a lift. *Anyway, you don't see many hitchhikers these days. You have legs, Charles, and they are more or less fixed now, thanks to Jane.* He challenged himself to see how far he could go by evening.

Arriving at villages with a glow of satisfaction – villages which he had glimpsed kilometres away, their church spires spiking the horizon, reached through his own efforts – led Charles to think of his forefathers, who probably did not think twice about walking such distances along rough tracks.

'Forefather, father, strange idea.' He was talking aloud to himself more these days. Sometimes, he heard himself mutter a phrase and was not sure what he was talking about, like, 'What a shame, what a pity.' When he thought of his father there was always a gap, or sometimes a fog, but now he tried to think about the line of fathers that had inevitably preceded him, and about whom he knew nothing. It was like trying to follow a trail in the dark.

There was a buzzing sound in his bag. It took Charles a few seconds to realise that Jane's mobile phone was ringing. Hesitantly, he answered it.

Hearing Jane's voice was like a strong rope that connected him with his new resolutions to turn his life around. But then, he sensed her distance too, and she only wanted a friend's number. She hadn't really wanted to speak to him. Again, he was confused and did not know if he was being used.

Just like the other day, when he had intended to phone her back with her friend's number, an electronic voice in English said something about 'credit', and he realised that he did not know how to top it up, there in the middle of nowhere.

He felt frustrated with the whole strange set-up, but sensed that there would be other chances to be in touch with Jane.

Having slept in the car in a coppice the night before, he resolved to find a simple *chambre d'hôte* that evening.

In the small town of Valence-sur-Garonne, in his attic room, Pierre had a shower and decided to shave his beard. He wanted to change his appearance. This was not entirely to escape the law; it was also part of his wish to get back to his more honest self. The newly exposed skin was pink and raw, in contrast to the rest of his tanned face, and looked altogether odd. He smiled at his reflection, like Neapolitan ice-cream, and shrugged. He trusted that the sun would soon make it blend.

He ate a simple meal in the restaurant – with its bistro-look chequered tablecloths and pine chairs, candles in encrusted Chianti bottles, and a menu chalked on a board. Steak and chips, salad, a glass of red wine, followed by crème caramel. He went to bed early.

AUGUST 23RD, 2003

Charles awoke refreshed, bright and ready for the day.

In the town, he bought a cotton drill navy shirt and plain navy trousers in an outfitter for cooks and other trades. He was surprised at how inexpensive they were. He bought a beret and two pairs of underpants, and socks. Not wanting to arouse suspicion, he put everything except the beret in a bag, and later donned the new garments in a wood. He pondered whether to hide or bury the clothes Jane had lent him, the black t-shirt and white baggy trousers. But why? Yes, he had stolen a car, but there were worse crimes than that. Well, two cars, if you counted Giselle's. Remembering that his mother often said he was economical with the truth made him smile.

Charles sat a while in the shade, eating a croissant he had kept from breakfast, and thought about doing most things in his life by stealth, even taking the car that he thought should have been his as of right. The croissant began to feel dry.

But, but, if Giselle is dead… He stopped in his thoughts. No, that can't possibly be, she's just disappeared. With a pang, he wondered what would have happened if he had not taken the Renault. He must work out the dates of all this, must check the newspaper dates. Should he try and help the police with their enquiries? But then came the counter-thought that they would charge him for stealing – well, borrowing – the Hertz car, and probably worse, driving when he had already lost his licence for drunken driving a year ago. What if he came out in the open, stopped hiding, faced what he had to face? He might even be able to help them, help Giselle. He remembered Giselle refusing to give him her telephone number that night of the row, before he took her car, telling him that she was ex-directory because of him. He had tried to forget her words, that he was a 'parasite', that she had to cut herself off from him in order to make a life for herself; she had enough troubles of her own. Now he remembered her crying, as if it pained her to be so cruel. Charles' face paled now. He batted away small flies that repeatedly landed on his arms and face.

He did not know if he really wanted to go to those lengths to help her. Perhaps he was caught up in sentimentality. He enjoyed the flow of tears down his cheeks, not wiping them away, nor the dribble from his nose. It had been a long time since he had really cried. 'Shit!' he exclaimed aloud.

He found himself remembering a teacher, a pretty young woman, in his first school. *What was her name? Mademoiselle le Bruin!* There she was, shining through a cloud of chalk dust, resplendent in her glistening nylon stockings and high heels and curly auburn hair and red lips, smiling at him as he struggled with subtraction sums. 'Charlie, you can do it! Good boy! Well done! My clever boy!' Shivers ran down his spine at the memory. How he wanted her to clasp him to her bosom, then and now. *Thank you, Mademoiselle le Bruin, thank you, wherever you are. Encourager of children! You deserve a medal!*

Charles stayed there, his legs crossed, on a dry patch of ground in the glade, striated sunlight filtering through like the paintings he had seen in church of intimations of heaven. *And I'm not even stoned, or drunk.*

But where to start? Of course, he could not find Mademoiselle le Bruin to say thank you, but he could try to help Giselle, who must be somewhere, in trouble. And maybe contact the English woman, who was good, and alive. Yes, he might write to that lady who owned the property. A French woman, called, what did she say, Jeanette or Annette perhaps. He could remember the hamlet and would write 'opposite Templiers Chapel', and ask her to send the letter on to Jane. He thought about her saying that she was ill, very ill, with cancer. Unbelievable. Still, not all cancer kills; and there are miracles, like the letters people write in that book in church to Jesus or the Virgin, thanking them for curing cancer. But then, Jane said it was serious. He felt sorry for her.

He decided not to hide his old clothes. They might be useful. He breathed out heavily through his mouth.

'It's *hard*,' he said aloud as he strode forth in the sun. His old trainers would not last much longer. He would buy stout boots as soon as he earned some money.

The sun and the heat formed mirages on the road. The world gyrated before his eyes. He drained the water from his bottle, beginning to feel faint, despite some sun protection from his beret. He had eaten little in the last twenty-four hours. He admonished himself for being stupid and vowed to buy food in the next village. Charles hoped that Jane's mobile phone would ring again, that it would be her. He hoped that a phone without credit could still receive calls.

He had never owned a mobile phone. When he had a job in Lyon, he had decided against it, thought it part of the capitalist world that he had renounced.

He knew that he would give Jane a very different response from before. He would have a chance to explain that there was no more credit and ask her how he could top it up, without speaking English. But he did not hold out much hope for another attempt on her part.

As he walked, he considered phoning her friend 'arriet – whose number she had wanted – from a phone box, and asking for Jane's telephone number in England. But was that ridiculous – what on earth would the English friend think? The phone still had some battery life. When he envisaged the police taking it from him, he paused in the shade to try to access Harriet's number. He was pleased with himself for working out how to find it and wrote it on the back of the receipt for the clothes he had bought.

One day, he would send Jane the money he had stolen, and more, as compensation.

An undertow of conscience led him back to his sister. Perhaps she had been kidnapped, or… worse. But by whom, and for what? Knowing so little about her was part of the problem. Their paths had diverged; she seemed to be leading a respectable life in a city, but he did not know for sure. His sense that he was illegitimate, and she the rightful one, was shaken. He felt a wave of panic, panic at the deadly possibilities that could be operating in her life that he knew nothing about.

Only one thing made sense now: to phone the police. To see if he could help them. He bit his bottom lip hard. *If the world is collapsing around you, Charles, you either lie down and die too, or you fight back, struggle to have a decent life, and see if anything can be rebuilt.* Not being insured or licensed to drive her car, taking it without her permission, giving people the name 'Pierre', all seemed like minor irregularities now.

He pushed open the resistant doors of a phone box, dialled the police and waited for the certain response.

He said he was the brother of Giselle Baudier and may have some useful information. In a faltering voice, he told them that he was somewhere on the road near Valence, in the village of Fontane, and would wait by the side of the road for them to fetch him.

While he sat in the shade of an oak tree, with his bags at his side, undulations of sadness at his mother's death swept over him. He felt powerless about what he could do to change things, but knew he had to try. The attempt to help the police now felt paper-thin.

He wished he had water to drink. He scraped the ground with a stick, uncovering the dark loam beneath dried leaves.

His helplessness led to a memory of when he was a boy, of a fire breaking out on a dark evening in a cottage nearby, and all he could do was watch it burn down. Everyone knew that a cat and her kittens were in there, in the cellar, and probably had not escaped. He had been mesmerised by the orange flames dancing triumphantly towards the sky, devouring and surmounting any obstacles in their way. His focus blurred as he remembered the sound of the flames' urgent licking, like great bats' wings flapping in the wind. The fire brigade did their best, but could not arrest the fire by the time they got there. Charles, you useless idiot, he thought now. But he also knew that he had felt a frisson of excitement then, something that he should not have felt. He had held himself in the dark through a hole in his shorts' pocket and rubbed in time with the flames until a great shudder of something erupted, and only then could he walk away thrilled and bemused.

He did not know if what came out of him was bad, like pus, or good like milk. He felt it had to be bad, even though it felt better than anything he had ever imagined. Bad because he knew it had to be a secret, that no one else could possibly have the same problem. He thought that the flames had made it come. The next time he saw a fire, a bonfire in a field, the same thing happened to him. But by then he had made it happen countless times, to the accompaniment of the darting and dancing flames and the crackle in his mind.

You can't really help terrible things. He had known this feeling all his life. *Why should it be different now?*

They call this an interview room; they could make it more congenial than this. Why not a few magazines, a plant maybe – even a plastic one would be better than nothing. And surely, an interview room needs more than one person in it. His wry humour made him smile.

Charles Baudier sat at a grey Formica table in the police station on a wooden chair that felt too small for him.

Waiting.

A chair of moulded plastic on the other side of the table looked more comfortable. He considered exchanging his chair for that one. Would they hold it against him, wanting to improve his situation? He gave a little chuckle. He perused the walls and ceiling and iron grille in the door to see if he was being watched or filmed. Probably not – unless they were very sly about it. *They had bigger fish to fry.*

He could hear a low buzz that clicked now and again. Perhaps it was the light.

By the doorway, areas of grey linoleum had been worn through to the brown below. It reminded him of his grandmother's cottage. The table had biro marks and scratches, and one cracked patch where wood showed through the plastic. Charles ducked his head to observe the solid iron legs. He noticed scuffs on walls, a dado of a stripe of dark brown paint that demarcated the unremarkable lower area of dark green from the unremarkable upper area of light green all around him, save for the metal grey door through which he had come. He peered again at the grille and the peephole. He began to feel he was getting a grip on the situation. One bright unshaded light bulb hung from a brown short flex of twisted cord. They probably made the cord short, he chortled, so that people couldn't hang themselves. But then, could someone electrocute themselves? The ceiling seemed very high.

Would I be able to reach the light if I stood on the table? What if I stood on the chair upon the table? What if I needed to pee?

He wandered over to the grille and stood on tiptoe, trying to peer out. All he saw was blackness. There was probably a shutter or door on the other side of it. The peephole seemed to be blocked. He shivered at the thought that someone could be observing him the whole time.

Returning to his chair, he heard shouts from outside the room and a clanging noise. His inability to interpret the sounds disturbed him further.

Now Charles felt confused about the circumstances in which he found himself, especially as he had chosen to give himself up, to begin a different journey. How it could lead to a different life he did not know, especially as the police officers who brought him here were not in the least interested in what sort of a person he really was. All they seemed to want to do was humiliate him and corner him, not show any gratitude for the return of the car, or his wish to help in their enquiries over Giselle.

Giselle. He tried not to think of her now, but her presence, or was it her absence, throbbed like an abscess that he tried to ignore.

Perhaps the police were short-staffed? He felt generous in this explanation for being kept waiting like this.

Sitting sideways to the table, Charles stretched out his legs in front of him. He considered that he looked quite good in his new navy blue drill trousers, navy shirt, and new socks. He wished there was a mirror here. He gently squeezed his thigh above the injured knee, testing it. They had inconsiderately removed his trainers when they put him in here, but he was sure they did this to everyone and would return them – as well as his beret, watch, razor, some cash, even his comb, and canvas bag... But, of course, they would not return Jane's phone.

He felt a qualm at the thought that they might see his... his misdemeanours – surely, they were not real crimes – as serious. That they wouldn't look sympathetically on the turmoil that had led him to take his sister's car which, after all, he had as much right to as Giselle – and then to borrow, well, to take Jane's car. Without a valid license. He sensed that if he went down the path of what they might think, of the Law, he would become frightened and even panic. He couldn't help but conjure up pictures of men in uniform with guns, like the men who picked him up in a police car, only much burlier and more aggressive. He told himself that it would probably be alright in the end; after all, that good English woman had believed in him, had liked him – more than liked, it seemed. So, he can't be all bad. Perhaps she would be putting in a good word for him at this moment.

Charles felt hungry and thirsty. And shabby, not because he had not washed properly or shaved, but in a way that had become familiar this past year or so.

If only he had his trainers back. No one can feel confident without their shoes.

He thought of Giselle with a jolt.

It was a relief to hear the door being unlocked and to see two men entering. Now the room felt crowded. One wore a light blue shirt and royal blue trousers that denoted uniform and stood in a corner. A gun was slung from his belt, bulging through a black holster, like an ill-disguised erection. The other man, wearing a creased grey suit over a nylon shirt with a loosely knotted plain maroon tie, had blonde wavy hair darkened by pomade that tried to tame it. His fleshy face was quite soft, almost womanly. He sat opposite Charles at the table, placing a pile of forms and papers in front of him.

'Your name?'

'Charles Baudier'.

'Can you spell "Baudier"?'

Charles complied, his eyes shining brightly, like a child giving the right answer. The Inspector wrote rapidly on a top pink form, checking that a copy was coming through on a green one below.

'Any other names?'

'No. I mean, well, yes. I sometimes call myself "Pierre".'

'Date of birth?' 'Address?' 'Nationality?' He continued methodically to go through the form in front of him: 'Mother's name?' 'Father's name?' 'Place of birth?' 'Religion?' Although Charles had already been through some of this when they picked him up by the roadside, he dutifully supplied the answers again.

'Occupation?'

He gave a little shrug, 'Lately, odd jobs. Worked in a *boulangerie* in Arles for six months, about a year ago. Since then, this and that. Washing dishes in restaurants, mainly in Lyon.' The Inspector looked up at that point, directly into Charles' eyes.

'Which restaurants?'

'Oh, one called *De Fourvière*, in Place de Fourvière; another, what was it called... yes, *Les Lyonnais* in Rue Tramassac.' Charles was pleased that he could give such authoritative answers, spelling out names where necessary.

'Why Lyon?' the older man asked. Charles was not sure if it was the man's unbidden dimples in both cheeks when he talked, or a twinkle that lightened his penetrating eyes at times, that gave him an air of good humour.

'Because... because I know the city, one or two friends there – well, acquaintances really. I thought of enrolling at the university, to study.' Something about this older man, his earnestness, connected Charles with his resolve to be more sincere, to begin to do something with his life. So he divulged something that he had never shared with anyone, 'Always wanted to be a landscape gardener.' He paused, half waiting for a snigger of disbelief. All he found was an open seriousness. So he continued, 'Or an artist. I draw a lot. Used to go to the *Musée des Beaux-Arts* to draw.' Like a balloon that was rapidly deflating, he looked downwards, 'Can't really make money that way.'

But he felt the interviewer beginning to relax.

'Any other reason for being in Lyon?'

'Yes, my sister lives there.'

'Yes?'

'Well, you know that too, I think. Giselle. But can you tell me, please, Officer, if there's any news of her? Of course, I'm really worried about her. Saw the article in the paper. She can't be… must be… kidnapped? Or … or what? Please?' Charles sat on his hands in his agitation, squashing them on the wooden seat beneath him.

'No, no sign of her. We have made enquiries throughout the country, and beyond. We're beginning to treat this as a possible murder.'

The two seated men looked at each other, the Inspector maintaining his stance of alertness and acute observation.

'Oh my God,' was all Charles said, shaking his head, his eyes petrified. How he hated this 'reality' he had resolved to follow, how much easier to tell himself that it would all be alright in the end, to smoke dope and drink, and drift, and smoke some more.

'Monsieur Baudier, can you tell me anything more about how you came to take the car, your sister's car?'

And so Charles told him shakily, but as truthfully as possible, about the family situation, how he had felt rejected by his mother, even though she died years ago, for leaving money to Giselle and only a small amount to him. He'd been angry with Giselle for getting on with her life, not looking after him. She was four years older, but always seemed much older. 'Girls are like that,' he added. And how he wanted to show her that she was being selfish, all stuck-up, working for a bank, with her classy friends and tidy flat, and he thought she had some liaison with the bank manager – he'd heard a rumour, seen her out in the man's big black Peugeot. But the last time he'd seen her, when they had a row, Giselle denied all that. She had laughed at him, saying that the man was married.

Now Charles removed his hands from under his thighs and observed their whiteness.

'That man, was he the manager of the bank she worked for?'

'Yes, I think so.'

'Do you know if she had a boyfriend or boyfriends?'

He thought for a moment. 'No, Monsieur. Pardon, Officer. I can call you Officer?'

'Inspector, actually. Inspector Taillandier.'

'Pardon, Inspector. I mean, I don't know, about boyfriends and all that. You see, in recent years, Giselle and I were not close. That's part of the problem, I mean, from my angle. She may have wanted it that way. But how can I be talking about all this and forgetting what you said, about a possible *murder*? Please, please, let her be alright,' he added, fighting back tears. 'Perhaps she's lying low for some reason.'

'Can you see any reasons why she may not have wanted to have much to do with you?'

'Well, not really, other than what I've implied, that I was a bit of a layabout and she was getting on with her life. But I guess she felt that I had a chip on my shoulder – she said as much – that I always said she was Maman's favourite. It's hard to know, with a chip on the shoulder, if it really is an unfounded grudge or if it's real.'

The Inspector nodded in agreement while he wrote.

'Another thing, Inspector, I smoked dope – weed – a lot. She didn't approve. Nor did Maman. I don't anymore; can't afford it for one. But anyway, I don't want to now. But I think she gave up on me because of that, partly.'

He interrupted his narrative anxiously, 'Excuse me, Sir, but is there a toilet I can use?'

The Inspector indicated to the policeman to accompany Charles.

They soon returned. Charles had managed to spruce himself up by splashing water on his face and hair. He again sat at the table, like a serious schoolboy who wanted the teacher to like him. He raked his hair back with his fingers. The Inspector gave him a little smile and then resumed the interview.

Holding his biro at both ends and gently rolling it with his fingers, the older man asked, 'Have you ever been involved with any societies, like Church groups, or secret societies, or the Knights Templiers?'

Charles wrinkled up his nose and shook his head, 'Not really. No. Not at all. Never appealed to me. Never even joined the boy scouts, or the cadets, when I was a boy. Was a bit of a loner, I guess. I don't see the point. They often seem to be ways of making the individual feel important, perhaps substituting for a sense of family.' Something about this other man enabled Charles to find interesting thoughts. He did not want the interview to end.

'Even religion can be seen that way,' he continued. 'Although people then often feel small and helpless, like children, with God the father and the Virgin mother looking after them. I guess I've never really bought into that either. Maybe I'm still looking for the real thing, the family, the real mother and the real father – I don't know... if that's a good thing or a bad thing.' He looked up at Taillandier, as if expecting an answer.

'That English woman, Dr Samuels, who helped you, can you tell me about your contact with her?' Inspector Taillandier did not refer to her as the woman whose car he had stolen.

'Oh, Jane. How did you know that I was thinking of her just at that point!'

'Not so difficult; I'm not a mind reader. Just that you were talking about the need for a mother.'

'Oh yes.' Charles blushed slightly and rubbed the bristles on his chin. He talked now about the English woman's kindness, how she seemed generous and wanted to help him get back on his feet, literally. He paused.

'Yes?' asked Taillandier patiently.

Charles looked up at the policeman standing in the corner. It seemed wrong to talk about intimacies in front of that stranger.

The Inspector waited.

'What shall I do?' asked Charles, cocking his head towards the other man.

'Yes?' asked Taillandier again.

Hating the presence of the other policeman when he wanted to be alone with the Inspector, Charles forced himself to continue, but in a lowered tone, 'Well, perhaps you'll be interviewing her – Jane – too. That would give you the whole picture. Anyway, as the saying goes, lies have short legs, so I am being totally honest. You see, from my point of view, I was done for: almost killed myself – not intentionally, but perhaps there's always some "intention" in driving when drunk. I used to say, "It's not my fault," about practically everything. Certainly, I had sunk pretty low when I had that crash. Jane was like… my guardian angel, her face appearing above me in that wrecked car, calm and good. And… beautiful.' He straightened his back to continue with his story. 'You see, I'd spent the night in the chapel, the ruin, near where my mother is buried, wanting to die too, in a way. I didn't realise it at the time – I just got drunk after repainting her grave. Did more than repaint it: I changed the wording on the inscription so that it looked like it was from me only, and not me and Giselle.' Charles noticed Taillandier stopping his writing to look up at him. 'Really bad of me, I know,' he continued. 'Doing that only made me feel worse, made me think, "What's the point of anything?"'

'But then there was something between me and the English woman… a kind of magic.' Charles sat now with his elbows on the table, his hands forming a tunnel of vision towards the Inspector, screening out the harsh light and the other policeman. 'She said she was ill, very ill, with cancer.'

Charles paused, collecting his thoughts. 'That wasn't so significant at the time, in fact, she seemed quite well. But I've been thinking about it more since...'

Taillandier, who had stopped writing, watched, waited, and listened.

'Anyway,' Charles continued, taking a big breath, as if pulling himself up to the surface after diving deep. 'In this "magic," we became... intimate, quite soon, and it was good, for both of us. Of that, I'm sure. I haven't known anything quite like that ever, with any woman. Not that there have been that many. It didn't matter that she was old enough to be my mother. She didn't tell me her age – but she did tell me that she was a grandmother. I even imagined staying with her, forever..., she had a way of making me feel real.'

Charles thought that this man Taillandier had a similar quality but, of course, he could not say that. Why, all of a sudden, was the world full of people who made him feel he counted, when all his life that had hardly been so? Mademoiselle le Bruin flashed before his eyes again in that small first school, her moist violet eyes shining their light on him.

'You mean, you usually don't feel real?' Taillandier's eyes looked deeply into Charles'.

'Don't know,' shrugging. 'Am I going on too much? Sorry. It must be hard to make sense of all this. Perhaps you should just ask me questions, and I'll answer, straightforwardly.' Sitting back in his chair, Charles folded his arms.

The Inspector smiled. 'Okay then. Why did you take the car? Especially after all that?'

Blushing again, 'It was unforgivable.' He shook his head. 'You see, you must understand, Inspector, there's the old me, and the new me.' He banged the table hard with the side of his hand, and then repeated the action with his other hand, to make his point. The attending policeman stiffened. 'That was the old me – the me that could be ruthless and feel sorry for himself, and felt that the world owed him a living. And then there's the new me, that hasn't been properly... *born* yet, that can switch into such a different world, a world which is… oh, I don't know.' His speech quickened, ' A world with people like you in it.' Withdrawing his hands he looked down, embarrassed, and wiped his eye with his fist.

'People like me?' the Inspector asked, raising his eyebrows.

'Pardon, Inspector. Can't explain. I mean, I had a feeling that I could either die, you know, completely give up, or pull myself out… No, that came later, when I read about Giselle in the paper. With Jane, the English woman… To be honest, I think that I felt hurt, more than hurt, wounded, when she wanted to get rid of me, wanted to see me on my way. Despite her kindness, I felt at that moment that she had used me and was keen for me to go. Now, I can see it's more complicated, of course. But in that moment of hurt, I decided "fuck you". Excuse my language. We had had a good time, you know. In bed. And then, as I said, she wanted me to go. She was rich anyway, and could always get another hire car, and I needed the car more than she did.' He paused. 'Almost as if she became Giselle.' More to himself than to the Inspector, he spoke quietly, 'It's amazing how the old me could justify anything.'

Taillandier resumed making notes. The only sounds were of pen on paper, Charles breathing heavily, and a background electrical buzz.

'I think we can leave it there, Monsieur.' He stood to leave while gathering his papers.

Charles looked up, 'You're not going, are you? Just like that? What happens now? What do I do now?'

Taillandier said kindly, 'Monsieur, I have my job to do, others have theirs. My colleagues will be taking over now.' He looked at his watch, and then at Charles' crestfallen face.

Charles stood up, 'Didn't I do well enough then, sir? I mean, didn't I… give you the answers you wanted, the correct answers?'

'You'll get more used to our ways in due course. The world is not always a kind place. One day, when you're free of us, you should go to that university and study landscape gardening.'

'You remembered, Inspector,' said Charles, his eyes illuminated. 'Can I just ask you one little thing, please?' He gauged the other man's silence as agreement. 'Will I see you again?'

'Monsieur, I'm not sure. It depends on what we decide. Perhaps.'

'Thank you for that. You can go now!'

Both men smiled at Charles' attempt to gain control of the departure.

AUGUST 24TH, 2003

Again Jane dialled her familiar mobile phone number, one that had taken her a long time to memorise when the phone was new. The church clock in Ceneyrac had struck twelve with its long announcement of metallic chimes, some notes were more resonant and reverberating than others. The bell's ancient workings followed their own rhythms, as if man's imposition of order could be softened if not effaced.

In the dog-barking cicada noise that followed, she waited for an answer. She heard her voicemail message. And then she spoke, less confidently than the time before, 'It's me, Jane. Again!' She gave a little laugh. 'Just to let you know that you now have thirty pounds credit, thirty English pounds. I think that's about forty-five euros. And, and, I'm at the same phone box, 05 65 217 899, for the next few minutes, in case you get this message and can ring me to give me my friend Harriet's number.' She repeated, '05 65 217 899,' her foot scraping the cigarette stubs and an empty Marlboro packet on the ground as she said, '*Au revoir.*' She tried to sound upbeat, knowing how unattractive neediness could be. The heavy receiver was returned to its bracket.

In the stifling silence that followed, she dared not think what she was doing.

A lorry rattled past, the roar of its engine shaking the small village out of its Sunday sleepiness for a few seconds before it disappeared. A cool breeze fanned Jane's neck and arms. She wiped her wet upper lip, raised her elbows to allow the breeze to reach her armpits, and lifted her short hair from the back of her neck.

'Of course, I'm mad,' she told herself now, 'pathetic and obsessed, but I can't help it.'

Sitting in the shade on a low limestone wall near the phone booth she waited, deciding to linger until the clock reached a quarter to one. Her hand stroked the encrusted roughness of the wall, accretions of black from long-dead lichen.

It was quite pleasant now that there was a breeze. Closing her eyes, she listened with her basket propped between her feet. Dead leaves clattered loudly on the paving stones. She could hear one of her favourite sounds: the crowing of a cock. She squashed an ant that was crawling across her neck and looked sorrowfully at the crumpled body on her finger. The smell of what she thought was someone's lunchtime soup led her to wonder what she would eat.

Her self-sufficient state of mind, of enjoying solitude and cooking for herself, had been shattered by Pierre, for now she thought of finding a restaurant to eat out that evening – to brave being the only single person, to take a book and look as if she was quite happy to be alone among families and couples. She did not know if she could salvage the days left and even enjoy them when she was left with a freshly exposed disturbing longing.

Years ago, she had covered that longing, like sewing patches of different fabric over holes in a quilt. After a while, a new patch would wear thin, and then she would re-cover part of it with another, not matching, so the hole would become less and less conspicuous. She almost forgot it was there beneath all the layers. Other holes or tears would appear in other parts of the quilt. The various remnants acquired a beauty of their own, the fabrics becoming old and soft and faded with age, the different patterns no longer discordant, despite their randomness.

The contact with Pierre had torn off the layers, and now the wound was exposed. She questioned going back to the patching and grafting like a poor housewife who had to 'make do'. You only do that if you live under the illusion that you have forever, she told herself.

Or feel that you have no choice.

Or cannot risk change.

Or feel that it is alright, that the motley quilt is the fabric of your life, and that is the way it is. That it can be beautiful, like the landscape in Tuscany, with its patches of small fields worked in different ways, so that the whole is broken up by differing textures, tones, and directions.

Jane allowed a small thought to form itself as she gazed at the heat-wilted leaves of a walnut tree. *What if I left Lennie? What if I tried just being me again and took myself off, somehow?* Before fully allowing this thought to emerge, as tentative as a baby mouse creeping out of its hole for the first time, she shooed it back into the wainscoting of her mind with a cold draught of counter-thoughts. *You know that's crazy. Lennie doesn't deserve that. What about the warm thoughts you had when you heard the* Traviata *overture the other day? What about the children, and the grandchildren? And the house? And now, with the cancer, and maybe death, what a time to choose!*

But perhaps that's why I'm thinking this now.

She had gone almost straight from Mike Shand to Lennie – from home to living with Lennie – with some excursions along the way and then marrying him when she was only twenty-one. They had evolved like two young trees whose branches entwined, and whose bark became joined in places. The only way of separating them would be a drastic cutting of some of the branches and of the bark.

A further counter-blast told her how selfish she was, and how it would have untold repercussions that she would sorely regret.

The persistent little mouse stuck her pointed snout out, its baby teeth already long and thin against its lower lip, and suggested it might have a right to be selfish, especially now, before it was too late.

No one is an island, we all need people unless we are isolates, and I certainly am not. And my work would suffer.

There was an '*ah, but*' twinkle in the little mouse's pink eyes when she thought that it would be interesting to find out for herself what it felt like to be free and to make decisions that were based on... based on, she was not sure what. The tiny mouse was too immature to connect its thoughts with that deep aliveness that Jane knew existed in her womb. The tiny creature was not the same as the young adult Jane who, with tears of bitterness at times, or self-pity, or with a valiant smile, or with a sad bewilderment, or a crazed hatred of life, or an energy in other pursuits, had patched and repatched that great longing over the years: that open womb, wet aliveness, that primordial yearning for that which would assuage the need.

But the timorous little mouse could risk the 'what if' trail, for it could always bolt back behind the skirting boards.

Now this 'what if' trail was made of fresh morsels of cheese and walnuts, in a zigzag fashion, that the mouse sniffled and followed, heady with excitement and the possibilities of where this would lead. It sensed open fields where the grass was long, where it could feed on fat grain, where it would not fear the whispering whiskers of barley nor the red poppies that turned black at night, nor their shadows cast by the full moon. She would find another mouse...

In a light ochre silence, a cool silence after the sun had set, but when the stones were still warm, she saw that she could be courageous, she could manage her guilt, the inevitable guilt, and find a *joie de vivre* that was not going to be squashed by anyone else, and not by Lennie and his neediness. After all, there was no universal pattern laid down from on high, no absolute rule that dictated her life. She could still find her soul, her joyful soul, and if one day, she rejoined with Lennie – though that was unlikely – she would have known what it was like to swim upstream against the tide in dappled sunlight, and to have danced through the night, not intoxicated with alcohol, but with the pulsing thread of life that connected her with the child who once ran among the towering cosmos daisies, pink and sky-blue and amethyst, until she reached the glinting lake.

For the first time since she was a very young adult, she saw her life as an adventure. Her heart beat faster, her mind awash with images, russets and golds with glints of silver, brocaded fabrics, whirling, heady, possibly dangerous.

When she was seventeen, William Golding's *Free Fall* became her favourite book for it tackled the issue of free will versus pre-determination in a way that she had never fully considered before. But she had not been able to stay with that tension, or to feel truly free. She had allowed herself to follow the path of 'predetermination' for it was easier. It was what was expected of her by her father with his conservatism despite, or because of, his Communism and by her mother with her conventional views of 'normality' and anything that deviated from it being pitiable or shocking. Children seem to be cursed or blessed with such differing degrees of a will to please versus a will to question, attack, or discover. She was overendowed with the former. And yet, Jane sometimes wondered, if she 'chose' predetermination, did that not contradict the term?

Sitting by the side of the pool, in the still time of evening, Jane thought soberly that she would not be able to ask Lennie for favours or want him to fetch her from the airport, or ask for anything now, if she was going to be so traitorously independent in spirit and body and soul. As he often said, 'You can't have it both ways.' These thoughts made her smile as she tasted the almost black Cahors. The only movement was a turquoise dragonfly skimming the mirror-surface of the pool, its colour and the water almost as one. Holding the glass up to the bright part of the sky where the sun had dipped below the trees did not lighten the dark ruby. Again the feeling of an adventure suffused her, a journey with an unknown destination. A strong tenor voice, like her father's and Adrian's, passionate and intense, wrapped her in its timbre and gave her the buoyancy she needed.

Now Pierre was not so central. She felt a slight wave of shame at recontacting him a few hours ago, topping up his – no her – mobile. Of course, he had not called her back. He was a means to an end for her, a significant catalyst that had torn off her years of hiding behind convention and expectation, and she now felt grateful to him. It was a relief that she would never see him again. The sudden thought that she might have to see him in court shocked her. His bizarre behaviour and the police involvement were more than the shadows of a bad dream.

Lennie would never understand what had taken place with Pierre, and that was why he should and would never know. Yet she felt grateful, immensely grateful and loving to Lennie, for the years of fun and companionship and hard shoulder-to-shoulder work they had undertaken. However, if there was someone who was going to flag when there was a job to be done, it was always Lennie. It was Lennie who would need to retire with his cigar, a double whisky, and music and a snooze. Despite his gender, it was as if his skin was more delicate, his hands softer, and his muscles weaker. Even when she had her first cancer, she felt stronger than him. At times, Jane knew she envied his capacity to sleep whenever and wherever, to be so healthily selfish, like an animal. Lennie's golf held supremacy over other events in the family – even if one of the children was ill. She wondered if she was being unfair in these reminiscences: her friends, and sister, Ruth, had a special place in her life, separate from her marriage, and sometimes they took first place for her.

Now Jane thought that the very thing she needed from that slip-of-a man Pierre, and had found, was the very thing that Lennie had not given her: the connection with her younger self, her pre-Lennie self. This passion did not have to be consumed by the cancer and by ageing, whichever came first – though the cancer was winning the race.

She pulled herself up from the chair with effort, pausing to notice, poised on the buddleia, a small cobalt butterfly whose black dots lent it the appearance of filigree lace. How delicate some things seem, when really they must be strong to withstand buffeting.

As she chopped onions, fennel, fat chunks of courgettes, and sliced the top husk off a whole bulb of garlic and added it to the roasting dish, sprinkling all with fine walnut oil, a dash of balsamic vinegar, and fresh coriander, she felt a wave of pity for Lennie. She saw him as so sad, eating alone, drinking too much, feeling depressed, not knowing what to do to lift his spirits, perhaps booking expensive seats for the opera, perhaps turning to further material pleasures like a new Jaguar or planning a luxury trip on the Orient Express, but so lonely without her. Yes, he would find solace in taking Max out for meals – Max, the child he was closest to. But most of their friends were really her friends; he would have few friends if they separated. Unless he had more of a secret life than she realised, as she sometimes suspected. She did not want to think about that now.

She felt a cold draught of fear that made her worry if she really could do this to him. Perhaps she was really fearful for herself, her own bereft feelings. She would not convey any of her thoughts to anyone, not yet. The word 'traitorous' came to her mind again.

Jane knew that she had not fully considered her children's reactions to what she hardly dare call her 'decision' yet, and she was postponing the telephone call to check on the safe arrival of Theo, trusting that 'no news was good news'.

But he was now about a week past the due date, and she began to worry.

She decided to drive to the telephone box while the supper cooked slowly.

Closing her problematic eye that blurred her vision, she peered at the chrome buttons which she had to press.

She telephoned Air France and postponed her flight by twenty-four hours, disregarding the surcharge. She needed more time to catch her breath.

Then she dialled her home number. She never thought that she would find the English ringing tone so reassuring, like a mother's heartbeat.

'Lennie, is that you?'

'Yes, darling! How *are* you? Was about to ring your landlady – about the baby! Guess what?' Jane could hear the pleasure in his voice.

'She was born at midday today. She! A girl!'

'Oh my God! Amazing, wonderful! Oh gosh...' She had nurtured a secret hope that this might be a girl, that the scans were misleading. 'All fine? Both well? What does she weigh?'

'I think Jack said 7lbs something. They're not sure about a name yet. I think they've mentioned Violet, and another flower name, can't remember what. Possibly Rose or Rosa. Alice had quite an easy time of it: only four hours' labour, I think. Jack got her there just as it got strong. You'll be back to see the baby soon enough, won't you?'

Jane was just beginning to take in the fact of the baby's femininity: her tiny femaleness already there, growing secretly in the dark over the past nine months, a gift for Tom and Will, a little sister. She pulled herself out of her reverie while Lennie gave more details that she could not take in, not yet, and then interjected,

'I'll be drinking to the baby tonight, 'wetting the baby's head', as your Dad says. I'll ring Alice – is she home yet? Perhaps I'll ring Jack on his mobile. Midday did you say? Oh darling, it's so wonderful. Wish I could see the baby sooner than planned.' Unexpected choking feelings welled in Jane's throat. She knew they were unprocessed lumpy feelings about the unbearableness of dying, but she could not possibly allow them to surface now, and not with Lennie anyway.

'And how are *you*?' he asked.

'Fine. Absolutely fine. Very well. Well, you know, under the circumstances – pretty good.' She put an effort into sounding normal. She thought he would believe her.

The words they exchanged about the weather, about the aftermath of the theft of her car, about her plan to return to London on the 28th, all seemed so unimportant after the monumental news.

She leant with her elbows on the shelf of the booth after saying goodbye to him. Imagining.

Tiny pink ears like shells; transparent minute fingernails; skin so fine and of a delicacy that coarse older skin could barely register – as soft as a breath of air; pale lilac eyelids, like petals, flickering over filmy unfocussed eyes; wispy hair. Jane knew she was being romantic and fanciful, but she needed all that now. She tried to evoke the smell, that inside-womb puppy smell on the top of the head that she never wanted to wash away from her own babies.

Even saying 'she' and 'her' seemed a treat, imbued with *petite*-ness and delicacy. 'Girl' rhymed with 'curl': she imagined soft light brown curls; Alice had inherited Lennie's thick curly hair. Yes, pearl, a pearl of a girl. Her thoughts were as numinous as a soft breeze through leaves, leaves illuminated by the sun to the brightest lime.

Sitting in her car before driving back, she began to allow herself to imagine what the baby would look like as she grew into a little girl. Perhaps she'll turn out to be a solid tomboy, Jane countered with a little laugh. But a golden-skinned girl with sturdy legs, wearing khaki shorts and tough sandals, was just as appealing as the delicate girl she had first imagined.

She knew how thrilled Alice and Jack must be, and Lennie too, and how this sense of three generations of women she had always wanted to be a part of was now a reality, before she died. Jane's own mother had died before the birth of any of Jane's children.

Driving slowly along the winding lanes, back to her supper, she knew that this was one of many considerable milestones that made up her life: the things that she and Lennie shared. When she thought of the catastrophic shifts to the whole structure if she decided to pull out, the pressure behind her eye returned, as well as a strange headache which she had tried to ignore over the past few days.

Jane stumbled upon the thought that withdrawing from Lennie might be an excuse, a way of easing her contact and preparing to leave this world. This idea felt indigestible for now.

Before leaving the car, Jane opened the notebook she always carried in her backpack, to look at the delicate *convolvulus* she had picked a few days ago, an omen for a granddaughter. 'Granddaughter,' she murmured, feeling entitled, for the first time, to use the word about her progeny. It had such a different ring from 'grandson' and seemed to carry within it whorls of herself. The flower's fragility had increased with drying and pressing. It trembled as it had that day in a faint breeze. She touched it gently with her lips and carefully placed it back in the notebook between blank pages, separate from the dead butterflies found on previous holidays, and from other pressed flowers, their petals drained of colour, their sap as dark as dried blood.

As Jane was locking the car, Annette appeared. In a halo of evening sunlight, the French woman clutched a tiny kitten close to her chest and talked about its bad mother abandoning it.

'Oh dear, wouldn't the kitten be better left for its mother to care for it?' Jane ventured. 'You know, they often change their minds.'

'No, no, the mother is a bad mother, it happen before. I was chestfallen last time. Makes me... like a red bull. No, I will look after this one. I don't think there are any more kittens from this litter. I found this one over there,' nodding towards the low wall near Jane's cottage. 'Can you carry it please to my house while I find a... a thing, you know, to give it drops of milk?'

The tiny creature in Jane's hands felt strong and desperate in its search for milk, but every few seconds became still and quiet. Jane feared that it was really quite weak. It cried loudly like a distressed bird. Its eyes were closed, the small ears so low on the sides of its round head, the tabby markings already fine and distinct, with a worm of a tail. The poor thing seemed to be rooting for a nipple on Jane's chest, its needle-claws outstretched.

Annette seemed to try to force its mouth open to receive the full syringe, but the creature resisted. Some milk spilt onto Jane's hand, which the kitten licked. Jane suggested that Annette squirt more milk onto her hand, but Annette had a preconception that she had to force the tiny mouth open.

Jane felt helpless in the face of the French woman's wish to be the feeding mother with her syringe. Her inability to follow what the kitten was demonstrating in its instinctive way of licking the milk reminded Jane of Annette's own childlessness.

'Can the kitten manage this cow's milk? Doesn't it need some special formula from a vet?'

Annette did not reply but continued to try to force the creature's mouth open.

Jane tried to sound supportive in her questioning. 'My goodness, you'll have to feed it every hour or so through the night.'

The French woman responded challengingly, 'Well, would *you* like to keep the kitten then? To care for it?' She can't be serious, Jane thought, but for a brief moment considered that possibility.

'I've done this before. It will be fine. One has to have the faith,' Annette added with religious fervour, pushing her glasses higher up the bridge of her nose, her eyes glinting. Jane discerned a fieriness in the other woman, a sense of a mission, as if all her cleaning and scurrying now had a proper outlet. Her plain features became more alive and attractive.

Jane offered to go to the *pharmacie* or a vet the next day if Annette needed anything for the kitten. Annette thanked her in her usual fusty English but with French formality: her husband 'Stevern' would be able to do that. 'And now you go and 'ave the dinner'.

The kitten was now in a small box lined with a tea towel, crying pitifully, while Annette scrabbled in a cupboard for something. Jane bowed out, wishing the woman good luck. She could not bear to think about the small creature's next few days.

Over supper, Jane thought she could hear the crying of the kitten, but then thought it was a bird. She told herself she could not take on concern for a kitten as well. How she longed to ring Alice, or Jack, to make contact with the real, wanted baby, rather than this 'kitten-napped' one with a disturbed 'mother' who, she was sure, was pushing her own disdain for mothers onto the mother cat.

Which flower name had they chosen for the baby girl, she wondered, turning over names delicately, as one might examine a jewel from various angles to see how the facets caught the light, to see which ones cast a translucent glow. She silently intoned a litany, Iris…, Lily…, Holly…, Ivy…, Primrose…, Rose…, Rosie…, Rosa…, Poppy…, Daisy…, Hyacinth…, Jasmine. Each one evoked different seasons and shades of different colours. And then she remembered Violet, which Lennie had mentioned. She liked them all. She tried them out with Jack and Alice's surname, 'Lewis'. Then there's Rosemary, she thought, but rejected it. Or Olive? She wondered why people didn't call their girls Tulip, or Daffodil, or Chrysanthemum, or Crocus. Or perhaps they did? Or Peony, Hydrangea, Carnation, or Hollyhock, for that matter, she thought with a smile. Oleander, Hibiscus, Geranium. She remembered the names Saffron and Amber and Scarlet and Ruby and Willow, which had become quite popular these days. She thought of Pearl and wondered if that would have a revival. And how boys were spared flower, tree, spice and jewel names.

That night Jane dreamed of coming to a large house, which was her house, a new house that she would occupy, but the rooms had already been appropriated by lodgers. The only vacant room was small and crowded with children's bunk beds, which she thought would have to be her consulting room. She wondered if she could manage in it. She then walked into a big, rectangular room with a large picture window, from which she could see a beautiful, green pastoral scene, like the background of a Fragonard painting. She imagined how lovely it would be to sit there every day with that view as she worked. She did not know if she had a right to take over that room.

After speaking to Jane, Lennie clicked off the handset and put the phone down. He could not fully rejoice in the birth of the baby girl on his own; he did not really know what to feel without Janey.

Her break in France did not really make sense. She was always on about 'space', and 'finding herself' – it all sounded so New Age, even hippy. Sitting on the edge of their bed, on Janey's side, he ran his fingers through his thick, dark hair that was barely greying. He shifted his head to catch his reflection in her dressing table mirror, pleased at how like his father he was beginning to look. George had thick black hair, wavy too, and was considered handsome, even now, aged eighty-seven.

Lennie asked himself if he wanted a drink... or what.

And now Janey was delaying her return by twenty-four hours. She was pushing her luck. He had to appear reasonable, or she would chafe more at the bit. But that had never been the arrangement, had it, for each to go their own way? He could understand her reasons this time – up to a point – but after all the residential conferences and teaching abroad, she had used up her credit.

The idea of 'credit' led him to wonder if she had indeed used up her lives, like a cat. He thought of the cancer. And shook his head. He knew he was 'in denial', as Janey called it, 'defended', and all that psycho-babble. But what is a bloke to do, wallow in it?

After the death of Timmy, Lennie never saw the point in grieving. He had reached the edge of madness, an infinite arctic wasteland when Timmy died, and in the baby's wake he lost Janey too.

Then, he had hauled himself back with Wagner; Wagner, while he lay in the bath until it was cold and he was numb all over, his fingers white and wrinkled like prunes. Heavy as a porous brick, he would haul himself out and lie on the tiled floor in his own puddle, with *Tannhäuser* on repeat. And then he would crawl out of the bathroom to find Janey on the sofa staring into space. All he could do was sit on the other sofa, wrapped in a towel, shivering. Luckily, there were two identical cream linen sofas. They had bought them at a special price at Habitat only a month before – everything began to be defined by 'before' or 'after' Timmy. Who would have known what use these sofas would be put to, at right angles to each other. And he would stare into space too. The precise positioning of this furniture was the only thing that made sense, like the dovetail joints in the wooden bookends he had made as a kid.

Sometimes, there would be other people around, flapping like crows, bringing food. Janey's sister Ruth, and Harriet, her best friend. And Harry, Janey's father. And well-meaning Tina. And others he couldn't remember.

Janey continued to suffer, to be broken, but one day he decided enough was enough. The idea that some cultures give you forty days, or whatever, to grieve and then that's that, back to work, as well as the Wagner – with its tragic *leitmotifs* and its monumental themes of pain and redemption that you just have to accept, no need to go on keeling over like a boat in a storm – helped him to right himself.

He had begun to feel that Janey's protracted grief was self-indulgent. And so the gap between them widened. She found comfort for her sorrow in her psychoanalysis and in her friends, and he wondered if she found it in secret affairs. He could not really ask while he was finding solace from young women – ex-students and secretaries, and one junior colleague – at his college, who were flattered by the attention of a senior criminologist.

Although Lennie would never admit to anyone but himself, the main attraction to these young women was not their minds, but their breasts. Young plump breasts that drew him to them inexorably. He would flatter these women and soon they would feel that a fling with an attractive, older man with all the accoutrements of power was irresistible. He sensed that some young women imagined that they would succeed in wooing him away from his wife. Much of his sexual energy went into these 'friendships', which were less knotty than his relationship with Janey, for Janey was always complicating matters, never satisfied, always undermining him.

When his father, George, retired – George had shrewdly bought a wine farm in the Western Cape and sold it when it was flourishing – Lennie and his sister inherited a fair amount, which kept him in the manner in which he felt he deserved, including membership of a good golf club. It wasn't only the well-kept 18 holes surrounded by velvet lawns, but the *belonging* that gave him smug pleasure. He had to be nominated by someone and vetted by a committee and, of course, he had sailed through. They were glad to have him, he was sure. Always the best Havanas, bespoke suits, a flamboyantly coloured silk handkerchief flopping out of his breast pocket, Bond Street brogues, cufflinks from that little place in Sloane Street, to which he added plenty of confidence and charm.

Both he and Janey sometimes wondered why they had stayed with each other all these years. There were the children, of course, the three children after Timmy. And now the grandchildren. And the social circle, and the extended family, and comfort, and familiarity. And the big house.

In a way, he thought he loved her. He did not analyse things the way she did, but he sensed a deep connection with her despite the gap. A connection that he felt when their bodies lay together – his hands cupping her soft breasts, her buttocks pressed against his genitals as neatly and as comfortably as two bodies cut with a jigsaw from one block of wood. When he stroked her smooth skin, she would fairly ripple with pleasure. They talked in the navy-dark night, about whatever, but never about their sex life, shared or otherwise – he steered clear of that whole area, felt it was a minefield. Things could tootle along pleasantly without excavating. And they laughed together, usually at his spontaneous jokes, sometimes at quirky ways of seeing the world that they construed together, each providing one brick at a time until the final joint edifice was hilarious. Lennie half-realised that he had to claim credit –for his part in the jokes, his part in the anecdotes that they recounted, his part in the conversations, his part in helping the children – to avoid being overshadowed by Janey. He felt connected when they remembered things they had shared from their packed dossier of thirty-three years of marriage plus one year of courting. And when they shared worries about the children. And when she cooked his favourite Italian dishes with fresh ingredients and they drank good red wine, or when she brought him the perfect chocolate cake from *Maison Blanche* with a cup of espresso coffee. Or wore certain under-garments for him – occasionally. (Although, with the rarity of that, he wondered if she was 'getting it over with', keeping him quiet, but he never asked her if she was doing this because he wanted it and that she didn't seem to, for he was not the asking type, and never wanted to be.)

Now, as Lennie stood up he put a hand down his shorts and scratched his scrotum with a delicious pleasure; as satisfying as scratching an itchy bite, as good as sneezing, or a good crap, he thought. At least he could do what he liked when she wasn't here. He felt like a boy whose parents were out, having the house to himself. His cock began to stiffen.

Fuelled by resentment at her taking herself away like this, not really caring about him, not acknowledging him enough, he went to his study, pulled down the blinds, and logged onto a cyber world which he knew always led to a particular outcome, the glimmering screen taking all his attention. Within seconds he found his favourite, and buried himself in a world of young girls with all the breasts he could ever want until he needed them no longer. For the time being.

Then he wandered downstairs, his brain feeling slightly mashed, not wanting to think about where he had just been, and unsure how to spend the evening. *A video?* He glanced at the disorderly collection, knew that there were some hidden at the back of the shelf that would take him back to the world he had just been in, or a similar one, but he felt that he needed to find something more nourishing. *Music? Phone a friend?* laughing at the phrase that would never be the same again after the television quiz show had exploited it.

He considered working, finishing a book review whose deadline was looming, or beginning a paper he had promised the *British Journal of Criminology*, but he felt he deserved a relaxing evening.

The ice cubes cracked as he drowned them in whisky in a cut-glass tumbler. Janey returned to his mind. He pictured her getting brown, swimming, relaxing. The good life, despite everything. He was pleased for her. And then, pleased that he would have her back in better shape.

He thought, not for the first time, it was ironic that the cancer had begun in her breast. Its spread now was something from which he averted his whole being, as ghastly as that tray of rotten peaches he had seen teeming with wasps in France last summer. He had managed to avoid the scar too, the silky raised area where they had removed the first lump. What if they had removed the whole breast? Would she have had a better outcome, he had asked himself countless times since the recurrence. Had she opted for a lumpectomy partly because she knew how much he needed her breasts? He was frightened of voicing these thoughts to her. What would be the point of indulging regrets and anxieties?

What was she going to do, now that there was a granddaughter in the family, let alone the three children and grandsons? Of course, she'd have to have treatment – surely, she'd be sensible, he reasoned. He felt helpless at his lack of a say in all this. Janey had made it clear to him that she had to decide for herself.

At the time of the recurrence, he thought that if she were to decline treatment it would be selfish, and had begun to say as much, but her reaction was acerbic. 'It's *my* life,' she had said that day when they were driving to see Alice and Jack and the boys, putting *Don Pasquale* on in the car, loudly. He knew he had to withdraw and let her sort it out. In her own time, she would see sense.

It was still hot, at 7.30pm. Lennie put on a new CD of *Tristan und Isolde*, and stretched out on the chaise-longue in the conservatory. This was usually Janey's place. He closed his eyes, allowing the whisky and the music to meld in whatever way they chose. He felt waves of some force that he did not want to go with, could not ride, had to avoid being submerged by. He stood up, turned the music down, and phoned the better quality home-delivery Chinese place in St John's Wood. 'Menu C for two people,' he ordered.

And turned the television on looking for the Japan Golf championships. He favoured a rich Chianti now, too bad if it didn't really go with Chinese nosh. The golf was not on. He briefly cruised through the channels, but it was too much like the earlier surfing, which left him with a bad taste. Instead, he picked up the *British Journal of Criminology* to leaf through his latest article, to reread his well-chosen phrases and to marvel as he often did that he had actually written that, when it seemed so good. Pity that Harry was no longer here for him to show it to. When he died, Lennie had found all the articles, papers and book reviews he had ever written in two big box folders in his father-in-law's study. Janey was never that interested. Pity. And now she never will be, he thought, with a pang of anguish that the Chianti and the whisky had not banished. Perhaps he'd send a copy to Max, Max would be interested.

AUGUST 25TH, 2003

Jane awoke early. The pain in her side nagged, and another in her back and one deep under her right breast. At times like this she was unsure which pains were new and which were recurrences. The rusty metal sign she had observed the day before that someone had used as target practice came to her mind.

The prospect of phoning Alice as soon as the time difference allowed brightened her. Opening the shutters on another blue-washed sky, she looked at the chapel that had become her beacon, her fixed point, when all else was uncertain. Even if it was crumbling, it would easily outlive her. She dressed in a rose tiered skirt and white camisole, which she did not want to have brought for nothing.

Jane knew that Jack's mother, Rita, would be staying with the young family, as planned, for a week after the birth. The couple had planned to give Rita her turn to help, as Jane had assisted after both previous births and Lennie had felt unable to offer more than visits. Jane did not know if it was really her illness that had led them to spare her this time, or Lennie's difficulty in involving himself with young children beyond cooing at babies and play-fighting with toddlers.

Jane often felt that Lennie found it hard to share the limelight with a baby or young child, that he seemed envious of the baby, and so withdrew. He would smilingly talk about childcare being 'women's work', in front of Jack who was as involved as any father could be (and, unfortunately, Jane felt, in front of their sons Max and Eddie, unaware of how formative all this was to these young men who might become fathers one day.)

A loud knock at her front door startled her. She saw from the hall the same older police officer, with the younger one like his shadow behind him.

After polite apologies for disturbing her at an early hour, Jane responded with formal protestations that it was fine. She intended to convey within the permitted etiquette that actually it was not fine, that she was otherwise engaged.

The men trooped in, their hats tucked under their arms. They seemed to take up so much space in the room. The Inspector said that they had further questions, but would she prefer to come with them to the police station in Mapenche, only twelve kilometres away? She asked if they meant that she had to accompany them, feeling stupid as she did.

'No, Doctor, we can interview you here, as before, especially at this stage. We only want to ask one or two questions. But you will need to sign a statement, to agree to what you tell us to write down, if you don't mind, please.'

Jane thought for a moment and asked herself what a French woman would do. Was it because she was British that she was being treated differently?

'No, not really,' she replied.

'But we are aware that you intend to depart very soon, so we thought we should see you to clear up one or two things before you go. In fact, we need your UK details now, please, like address, telephone number, passport number, etc.'

'Sounds serious,' Jane replied. She took a deep breath. The news item about that young woman came to her mind. She was unnerved by the younger man watching her obliquely again.

The Inspector asked for practical details, including her place of work, email, fax number, profession, how long she had lived in her present house, number of children and their ages, for he was filling in yet another large form and had to oblige all the boxes that were awaiting information or, he said, the computer would reject all of it.

'Yes, computers can be most unreasonable, can't they,' Jane replied. 'I still prefer people.' The Inspector clearly resisted the temptation to join her chitchat. Today he seemed more business-like. Jane wondered what theories he and the other man, and no doubt a whole team behind them, had by now.

He asked if she had any previous convictions.

'Police convictions?' she asked.

'Yes, of course.'

'Well, you could have meant religious or political convictions!' She noticed their reluctance again to relax into more light-hearted banter, but decided that that did not mean that she had to lose her sense of fun.

'Forgive me, Officers – but I've just heard about the birth of my first granddaughter, and I am, how do you say "over the moon" in French? "*Dessus, au-dessus, sur la lune?*" No, that can't be right. But you know what I mean.' They looked blank.

Feeling childlike and trying to keep a straight face to suppress waves of giggles, she said, 'No, I do not have any police convictions, except speeding, *slight* speeding, recently, in England.'

'Speeding is speeding, Doctor. But nothing else?'

'No. But I'm sure you will check anyway. Interpol, it used to be called. I wonder if it's easy nowadays for you to do a police check, now that we're all part of Europe? That's not a real question. Just thinking aloud.' Yes, she thought, the slightly dotty older woman. Easy to play that part. *Just keep calm Jane, keep calm.* Flutters rose from her heart into her throat, unbidden.

The Inspector asked her to sign the form he had completed. She complied with apparent willingness, reminding herself aloud, 'But I must ring my daughter soon – haven't spoken to her since the birth.'

As predicted, as sure as a cat waiting to pounce on the mouse it had been gently playing with, they now asked her what her relationship with Pierre – actually *Charles* – Baudier had been and how long he had stayed.

Jane replied in a measured way that she had already answered them the other day and she did not have anything to add. They may think it strange, she said, but she had disregarded any risk for she believed that the young man was in need, she knew what that felt like because of her own circumstances, and she was a shrewd judge of character and sensed that he was a simple boy who had had a hard life and needed a bit of help. She now added that she did get a whiff of something odd, something 'hunted' about him, but she had not wanted to get involved.

She gave a little laugh, 'Huh! Seems like I am involved now, whether I like it or not.' She shook her head slowly from side to side.

'Doctor, you have not answered my questions, please. Where did he sleep? And why did you invite a stranger in?'

They seemed to be trying a different technique now, of multiple questions, in the hope of something slipping out.

'What…? Oh yes, well, he slept here on this sofa. I lent him that blanket. He was here for only one night, the night you know about. I forget the date. Was it last Tuesday, or Wednesday? While he rested I carried on as normal: going for walks, swimming, shopping, some cooking. He slept a great deal. I think he was exhausted. I told you that before… And I have already answered you, just now, about "why", surely!'

'Do you know anything about a red Renault Clio, the 1998 model?' the Inspector interrupted.

Jane distanced herself from the question, frowning. She was used to doing this in her work when a patient surprised her with a personal question. She could step back, and try to think what it meant, what the question told you about the questioner.

'I don't think so. Why? I'm not very good on makes of cars. The only red Renault that comes to mind is a neighbour's, in London. I think it's a Mégane, though. Wouldn't be as old as… 1999, did you say?' Feeling hot, she hoped her throat was not betraying her by reddening. The silent officer was as inscrutable as ever. She resisted an impulse to make him laugh. 'But why do you ask?' she persisted.

With a suave smile, as if he would burst out of his tight shirt, the older man said with the utmost seriousness that they had their reasons, and it's one question among many, an attempt to tie up lots of loose ends. Jane thought that was a clever non-answer, and looked at her watch pointedly.

He asked her now what the young man had told her about his life – adding that anything at all might be helpful. She did want to help them, didn't she? 'You see', he added with consummate skill, 'there is the recent disappearance of a young woman, last seen driving her red Renault, which you may have read about in the local paper. The woman was, is, Giselle *Baudier*,' emphasising the surname. 'There could be extremely serious implications. Both the car and the woman have disappeared.'

'My goodness, no,' Jane exclaimed in English before responding in French. 'No, sorry – didn't know about that. I don't buy a paper when I'm away. Oh dear. Well, I'm sorry I can't help you,' not mentioning that she thought she had seen the item on television. Surely, there had not been a mention of a red car on the news. She began to feel that the police were being tricky with their facts in order to trap her.

'Then the car was discovered, crashed, very near here. We traced it from the licence to Mademoiselle Baudier. '

'But why didn't you tell me about that, about the car, before?'

'It was in the newspapers, Doctor.'

She hoped that they did not have a way of detecting lies. Her heart was racing. Why did they leave this piece of information until now – like patients who come to the main point a minute before the end of a session, sometimes to leave you with anxiety and helplessness. She weighed up whether the policemen could be using sophisticated techniques, or whether they were really as simple as they appeared. Wondering if perjury was a serious crime, her heart missed a beat.

Jane realised that this time the Inspector had not transcribed the interview after all. Perhaps he had been taping it secretly. At least she had not lied further by signing a statement.

He asked exactly when she was leaving for England. She told them that her flight had been for the next afternoon,

Wednesday, but that she had postponed it until Thursday afternoon. He gave her a printed card with his name, Chief Inspector Lagarde, his number in the force and telephone number, should she wish to contact him with any more information. She said that she realised how serious all this could be.

She wondered to herself if French law was the same as English law and you were innocent until you were proved guilty. And she was not thinking of Pierre.

When they left, she felt like crying, crying that she should be caught up in something that may involve a murder. She felt sorry for herself, knowing she already had far too much to deal with, and all because she had been so naïve and impulsive with Pierre.

She wondered whether to confess all, to tell them that her illness made her act irrationally and ask if they would take that into consideration. She now felt that she should consult a lawyer, but feared that he or she would persuade her to tell the truth about finding the Renault, and about becoming sexually involved with Pierre. What difference would her involvement make? If Pierre had behaved criminally, she had not actually been an accomplice, she reassured herself.

I must ring Alice, surely, she told herself, but now felt quite unsteady.

On the familiar drive to the phone box in Ceneyrac, Jane was behind a large black shiny car with darkened windows. It cruised slowly over the undulations of the country road like a large liner on rolling waves. After her conversation with the Inspector about cars, she peered to read the make. She could just discern that it was a Peugeot 607. It suddenly accelerated and sped away into the distance.

She was aware of a persistent low helicopter that she thought she had noticed on and off over the past few days.

Jane felt slightly guilty about ringing her daughter from the same little dusty booth that she had used to call Pierre. But as soon as Alice's calm voice answered, Jane's euphoria took over,

'Darling, it's Mum! How are you? Congratulations! *Wonderful* news!'

Alice sounded serene, her voice soft. Jane was astounded at how young women these days seemed to revert to normality so soon after giving birth, how the days of 'lying in' no longer existed.

The two women rejoiced in baby Daisy, and in her gender. Alice now shared her secret sense that it was a girl during the pregnancy. She talked about the labour, and about the other two boys' reactions, although she said she would tell her a great deal more when they met.

Alice said that they had wanted to call the baby 'Lily', but 'lilly' was Will's word for 'willy' or penis, and his puzzlement when they told him they may call the baby that, compounded by his dawning awareness that she did not have a 'lilly', left the parents feeling that perhaps another name would be better.

'I wish I could see you, darling. And the baby. It's hard being so far away. Of course, we'll find time to be together when I'm back.' Jane's voice was strong and full of energy; her sense of where her real priorities lay made everything clearer. 'I want to hear more, much more, about the labour. And the birth. I'm sure you'll manage a blow-by-blow, or contraction-by-contraction, account. But when is Dad going to see you all – or has he, already?'

'Tomorrow, he said. Just for a few hours. I think he's worried about adding to our pressure. Also, he has a slight cold. But really, it's very relaxed here. I try to sleep when Daisy sleeps.' Her voice sounded mellow, a rich caramel colour. 'Jack's been wonderful, and Rita's great – mainly looking after Tom and Will. But, of course, it will be so good to see you, Mum,' she added.

Jane could hear a creaking sound, like a gate that needed oiling. 'Is that the baby?'

'Yes. Do you want to speak to her? It's Granny, say hello to Granny.'

Jane cooed gently into the mouthpiece, sending her love through the wires and across the Channel. The baby gave a little husky cry. Jane could picture the tiny one on her mother's shoulder, raising her wrinkled brow, turning her head to search for the breast.

Alice came back on the phone.

Through a film of tears, Jane began to say goodbye to her daughter. Alice asked how she was, as Alice always did, genuinely, and not just because of the cancer. This side of her daughter always moved Jane. The children knew about a recurrence, but did not yet know quite how serious it was, nor the dilemma about further treatment. They all assumed that their mother would have whatever treatment was possible.

'Oh, by the way, Dad said I must tell you, he did manage to rearrange your hospital appointment,' she added.

A few chalky-ochre leaves slanted down from a tree having an early autumn, whispering loudly, and then they stopped, and all was still again.

Jane had not wanted to take any more energy from her daughter, who must already be so stretched, even though she was remarkably gifted at mothering small children and now a tiny baby as well. Jane thought how different Annette was, with her rigid way of trying to force the kitten to feed.

The thought that perhaps she herself wasn't a bad mother, if Alice was so fine, buoyed her up on the drive back to *La Retraite*.

That afternoon, Jane was tempted to buy a local newspaper and to put her ear to the ground by talking in the *boulangerie*

in Ceneyrac about the young woman in the news. And yet how ridiculous that would be. She knew that, like the dream of moving into her house, she could inhabit a little cramped room still crowded with her own child-paraphernalia, where she could not 'work' properly in all senses of the word, or she could rightfully inhabit the much bigger room with a leafy view through a picture window. If she stayed with the speculations and intrigues around Pierre, maybe she would be increasing the progress of the cancer, she risked thinking. Yes, she would have to oust the lodger that had already appropriated that lovely room. It was her house.

Of course, she should hand over responsibility to people who were trained and paid to do the job of investigating Pierre.

She cast her mind back to how Pierre had bargained with her from the very beginning, adamant that she was not to pry, threatening to manage on his own if she did not keep her nose out of his business. Why had she gone along with that? She was reminded of her negotiations with Max when she was sure he was using drugs, how she had to gain his trust in order to be able to help him, without having access to all the facts.

And then, she remembered speaking similarly to Lennie – that it was her life and her decision – over whether or not to have treatment. His counsel could not be impartial. Yes, that was why she had respected Pierre's imperative that she keep out of his business.

And yet, she could still feel the young man who she had slept with, feel him deep in her body. Sometimes, the feelings would come unbidden, sometimes, as part of a memory. Pierre – who she had felt recognised by, who had not taken away anything that she had not willingly given – how could he be someone who had behaved criminally? She churned this over in her mind again and again until she was sick of her speculations. Not for the first time, she wondered what 'papers' had been in the boot of his car, and whether that had been a ruse to get her out so he could steal her car.

Again Jane retraced events, needing to find out whether their contact could still be good in her mind. She tried to think that the police and their enquiries were one thing, but her own experiences with Pierre were another. The two did not have to be confused. The familiarity of this internal debate exhausted her, for she knew how circular her thinking could be, how she needed to talk with someone over the legalities of the situation, let alone the emotional implications. How Lennie would berate her for her foolhardy stance with 'someone like that', even if he were not to know about the sexual aspect. If only she could talk with Adrian or, in a very different way, with Harriet. It was not mere coincidence that she called her 'Harrie', almost her father's name.

Jane swam breaststroke and sidestroke covering big ovals and figures-of-eight in the pool, clockwise and then anti-clockwise, using different muscles, feeling so much stronger than when she first arrived. She relished not setting herself a number of lengths, but instead followed her body, and her instinct, in when to push a little harder, when to make her heart race, when to go steadily and slowly. She did not believe in the slogan 'no pain, no gain' seen in gyms and magazines when it came to what her body needed. Maybe, she thought, she did not want the pain of chemotherapy... or why bother to stretch herself, when time was running out?

Her recent resolve to separate from Lennie returned to her mind. Her visual impairment increased, clouding her vision.

She opened her eyes underwater, to defy what was happening to her sight, to marvel at the large silver shapes like nets cast by the sun beaming through ripples in the water, vibrating and waving on the bottom of the verdigris pool.

Her thoughts were disturbed by Annette appearing with a yellow hosepipe to water shrubs nearby. *Why are French hosepipes yellow, while English ones are usually green?* Annette had recently had her hair severely cropped at the back, characteristic of French women. It made her nose look bigger.

'Is the water good?' Annette called.

Economical in her response, so as to discourage unnecessary chit-chat, Jane replied, '*Oui!*' feeling satisfied at her mastery of the French pronunciation: making it sound breathy and brief, more like 'way'.

Now Annette was harvesting fallen plums, placing them in a plastic bucket. Jane decided to swim underwater. When she surfaced Annette was returning to her house. She felt churlish and decided to enquire later about the kitten.

That afternoon, Annette called to her from the washing line that the tiny kitten was doing fine, it was a girl, and she was calling her Ursula.

Another girl, Jane wondered if Ursula would have suited the new baby; it was a name she liked from Lawrence's *The Rainbow* and *Women in Love*.

AUGUST 26TH, 2003

Jane was surprised at how difficult it was to get through to Inspector Lagarde. When eventually she heard his sonorous voice, she asked if he would phone her back, as she did not have much credit left on her phonecard. The truth was, she resented the minutes she had already been kept waiting, at her expense. Her difficulty in sleeping the night before and torment over what to do about the possibility of a serious crime had made her more impatient than usual. As well as the pains in her side she felt nauseous.

The loud ring of the phone shattered the soporific silence.

'Inspector, it's Dr Samuels. Yes, sorry, of course, you know who I am. I've been a bit stupid really. I do have more to tell you about that young man.'

But Pierre's earnest expression, the feel of his tender embraces, his young skin, pushed back the information she was going to offer into a corner of her mind. How could she betray him when she could not get him out of her body, when she felt more truly herself than she had for a long time, and even had tangled thoughts of seeing him again. Surely, he had nothing to do with the disappearance of his sister. Giselle disappeared after he had taken her car, didn't she? He was just a poor young man struggling against difficult odds, and the police may be brutal with him.

The Inspector waited, 'Yes?'

'Well, you see, he did tell me that he had a sister, called Giselle, and that he had rowed with her.' The thought that this conversation was bound to be taped made her hesitate further, but then she knew she was telling them things they probably knew anyway. Confused as to what she had already told them, and what she had not, she continued, 'He seemed to be jealous of her. He said their mother, who had died, had left Giselle money and… and did not leave him any. He said he had rowed with his sister but, but wanted to go back and sort things out.'

On television and in the papers, people who plead guilty are always treated more kindly than if they lie, aren't they, she told herself. She went on, 'I didn't tell you before – or did I? Oh dear, you see, I am getting confused. You see, because, because, well, because I felt sorry for him, and I had promised him I would not be curious about him… '

There was a silence. She felt annoyed at the other's lack of response, so she asked provocatively 'Are you still there, Inspector?'

'Yes, yes, of course. Well, I think I should collect you and bring you to the station so that you can assist us with our enquiries.'

For a moment, Jane thought he meant the train station. She quickly composed herself, 'Surely, that's not necessary, Inspector. I can talk on the phone, can't I? You see, I think I am just a bit disturbed, you know, emotionally, by my illness and other personal things, and so I got caught up in the boy's… the young man's drama in a stupid way. I tell you what,' she went on, trying to sound as lucid as possible, 'why don't you and your colleague come here, again, and I'll fill you in? Well, I don't mean here, in Ceneyrac, clearly. I mean *La Retraite*.'

'One second, Doctor. Please hold on, while I discuss this with a colleague.'

She waited, imagining a whole room of uniformed men in front of flickering screens with the latest details of the case, and now a discussion about the lying *anglaise*. At least they couldn't see her blushing. She was grateful for the distance that the telephone afforded. The heat in the booth was rising.

Just as the church bell rang out the ninth stroke of ten o'clock, the man came back on the line. She could not hear him until the bells had stopped.

' …come to your house, at midday today. Alright?'

'Yes, fine. See you then. 'Bye.'

At least she was beginning to be more honest.

She left the phone booth and sat on the grey wall to draw breath before driving to the little supermarket on her way back. A crow's raucous call seemed to mock her. Her guilt led her to want to buy good quality chilled apple juice for the men, and the best custard tarts, but she knew they would not accept them. Jane feared that once she began to disclose more there would be no stopping the divulgences: that sooner or later, they would know her private connection with Pierre, and then, somehow, Lennie would get to hear all about it.

Again, she could hear Lennie's prejudice, belittling someone like Pierre, damning his character, talking about 'people like that,' as if he was the real expert.

In a moment of relative objectivity, she thought that it was amazing that the course of justice could be affected by subtle affairs of the heart, and how probably that was often the case.

Realising that she would have to give those police officers a bit more information to keep them happy, she anticipated telling them about Pierre smelling of alcohol, and sleeping rough, possibly in the ruined chapel, the night before he… before he… knocked on her door. She still didn't have to say that she rescued him from the crash. She was worried about what they would make of what they found in the chapel, the spatters of paint by his 'patch' on the flagstones and his mother's freshly painted grave.

She realised that people sometimes assumed that the police knew more than they did, but the more Jane wondered, the more confused she became. She remembered Pierre's unkind way of agreeing that she thought too much.

She closed her eyes and tried to breathe deeply. She decided that she had better drive on, in case the police were watching her.

Jane sat on the patio, bored with waiting for those men again. She had better ways to spend her holiday.

The church clock in the next hamlet gave its long toll for midday, the chimes structuring the landscape with a calm orderliness that she craved. For the first time, she wanted this holiday to end, wanted to be back in England where she could see the new baby, and the little grandsons, and Alice and Jack, and Max and Eddie. Thoughts of seeing Lennie were far more complicated.

The men were late.

In this space of time, waiting time, thoughts about treatment came to mind. She knew she would go to the hospital for a rearranged appointment on the 30th, assuming that her request for a change of date had been granted. But she but did not know if she would be asking them if she could start treatment. Jane knew how ill that had made her previously. And now there was little hope of a real remission, let alone cure. She was fearful of entering that whole cycle of expectation, or bargaining, of wanting what she probably could not have, and the disappointment when a gain was not forthcoming.

And yet, after years of patching over the holes in her life in order to avoid feeling need, perhaps now that Jane had begun to pull off the protective layers, she could allow herself to want, to desire, to really want to live more?

Increasingly, the possibility of a more sincere life, even if it did not involve a relationship with a man, was something that she did want to give herself: that open big room in her dream with a luxuriant view beyond, where she could really breathe. The shape of the room – rectangular, not square – suggested to her a 'double room': as if she had mental space now for something more.

Perhaps she would discuss with the doctors if she could try a few cycles of something. She did not know if this compromise was a way of allowing for the bigger space in her mind, or not. You can't paint a picture if you don't have the canvas, she thought. Yes, I need the time, the space, to find out what there is, what could be.

It was now or never to paint a real painting, where she could see and feel the colours, and make mistakes, but at least it would be rendered before her eyes. It did not have to involve a relationship with an actual other person: it would be her painting, about aspects of herself, which others could see if they wished. They may not like it she mused – thinking of Lennie – but that would be them, and the painting is me.

The men were now twenty minutes late. She felt like going out, leaving them a note – but that would only prolong the saga.

Annette's cat, Sweet William, small, ginger, and stripy, came up to her expectantly. He swaggered as if he owned the place, his little furry testicles proudly on show. She marvelled at the close-fitting fur suit he wore, no seams or zips anywhere. His body and tail brushing her legs tickled like a feather, sending shivers up her legs. She knew how she longed for human touch. Since Pierre. As she stroked the cat, he easily swayed with her caresses, as if he could not stand firm. *Just when I have to return, he's becoming friendly.*

Sweet William's purr was now as loud as a motor. He leapt onto Jane's lap and pawed her belly as she reclined, his needle claws pricking through the thin fabric of her skirt. She stifled a yelp, understanding how he needed this, and so did she. 'But stop, please, Sweet William,' she whispered in French when English would have been just as effective. 'Settle down! I'm not your mother, you know.'

A rough dry-stone wall, draped with patches of thick moss like swags of old mouldy velvet, greens and golden browns sunlight-faded, formed part of the perimeter to *La Retraite*.

Jane had been attracted to this wall for days. Now, with a little unstructured time – what she had come away for – she decided to draw it if her eye problem did not impinge. All her observations of this wall would be channelled into a rendition; hopefully, with more meaning than a mere copy of limestone piled in a particular way. Somehow, for Jane, it carried a presence of the people who had built it, however long ago. It was looped with ivy, some of which was dead, bedecked with fallen oak leaves, and housed crevices deep enough for a delving hand, where leaves had lain for seasons. One might think that the stones were placed nonchalantly, yet so skilful was the fit of big and little, fat and thin, that most of it would last hundreds more years. Some had slithered and slid, some may have been knocked, leaving the top as irregular as the craggy peaks of a mountain range. Rubble and beauty, chaos and order, the softness of the moss and the hardness of the rock, again.

She chose heavily textured paper that would give the drawing a unity on which she could impose the irregularities. Lightly sketching the lines and angles, her eye problem abated.

'Knock knock,' broke through her concentration, causing Jane a moment of panic. Ridiculous woman, she thought, as Annette appeared, looking quite old and distant, as if in a cloud of mist.

'Some sad news. The kitten has died. Last night. I buried her in the garden, at the back.' The sky seemed to darken.

'How? Why, did she die?' Jane asked, unable to disguise her immediate upset. 'What happened?' Although Jane knew.

'Too young. The vet said a kitten of that age cannot manage away from its mother. Though, I don't know about that... Her stomach swelled up, you see, became... balloon. Because the mother cat normally licks the baby's bottom to keep things... what do you say in English, "progressing"? Moving.'

'How long was it, then, has it been, that you...?'

'Two days, I think. Not sure. I did take her to the vet yesterday to pluck his brains, thought she wasn't crying for milk... ' Annette shrugged and turned away before Jane could force herself to say,

'You did your best, Annette. You did try.'

The French woman had gone. All Jane's reservations surfaced about the landlady's determination to take the kitten, her supreme confidence. What good were my earlier doubts, my analysis of Annette's motives, she now thought. A lump of discomfort rose in Jane's chest, at not having found a way of persuading Annette to see if the kitten could be left for its mother to reclaim it; giving nature more of a chance. That perfect healthy tiny creature, with its domed furry head and low-lying tiny ears, mackerel-patterning already laid down on its tabby fur, all as useless as a stuffed toy.

A small bird endlessly repeating its cry irritated Jane, as she scratched at an old mosquito bite on her neck.

'Ursula.' She whispered as softly as her fingertips had stroked the kitten's tiny head, 'Ur-su-la.' She hoped that Ursula's few days had not been too unbearable. At least she's not suffering now, she comforted herself; pleased she had not suggested that name for Alice's baby after all.

Jane tried to continue with her drawing, delineating some of the stones, thinking how the shadows and crevices defined the solid shapes. Worries about the new baby in England jostled with the sketch before her. Anything could go wrong; how vulnerable small creatures are. With a slight snort, she thought of her own cells going crazy, changing the pattern they are programmed to follow. Nothing in life is certain or reliable. Except for its cessation: the inevitable end of every creature, plant, and living cell. If that is so, she thought, it makes tiny Ursula's death more bearable. The kitten was like a small bud that had hardly opened before the frost killed her. As simple as that.

Jane drained her mug of the bitter dregs of coffee, down to the thick slurry. She needed the pick-me-up even though the metallic taste made her grimace.

But no, she protested. The kitten's death was because of Annette's intervention, her omnipotence. Even now, the French woman had disputed what the vet had said. If she had left the kitten on the wall, crying, surely, the mother cat would have picked her up by the scruff of her neck and continued to nurse her. Jane remembered how healthy the tiny creature seemed that day she had held her.

Some things we can affect, some we can't, she thought weakly, providing there are the right conditions. This was what she had tried to do with the children, but there came a point when it was up to them. Hopefully, though, the parents are still there, even after they die, like the pole star, to help the children navigate their lives, she thought falteringly.

Jane went inside for a glass of grape juice. In her 'bottle store' under the stairs stood the missing Chablis. She felt relieved that Pierre had not stolen it. How easily we blame others. We must be mistaken so often.

The wall in front of her ceased to be rich with texture and depth as it blurred into meaninglessness. She felt weary, despite having more sleep than she'd ever had in London. She looked above the wall, across the stubby field to the chapel, to the pair of white stone crosses that peered above the perimeter wall like two beckoning faces. She was drawn to the place in the way that one may sniff an old sprig of lavender hoping to extract the last of its perfume, before it crumbles into dust.

Aren't you sick to death of it? Why are you still drawn to it?

She bundled a small quiche into a plastic bag, and placed it in a shoulder bag with a bottle of water to take with her. It was 2.30. She tucked her drawing into a sketchbook, which she placed under the seat of her chair and wandered off for her last visit.

It was less hot as Jane sat once again on the low plinth of a grave to look up at the chapel and the tumble of brambles and ivy all around its base. Her fingertips stroked the delicate skin of her inner arm while the warm sun and soft breeze played upon her bare shoulders. She thought of Pierre and closed her eyes. The staccato cry of a bird rose above the background murmur of bees. There was an aeroplane high up, distant fat cumulus clouds. This cemetery wasn't about death, she realised, but about life, here in this spot that she had grown to love in so short a time.

And Pierre, where is he?

Her eyes focused on his mother's grave.

A background drone of bees seemed to become louder, insistent. The sound was not quite like bees though, more like big flies. It seemed to come from the one large stone shrine, as if an engine was revving inside it. Now she detected a putrid smell, like a blocked drain.

She darted a look around the little churchyard, and at the fields beyond. All as deserted and still as ever. Drawn towards the shrine, she removed some plastic orange roses that blocked the entrance – *I'll put them back, in a moment* – and peered into the stone house, above a small iron gate, expecting to see concrete slabs covering sarcophagi, like neat bunk beds. The fetid smell was stronger, much stronger.

Sweat broke out over her whole body as she struggled to see into the deep shade. A smell, a rotten stench was trapped in this vault, a smell worse than some of the odours on that ward where her father had lain dying. And through the smell, she discerned a shape on the floor that she could not see for her eyes had not adjusted to the gloom.

She had to escape into the bright light. Her shoulder ached. What should she do now? Call the police? But what if it's nothing. What if it's just… a dead sheep, or something. She told herself to have a proper look, first, before ringing the police. Memories of her own bravado in counterpoint to her sister's terror when they were children now spurred Jane towards bravery. Why do we have this great reverence, or fear, for graves anyway, she asked herself.

She looked around furtively at the landscape. How near this was to the Baudier grave. Why should there be some rotten carcass here, not even sealed inside a tomb? A frantic curiosity overtook her, a need to know at whatever cost, like the times she had watched horror films with her face half-averted, unable to stop.

Holding her breath she opened the iron gate of the small stone house and entered the tiny space.

The smell and a loud buzz everywhere, inside her head and outside. She breathed shallowly through her mouth. Her eyes began to adjust to the obscurity.

A tangle of hair at her feet, black curly hair that seemed to be moving and whining, so alive was it with insects. And then shoulders, in what looked like a kingfisher-blue dress. It became a woman, a young woman, a woman who seemed to have chosen this peaceful place, despite the flies, to have a long sleep. Just lying down on the stone floor. And, in the murky space beyond, an arm at an absurd angle. The skin purplish, like the blush on a plum. No face. That was downwards, mercifully. Jane sensed, from the alive drone of insects, that they were working on parts she could not see.

She pulled back. She began to retch, though her mood was detached.

She felt compelled to take one more look, caught between curiosity and revulsion. She peered again into the dark depths, at the crumpled dress – how it twisted around the body like a shroud. All this clinically observed, 'the arm', 'the skin', before the shock and the horror began to punch her. Her own skin began to crawl. She wiped her arms and neck and scratched her scalp, returning to the light.

Tu es folle, Jane, *complètement folle,* came the phrase from an alter-ego that had to proclaim and denounce her as a first step towards reality before she could think and feel in her mother tongue how shocked she was.

She turned away from the house of death feeling full of corruption. A pain like a metal band constricted her head, punctuated by an insistent pulse beat. The world twirled, the cypress trees tipped, the crows flapped and laughed in callous caws. She felt like crying but could not.

Crumpled over on the ground, clutching her bent knees, her head in a black and purple exploding world.

How long she stayed like that, frozen with horror, she did not know, before registering that she had discovered something that had to be uncovered, something that was not part of nature's plan. She looked up at the same blue sky, the same chapel, the same cypress trees.

A tractor clanking along the road dragged her back to the real world.

And a deep sorrow filled her, for the girl, for the kitten, for baby Timmy, for herself, for any life that is snuffed out, especially when it's tender. That is the outrage, the inexplicable unbearable thing.

'No, no, no, no,' she wailed now, remembering.

Still curled into a ball on her side she lay on the ground, seared by seismic sobs. She felt more nauseous, felt as if she was leaking fluid, like amber liquid from a rotting pear, from every orifice. She did not feel the tiny sharp stones sticking into the sides of her legs.

'I'm sorry, I'm sorry,' she cried. Sorry for all the times she had been cruel, had not given more love, to Timmy, to the other children, to Lennie. The only thing we have is love. We must stay with it, nurture it, it is the honey that makes all the bad bearable. And beauty, whatever is beautiful. 'Poor girl,' she moaned, with fresh incredulity. *Poor stranger, so close by, so unmourned, so alone.* 'Sorry, sorry to you,' she said softly, sorry for whatever had happened in the young woman's life. She could not wonder who this person was. Not yet.

'Oh God, get away from here!' she growled to a passing car, shielded by the surrounding wall. The thought of someone coming, finding her, interfering, forced her to get up.

The fact that her big toenail was cracked, that a small ant traversed her trousers unhampered, that a thread of dried grass was blowing across the gravel, that the noise of insects could be heard like a mower, was all registered sharply by Jane, all part of the fabric of the last half hour. She saw as if she were a film camera, without understanding.

'Rest in peace,' she muttered, shivering, now desperate to call the police and escape to the privacy of her bedroom, away from Annette and the whole cruel world. The thought of more hours here in France was torturous.

Of course, she would contact the police and tell them everything. All about the crashed car, Pierre, everything, despite the 'too-lateness' – a phrase that a couple she had worked with in therapy coined as a noun. The rank odour was still seeping out: putrescence was in her, filling her head, her very pores; no amount of soap or fresh crushed mint or lavender, all the smells she loved – orange blossom, oregano, basil, sweet peas, the deep smell of some roses – nothing would ever fully expunge that smell.

She replaced the plastic orange roses on the front step of the shrine, stepped back briefly, and bent to straighten them.

She felt dizzy on her short walk back to the house, unsure if she had her keys or if she had locked her door. Her head pounded. She vowed not to ring Lennie, she wouldn't even if she had a direct phone line. She was really alone now.

The darkness inside the cottage was so like that murky place to her unaccustomed eyes. She did not know if she wanted to be outside or inside, when she should ring the police, or what she should do. She seemed to be losing her practical nature, her resourceful self.

Drawing the curtains in case Annette was on the prowl, she knocked over a lamp, and lay on the sofa, pulling a blanket over her.

Try to recover, she told herself, her heart still pounding. She curled on her side and closed her eyes. At least *I'm* safe… safe enough, and… comfortable.

But the tumble of tangled black curls, the thrum of busy insects, the stench, swept over and into Jane.

'Disgusting!' burst from her in an angry explosion. It had to come to this before you see reality: the reality of death staring you in the face. *The car crash, Pierre's behaviour, all the police enquiries – all that was not enough to stop you in your basket-case tracks!*

Shakily, she rose from the sofa. She had to go to the police immediately. Anything else was self-indulgent and criminal.

She ran around to Annette's house and pounded on the door.

The French woman appeared with a basket of washing, 'Must make grass while the sun shines… hang this out. Might rain la—'

'Annette, can I use your phone for a quick call?' No apologies this time, no humbling offer of money.

'Sure. Nothing wrong, I hope?'

'No, well, yes. Sorry, can't talk now. Thanks.'

Jane walked across the room to the telephone clutching the number she needed, bumping into the sofa; Annette's expression a blur, an irrelevancy.

During the wait for Inspector Lagarde, she opened the curtains, picked up the overturned lamp, washed her face and hands, and looked in the mirror. She saw a worried old woman and shrugged, narrowing her eyes to focus on the important things she had to face.

Glancing around the room, she remembered her sketchbook under her chair outside and brought it in. When she thought of Pierre's drawing in the book, she wondered how much she would be under cross-examination now, how much she would feel even more like a transgressor.

She began to make a list, something to hang onto, of all the things she had to do once this interview was over.

1. *Tell Annette*
2. *Agen (baby – present?)*
3. *Haircut – Agen?*
4. *Lennie? Ring?*
5. *Ring Adrian (consultation)*

And she made herself a cup of tea with the last teabag brought from England, put away dry saucepans, wiped the draining board, and picked a fragment of onion skin off the floor.

Once again, the three of them sat in what had become their usual seats in the airy sitting room. The previous meeting felt so inconsequential, when Jane threw them some bait, only to withdraw. This time Jane was not full of her own thoughts about what they made of her, what she should and should not say, or what the consequences would be, for she had become the supplicant who knew she had to confess if she was to have any hope that she could rediscover some peace of mind.

'Yes, it is serious, very serious' – the French word *'grave'* felt chillingly fitting – Jane announced, avoiding eye contact with either man. She began to tell them as succinctly as possible about the sound she had noticed in the graveyard, and how she had been curious. 'Perhaps it was crazy,' she added. 'I should have called you at that point. And of course,' she hurried on, 'it was near the Baudier grave, of Pierre's – Charles' – mother, or so I assumed... And yet, yet, it was just as well,' she hurtled on, yet stalled, 'Yes, it was just as well that I am observant because it led to my finding what I found.' She gently supported her brow on the tips of her fingers, her head down.

'I'm sure you and your men want to get on with finding the body.' Jane looked up now at the Inspector for the first time during this meeting, 'And all that. I've lots more to tell you, though, about that young man, Pierre. He may not have anything directly to do with the death, but... but...' Her courage faltered, without knowing why, just when she was determined not to lie, except, except about the intimate things that had happened between them. She knew she felt shame, shame at what she had done with such a young man.

The Inspector's impatience broke through his effort to remain calm. 'You say "body". What do you mean? A body in the cemetery, you mean, a body that has been uncovered?'

With eyes closed, as if reciting prose she had memorised, she calmly said, 'No, yes, a young woman, newly dead, well, fairly recently I think, in that stone house. What's it called, a catacomb. No, a shrine. I mean, dead for sure, recently dead probably. Not uncovered; probably never buried, you see. But, maybe, suicide? Maybe not... murder?' Jane stopped in her tracks with a hand cupped over her mouth. Her startled eyes looked ahead.

Lagarde, looking more flushed than usual, asked Jane when exactly she was returning to England. Surely, this was a *non-sequitur*, but now nothing would surprise her.

She told him the time of her flight the next day.

He asked if he could see her passport.

She rattled off that he knew it had been stolen when her car was stolen: it had been in the boot with her purse and flight tickets, and other things, but she had been in touch with the Home Office in London and the consul in Paris, who had agreed to offer her a travel permit which she would pick up at Blagnac Airport. 'I'm sure you don't want to know all this now, with all that...' waving her hand in the direction of the chapel. She added that they would also fax her a document by this evening, via Madame du Plessis, the landlady here. She surprised herself at how lucid she was.

The Inspector looked troubled. He glanced at his colleague and said that he and Officer Bonnet would have a 'small conference' outside and would be back in a moment.

Through a sheer curtain, she noticed Lagarde with his back to her, talking on his telephone, then talking to Bonnet, and then returning to the phone.

The sensation reminded Jane of seeing penguins swimming underwater at Harewood House, near Leeds: unclear, murky, the creatures getting close and then disappearing. Jane had looked above the water surface to see if they had exited. The police, like the penguins, were alien and always would be, interesting but not really something she would wonder much about.

Then the two men re-entered the sitting room and sat down.

'Yes, there is a great deal to ask you, Doctor, but, yes, we have sent some men over to the cemetery. As you must realise, we are considering if we need to detain you for a longer time.' He looked at her in a different way, as if perplexed and disappointed in her.

'Here? Where?'

'In France.'

'Oh. Oh no...' she muttered.

Jane could not focus fully on what he was saying, nor explain how shocked she was by her discovery, how the horror had hardly registered, and yet it affected everything.

A cold sweat came over her. Tears filled her eyes. She said nothing. They both looked at her, and then Bonnet looked at the ground.

'Perhaps we should bring a policewoman next time?' Lagarde asked, surprisingly kindly.

Jane began to tremble, and then to shiver.

'You said you were ill, before.' He cleared his throat, 'Cancer, you said?'

She nodded, giving a flicker of a wry smile. All that had faded. She pulled the rug around her shoulders. *If they ask me what I'm thinking, which they won't, I'll tell them about the penguins.*

'I'm sorry, Officers. I will try and help as much as possible. I don't mind who questions me. But I must get back as planned. You see, I have to start treatment, chemotherapy, and perhaps radiotherapy. They say that any further delay could make a big difference. And I can help you from England, can't I? Surely, nowadays, with... Europe... it's all like one big country in many ways. What with International police, surely? I don't know what happens to the different legal systems, but—'

'Madame, I mean Doctor, we would like to speak to your doctor in London, your cancer doctor, if possible?'

"Curiouser and curiouser," said Jane dreamily in English. 'Sorry – that's a quotation. Just that it all, the world, seems very strange. I can't keep up with everything. Perhaps I should have a lawyer, just to help me, and help you, but I haven't the energy to find one.

'Yes, of course, you can ring the hospital,' she continued. 'It's St Catherine's, in South London. My doctor, the consultant, is Dr Greenberg, Gerald Greenberg. Actually, he is called 'Mr', but people often stay with 'Dr.'' As Lagarde was writing this down she slowed and spelt it. 'I know the main number off by heart – it's 0208 663 9627. Plus the code from France, of course. You can ask for him or his secretary. But perhaps I should first give permission for him to tell you whatever you want to know? Yes, I think I should ring him first, to pave the way.'

She realised she had stopped shivering and had begun to be able to think. 'You know, doctors' confidentiality and all that,' she added.

Jane noticed that Lagarde seemed confused, as if his world of imperatives did not mix with a world where confidentiality was the rule.

Again she sat still, unable to maintain her input.

Lagarde said that she should ring now, looking at his watch. He produced a mobile phone from a back pocket and asked her to dial the number.

'That's very handy,' Jane remarked. Bonnet looked up, clearly wondering if she was being sarcastic. 'How come you get a signal when I can't? I've just realised, though, Inspector – what if Dr Greenberg doesn't speak good French. How's your English? Oh well, that's up to you. I can do the first bit, about permission.'

Lagarde frowned.

'It will be a miracle if I get through to him. It's worse than trying to get hold of... of... Prince Charles.'

Officer Bonnet smiled weakly. She wished she had not come up with that name.

But Jane did get through, surprisingly, and did speak to her consultant. She told him rapidly that she had an awful, unbelievable brush with what may be a serious crime here in the Lot-et-Garonne, and for some reason, the Inspector on the case wanted to speak to him. She added that they were thinking of detaining her, to help with their enquiries. She said that she wanted him – Dr Greenberg – to know that she had no problem with him talking to the police about her medical situation. She thought the consultant sounded bemused, but felt he had always liked her, and now seemed to take the whole story in his stride. He responded that he would not ask her now about her health, but he thought she was coming to the clinic next week.

'Yes,' said Jane, sounding decisive. 'Next week. To start treatment.'

'Oh, you've decided to go for it, for us to give it our best shot?'

'Oh yes, Dr Greenberg. Yes.'

'Fine, fine.' Jane could picture his bronzed face, how he always looked as if he had just stepped off a golf course; saw him as a symbol of sanity and hope at that moment, a vital link with a world that was so different from where she was now.

When the doctor wished her a good end to her holiday, she almost laughed. They said goodbye.

As Jane clicked the button to disconnect she realised she had interrupted the link that Lagarde could have had with Greenberg.

'Oh sorry, Inspector. Do you want me to retry? He knows I'm fine about you talking with him.'

'Don't worry. I will need a translator. I'll do it from the station – make an appointment to speak with him.'

Jane wondered why there was to be this enquiry, but her curiosity was not strong enough to pierce the numbness spreading through her. She pulled the rug around herself again, and half nodded to Lagarde.

The men rose hurriedly, and said they had urgent business to attend to as she knew. Someone would speak to her early the next day, perhaps at the police station. She nodded without looking at them.

She did not get up when they left.

Jane drank grape juice and nibbled cold roast potatoes, knowing she should not drink wine or give into the overwhelming tiredness she felt. She wanted to ring Harriet in London, but did not have the energy.

She refocussed on Lennie, to wonder if she was throwing away years of something, some understanding between them. Now wasn't the time for new beginnings perhaps, she reasoned, when she felt frail and limp, and nauseous. It wasn't surprising. No, she told herself, I must get back to London soon, no matter what. 'Here' was horror, fear, even craziness.

It was only five o'clock. The only thing she could think of was driving to the phone box and finding an earlier flight from Toulouse. Even a few hours sooner would help. Without a credit card, it would be difficult. She would have to enlist Lennie's help.

She knew she should be telling Annette some of the main events, but did not have the strength now, and would have to avoid using her phone. Annette would find out sooner or later.

The short twisty journey was like driving a dodgem car without the fun. Jane held her breath, in danger of bumping into walls and trees.

A seat was available at eleven in the morning, only four hours earlier than the existing booking, for a further supplement. Yes, she would take it. Her husband would phone with the payment details, she said, writing down a reference number. The young man at the other end of the phone seemed so kind that she felt like crying for the first time since sobbing in the cemetery. He said he would hold the ticket for six hours.

'Lennie, is that you? Thank God. I feel quite ill. No, well, don't worry – not the cancer and all that. Just… so much has happened here. To do with a death in the neighbourhood. Yes, a suicide, well, I don't know, or maybe murder, of all things.'

Jane resisted saying that was all she needed, for that sounded callous, as if her cancer was always more serious than other dreadful things. 'Coming home a bit earlier, tomorrow, tomorrow afternoon. Flight at eleven in the morning.' Again tears rose to the surface. She knew that she would have to take a hold of herself or she would not be able to tell him anything. Feeling sick, she took a deep breath.

'Darling, I'll explain soon enough. But in the meantime, can you please ring the Air France desk at Toulouse airport – called Blagnac – and pay the supplement for my ticket? About forty quid.' She gave him the information he needed. 'I know I keep changing my return time. If there's any problem about securing the ticket ring me via Annette.'

'But Janey, I don't understand. What's "Blandnack"? I thought you said Toulouse? Toulouse airport, surely?'

She did not know if he was being obtuse in the way he often could be, digging in his oar so as not to facilitate something.

'Oh sorry, Lennie. Blagnac is the name of one of Toulouse's airports, you know, like Heathrow. B-L-A-G-N-A-C.'

'What? Yes, I know you're coming in to Heathrow.'

'Maybe it's a bad line, Lennie. But I can hear you perfectly. I know all this is hard for you too. But just say if you can't ring Air France.'

'Okay, sure, that's no problem. You just weren't being clear. You had said Toulouse. And of course, I'll meet you at Heathrow.'

'No, I really don't want you to. Thanks anyway.' She was not being heroic or stoical now, she just knew she needed time, as much time as possible, to see if her thoughts about claiming more separateness from Lennie still mattered, to take one tiny step towards her plan.

This same phone booth with its suffocating atmosphere sickened her. 'Sorry, can't hear you,' as a large lorry clanged past, sounding like loose sheets of metal. She cut across Lennie, who was asking if that death had anything to do with her car being stolen, for she did not have the strength to talk further. 'Blast. Noisy here. I know it's tough on you too. Can't easily ring you. But I'll see you tomorrow afternoon.'

Minutes later, sitting on the familiar wall, Jane did not know if she should ring the police and tell them she was leaving a little sooner than planned or let them find out. No, it would make matters worse if she left on a flight they had not known about – they may even stop her at the airport.

She forced herself to dial the police station and asked for Lagarde. As he was not available she left a clear message.

She telephoned the consulate in Paris again to check that a letter from them would be waiting at the Air France desk at the airport. At least that was in order.

As she parked on the grassy verge she looked across at the cemetery, despite her wish to avoid it. A plastic tent had been erected over the shrine and a small area around it. Two cars and a police car were parked outside the perimeter walls. She could hear the insistent drone of a motor, horribly reminiscent of the other hum that had alerted her. Two men walked away from the tent, talking, one carrying a hard black case. Then someone wearing a hooded white baggy suit like an astronaut's emerged from the enclosure. Bright orange tape had been tied to metal stakes, which the men moved as they exited.

A large cloud eclipsed the sun. Now Jane could see a generator outside and that the tent housed a bright light.

Her curiosity almost pulled her out of her numb state. But the re-emergence of the sun was too reminiscent of that sun shining down on the old stone structure, and the secret that the shadows had not been able to hide.

She saw Annette walk towards the cemetery, watching, holding her elbows behind her back. Annette turned to peruse Jane's cottage, frowning. Then the woman returned to her house, shaking her head.

Jane left her car, turned back to her cottage, where she curled up on her side again on the sofa, and this time did not stop herself from giving in to her exhaustion.

When she awoke, she longed for a delicious meal, something substantial and sustaining. She realised that this emptiness wasn't only about ordinary hunger. She knew that something healthier and resourceful was there inside her, deep down. All her discoveries during this sojourn could not have come to nothing. She just had to survive this appalling encounter with death before she could connect with her robust self.

She rose, closed the curtains, and threw off all her clothes. Stepping over the crumpled pile, she stood under a warm shower, allowing the water to pound her head, her face, her back and her breasts. She shampooed her hair, washed her body, and then stood under the flow for several minutes, gasping for breath as it flooded her face, washing away the cemetery and its contents. Soaping herself between her legs, she remembered Pierre with a surge of pleasure. And smiled that she was still alive, that not everything was dead or dying.

She turned the faucet to cool and then gradually to cold, until it was icy. After a few gasping seconds, she turned it off and stepped out, almost laughing with the tingle throughout her body, knowing that she could be ill and old and a bit mad, and shocked, yet vibrant.

As the day was still hot, she did not dry herself. Wearing a sarong around her waist, she left a trail of drips. Just as she was deciding whether to have a cold glass of white wine or a cup of green tea, there was a knock on her front door.

'Who's it?'

'Inspector Lagarde, Doctor.'

'Can you wait five minutes? I'm changing.'

Blast, the saga never ends, does it? Who'd have believed it? Crazy, crazy place, or is it me?

She pulled on a crumpled long skirt and a blouse, and half towel-dried her hair. When she glanced in the mirror, she thought she looked so healthy.

But she was trembling all over again. The difference was that she was no longer numb. Jane was as straightforward as she could possibly be now, and explained that she was returning a little earlier because she felt so shocked, so disturbed, on top of everything else she was going through.

'Doctor, you realise that, if not for your illness, we would be detaining you here. We want you to know that. We, well, I spoke with Doctor Grreen-berr' – his pronunciation glamorising the name – 'earlier, and yes, of course, we will let you start treatment. In the meantime, I need to ask you a few things.'

And so Jane told them, a little as if it was not her but someone in a play, about Pierre's sister again, and his row with her, his mother's money buying the car, his resentment, his wish to hide things from Jane.

She tried to focus and to be more specific. 'I think he said something about his sister being quite affluent, and that his mother must have left her quite a lot of money, or she had got it from other sources—'

Lagarde interrupted, 'Do you mean that that is your speculation? I mean, are you having difficulty remembering what he said, or did Charles Baudier, in fact, suggest that other sources, mysterious to him, may have "given" her money?'

'Oh, yes, I mean the latter. I think he speculated upon the latter. But Officers, the main thing I must tell you is about his car, the red car, the Renault, crashing over the precipice near here, and… and I went to rescue him.' Jane's eyes filled with tears. She cupped her cheeks and nose with her hands and looked at the wall ahead.

There was a silence.

'And then the car disappeared. A day or two later. Just wasn't there. So perhaps you know about it anyway.'

Everything Jane said now carried a staleness, a sense that she was a few days behind in all her statements, through her own stalling, her wish to divulge at her own pace, to retain control in this way. She felt the futility of it, how these policemen must see what a liar she was, through what she repeatedly left out. Her dislike of herself returned.

Jane noticed that Officer Bonnet was writing everything down. 'You two are very versatile, aren't you. I don't mean to be rude. Seriously – one day, the Inspector is the scribe, another it's you. Don't know why I'm saying all that now, though.'

'Saying what?'

'What do you think? About who does the writing here, of course.'

'Do you know anything about the Knights Templier, Doctor?'

'Why? No, not much. Only, that chapel, it's a Templier place, isn't it. Annette, Madame du Plessis, mentioned it. But why?'

Lagarde gave a slight sideways shrug of his head.

'Sorry, I forgot. You don't give much away, do you?'

'Did the young man, Charles Baudier, say more about his sister's associates or friends?'

'No, no, not that I remember.' Jane shook her head. 'But when did you know about the crashed car and all that? Did you find out, I mean the police, or someone else? You can tell me that, can't you?'

The Inspector remained silent, and gave a little Gallic shrug and a crooked small smile.

'Oh dear. And I'm supposed to go back to England carrying all that mystery with me. I know I haven't been very helpful up to now, but I could explain my reasons. And surely, now that I am helpful, you can just tell me how you knew about the darn car?'

'Sorry, Madame, I mean, Doctor.'

He always makes that mistake, she registered. She wished he'd just stick with 'Madame' and be done with it. Jane shook her head, knowing tears could easily resurface if she stayed with this isolated feeling.

'Okay, then, gentlemen, another question. Not that you'll answer me. The woman, the young woman...' Her voice faltered. 'In the shrine. Is she Pierre's sister? Is she? Please, please tell me if that is what you suspect? I have to know, I can't stop thinking about it.' She made no attempt to hide her tears.

Yet again coming up against their inscrutability, her frustration surged onto the next anxiety, 'And have you found Pierre, Charles? Has he been caught yet?'

'You will no doubt be able to read about our findings in the newspaper in due course. With respect, Doctor, at this stage we cannot say much.'

'Hmnn, I suppose that was meant to be helpful,' she said more to herself, in English. She wrapped both arms around her shoulders and looked through narrowed eyes into the distance beyond the garden, while the unanswered questions eddied like a whirlpool in her chest.

AUGUST 27TH, 2003

The heat oppressed Jane as she boarded the plane the next day. Not buying a present for the baby, not really explaining much to Annette, were minor loose threads compared with the major questions. Her relief at being allowed through passport control, and to be on her way home, surmounted all the other anxieties for the moment. Jane felt as if she was stepping across an abyss into which she might fall, from one world to another, as she carefully climbed the gangway to the plane. But, she thought, perhaps the two worlds were not so different after all, for they are both full of irreconcilable elements.

She ordered a gin and tonic, followed by a second when the first hardly touched her. The magnificence of Rossini's *Stabat Mater* on her CD player worked its magic: the heavens rolled into view and her blood thrilled with the glory of life. She remembered Pierre saying that he did not like choral work, certainly not anything that was devotional, when she had played part of the Matthew Passion during his brief stay. And he had said he did not like poetry. How could she have found such an intimate connection, in so many ways, with someone who spoke another language?

Now, she thought of moments with Pierre, instances of his being there with her, not making demands, but simply responding to her with what seemed like a kind of love. An alive longing readily suffused her lower body. Yes, the body does not forget. She smiled.

Jane and Lennie stood in the kitchen, its deep terracotta walls and ceiling blushing in evening sunshine.

The dusty-pink cupboards seemed to welcome her back. Lennie had clearly made an effort to tidy up: the ceramic sink was pristine white, the slate floor impeccable, even the Tuscan bowl was full of peaches and nectarines. But how unappealing the fruit looked, after her sun-ripened feasts in France. She felt churlish and ungrateful. The geraniums all had their wan cream faces pressed against the window pane, as if they longed to be outside. She deadheaded the plants and carefully turned each one round while he was out of the room, fetching her a pile of mail. She knew he would see her action as a reproach.

'Would you like a cup of tea? Or a glass of wine?' he asked, his efforts at cheerfulness betrayed by something pensive in his manner. She knew that he was puzzled, rebuffed, by her arriving home without his assistance.

Jane had forgotten how handsome he could look. No wonder other women seemed to find him attractive.

'No thanks, love. I feel pretty tired. Good to be home.' She breathed out expansively through her mouth, puffing out her cheeks. 'Yes, I'll have a cup of herbal. Any kind. Perhaps I ought to have a little rest. And then we should talk.'

'Yes, lots to catch up on, I'm sure.'

'Any latest news of the baby? I rang Alice – she probably told you. Any recent news? All well?'

He shook his head from side to side in a way that Jane knew all too well while saying, 'Fine, all fine. Spoke to Jack today. Baby beginning to gain weight. She lost weight at the beginning, but Jack said that was normal.'

Jane smiled to herself. *Didn't he know that by now? Three children, four really, of course, and now three grandchildren.* She sighed, this time through her nose.

'I'll give Alice a ring later, to tell her I'm back and catch up. And the others? How are Max and Eddie?'

'Fine. Saw Max a few nights ago. When was it? Took him out for a meal. Went to that Turkish place near the station. He's having problems with Natasha – nothing new. About

money, really, it seems. Don't want to go into all that now.
You seem so tired.'

Jane was surprised he had noticed; that he seemed for
once to stop in his tracks. She wondered if he simply saw it
as an obstacle to his usual pattern of pouring out all his stuff.
He seemed to say it resentfully.

'And you? How're you, how've you been?' she asked,
because that was always the easy path that patched over
her needs, and she did want to know about him – up to a
point.

His gesture of raking back his thick hair with his fingers
reminded her, with a shock, of Pierre. That connection, and
the guilt, made her determined to be kinder to Lennie.

And then he smiled and said that it had been strange
without her, he'd missed her. He had watched quite a lot of
telly, the news every evening, things he didn't normally do,
watched some late films on TV and then thought what a waste
of time. Jane thought that sounded more like her than him;
he never normally had a concept of wasting time. And she
wondered what late night films he had watched – probably
things she wouldn't feel comfortable about.

'Finished a big book review,' he added. And then he
looked at her.

She was aware of the gulf between them.

'But you – how're you feeling? Your health…?' he asked
with tentative concern.

'Not too bad. Really. As far as I can tell. Perhaps I will
talk now. Don't think I can rest after all.'

She noticed that he had boiled the kettle, but not made
her tea. She went to the cupboard and chose Bengal Spice,
reboiling the kettle. Lennie protested that he was going to
make it. Ignoring him, she carried on with the simple task
of filling her cup and suggested that they go into the sitting
room.

A sharp headache suffused the left side of her head.
She sat with her feet up on the aubergine velvet sofa with
cushions behind her back. She noticed that the plants needed
watering, but knew she shouldn't complain. She felt pleased

to see the Wagner CDs out of their cases, strewn on the music centre, pleased that he had that.

He had poured himself a whisky. With both hands he nursed the cut-glass tumbler. Well, it is 6.30pm, Jane thought. She asked if he had had supper yet. He said no, they could get a takeaway. She said she wasn't hungry, she had snacks on the journey. Air France had given her a meal, hours ago it seemed, but... She grimaced.

'Darling, I know there's lots to catch up on, but we can, we will, do that, over time.' She was aware that she sounded so formal. Now he had that furrowed-brow look that she disliked, a look he even had while opening an envelope whose contents were not clear.

'Lennie, I want to tell you... that I've been through one hell of a lot while I've been away, and some of it was bad, dreadful, but some of it was good, really... dare I say, an epiphany.'

'You'll have to tell me what that word means. It's one of those words I can never remember.'

Jane stiffened her lips into a straight line, and said, 'A turning point, a life-changing moment.' She suspected that he chose not to know certain words as a protest against what he thought was jargon, despite being an academic himself. In Lennie, it seemed inverted snobbery.

She looked straight ahead. *Hah, deflecting. Distracting me.*

She did not know if she could continue to take her courage in both hands without becoming as steely as Lady Macbeth, but sensed that if she softened she would break down, cry and dissolve. Then Lennie would get right back there at her side, or insidiously inside her. *Is this madness?* flashed through her mind like fork lightening in a black sky, disturbing her further.

'Shall I come and sit by you?' he asked.

'No. Please.' She closed her eyes, holding the cup of tea. 'Lennie, I've been through a lot of soul-searching, and... and, I've decided, more or less, to... to move out.'

She could not bear to look at him. She imagined him turning nasty, as she knew he could be, and showing his sarcastic side. She decided to plough on, 'Yes, you see, it's about this stage of my life. It's now or never, really, to find out who I really am.'

He could not resist a guffaw.

She resolved to stay calm and resolute.

'I knew you'd do that, I mean, mock me. That's up to you, of course,' she added coldly. *Let him dig his own grave.* She sipped her tea, taking in its warmth and richness. 'You haven't even let me explain.'

'Haven't said anything. I'm waiting. What do you think I'm doing?'

'Okay... I suppose... even if you did sneer just now, I'll carry on.' She began to feel sorry for herself, at how difficult this was.

'Look, even if I'm making the wrong decision, I've decided to separate. From you.' The last two words were said clearly but quietly. She swallowed hard. 'To see what it feels like. To... to give myself a different future, possibly. To not be looking back all the time, hemmed in... to have, to have a sense of space ahead of me. Even if .... Oh, I don't expect you to know what I'm on about.' She almost stopped, to allow him to react, but decided to continue, to do her best to explain – she owed that to him – even though her newfound search was tenuous.

She decided to take up a different angle. 'I know there's a lot that's good, really good, in our relationship, that it's... woven together... over so many years, a vast edifice: decades, children, grandchildren, friends, property, lots of good times – I really mean that – but somehow, somehow, now that I am dying – I can't help but add "probably" – I want, I need, to be alone.' She felt like crying but forced herself to continue, 'To find out who and what I am. Before it's too late.'

She risked a glance at him. He was sitting with his forehead in his hand, eyes closed. She did not want to start feeling sorry for him.

'Lennie, if this is what I need, it's also at some level what you need. I know that may sound crazy – there's a lot you probably think is crazy.' She ignored another little laugh that was more of an exhalation of breath from him. 'But what I mean is, if I'm not truly happy, happy in certain ways, about our relationship, then it can't be good for you either. If I leave, you may find all sorts of joy without me, in yourself, in other relationships.'

'Don't give me that crap, that shit!' he interrupted.

Here it comes, she thought, the anger, the black-and-white response. She knew that that was one of the reasons she was leaving him. But no, she told herself, it's bound to be hard, preposterously hard.

Quietly, she said, 'I'm sorry. Sorry. But I can't go too far down that path of being sorry, or all my hard work may be lost.'

'Perhaps that just shows how it's built on sand!' he exclaimed.

No, I'm not going to enter into all that with him, I don't have to, she thought. I owe him an explanation, up to a point, and if he can't bear it, so be it. She remained silent. And so did he. It felt like ages before he said, 'Aren't you going to say anything?'

'Sure. Okay. Or you could. Alright, I'll try and go on. I know this seems inexplicable to you, and may do to the children—'

'The children!' he interrupted. 'Have you thought what this will do to them? As if they don't have enough on their plates.'

'Look, Lennie,' she cut in. 'I'm agonised, of course, I am. I have struggled with this from every angle, for ages, if you really want to know. Now, I'm going to give it a go. It may be crazy. I may regret it. I may well fail, fail in my search to *be*. I know that sounds very New-Agey. But at least I'll know, at least I'll have tried.'

She felt her lips quivering, knew tears were not far away. 'I don't expect you to understand,' she said weakly. 'If you did, did understand, I'd probably not be leaving… ' Her words petered out, while she struggled to stay with some of her recent discoveries.

'Is there someone else?' Lennie asked aggressively. 'There has to be.'

Jane knew this was coming. 'No, there isn't,' she lied, or half-lied, because it's not about Pierre, she thought, not now. She went on, 'It's not like that. It's about wanting to be alone more, to find out my own lows and highs, my own needs, even my own thoughts. I have hardly had that, you know.'

'Huh! Rubbish! You've gone away whenever you wanted, on your own.'

'To conferences, yes. Residential courses, and once with Ruth to Paris, for two nights.'

'And all those years of analysis. What was that about? Wasn't that you finding out what you needed?' His scathing tone appalled her. 'Surely?' he continued, bullying. 'Why now? Why all this, now?'

Both were silent. The telephone rang. They ignored it, heard Max on the answerphone.

'Lennie, you see, so much happened in France. Some of which you'll have to know.' She looked at him, his head again in his hands, away from her. 'Do you want me to explain?'

She took his silence as permission to continue. 'I helped a young man – you know, I told you a little on the phone – who had been injured when his car crashed, and then it seemed he was up to something dodgy, I don't know what, and… This is hard to explain.'

He looked at her accusingly. She realised he thought she was going to confess to an affair, after all, so she quickly told him about her discovery of a body, a corpse, which she said she had also referred to on the phone to him, and how the young man may be implicated. 'I know this sounds terrible, unbelievable,' she went on. 'He may be guilty… or involved somehow.' Her heart was speeding. She glanced at him again, to gauge his reaction. She knew she had spent most of the marriage sensing his mood, tempering what and how she spoke, often not saying what she really felt about so many things. How that left a tangible gap between them. She thought she had better try to speak her mind now, up to a point.

'Well, the police were involved, are involved, of course. They interviewed me countless times. They only let me leave the country because of my illness and the need to return for treatment. I'm sure that's not the end of it: they'll be contacting me here in London.'

'But you haven't done anything wrong, illegal, surely?'

'Well, no. Unless housing him – the young man – for two days and not reporting him, is illegal, even when I was quite suspicious... And rescuing him from his crash in the first place, down a precipice, and – because he insisted – not involving anyone else. It's complicated. His plight reminded me of mine, somehow.' As she talked Jane knew that she could not share the extreme effort involved, because his disapproval would be even more extreme.

'Look, Lennie, I know I've got a lot to sort out about my side of things, as to why I acted like that. Don't think I haven't already been trying to analyse, endlessly... and I'll ask Adrian – Dr Thomas – for a consultation as soon as he can see me, you know, to help me understand.'

'Hmnn,' Lennie snorted. 'You clearly don't feel that I have any use whatsoever, that you and I can't talk about what could be a *murder* you've been involved with. You seem to think I know nothing about crime. And obviously, I'm no use to you in all the other things you're saying.'

The heavy silence that followed was broken by Lennie. 'It doesn't add up. I don't believe that you didn't have an affair with this, this...,' breaking off as he tried to compose himself. 'A complete stranger. And it wouldn't be the first time either.'

'Len, I'm not going to put up with your attacks. You can think what you like.' *Of course, he's right. The affair I divulged all those years ago, but I'm not going to start a tit-for-tat game with him.* 'Surely, we're not entering a tally? I don't think that's helpful: you conveying that I've been promiscuous!' Jane spoke calmly but her teeth were clenched. Her exhaustion returned. 'Perhaps that's all we can talk about now. Perhaps I'd better go and sort myself out. I'll have to have a rest, and then look at my post and messages.'

For a moment, she felt like saying how sorry she was, felt like putting an arm around him, telling him about the love she still had for him, but knew that she would topple back into comfort and lose the point – the point that she found and lost time and time again, the point about her place in the world. All she added was, 'Lennie, if you're still around, I may find myself coming back to you – only, only, maybe, in a different way. Who knows. I know you may be so furious, or so hurt, that you may not want that – but… and I don't have, may not have, much time, so all this might be concertinaed into a shortish time. Who knows.'

'I'd have thought this is precisely the time you need me, need things to be in place when you're up against your illness.' His voice was strained. 'I don't understand, Janey, I really don't. Sorry, but I think you are, um… out of balance.'

She laughed. Now it was her turn to chortle, 'At least you didn't throw your usual barb, plain and simple, "mad!" Fair enough. I can understand you thinking that. Yep. It's my job to try and find out if I am mad, or sane. The mad do not usually know they are mad, though, do they? Catch 22. It's interesting how often reactions to life-changing epiphanies – plural of *e-piph-an-ee* – can be seen as mad.'

In a further silence, she knew she had to try to appear definite, to hide her own uncertainties.

They both knew that she had addressed some of her frustrations in the marriage countless times in their first years together, and Lennie had always found her so unreasonable, said she was 'never satisfied', and had responded with despair or anger. Sometimes they were both on their best behaviour for a while after those scenes, but then the old pattern returned, of Jane patching over the tears and holes with remnants.

Some of her remnants were bright and richly patterned, some borrowed, some of the type that Lennie liked – silky and soft, some of a worn velvet with an aged patina she felt comfortable with, so that she eventually did not know whether the original fabric beneath would be better. Indeed, she could hardly remember it.

But it was when Pierre tore off the layers inadvertently, almost violently, and found something alive and true and delicate beneath, found the original fabric which had become almost unrecognisable to Jane herself, that she knew she was living a lie.

It was probably a question of degree. Perhaps everyone hid their inner soul, and it was only discernible through dreams, or works of art, or in private moments, or in psychoanalysis, or in rare intimate relationships. Not that her more authentic self had now been fully uncovered. But she no longer had to dance to please others. She would find her own music.

Jane surveyed some of this patchwork pattern as she sat with her eyes closed. Lennie did not know if she was asleep. He quietly left the room. She breathed a sigh of relief.

She asked herself again and again if she was deluded – could a young man, possibly a criminal, have been so important to her? All she could extract from this conundrum was that he was a catalyst, that if it had not been him it may have been someone else. She thought, not for the first time, how her body was corrupted by the cancer, and perhaps she had turned to him for repair.

She realised she had not told Lennie that she had decided to go to the hospital for a round of something, some cocktail – if they would give it to her – to ease her symptoms, possibly, but not for full-scale treatment. But what was the arrangement between them now? Did Lennie want to know? When and how would she move out? She had already considered moving out to the tiny flat that she used as her consulting room, even though she would have to live and work in the one room.

Lennie poured another whisky before padding barefoot to his study to check his emails. He thought of watching a programme about unsolved murders, but decided against it, even though it was something he usually enjoyed. He could not be bothered to tape it.

He stood in his study and looked out through the sash windows at the garden. The huge copper beech was now cast in an ethereal light by the last rays of the sun. No, Janey was not to be given the satisfaction that he was fine, when he was not.

He felt a ruffle of discomfort at what she seemed to have been through, and at how little she had told him. A corpse, possibly murder, he reiterated with incredulity. All that had been lost amidst the immediate shock of her resolution.

He did not know what to feel; whether this was a temporary blip or whether, yet again, she was saying that all was not right, as in the early years of the marriage and she would come to her senses. How was he ever to know what was real? Were all those years of apparent satisfaction a sham? A shadowy memory came to mind of Janey crying with such anguish when she watched certain films, often about lovers, or films that she said showed real kindness. And how she wept over some operas, and how he could never understand that degree of upset. He saw it as some terrible wound from her childhood that had opened up, which he could not do much about. If they discussed a film they had seen together they were usually on such different wavelengths that he had to state his views, his morality, loud and clear, for she would try and swamp him with a blurry view of relationships where anything was permissible.

No, that did not seem to be the problem. Now he did not know in the end who had a hazy view of what was right and what was wrong, he or Janey. Whatever it was, they usually ended up poles apart.

He logged onto his emails. There were five new ones. The only one of interest was from a colleague, Valerie, who was chattily, possibly flirtatiously, agreeing to an invitation to lunch together some time, to discuss a joint writing project that he had in mind.

> Your email made my day. Been snowed under (if one can use that expression in a heatwave) with proofreading and demanding relatives, and then came your breath-of-fresh-air invitation. Yes – I'd love to discuss your ideas over lunch. How about next Tuesday 2nd Sept.? Or otherwise Thursday? Suggest a place and a time. Looking forward to it.
>
> Love, Val

He printed it out, looked at the fuchsia coloured font she had bothered to specify. And hesitated about his tone in the various replies that came to his mind. He found some assurance when, eventually, he wrote:

> Great! Shall we say this Tuesday? I know a gastropub that serves good food in Islington – quite near you. How about the restaurant of The Buccaneer, in Essex Road, at 12.30 pm? It's on the right if you're facing north, by the traffic lights at a small intersection.
>
> I'll make sure I'm early so you don't have to wait in a pub on your own. Just confirm.
>
> Looking forward to seeing you. (Things not been easy my end either, on the whole.)

He returned to her email to see how she had signed off and added:

> Love, Lennie

He felt pleased at his thoughtfulness over being early. With another gulp of whisky, he marvelled at his powers of recovery.

He wondered if he should call her Val. How different the two names sounded. He was not sure which he preferred. Lennie realised that he hardly knew her, had always liked her at departmental meetings and the occasional college social gathering. He knew she was divorced.

He tried to remember her breasts. She was certainly quite a shapely woman, that he could remember, but to his surprise, he had not made a mental note of her breasts. He remembered that she wore rather loose clothes. He could see her reddish hair in a straggly bun, and then she seemed to have had it cut into a stylish bob. He wasn't very observant about most things. Except breasts. Usually he would look to see if a woman's nipples showed, gauging by her colouring if they would be pink or brownish, what type of bra she seemed to be wearing, whether her breasts seemed to be heavy or light, rounded or pointed, wide or narrow, whether they looked like breasts that had never suckled a baby, whether she had a cleavage and whether it was plump or slight, and whether the skin had begun to wrinkle if she was over about fifty-five. He never forgot his brief contact with his ex-student Mai-Mai: how her nipples were small and dark, like chocolate buttons. He could easily imagine a woman in his presence without her top garments, but this would lead to being aroused and he would have to stop, depending on the situation. And all without the woman knowing what his eyes and his mind and body were doing. He was skilled at shifting his glance to her face, or hands, or her eyes. But with Val, he had failed to compile a dossier. All the more reason to see her.

He began to feel hungry. He looked at his watch: 9.25pm already. He decided to order a takeaway from a new expensive Thai home-delivery place that had put a glossy menu through the door. Judging by their prices, they had pretensions of being upmarket, but perhaps that was where the similarity ended. He suddenly wished that Janey would join him, that all that had happened since her return was a bad dream.

He quietly entered the dark bedroom, thinking she must be asleep. The curtains were not drawn. He peered at the bed, but could not make out her shape on it or in it. He felt a pang of what was in store: an empty lonely house, with no prospect of her return. It was different when she was in France, he could easily manage, knowing she'd soon be back.

He went up to the spare room on the top floor. The door was closed. He did not know what to do. She was sure to be in there. He tried to peep through the keyhole, but all he saw was darkness. He decided to heed what she had said so forcefully before and to leave her alone.

In a surge of anger, he decided not to include her in what he ordered, to take her at her word, that she was not hungry. *If she does reappear and is hungry, what then? Do I have to give her half of mine?* He decided to order one extra dish, in case, which he could always manage.

While watching an old French movie on television, his takeaway on a tray on his lap and a glass of Chablis by his side, Jane walked in with a 'Hi,' as if nothing untoward was happening, and went to the kitchen.

'Hiya,' he replied guardedly. He heard the kettle being refilled, and a cupboard opening and closing.

He felt annoyed that his peaceful supper was being disturbed. He was feeling too churlish, too unsure to tell her how good the food was.

When Lennie went up to their bedroom later, Jane had taken her bedside clock and her dressing gown, and he knew she had decided to sleep in the spare room. That it should come to this! Her suitcase appeared not to have been unpacked.

He thought of checking his emails, in case Valerie – or Val – had replied, but he knew that connecting to the internet often led to his well-known sites, and to the inevitable outcome. What if Janey came downstairs and found him? What if she wanted to sleep with him after all? Why did life have to be so complicated?

AUGUST 29TH, 2003

Jane awoke in the little spare room at six in the morning, alert and anxious. She felt as if she had hardly slept. Whichever way she turned, she saw huge obstacles.

'Hi, how did you sleep?' she said to Lennie because it was easier to say what was expected than not.

He looked distant. 'Not very well. How about you?'

'So-so. Running a bath.' She avoided looking at him. 'Going over to see the new baby. If the French police ring while I'm away, give them Alice's number if they say it's urgent. And I'll spend the night there, with Alice and Co. I'm going straight to the hospital from there, tomorrow.'

'But Janey, this is ridiculous. You can't carry on like this, as if everything's normal. First of all, I can't speak French to those police. Secondly, we must talk. Surely. You know that, don't you? Come on, you must know that, you of all people.'

She remained silent, sipping her tea, looking at the floor. She hated the way he took on moral superiority, patronised her about her own good sense, talked to her as if she had lost the plot, as if he could coax her back to normality, his normality.

'Aren't you going to say anything?' He sounded patient, but she waited for his mood to flip into his particular brand of seething rage.

'I must ask you, Len, what time is my rearranged hospital appointment tomorrow?'

'Thought I told you. Three o'clock. Why do you call me 'Len'?'

AUGUST 29TH, 2003

How easily they could slip back to normal exchanges. But she knew she did not want that.

'It's your name, isn't it. Thank you,' she said formally, 'for rearranging the appointment. I must turn off the bath water.' She left the room. Lennie followed her into the bathroom.

'Lennie, I'm sorry,' she said, with her back to him. 'But what I said yesterday still holds, you know. Of course it does. About needing space. Alright, I will talk after my bath. But let's limit it to an hour. You know how we can go on and on, and not get anywhere, and how exhausting that is. Please.'

Lennie stared at his face in the mirror, his frown deepening, disappearing behind steam, and left the room abruptly. Jane closed and locked the door.

She wiped the area of mirror he had looked into, peered hard at herself and then turned away, not wanting to engage with the anxious image, trying not to allow the physical well-being she had gained in France to fade away.

Adding a few drops of her favourite geranium bath essence with its emerald smell to the water, she edged her way slowly into the too hot water, gasping. Submerging her body and then her head, she felt the water caressing her ears, and stayed still with only her face above the surface.

Jane looked down at her body, at the marks where her swimming costume had been. Her stomach was almost flat, her breasts plump and attractive. The raised edge of the scar had been eroded and polished by time. She pointed a toe up in the air and admired the firmness of her thighs.

What would have happened between her and Lennie upon her return if she had not met Pierre, had not taken a major step away from her marriage? If she had fallen into the old pattern, everything would not only be a great deal easier for Lennie, for the children, and for most of their friends, but for her too in many ways.

Can having cancer make you lose your mind?

She pushed away a wayward thought about brain metastases. Berating herself for not having telephoned Adrian yet, she closed her eyes and thought that he would only help her to find out what she did not fully allow herself to know. Taking a deep breath, she tried to short-circuit the process.

She felt a flutter of life in the depths of her body, low down, and tried to imagine keeping her sexuality alive but still remaining with Lennie. The only way that could happen was for her to allow a secret fantasy life, but to go through the motions of a relationship with Lennie, including a sexual relationship. Would that be sad, she wondered? Although reluctant to think psychologically about the cancer, knowing what a fraught path that was – especially if it led to self-blame for the disease – the thought crept in now: would the illness be more, or less, likely to invade further if she stayed with Lennie? She knew about some 'fighting spirit' research into lung cancer patients which showed that a patient's attitude of mind did not affect the outcome. But, if it did play a part – in case it did – she must do whatever she could to feel good, in body and soul.

She felt a fresh pang of guilt at what leaving Lennie would do to him.

Jane washed her hair and left the bath reluctantly. Looking at her watch, she decided to ring Alice first to finalise her travel plans. The prospect of seeing the baby and the other little ones, as well as her daughter, buoyed her up. But what if Lennie wanted to come with her? She couldn't stop him.

While she dressed, he knocked on the door, as if it were her own private bedroom, calling impatiently,

'Jane! Janey! Telephone – it's a call from France. Someone calling you Dr Samuelle.'

Jane's relief that it could not be Pierre quickly switched to anxiety that it was the police again.

She took her time going downstairs. She did not want to speak to them in the bedroom. And she wished to gather her thoughts.

There, at the end of the phone, was Inspector Lagarde. He enquired quite formally about her health, to which she replied, 'As well as can be expected, Inspector.' He felt almost like an old friend now, despite his stiffness.

She found herself transported back to that azure-skied fertile place, where ripe figs and plums weighed heavy on branches and scattered their overabundance on the ground, where there was enough goodness for all creatures.

Lagarde was saying something about 'further enquiries', and asked if she had been reading the newspapers. She felt the stench from the shrine creeping into her nostrils.

'No, I haven't seen the papers. Why?'

Again, he was not forthcoming with news. When would she learn to stop asking him questions?

'You may wish to find out by visiting the website of *France-Soir*.' Jane thought that was a remarkably modern idea coming from someone so provincial. But perhaps she was wrong in her assumption of his simplicity. Now she worried what his game was, why he wanted her to find out more.

'Look, Inspector,' she replied, fuelled by her surfacing anger that he should reach her here, should uncover the horrors of that graveyard, which she was trying to forget, 'I really am preoccupied here with major, yes, really major events in my life. I don't have the time or inclination to go 'surfing' – do you say that in French? – surfing the web. Really. But why did you telephone?' She wondered if Lennie was listening from the next room. She felt sure that he was.

'I need to tell you, Doctor, that this call may be recorded for monitoring.'

She remained silent.

After a pause, he said that the 'youth' had been picked up and was helping the police in their enquiries.

Jane said 'Yes,' in as non-committal way as possible. She added, 'You mean, Pierre, or Charles. Baudier.'

'Yes.'

'Well?'

Now she valued the distance between them, not having to worry about being observed, especially by that Bonnet man. She broke the silence with, 'I hope he is being helpful. About the girl, the young woman. You see, I don't know if that is, was, his sister – it probably was – but I'm sure you know.'

She realised with a stab of conscience that she felt nothing for Pierre at this moment, that if he was being implicated in the death, she no longer cared, other than a vague thought that if he really did such a thing then, of course, he should be brought to justice.

'Well, Doctor, we have to ask you if there was more to your contact with Monsieur Baudier than you have already divulged.'

'Why?' she asked as straightforwardly as she could, now angry with the way Lennie frequently listened to her phone conversations. His schoolboy French would not stop him from eavesdropping. 'What has it, that, to do with why?' Her sentence emerged clumsily, her knowledge of the language floundering.

'Pardon?'

'Oh dear. But why do you want to know? What possible reasons can you have for asking?'

Now Lagarde sounded patronising for the first time, 'Come on, Doctor. Everyone knows about the need for an enquiry to discover motives.'

Jane walked with the portable handset out into the garden, hoping for privacy. She talked softly, 'Yes, as you probably know by now from the young man, some intimacies did take place between us. On precisely two occasions. That's the way it is. Was.' The formality of her response was a direct reaction to the implied promiscuity. Now, she could legitimately wait for his response.

'Please will you hold the line a minute, Doctor. Won't keep you long.' She almost laughed at the men at the other end scurrying around, trying to decide which line of enquiry to pursue next. While she waited, she began to think that this was a secret she would not be taking to her grave after all. But perhaps if Lennie were to find out it would not matter that much, after the ground she had covered last night. All she would have to face would be greater contempt from him, and why should that matter? It may even make it easier to leave him.

Through blurred vision, she deadheaded petunias while she waited, irritated with Lennie for never noticing, let alone doing, little jobs like this. She half closed the eye that clouded her vision, wondering if it would be easier to wear a patch.

'Inspector?' she said into the silence of the phone. And waited.

When he came on the line again, he asked if Monsieur Baudier had talked with her about any contact he had with Giselle's acquaintances in Lyon?

Jane said that she did not think so, the young man had said he was from the Occitaine, or Occ, and she was not sure what that meant, other than some links with southern France or Spain. 'But I really don't know, Inspector, if he had a strong connection with anything. He struck me as a… a… I can't think of the French word for "will-o'-the-wisp" – a sort of vagrant, nomad, in a way. He was not really connected with his sister, it seemed – other than in anger and resentment. Yet he revered his mother, so it must have pained him – her seeming to favour the sister. He had hardly known his father, who left when he was young, I think. His mother sounded like a good woman, somehow, I think.'

Jane pulled off a few columbine seed heads to make way for the fiery montbretia while she talked, rarely doing one job at a time. The greyness of the day with its hint of autumn in the air, despite the orange and yellow flowers, led her to miss the saturated colours of the garden of *La Retraite*.

This conversation felt surprisingly easy. She found herself enjoying recalling aspects of Pierre, and wondered why she had been so reticent in France during all those interviews. She knew the answer as she formulated the question.

'Thank you, Doctor. Did you gain any idea that he could feel that…' He paused for what felt like a long time, and then Jane heard Lagarde's voice continuing as if there had been no interruption to the flow, '…*that* vengeful, or be part of a wider movement or conspiracy?'

'No, really. As I said before, he was merely vengeful towards his sister. But isn't it strange to be having this interview on the telephone? If an unexplained death is involved, shouldn't you be sending someone over to interview me, or engage a British detective?'

She might have known he would not reply. It was as if he only had a preordained number of sentences at his disposal, and had to use them judiciously. She had heard the idea that everyone has a certain number of heartbeats granted them at birth; would her quota soon be used up? Now she was keen to end this conversation.

'You still have my number, Doctor?' Lagarde asked. 'Please telephone me if you have further thoughts. Goodbye, and good luck with your treatment.'

Oh yes, all that too, she thought. She was frequently amazed that she could forget about her illness. She thanked him almost as if he were an old friend.

As she walked back towards the house, she knew it had been different before, talking to them. Now she no longer had to guard some precious secret.

Jane found Lennie in his study at his computer, checking emails, when she dutifully approached him for their appointed further talk.

She sat on the window seat, looking sideways at the magisterial copper beech. He often wanted to have it pruned, while she wanted it to take its course, even if it overshadowed half the garden and its roots pushed up the paving stones of a path.

She sensed that he was irritated that she had not divulged details about the call from the police, and that she seemed as resolute as ever in her remote stance. Pleasantly and matter-of-factly, she announced that she would be going by train to Canterbury, leaving at midday, and staying the night. 'But you know that because you heard me talking to Jack on the phone, arranging it. Or maybe I've already told you.' There was a silence, Lennie still looking at his computer screen.

'I'm not sure what else there is to say,' she continued, softly. 'I mean, more than we said only last night. There's always more, but right now I'm running out of steam. Anything you want to say?'

He shook his head in puzzlement and looked at her. They had hardly looked at each other all morning. 'You managed to find it in you to have a long conversation with that Frenchman.'

For a moment she froze, then realised he meant the police Inspector.

'I don't know, Janey. I don't understand. Really. You can't carry on like this.' Then, more forcefully, 'We can't carry on like this.'

She was reminded of the many times that Lennie had said that, how he easily rushed to catastrophic conclusions about the relationship when he felt unhappy or misunderstood or mistreated. And yet, now, he was right – although her view of 'like this' was different from his.

'What's that supposed to mean?' she asked.

'Well, can we carry on like this? What am I supposed to think, or do? What about the children?'

'It's up to you what you think or do, surely. For my part, I still need time, and space, and some distance from you. Then, we'll see.'

He sniggered as he had the evening before, hardening Jane further.

She imagined being in a dark arbour, through which bright sunshine shafted, white and glaring, illuminating a patch of earth. She did not know where this image sprang from, but knew she needed that piercing light; that the dark, dank forest-green would not feel peaceful for long.

All she said to Lennie now was, 'I'm sorry for being so confusing for you. Clumsy sentence – been speaking French too much. I can see you're in a dilemma over everything. But... I think you're choosing not to remember the years of my unhappiness, when you would insist that it was all to do with my past, or my childhood, or my parents, or even pre-menstrual tension. Yes, there was all that, but I also think something was...' She paused, suspended, holding her breath, before continuing. 'Something rotten in our relationship all along, and in my characteristic way I patched over it, again and again. So I was being false, in a way. And I take responsibility for doing that – then. It doesn't mean one – I – have to continue forever in that way.' She wanted him to hear the implications about her mortality in this. 'It's not just my limited life, it's yours too – everyone's life is limited by time – but it's also what I think you won't see: you know, what I've often said, that if I'm unhappy, you can't be really happy. So if I "up and go", you may be gaining something – in the long run.'

A long silence ensued. Jane had not anticipated making these speeches again. She had made them so often over the years, only they now carried a certain *gravitas*, as if she was saying them for the first time.

She looked at her watch and said she had better pack and go soon. A minicab was coming to take her to the station.

'It's so silly for you to get a taxi. For heaven's sake, you know I can take you to the station. Come on! What's the matter with you?' He spoke forcefully, trying to inject his words with wry humour. 'Or what do you think is the matter with *me*, that I can't pop you to the station?'

She shook her head slightly, more to herself, as she realised that there would have to be many such exchanges between them. Lennie was like a river that would find a way through or over or around obstacles. There was no stopping him. More reason to build a dam.

All she said was, 'I've asked Harriet to come with me to the hospital tomorrow.' After a pause she added limply, 'Sorry,' prompted by a sense of Lennie as being so helpless. There was another pause, before, 'I don't know yet what I'll say, or want, at the hospital – yes, after all this! But, of course, I know you're involved, and of course, I'll let you know and... I'll come to you if I want to discuss it, discuss anything.'

'I'm not sure I can put up with all this, you know,' was all Lennie said as he stomped out of the room.

Not such a saint, after all, she said to herself

AUGUST 30ᵀᴴ, 2003

Jane and Alice sat on the terrace sipping tea. Jack and Rita had taken the two older children to Sainsbury's. Will seemed to wear the new mantle of older brother with seriousness and great tenderness, in between uncharacteristic flurries of rejecting food and sucking the blanket he used as a comforter at night. His mother breastfeeding the newcomer was almost unbearable. His transformation from baby to middle child went in great surges, forwards and also backwards.

'I must go and see the baby again before I leave, darling. I know she's sleeping. But I just want to spend a few quiet moments with her. It's such a wrench to leave you all. If I didn't have the hospital appointment today, I'd stay. But you've got Rita to help,' Jane added feebly, knowing that having Rita at a time like this was not the same for Alice as having her own mother.

Baby Daisy lay on her back in a white Moses basket in a small room. Creamy-yellow sunlight filtered through white muslin curtains which, caressed by the warm breeze, billowed into the room like the joyful sails of a ship at last making progress on a long voyage.

Here, Daisy simply was, after so much expectation, so many counted days and appointments and scans. And now time seemed suspended.

Jane sat by the side of the crib, noticing the curtains first, before being drawn to the little face. It showed traces of features Jane recognised – Tom's forehead, Jack's chin – yet it was the baby's own, her own perfect assemblage of curves and hollows and creases, a miniature landscape that would evolve and absorb and radiate and grow.

Her powder-pink Babygro perfectly complemented her delicate pastel colouring. Pale lilac eyelids flickered almost imperceptibly, not quite closing over dark filmy eyes, fingers as delicate as sea anemones slowly swaying, opening and closing, as if carried by some current, her small chest rising and falling rapidly, a slight frown briefly clouding her brow, like an undercurrent pulling her away from the light. On her domed head lay breath-soft down, almost invisible but for the sunlight illuminating it as on a spiderweb. Plump cheeks pursed the tiny lips forward and then relaxed. Her whole being became so still that if anyone had been observing, they may have felt compelled to check that the chest was still rising and falling, and the cheeks were still rosy.

Her femininity, her petiteness, was so different from Will and Tom, and from Jane's own children when they were babies. Even Alice had been quite solid from birth, round and active. This little one had the delicacy of a shell chafed by the ocean to translucency, a shell with mother-of-pearl glints to the perfect evolved forms and shapes, inside and outside.

Jane felt a lump in her throat as she watched. She knew that this moment was going to be added to her selective store of precious memories that she would never lose. She could not help but think about her own predicament, the decision to be made today.

Now she knew she did not have a choice, sitting here with Daisy. Of course, she would have to try for more, at any cost. Yes, of course she wanted to see her, to know her, to watch her unfurl, to preside over her for as long as possible. How could she not? 'Thank you, thank you for being,' she whispered. And exhaled heavily at how obvious things can be, after so much vacillation. With the tip of her index finger, she stroked the delicate skin of the baby's hand, as soft as a silkworm, so soft that Jane could barely discern the other. Her own skin looked more wrinkled, its texture more like orange peel than ever.

She pulled the fluffy blanket higher up the baby's chest. Daisy did not stir when kissed gently on the forehead.

The grandmother took in a last look at the slumbering infant from the doorway.

On the train to London from Canterbury, Jane wished she had not asked Harriet to accompany her to the hospital. It seemed too soon to fill Harriet in, to tell her some of what she'd been through, even though Harriet would never press her to talk.

As the train rushed past neat back gardens, Jane was struck by people's efforts to use the space they had: to grow things, to personalise, to claim, to mark out territory, sometimes to excel and rejoice. Some occupants gave up, with their little patch taken over by dried scrub or '*garrigue*' – a new word she had learned in France – and stones, and bits of scrap metal.

She was grateful when the train stopped briefly, so she could observe one small garden on which the sun beamed. Its fenced sides were adorned by clematis and roses, as well as tier upon tier of bright yellow and orange and white flowers, and a black pond in the middle fringed with purple borders. Even the white water lilies were in flower. This creation of operatic grandeur, even on such a small scale, was as great as anything by Verdi.

We're not that different from ants scurrying around in their nests, each with a job to do. Such an apparently random set of circumstances could all seem pointless. Or all the more significant, because of its brevity.

She thought how Daisy did not ask anything of her, did not try to bend her to her will. She just was. Alice took care of all the baby's needs, so Daisy and her grandmother could just be. That, she realised, was what she needed from Lennie now. Yet that could never be. If it were the other way round, she wondered, would she be able to give Lennie the degree of freedom that she longed for? Or would she start making demands on him, or somehow convey disappointment? Yet by doing what she chose now, she realised, she was making demands on him: she was asking him to forbear.

Jane closed her eyes for the last part of the journey, hoping to snatch some sleep. That blessed garden of Eden returned to her mind's eye. She wanted to dwell in her soul's garden until she died, knowing that it was a way of resourcing nature, and the world of ideas, and what she had inherited, to be mined or nurtured or pruned or dug over. And adored.

Again, she tried to imagine doing that in some form or other with Lennie at her side, and immediately felt him as a deadweight pulling her away from the toil and joy of that garden. For in one way or another, he would say, 'What about me?' If she were to say, 'But Lennie, it can be our garden,' he would soon tire and withdraw. And if she were then to say, 'But Lennie, where is your garden? What is your garden?' he would laugh, and say she was always chasing rainbows, never satisfied, why couldn't she just settle down and grow old gracefully.

She came to the point she had reached many times, which was to resolve to work at that garden of life now, without him. It was better for one person to truly survive – even if her survival was to be short-lived – than for two to drown.

She smoothed her dark red floral dress over her legs, looked down at her bare brown arms and her reflection in the window, and thought she looked quite young and healthy.

'Busman's holiday for you, Harrie!' Jane said when the friends met outside the ticket offices at Charing Cross Station to begin the journey together to St Catherine's Hospital.

They hugged each other, Jane holding onto Harriet longer than she might usually. Harriet's clear aquamarine eyes with their darker halo looked penetratingly at Jane, and she asked as only Harriet could, 'How are you?' In that moment, Harriet put aside her own needs and was there entirely for Jane. How Jane loved her, how grateful she felt, and how aware that she could never be so selfless in return. Harriet always left space, like a painting on a white canvas with blank areas for Jane to fill in.

Harriet was wearing a hyacinth blue linen dress with short sleeves and a round neck, a style that suited her modesty and quiet good taste. Jane thought Harriet looked fresh and beautiful even on this clammy clamouring train with its worn upholstery and grubby windows. Instead of a handbag, she carried a small rucksack over one shoulder – as always, even when she went to the theatre. Jane saw it as a sign of her independence of spirit, not only because it was practical when she bicycled almost everywhere.

Jane was glad they had had a long telephone conversation, exchanging summaries of their time apart. So Jane said, 'Well, in short, I'm glad I went. But it was so intense – yes, even life-changing! Will tell you more. One day, soon.' But she probably would not share too much with her friend today. She simply wanted her there as another person, to hear the doctor's pronouncements and to clarify Jane's questions. It was helpful that Harriet was a nurse, but not essential.

As the train jolted along, Harriet said, 'You look different, Jane. Don't know what it is.'

'Maybe. Not surprising really. But do you mean, different-better or different-worse?'

'Different-better. Not just the suntan – though that's great.'

Typically, Harriet didn't press her. She sensed Jane's need for quiet now.

Jane asked Harriet what she'd been reading over the summer, and if she had seen any films or theatre shows. She asked for Harriet's sake, for her own mind was overfull. Harriet responded with her news and ideas. They compared thoughts about *The Story of Lucy Gault*, which Harriet too had just read. She found the narrative less convincing than Jane, but they both loved the spare prose and the sentiments left unsaid. Jane said that she found the story courageous, that it took twists and turns that many authors would avoid.

She thought for the first time that there was something of William Trevor's taut simplicity in this friend, a straightforwardness that was so refreshing.

All she could tell Harriet now was that she knew for sure that she wanted treatment, that there was no subtle Trevor ellipsis there; that so much had happened recently, some good, some terrible, and one day she'd share it.

'But now, yes, I feel... hungry for more life. I know that sounds clichéd, but I mean, simply, to... go on being. If it means short-term suffering from the treatment, as I know it will, and even the risk that it won't do any good, that's a price I'll willingly pay.'

A flutter of surprise came over Harriet's face – a mere widening of her eyes – at this clarity and change of heart in Jane, but she smiled softly and nodded.

Jane felt she would have to fill Harriet in on the return journey, about her resolve to leave Lennie, because Harriet would find out soon anyway. Harriet was one of the few people whose own reaction would not have to burden Jane: whatever she may feel, she would give Jane tacit support in whatever she did.

Dr Gerald Greenberg stood up from his desk to shake hands with Jane, and then with Harriet. He introduced Felicity, a cancer nurse specialist who Jane had not met before, explaining that she was part of the multidisciplinary team. Her straight blonde short hair and upturned little nose gave her a neat, sharp look that Jane did not warm to. She did not know if her irritation was because she would have preferred to meet with just one person, or because Felicity smiled too much, as some shy people tend to.

Dr Greenberg had worked with Harriet at St Cat's – as they called it – years ago, before she went to Bart's. The friendly banter between them was a relief for Jane, but she soon felt isolated in her position as 'the patient', especially when she noticed that Felicity was smiling again. As if sensing this, Harriet closed down the chat with the consultant and looked towards Jane.

Dr Greenberg had her file open on his desk. He paged through it rapidly, his other hand supporting his chin, a lock of grey hair falling over his tanned forehead. Jane distracted herself from the tension of awaiting a discussion by observing his strong face, as if hewn from rock: solid square chin, prominent cheekbones, suiting his broad shoulders and muscular body.

Jane noticed the framed photograph of three smiling children on his desk. A brown felt fedora on a shelf immediately made him more attractive to her. A child's drawing was pinned on the noticeboard among fire regulations and lists of telephone numbers. Two numbers were in big bold letters. She looked at the light boxes on the wall for X-rays and scans and wondered about the many awful images that had been displayed there, hers among them. Yet the atmosphere was one of calm normality; this hospital world could all too deceptively feel like the real world, as Jane knew.

She shivered slightly at the thought of being sucked into it again, like a vortex that purported to be inviting but was really insatiable for more victims. Fragments of thoughts about baby Daisy, slumbering with gentle life, and the grotto of a pool in France, with the sun on her back, fluttered through her mind. And intimations of Pierre simply being with her, not demanding or invading – when she discovered that she could bestow gifts because she wanted to. She nodded to herself and noticed Harriet glancing at her out of the corner of her eyes. Her arms were crossed and holding her upper arms in a position of self-containment.

Dr Greenberg looked up at Jane and nodded to her, 'How've you been then?'

Jane had never been sure how to answer such a big question since she'd had cancer the first time around: whether he wanted to know the minutiae of symptoms and worries or the bigger picture. All she said now was, 'Quite well, really. Old aches and pains – like in my side and leg – and my vision in one eye became variably clouded, but I think that's abated. I think some new bumps on my head – scalp – though I can't be sure. Don't know how much it's imagination, how much I'd be having twinges anyway, at my age. Everything else, fine: appetite, energy levels. Since I came off Tamoxifen about a year ago, I've felt relatively well, with hardly any hot flushes and no discharge, bleeding, as I said when I saw Dr… sorry, can't remember his name, Matthew somebody or other.'

Dr Greenberg nodded, 'Pretty good, then. Let me take a look at the eyes.' He walked round to her and asked her to look at the ceiling and to follow his finger. He covered one of her eyes and then the other. He said he couldn't discern anything, but they would monitor the vision.

The vision, again, Jane noticed.

'Could the cancer be causing the eye problem? In what way?' she asked, joining them in the impersonal approach.

Dr Greenberg cleared his throat. Always a sign of difficulty in expressing something, Jane knew. 'Uhm, yes, it could be, could be something, something that's affecting vision, in the brain.'

This was a fear that Jane hardly dared contemplate. She tried to file this information somewhere at the back of her mind to deal with later. But it scuttled out obliquely like a crab from behind a rock, and she wondered if the disease could spread absolutely everywhere. Even on a computer, you can install a firewall to protect it from viruses, so why can't they put up a barrier to stop the cancer from infiltrating? She decided to ask Harriet more about this later.

Instead, she asked about further treatment now.

'Yes, we can give you more treatment. Chemo and probably radiotherapy. Palliative.' The doctor nodded, not looking a Jane. 'We discussed that with you when you re-presented here – when was it, at the beginning of August,' glancing at a page of her notes. 'Oh yes, on the 6th. Then you were away, on holiday, to think about everything, I think. And when we spoke on the telephone recently, you said that you'd decided to go for treatment.' He was too professional to ask her now about the police involvement; Jane sensed he would wait for her to offer something if she wanted to. He was also too discreet to ask why she had brought her friend instead of her husband this time.

'But first, we should rescan you. You'll have to have a radioisotope bone scan, and a CT scan of your abdomen – tummy. And a brain scan.' While he talked he filled in forms. Jane was sure he was marking them 'urgent'.

'Go down to Ultrasound and see when they can fit you in. Maybe later today. Certainly, it will be in the next few days.'

'MRI or CT for the brain scan?' Jane asked.

And so she rejoined the hospital world, with its rules and regulations, its rituals, its own clock which decided that days started at 7am and ended at 9pm; its power and its power games; its efficiency and its inefficiency; its human kindness; its mandatory cheerfulness; its selflessness; its neon buzz, hum of air conditioners and fans, bleeps of pumps and monitors; its tangles of tubes and wires; its industry; its one-taste-suits-all pictures and curtains; its crisp white sheets; its good, bad and indifferent smells; its army of workers behind the scenes; its tea trolleys; its bland mashed potato, overcooked cabbage, and fish that tasted of nothing; its tiny packs – like a child's food-shop collection – of cheap jam, marmalade, butter, margarine, UHT milk, tomato ketchup and salad cream. She did not need an initiation period; frighteningly, she could hurtle back all too easily into this world. Perhaps that was why she had resisted, she thought – knowing how easy, almost seductive, it was to lie down and let them do things.

All this – but only because I want to live.

She was to return in three days' time. Felicity added that she would have had the scans by then. And, depending on the scans, would begin a cycle of Arimidex.

Greenberg had slipped in that this was palliative chemotherapy, hadn't he, she now remembered, applying the brakes, to stop herself from rushing forward. 'Palliative.' She disliked the word. She knew it was palliative, but to accept it was like temporarily cauterising a bleed that would recur and her life would seep away.

The consultant turned to Felicity to suggest that she explain the possible side-effects of the drug. The chirpy nurse talked about nausea, vomiting, loss of appetite, menopausal symptoms, and the number of cycles before they rescanned – all as ordinarily as if she was explaining the cycles of a washing machine. Through a foggy mind, all Jane heard was a list of things out there that hardly mattered anymore; grist to the mill now that she had taken the step of committing to treatment. Although she could not think of anything that would make her change her mind, she felt immensely heavy-hearted.

If for any reason the scans contraindicated this course, Dr Greenberg said he would ring her. Jane was relieved to be in the hands of a doctor she could trust, who would not forget this arrangement. She thanked him with genuine feeling.

Jane asked Harriet if there was anything else she should ask? Harriet hesitated before saying that perhaps Jane needed to know what Dr Greenberg thought could alter the treatment plan, what he meant by the need to check the scans first? 'Although', she added to Jane, 'you may already have an idea of his answer.'

'Oh yes! I mean, no. Why didn't I think of that.'

Dr Greenberg said that a contraindication may be a spread of disease that could alter their plans for infusions of Arimidex or, possibly, really good scans, where the masses had decreased and the treatment plan may need to be altered. He added that all these scans were markers with which they could make comparisons at later stages. Jane nodded understandingly, though her grasp at that moment was superficial.

This sense that the facts were eluding her was so familiar these days. How could she understand when the real question hung in the air like a scythe, hovering above her head. Treatment, yes.

But how long? Could she ask? She pulled herself up to the surface, forced the question that had to be asked, but felt as difficult as trying to keep out an encroaching tide.

'I know it's hard to say,' she stuttered, 'but what might I hope to gain from this treatment? You know, chances of… of survival? I mean, how much time, really – roughly?' Even now, looking into the jaws of death, Jane felt the need to ease the way for the doctor, to phrase her questions indirectly, to protect him in his awesome task by adding, 'I know it's hard for you…'

Now he really needed to clear his throat. 'Again, it's even harder to say without having rescanned you.' He looked sideways at the wall and leant back in his chair, his desk a vast barrier between them. 'But let's say that the scans are more or less as before, I think we'd rescan after four cycles and have some idea of the response. If you were tolerating the drug reasonably well and there was a response, we would proceed to six to eight cycles altogether. If there was not much response, we would ask if you wanted to continue with the treatment.'

For the first time, Jane had to register that her body may not respond at all to the new treatment. She hadn't bargained for that. In the silence that followed she realised how much she could hide behind defences, but then reality would jump out at her and frighten her.

Jane knew that he knew that she knew that he had not answered her question. She sensed that he was gauging her expression, her need to know, for he went on, 'The best we could hope for would be…' – scraping his vocal chords again with a loud *agh-haa* – 'to hold the cancer, not cure it. At a guess… we may be able to hold it for about nine months to a year. But as you know, we can be wrong, either way.'

In her mind, she had already accepted she may only have six months. This was a time when her pessimism had paid off. She had been granted a potential gift, but remained silent, nodding slowly.

'I think this must seem vain, but what about hair loss?' she asked after a short while.

Harriet nodded as if approving the question.

'Not vain at all! It's some women's – and men's – main concern. Well, we can offer you an ice-cap – scalp cooling – which may postpone or lessen hair loss, at the time of the transfusion. Felicity can explain all this better than I.' He looked at his watch. 'But, usually, people do lose their hair eventually. It does grow back though.'

'Ah yes. If there's time for that. The icing on the cake. 2nd September, start date, then! Sounds a good date to me!' she concluded to Dr Greenberg as she rose to leave. Jane could be as good at cheery banter as any of the inmates, paid or unpaid.

Harriet put a solid arm around Jane's shoulders as they walked towards the station. Both were silent until Jane spoke.

'Actually, you know, that's not too bad. I don't feel bad. Before… before I went away, with this recurrence, I really pressed that junior doctor, the senior reg., Matthew. He was very reluctant to say, but I sort of wheedled it out of him, poor chap. You know, by saying that I'd heard of another case like mine, where the woman had only a few months and she needed to know, and I wondered if I was in the same boat. I think I wore him out. And he said, "Probably a question of months." Now I know where I am – more or less. Now I know that I'll see baby Daisy learn to sit, hopefully. And I can begin to think what to do with my patients: end with some, refer others on. Clear the decks. Plenty of time!'

Harriet laughed warmly, 'You are amazing, Jane!'

'Why, what do you mean?'

'You always have this marvellous capacity for life. That's what's so attractive about you.'

Jane was taken aback, unused to such a compliment from Harriet. She flushed with pleasure. 'I hope it's true. Not sure I deserve it, really feel that, through and through.'

On the train, Jane said loudly, above the din of the wheels and the rattling, that surely Harriet had known so many patients with similar predicaments and similar responses in her work. Her response was, 'Maybe. But I don't know them in the way I know you. Or care about them in this way.' It seemed to be an effort for her to be so forthcoming.

Jane was reminded that Harriet was one of her few friends who managed her own feelings so well, even now. If it were her sister Ruth, or her old friend Bella who she rarely saw, or certainly Lennie, she would be made so aware of their response, their fears, their sadness, their loss, that there would not be much room for her to know her own.

She decided not to talk with Harriet about her resolve with Lennie, after all, not today. It would feel as if she was overusing her friend's goodness. Harriet noticed Jane becoming more withdrawn, and when they parted at Charing Cross she said, 'Ring me any time.' Jane knew she meant it. 'Really, Jane. Any time.'

On the last leg of the journey home on her own, the thought, unbidden, came to Jane's mind: What if the scans show a great lessening of the cancer? She thought of her father's lung secondaries disappearing for a while, confounding the doctors. This had occurred when he wasn't on treatment, but was using a visualisation technique. What if… it was not a cure, but remission? It had been known. But when does hope slip into denial? She remembered Pierre telling her that his mother used to say, 'Never say never.'

Her mind wandered back to when she had said to Pierre, after the first time on the floor downstairs, that their liaison was unbelievable, as she chuckled at his side. And then he invoked his mother. That made what happened between them more preposterous, but also more understandable.

She looked at her reflection in the tube train opposite, a middle-aged pleasant-enough woman. Who would guess about the cancer, and who would guess about her time in France?

She walked home from the station, past attractive houses, some with well-painted doors in subtle sludge colours. One or two were stripped, with their doors retaining original Edwardian stained glass in all its intricacy and richness, and their front gardens boasting tubs of petunias or lavender, or gaudy Busy Lizzies, one garden with a thick show of cornflowers surrounding a tall column of late sweet-peas. She would have felt lighter if not for Lennie. She could not shelve that forever, now less than ever.

She stopped by the pretty garden and wondered if she would ever see sweet-peas and cornflowers again, another year. Probably not. Maybe, if she was lucky. What was it about sweet-peas that she loved? She should have persisted in growing them herself, like her father did; their femininity, their fragility, their fine tissue-paperiness, their irregular, almost wild shapes, and yet with some sense of structure, their old-fashioned perfume which always took her breath away.

Lennie called out to her from the kitchen as she entered the hall, 'How'd you get on?'

Jane placed her keys in their place on a small ledge, put her bag down and glanced at the answerphone to see if the red light was flashing with messages before replying, 'Fine! Well, I'll tell you, of course.' She was surprised that he was not sulking – that he saw how significant her hospital appointment was. Of course, he would realise that. Why had she doubted him? She did not know if she wanted him to rise to the occasion now, to hope that he really could. But then, if the boat rocked, as it would, what would she feel then, if he was easily thrown, again. A wave of exhaustion dragged her down.

He asked from the kitchen if she wanted a cup of tea or a glass of wine. She walked in to see him, with a smile already on her lips.

Lennie looked handsome in a russet linen shirt and stone trousers, his wavy dark hair, thick and lustrous. Not for the first time, she thought that the tinge of silver on his temples suited him. The lines on his forehead seemed to have deepened. Although he had not had a holiday recently, he looked tanned. He stood hesitantly.

She half-smiled at him.

They had not really embraced since her return, other than a brief peck on the cheek, more like brother and sister. They barely embraced before she had gone away, either. Indeed, hardly ever these days. She knew she turned away from him, maybe that was why he rarely approached her. Sometimes, she worried that he was repulsed by the cancer. But then it was difficult before, even before the recurrence.

'I better not have a glass of wine. It would finish me off. Choice phrase!' Jane gave a mild laugh. 'Pretty tiring day.' She resisted her usual pattern of deflection, of asking him how he was. 'Cup of tea would be lovely. Earl Grey.'

She sat at the kitchen table, avoiding the sitting room, which had too many associations of excruciating sessions between them. He brought her the tea in one of their best bone china mugs and had unusually taken the trouble to steep the teabag for long enough.

'Darling' – she could not help that endearment, it would have felt callous not to – 'I'll tell you, of course, all about Dr Greenberg, and about my stay with Alice, and the baby – what a relief all that is! – but we, I, must sort out what is to happen with us, you know…'

Lennie could not resist replying, 'I've been saying that all along.' Although his point was true and logical, it avoided the complicated reasons why she could not simply be straightforward about their relationship. Now she ignored his inevitable need to assert himself.

Despite her wish to focus on their marriage, she began with the task of relaying the plans for treatment, and how that impacted on her patients. 'And about the prognosis: I asked him, if the treatment goes ahead, if it's not contraindicated by scans, what span I might expect.'

Lennie looked and listened, his face conveying shock and yet he was impressed by her capacity to be so direct. She knew he could never comprehend it.

'Well,' Jane continued, 'Dr Greenberg said, about nine months, maybe a year – with the usual provisos about no one really being able to predict.' She talked breathily, attempting to sound matter-of-fact. 'Doctors, good doctors, hate playing God in this respect. And you know, I feel quite liberated by this, because I'd thought he'd say less than that, like that young doctor – Matthew – said before. You know, I can see nine months as an immense gift – well, a gift anyway, perhaps not 'immense', if I'm honest. A time to do, and feel, and...,' hesitating, 'and sort out, and experience so much.'

She felt she was describing something like a play which she would be directing, without telling him if there would be a part for him other than in the audience.

Lennie stared into the middle distance glassily.

Jane purposefully filled the space between them with her positive view, for she did not want his distress to take over, nor for him to question her optimism. She sensed that she was teeming with doubts and fears and rage at the 'gift' of nine months, which could easily feel like the death sentence it was. But not now.

'Funny, it's nine months! Just realised the obvious: gestation period. Talk about irony,' she added more to herself than to Lennie. 'Though with a pregnancy, there can be a little more certainty about the number of days.'

He scratched his chin and seemed to be looking at the newspaper lying nearby. Then he said, 'But you tell me all this as if it's absolutely obvious to you now, to go for treatment – when a few hours ago I didn't know you were certain you wanted it.'

'Oh my goodness! You're quite right. I left out a big chunk of the story. Sorry. Not surprising really, if you knew the state of my mind and all my circular thinking. Of course. Haven't really explained about the baby, Daisy. How she played a part, a vital part – that word "vital", now has real meaning, doesn't it – in my decision. I'll tell you, try to anyway, about that, but first what shall we do about supper? We should eat something.' She could not ignore the rhythms of the day, the things people do routinely – especially now, when the universe was shifting. Even though she did not feel hungry.

'Didn't know what you were going to do. About supper, I mean.' Lennie was clearly baffled by her quick return to the mundane. 'I could have cooked something. What would you like?' he asked.

'What would *you* like? What do you feel like?'

With a shrug, he suggested a takeaway curry. The idea appealed to Jane. While he telephoned the order, she put the oven on low to warm plates. And fetched a cardigan.

Again, she sat at the kitchen table, this time with her fingertips on her temples.

She said to Lennie that she would try and explain how she felt now about him, 'About 'us',' she added.

Again, she began with 'Darling,' not looking at him. 'I'll try and say what I have to say. I know this is hard for you. You've been pretty good so far with all my toings and froings. With such a short life ahead...' She sensed him shifting in his chair. 'I'm not going to say what you think.'

'I don't know what you're going to say. Just get on with it,' his tone kindly, soft, belying the content of the words.

'With such a short – I know I said it was long just now – timespan, I think it would be crazy to move out, but – and you must listen, there's a big "but" – I'd like to continue here, with you, but in a different way.' Again she was aware of his fidgeting, his change of breathing; if he were a dog, his hackles would be rising.

'Please just try and listen, Lennie.'

'What do you think I'm doing?'

There was a silence. Years ago she would have cried, turned away, despaired.

'I find it difficult to explain because I'm just finding out for myself what I want as I go along. I think I want, I want us to be friends, of course, good friends, and not to make assumptions about expectations, and… sex and all that, to be decent to each other, of course, but, I suppose, to have more separateness. To have separate bedrooms for one, for us to choose to be together sometimes, like sharing a curry tonight, and seeing the children, going to a film, whatever. Sorting things out too, practical things, the usual responsibilities, to continue with what we're good at, but privately, for there to be an understanding that we each do our own thing more.'

Jane waited, looking down at her lap, surveying the flowery shapes on her dark red dress. The old station clock ticked hoarsely above them. Some things go on and on and on.

Now Lennie spoke. 'You've said this before, in a way. It's not new. I don't want that, but if you do, that's the way it will be.'

'But what do you really mean now? If you feel resistant, it will be difficult. Even if you say okay, I'll be able to tell.'

'Well, I can't help that. Can't hide the fact that I don't want this. But I'll try. Try to make it work.'

Again there was a silence.

'But I'll never know what you feel. If you're making it "work" – this new arrangement – just for my sake, but are unhappy, well, I will sense it, and that won't feel right. Perhaps I'm asking for the impossible.' But while she talked, she felt a brick wall crumbling and saw that what had been an obstacle, could be viewed as Lennie doing his best, in good faith now, when up against such a curtailment of her life. How, perhaps, he was being remarkably selfless. Why shouldn't an awareness of death change his perspective too?

She put her hand on his. He smiled bravely at her and grasped hers. She knew that everything could be seen in a different light, and sometimes we had a choice about the light that we chose.

'Thank you,' she said. He put his arm around her shoulders. She responded by holding his hand. From where they sat, side by side, at the table they hugged, deeply.

'Is this allowed? Can we still have hugs?' he joked.

Jane felt she was finding a part of herself that was warm and strong and wholesome, that was utterly familiar. Just as she was taking in a deep breath the doorbell rang. 'The bloody curry.'

'That's okay,' said Lennie. 'Plenty more where that came from.'

Over food and beer, she talked about her trip to Canterbury, and about the baby. She tried to share some of her wonder, the way the baby opened up a profound need to buy more time. How the little being just lying there – sleeping so peacefully and delicately, her tiny life ticking on, unfurling – had led Jane to feel that she had to try to stay alive to witness more of it, at least until Daisy was older, more robust, older than when Timmy died, if she was lucky. But while Jane talked, she knew she could not fully explain this to anyone.

'You see, I had that awful – awful's not the word – ghastly experience by that grave in France. And then this, with Daisy. Seems wrong to utter them in the same breath. The first shocked me into realising what a tragedy it is when someone's life is brutally cut short, and how I wanted – but hardly dared then – wanted greedily to snatch as much of mine as possible.' Jane pushed her plate away, unable to finish the food. She glanced at Lennie. He was looking at his plate and chewing. She didn't know how much he understood.

She continued, 'But then Daisy, you see, Lennie, *Daisy* in her pure, sweet, fresh existence... her *existence* is enough for me to feel something like... Well, you mayn't understand what I'm trying to say, but, I mean, almost a religious experience of adoration, of worship, of life.'

She knew, with a corner of her mind, that she was leaving out the part that Pierre had played in her reawakening, how fiercely and yet tenderly she had reclaimed life with him.

Jane, plucking up courage now to look at Lennie properly for the first time since she had embarked on this attempt to explain, was fearful that she would meet a blankness, or worse, some kind of subtle, disguised mockery. What she found was a huge effort on his part to listen sympathetically – similar to the moment a few minutes ago, when a familiar impasse between them had shifted and she could suddenly see him differently.

There were no frowns or fleeting irritation, but she was not absolutely sure if she had missed them when she had avoided looking at him.

'I guess it's hard for anyone to really know what I'm on about,' she added with a small smile. 'But I had to try. Thank you – and I mean it – for listening.'

Now he smiled at her weakly, uncertain. Jane assumed that what she was saying aroused unpleasant memories of what he called her dramatizing things, or seeing everything too psychoanalytically. He had said years ago that it was fine for Wagner to convey these grand themes of life and death, but when ordinary people tried to apply them to their lives it sounded false.

Nevertheless, she persevered. While nibbling a chapati, she told Lennie about a video that Jack had taken of the boys' first moments with the baby; how Will looked with wide-eyed wonder at Daisy and exclaimed, '*Tiny* hands... *tiny* fingers... *tiny* buttons!' She talked of Alice being so calm, lovely and capable, and what a natural breastfeeder she was. She recounted that Rita seemed so keen on doing things properly: like the way she changed the baby's nappy with meticulous attention to the bottom while not looking at the baby's little face – but added that it didn't matter, it wasn't important on the scale of things. 'Though perhaps that's why Jack married Alice, to get away from such a strict or restricted world,' Jane added.

'Yes, but why did Alice marry Jack? Because she needed some of his sense of order and routine?'

'Maybe.'

'And why did you marry me? Because I'm not as up and down as you are; you need my stability.'

'Let's change the subject,' Jane said, trying to sound friendly, but beginning to feel that unpleasant tension in her throat. *Here he goes again, always trying to score points.* 'I'm exhausted. Must go to bed.'

She made herself a cup of camomile tea and coffee for Lennie, and went up to the spare room. She did not kiss him goodnight.

In the small room at the top of the house, under the eaves, it was a relief to draw the curtains on the amber glow of the street lights and houses opposite, the air that was never fresh and nights that were never really dark, the city that was never silent.

Jane recalled her patch of France. Night-blue breezes, as if brushed by warm down, the hushing and shushing of fig leaves outside her window. Clematis tendrils shyly edging their way around rough thick stone into her bedroom, and when she closed the shutters she would carefully move them back out of harm's way. Otherwise, it would be like trapping someone's delicate fingers.

Lennie went to his study to check his emails, with his coffee and a brandy. It was midnight, but he had become used to staying up late until the early hours.

He felt left in suspense by everything that was happening between him and Janey, as if he could not grasp it and had to go through the motions. Perhaps she'll see sense, slip back into the old pattern, after all, he thought. Surely, that wasn't so bad, was it?

He felt a stab of disappointment that Val still had not replied to his email, suggesting a lunch date. The proposed rendezvous was not far off now. Perhaps she was away for a few days. But surely, she was the type who'd check her emails, wherever she was. He wondered if he would appear too keen, even needy, if he emailed her again now. The trouble with emails was that you could never be sure that someone had opened them.

As he was scrolling through messages he had recently sent, a new one popped into his inbox.

> Len,
> Many ta's for the thoughtful response. I know the pub. Yes: to confirm Tues Sept 2nd as you propose. Can we make it 1pm? I'll assume that's okay unless I hear from you to contrary.
> Looking forward 2 c'ing U,
> Love Val

She must be online now, judging by the time and date. He found her tone quite distant, despite the 'Val' this time, the fuchsia ink again, and considered ringing her on impulse right away. But then she might not be alone, and she may wonder why he rang when he could email. He wondered if he should reply at all – there was no need to, the arrangements had been finalised. But he wanted to connect with her; one, possibly two, lonely people emailing each other at this time of night.

So he wrote:

> Is this what they call 'chatting'? Coincidence we're both online at this time.
> Or is it?
> C U then!
> Love Len

While he waited for a reply, should there be one, he felt angry with Janey for her complicated ways of seeing the world, her stipulations about their relationship. Why was it always that way round? Why was it always Janey who called the tune, and decided when she was going to direct her music elsewhere? He wondered cynically who the beneficiary would be. Perhaps that scummy man in France. He wanted to know more about him, why on earth she had accommodated someone like that. No wonder she got mixed up with the law. She would have to sort it out herself now, he wouldn't help, even though he knew far more about the workings of the law than she.

No reply came from Val when he checked half an hour later. He felt like finding his familiar site, with a reliable source of excitement. Instead, he poured another large draught of brandy and took it with him to bed.

His head reeled from the alcohol and exhaustion, but he needed to reassure himself that he could find pleasure, regardless of Janey. He pushed back the duvet and touched himself and then followed a fantasy of going to see Val, undressing her, seeing her breasts, and being surprised and overwhelmed by them – with the predictable result. After the relief, he felt cheated and tearful. He stumbled to the washbasin to remove evidence, in case Janey were to come into their bed.

He was sure he would at least sleep deeply now, but was disturbed by brief half-waking scenes of Janey and a doctor talking; Janey without hair; Janey being sick from the treatment; flashes of her looking very thin; Janey full of something like brown mould which seeped out of her eyes and ears and nostrils and mouth. Her belly was distended and it was not a pregnancy. He could not sleep, but could not be sure he was awake. Fretfully he knew he had to do something, not just stand by and watch; somehow he had to either go far away or help her.

August 31ˢᵀ, 2003

Lennie was awoken by the telephone ringing at nine in the morning. The French police again. He asked them to ring back in an hour, saying in loud French that sounded uncompromisingly English, '*Ma femme est mal, malade, dix heure* okay? You, *vous, telephone à dix heure? Oui?*'

He looked in the mirror at the grey rings under his eyes and growth of stubble on his chin, and decided to have a shower and a shave. He felt unattractive and in need of a haircut. The waking dreams returned while he stood under the hot jets of water. Repulsed by the images, he knew that they were more about something bad and hopeless in Janey that was not necessarily of her making, but more of his. After years of living with her, he knew he had to try to take responsibility for his dreams.

He would try to help Janey somehow, even if she spurned him.

And when he saw Val on Tuesday, he would keep it friendly but no more. One day he may need or want Val, but not now.

Just before ten o'clock, he took Jane a mug of tea, knocking on the door of the spare room, calling that the French police would soon be ringing for the second time that morning, and maybe she'd have to speak to them.

Jane had been annoyed that he was waking her, breaking the beginnings of an understanding between them about separateness, but then realised that she would have to receive the call. She remembered the previous call from the Inspector, and how she had half intended to look up the events surrounding the possible murder on the *France-Soir* website.

Downstairs, she stood in the hall in her grey silk dressing gown, holding her mug of tea. She raised the cotton lace curtain to take in the salmon peach – or was it 'peach salmon' in the catalogue – hollyhocks outside the window. She remembered joking with Lennie before she went away that they were the colour of old ladies' knickers.

The telephone rang. Lagarde's familiar voice apologised for disturbing her. Could he trouble her with one more question? She was struck by how polite he was, as if his approach had altered. Yet again she wondered if this was tactical, or if circumstances, maybe the evidence, had altered. She conveyed a pleasant response and waited for the question.

'Doctor, I am sorry to be asking you to put your mind back to your… discovery… in the shrine.' He paused, perhaps waiting for her to object or react.

All Jane said was, 'Yes?' She knew she sounded detached.

He continued, 'Well, do you have any recall of anything else you saw nearby?'

'No,' she replied spontaneously and unhesitatingly, the dreadful image coming back to her. Allowing the curtain to fall back in place, she walked away from the window to sit hunched on a chair. She could easily, too easily, recall the stench, the flies, the dress, the hair, the colour of the arms, but nothing else. 'Oh, but at some time before then, I think I saw someone lurking in the cemetery, half hidden. I'd forgotten about that.'

He remained silent. So she continued, 'No, Inspector. Really. About the… the corpse. I didn't look, mind you. Too shocked. But no.' She tried not to dwell any further on the images. 'But why, why do you ask?' Surely, they could tell her now, surely, not that cagey business again, now that she was here, out of the way?

'Well, you will find the information you require on the website. *France-Soir* and *Le Figaro* are both running stories on the whole business. It's become a national news item. I'm sure you can buy French newspapers anyway in London. In "Pic-a-dee-lee"?' he added in an attempt to lighten the mood. Jane thought he was simply covering up for his ungenerous response to her questions.

She remained quiet, and then ended the conversation as soon as possible, realising he had no further need to detain her, nor she him.

She wandered into the kitchen. The sun was streaming through the etched ultramarine and carmine glass panes in the old window that she had found on a builder's skip years ago. It cast a rich jewelled pattern on the deep terracotta wall opposite. Lennie was at the sink washing a saucepan. He glanced at her uncertainly. His shoulders were hunched, his head hung low.

She hesitated, then broached what was on her mind, 'Lennie, that Inspector – Lagarde he's called – keeps telling me I can find out what I want to know about that case – you know, the girl who died – by looking it up on the website of certain French newspapers.'

Soon they sat, side by side, at Lennie's computer, slipping back with ease into their old pattern of working together on something.

They perused the 'Home News' of *France-Soir* and soon found a large article headlined, 'Bank fraud implicated in death of Lyon woman.' 'Man arrested over dead Giselle' ran the sub-heading. The article stated:

> *For the past six months, auditors working for the banking committee of Credit Lyonnaise have been*

investigating the disappearance of millions of euros. Their findings have not yet been fully disclosed.

The Director of the Midi France region of Credit Lyonnaise, Jean-François Cousin, a local man living in Lyon, is being held in custody while further enquiries are underway. Monsieur Cousin supervises the running of Credit Lyonnaise's Pension Funds Authority account. The PFA is their largest customer. Staff were being questioned over his personal relationship with the dead woman, Giselle Baudier, with whom he worked. He is described as wealthy and influential.

For further details of the suspected fraud, see page 3.

'Oh my God! That's terrible!' Jane erupted. 'I'm not sure I understand, but how awful, if that's true, if she was murdered because of some terrible fraud that she was aware of… or may've been involved in. Maybe she wasn't so innocent,' she muttered, her voice trailing off.

'Oh Janey, look, another column, under *"Developments"*.' Jane rapidly read on,

Forensic experts in the Lot-et-Garonne region, where Mademoiselle Baudier's body was found, are still unsure if an excess of potassium and a trace of cobalt nitrate in the deceased could have caused her death. It appears that she may have died from hyperkalaemia. This raises the possibility of suicide or poisoning. Further tests are being carried out.

As the body was discovered in an open shrine, and no attempt was made effectively to hide it, police are now thinking that it is unlikely to be murder.

Jane was unsure if she could bear further exposure to the crime. She changed gear, becoming matter of fact, and translated the article for Lennie, who had only gleaned the basic outline. It was easy not to look at him, as she translated that Mademoiselle Baudier's brother, Charles, was helping the police with their enquiries. She could not really register her shock, now, even though she had half thought this before. Oh God, what would Pierre feel, she began to speculate, if it was suicide – if he felt that he had driven her to it? She continued to read a statement by Detective Chief Superintendent Paul Grenon:

> '*In order to avoid unhelpful speculation, I can confirm that the individual, Monsieur Cousin, is not Giselle's boyfriend or indeed a member of her family.*'

Jane glanced back at a summary of the case at the beginning of the article – but did not translate for Lennie this time. She read how the police had become aware of Mademoiselle Baudier's car at the bottom of a ravine when a local farmer alerted them to it and removed it for investigation. The article explained that her brother Charles had made a miraculous escape, as he had been driving the car when it crashed. Jane was disappointed and yet relieved that she was not credited for her part in the rescue.

Some of the mysteries were becoming clearer, and now she could probably deduce that Lennie might never know, nor need to know, that she had clambered to his rescue.

She pushed her chair on its castors away from the computer and from Lennie and faced him. Jane felt she had to explain more, more about her shocking discovery, although she herself could not understand if her curiosity about what was in the shrine was normal. Tears began to spring from her eyes unexpectedly.

'Lennie, I'll try and explain. Don't know if I can, but… I felt sort of crazy for some of the time, as I've told you. Overloaded with too many major things on my mind. Didn't know if I was derailed mentally, or if I was finding my own way through… through the chaos. Anyway, that ruined chapel that I told you about, it had such a… I don't know, such a hold on me. You know how I'm drawn to ruined places. Well, it looked ghostly, sort of blurred, in a certain light, even in daylight. And then there was the chap I helped – you know,

Pierre, who's really 'Charles' – who'd had a crash, and who had hurt his leg quite badly.' She looked at the floor now, not risking seeing any negative looks on Lennie's face. 'And I was helping him to get sort of rehabilitated – yes, I know it was crazy of me – and the bastard went and stole my hire car, as you know.'

She looked up at her husband as he sat and faced her full-square, calmly listening, his expression one of friendly interest. Jane knew she was not being very coherent, but that she should go on. 'But he… he, Pierre, was the brother of the girl who died. You gathered that? That's the extraordinary thing.' By speaking out loud she was also helping herself to understand. 'Well, one of many amazing events. But it's not altogether surprising: he'd come to the ruined chapel – near where I was staying – because that was where his mother was buried. He'd felt the need to "talk" to her, I think. He'd rowed massively with Giselle, left her in a bad way, and then crashed his car – hers, actually – near my place. Do you understand?'

Lennie nodded but Jane was not sure how much he was really taking in. 'And soon – I don't know how soon – after that, she, Giselle, got bumped off or killed herself. I don't know which is worse. Of course, the police suspected Pierre. But he was, it seems, quite innocent – other than being a bloody car thief. I don't understand why she might have killed herself – that's none of my business really, except I feel… sorry for her. Oh, I know that sounds so inadequate.'

The light in the study became gloomy as rain clouds gathered. She looked at Lennie. At least he wasn't being judgemental.

Now she called on his experience as a criminologist, partly to humour him, partly because she did want help in understanding more about this case.

He reread the article on the screen, asking her to retranslate a few words. He asked if she wanted to print it out. She shrugged and shook her head, reluctant to have the whole story more in evidence than it already was.

Lennie talked briefly about major fraud cases such as this one. 'I can show you similar ones in my journals,' he added. 'Those who were involved may indeed have decided to bump off the young woman if she knew too much, if she was involved in a way that threatened them. Such huge sums of money seem to have been involved in this; they must have calculated that if they killed her, they could get away with it. Maybe she would have been a chief witness. The really odd thing is, though, dumping her near her mother. I don't understand that at all. Makes me think it probably wasn't murder, but suicide.' He smiled at Jane with a mixture of admiration and incredulity, a look she could not understand.

All she said was, 'I'm not sure what to make of all this. Not sure if I have any emotional energy left. Starting treatment in two days.' Her eyes travelled over the objects on his desk.

Remembering his sleeplessness and his thoughts in the night, he said, 'Janey, Jane, you know I'll do whatever I can to help you. But with all that you said yesterday about going our separate ways, I'm not sure what you want.'

At that moment, she felt touched by his orderly desk with its silver lamp; the expensive fountain pen she had given him years ago placed centrally above his padded leather blotter; the neat 'in' tray and the postcards of Brunel and of a Nordic country scene propped up on his bookshelf; the pot of beautifully sharpened Florentine pencils; and the best-quality embossed printed cream stationery complete with his full title, proudly upright next to a pile of Conqueror envelopes to match. There was something defenceless about Lennie, the way he clung to certain things, even though these objects were meant to convey confidence.

'I'm not surprised you're confused, Lennie. I am too. But thank you for trying, for what you just said about helping me.' She sighed. 'I think I'll need – and appreciate – your support in lots of ways, but at the same time I wonder if we can both try, as I said before, to give each other space.' She could not help noticing a slight frown pass over his face, and then an attempt to hide it as he swept his hair back with his fingers.

She decided to continue, 'You know, a bit more... respect for our own ways of thinking and being. I guess I must sound like an old gramophone record.' She knew that in some ways there would always be this tension between them. Maybe that's the way it is, she said to herself. 'I'm sorry that we always – well, you'll criticise me for saying "always", but that's my way of expressing something,' she said softly. 'We always reach a point where you seem to feel I'm speaking another language, or want something that's already there. Or I'm "never satisfied". I don't know what we can do about that except live with our differences. It's not that serious, is it, on the scale of things?' Jane did not know if she was betraying herself with this statement, betraying the ground she had fought for.

He smiled and said that she was quite right. She felt his response was bland, that he was upset and holding back. And yet she was relieved that he was, in his own way, calling a truce, if not really agreeing. She knew she had to conserve her energy for all that lay ahead.

In a friendly tone, she said she was going to get dressed and then make a few phone calls. Just as she was leaving the room, she added, 'By the way, Len, could you please find that further article on… what did they say? Page 3? And print it out for me? I would like to reread it another time. Feel I ought to, to be able to let go of it in the end.'

She left the room, after having wondered if she should hug him. She knew he wanted that. But she did not.

In the bedroom, she closed the door and raised the sash window. It had been raining. The air was fresh and birds were beginning to try out their voices. The weak sun sequined the wet leaves of a cherry tree. The drip of rainwater evoked the opalescent light that can be seen after rain in France, that abundance outside her window that she never wanted to forget, especially with what she had to face now in London. Well, in Kent, to be precise, thinking of the hospital treatment.

She wondered if she would return to that place, that very cottage by the chapel, despite the horrors there, maybe to expunge the trauma. It would have to be quite soon. 'Before… before I die,' she voiced softly, trying to get used to thinking that way. *After all, we could all do with thinking more that way, couldn't we, even if we didn't have....* Her thoughts trailed off, but then she gathered them up and continued. *The difference was, others did not have to be so focussed.*

Her fantasy ranged over the possibilities of who she could return to *La Retraite* with. She thought of Harriet. Always solidly there. How wonderful to share that place with someone on an equal footing. Or Ruth, as a way of rediscovering something warm and sisterly that had been lost in recent years. As long as Ruth didn't bring her own fears, confuse them with Jane's situation. Or Alice, but then she would have to include Tom and Will and baby Daisy, and Jack. Or Max, with his neat haircuts and preferences for ties instead of open collars, or Eddie, so different, with his long wavy hair. Perhaps she and Max would resolve something of his dissatisfaction with her, so that he would carry a more loving picture of her into the future.

Lennie, she wondered, perhaps she could go with Lennie?

She laughed at thinking of him now in this way, when she had sought *La Retraite* partly to get away from him. She left that thought hanging in the air, like the drops of water which were at that moment suspended from leaves, forming tear shapes. Some would fall and some would retract back into a wetness without surfeit.

She looked at her naked body in the mirror. She did not look too bad; yes, her thighs and stomach were firmer. 'All the better to...,' remembering the horror of the Little Red Riding Hood story, and changed it to, 'to start chemo with.'

Pierre came to mind now, but there was no physical sensation in her body. Instead, she contemplated where he was, and how he was, and if he was being detained by the police. How would she ever find out? Would he have to go to prison for stealing a car – or, really, two cars? Surely not. And surely, he had nothing to do with all that fraud. But then Jane remembered his vehement objections to her seeking help when he'd crashed, and her suspicions returned. She knew how alone he was.

She pondered if she would like to see him again, at *La Retraite*. No, she was sure that she did not want that. The question was what to do with him in her mind. And what about the frissons in her womb, the powerful surges like a falling into her very centre, what would happen to those now? Would they dry up again? Perhaps there wouldn't be enough time left for them to fade completely.

Jane had driven off to her consultation with Adrian. Lennie closed the door of his study and switched off the phone.

He felt a deep anguish that he could not name, and longed to submerge himself in whisky and listen to Wagner or Mahler, to draw the curtains on this uncertain day. It was not surprising he felt bad, he told himself.

With music and whisky, maybe he would find what he needed, know what it was he missed. Janey had her path cut out now, and if she ever felt lost, she went to see that Adrian person or one of her many friends, or could go away to France. But he had nothing, nothing like that. He considered going back to Robin, the psychoanalyst he had seen a few times at Janey's suggestion. To his surprise, Robin had been helpful in an ordinary common-sensical way, telling him what he thought he knew already, but had validated some of what he was going through when Janey was first diagnosed and had her lumpectomy. Years of being unkind to Jane, treating her as someone who was there to serve him, began to surface in meetings with Robin. The ensuing guilt was new to him, horribly uncomfortable, but had led him to feel better within himself when he tried to repair some of that.

Now, with her cancer, the world focussed on Janey, and he was expected to hold the fort, support her and the children. But he knew that he failed in Janey's eyes. Although he had tried his best. He could not become the pillar she wanted, especially when he needed her more than ever. The unbearable thought of six years ago, of her beautiful breasts being mutilated by cancer and then by surgery, flashed through his mind.

When he and Janey married all those thirty-three years ago, it had never been the agreement for him to give up his routines, his comforts, his need for her to look after him. When Harry had died, and Janey was heartbroken at the loss of her father, it had reminded him of the death of baby Timmy, the sense of devastation they had both felt. Harry had been someone he had admired and loved, in his way. After Timmy died – how long ago was it? – thirty-something years ago – Lennie had decided one day, when he had felt wrung out, with no more grief in him, to simply get on with his life. But when Harry died only six years ago, it was profoundly different from the death of Timmy.

This time something was torn from Lennie, from inside him, something strong and straight that had held him up without him knowing it. Harry was the only one, other than occasional colleagues, who read his articles and academic papers, read them properly and came back to him with ideas, tried to encompass the body of his output. And how unfair it was that, with Harry's death, when Janey had collapsed and needed him, he couldn't come up with the goods.

Yvonne, pretty and pink, like a celebratory iced cake, smooth too, smelling of roses. Being an ex-student, she put him on a pedestal that he liked. Of course, Jane would never see him through those eyes.

Yes, Harry's death was like the loss of the armature around which a *maquette* is built. He remembered that from Janey showing him her studies for a sculpture class she had attended then. Perhaps Yvonne would repair that, his wound. But she didn't, not really. 'Variable impotence', it was called on the internet.

It's your own stupid self, Lennie. Why should anything be easy? But it had been with Jenny, hadn't it? Jenny, with a thick straight fringe, black hair, ivory vellum skin, and of course, full breasts. But she turned away from him, went back to her old boyfriend, leaving him feeling scummy. So he turned to safer pastimes, where there was no embarrassment, only some guilt and some shame, securely on his computer late at night.

Soon after that, Janey was diagnosed, first time around. She had to make decisions about the whole breast being cut away or only a part of it. He asked himself, as he had often, if he had influenced her towards a conservative approach, because he didn't know if he could ever love her again if she was maimed in that way. Even if it was reconstructed later. He would not admit that to anyone except, eventually, to Robin, and Robin did not judge him. Still, that did not stop Lennie from worrying that if she had opted for a total mastectomy, this recurrence may not have occurred.

He felt a familiar deep loneliness, his parents on the perimeters of his mind, beyond the boundary as he would say in cricket, oblivious in their comfortable life in South Africa, growing old and wrinkled in the sun, more keen on their comforts and the maids they still kept than his life in London. He pictured his mild mother, wearing a lemon yellow summer frock and white court shoes, with her white handbag – not that there was ever much in the bag, except for a few rand, so that any mugger would not feel too angry and cheated – going for her daily walk to the seafront. Dominated by his father. And how his mother adored Lennie above all others when he was a boy. But then she became ill with diabetes and began to look to her husband for everything, even daily injections. And there was his sister in Hong Kong, living life in the fast lane, unmindful of him.

He was aware that he was becoming more and more morose, that he had to find a way out that made him feel better. Again, he recalled the hideous images of an ill, suppurating Janey in his half-awake state the night before. They say that no one really gets away with crime, he told himself.

If I'm treating her so badly in my mind, then, of course, I'm suffering. But then if I were to treat her better, would it be ultimately for my sake?

Could we refind each other, he ventured to think. Could we tenderly reach out and discover, and be found? Maybe that's what Janey would say. But that's impossible. We're both too jaded by life, by age, by everything. He wondered if life always had to dwindle in this way, into a sad loss of so much potential – some, or most, never realised.

He knew that was why he sought, or half-sought, women like Val… or Yvonne. Or Marie, so much younger, all those years ago. Women who offered him fresh hope of something untrammelled by time and disillusionment. He knew that all the women he was attracted to had a quality that Janey did not, which was not just their ample breasts – for hers used to be lovely, until she had children – but a gentle naivety, a gauche untutored quality, so that he was indubitably the one in charge. With Janey, if anything, she was the boss. As he told himself this, he knew she saw it the other way round. He reached now for one of his best Partagas cigars, even though it was still morning, and poured a whisky from the cut-glass decanter.

Through the blue-grey smoke that obscured his view of the copper beech, he longed for Janey to be the one with whom he could journey in this last stretch of her life before it was too late. Even if he wanted this partly for selfish reasons, he knew the regrets would be there anyway, afterwards, but more so, much more, if they didn't find a way of reaching each other now, nakedly. It would be different from anything he had had before with her or with anyone, except in his dreams and in his reveries listening to Wagner. Breathing in music, he sometimes cried at the purity of the female voice, at the perfection of his mother's golden love for him, singing him lullabies.

He smiled at this turn of events, at his imagination soaring so high, about him and Janey. And yet his thoughts were ordinary and human too, of two souls in need of something authentic after so many years of drought. If they had not had precious months here and there, over the years, of what he sensed they both yearned for, he would not have thought it possible.

But how would he ever convey any of this to Janey? He would stop calling her 'Janey' for a start, knowing she did not like it.

In his logical way, he wondered about his liking for women who wanted to be led by him, and why Janey... Jane... would never allow that. He remembered the years of variable impotence early in the marriage, and how his body stopped being able to give her what she wanted. How that was rarely a problem with the other women, or girls as they seemed. He closed his eyes, drawing deeply on the cigar, the whisky coursing through his head.

He imagined being led by Jane some of the time, and now, sometimes leading her. But he paused and wondered if relationships were inevitably about leading or being led. He wondered what Jane would say.

He returned to his earlier thoughts, of a kind of nakedness, of two people discovering each other. There could be surprises. This was a new idea to him, which seemed like a gift from somewhere. For within it, he could imagine the freshness of discovery, of risking seeing what was there in her, and maybe she would feel the same about him.

He poured another drink. Val's smile came to him, her slightly flirtatious look, with her teeth showing.

He shook his head, struggling to return to Jane. Perhaps that's enough for one day, he told himself. But he felt like someone who had partially unwrapped a wonderful gift and needed to really see what was inside.

He sat back on the leather sofa and looked up at a picture Jane had painted years ago of a small street in a village in France, in the Languedoc, where they had stayed: pollarded trees led the eye right into the heart of the picture, where there was a church, and he knew he had to get beyond these imaginings into some way of readying himself for Jane. Some way of finding how to relate to her that would be different, which she would notice and take in the right way. In his inebriated state, the church now looked like an angel: the buttresses were wings, the sky-reaching steeple became a head surrounded by the halo-sun, the little windows in the tower were the eyes. It was as if he first needed to sweep away years of cobwebs in his mind, and then... perhaps... hope. Hope that she would see the brightness in him, and maybe he too would see her differently. Yes, in a way he would have to be a petitioner, to show her that he was open to something different. He was not too proud for that. He smiled, but an anxiety that she would be irritated by him crept into his mind.

Lennie knew he had drunk enough whisky, so left the glass half full on his desk. His heart felt warm and full and tender. Even if he was hurt or misunderstood now, this was a good feeling. It reminded him of the way that he had allowed himself to feel the supplicant to Harry: the one person in his life who he had really admired, and was happy to show gratitude to, and to be small when he was with him. And yet, there was something about Harry that always gave Lennie a sense of his own real worth, so that his insignificance never lasted long, but was transformed by the older man into something like a sharp arrow held by Harry's taut bow of a mind.

And Jane is her father's daughter.

He opened the study door and looked out from the landing to see if Jane's car was back. He was relieved he had time to consolidate his thoughts before she returned.

Returning to his computer through the haze of alcohol, he managed to find the *Figaro* site, remembering they had not researched it. He found a page of that day's news, and not the previous day, which was all *France-Soir* had been able to provide.

He printed out the article for Jane: *Giselle Mystery Solved*.

Skimming the summary in the first paragraphs he cut to the conclusion. His sketchy knowledge of French gave him the general picture.

Experts have now agreed that the young woman took her own life. The questions posed by raised levels of potassium and an unusual trace of cobalt nitrate are now explained by a note, which has been validated as authentic, which Mademoiselle Baudier had deposited in a building society, dated 21ˢᵗ August, three days after her disappearance. The note states:

To whom it may concern,

I do not see the point of struggling any longer. As soon as I climb one mountain there is another. I had thought that if I bettered myself financially, life would be easy. But now I realise that was a false goal. I do not think other paths are open to me. Certain people are conspiring against me. I will not give them the satisfaction… but will get there first. At least, this is one thing I will do well: cobalt is an underrated poison, yet artists and paint manufacturers have easy access to it!

My will is with my solicitor, *Verfeille et Frères*. I want all my possessions and assets to go to my brother, Charles, except for a donation of 1,000 euros to the maintenance of the cemetery of the Templiers chapel at Dominipech, near Ceneyrac.

Too caught up in his own thoughts to try to read it properly now, he knew Jane would translate it later for him.

'Thank you for seeing me', Jane said in a dignified way as she sat down, her handbag at her side. The room was sombre as always, whatever the weather.

She glanced at Adrian, pleased he looked tanned, as if he had had a holiday.

'I'm glad you're back now. That is, if you've been away.' He gave a fraction of a smile and looked on.

She knew she could waffle on, waste time. So she tried to come to the point, but didn't know quite what the point was.

She looked down at her lap. How many times she had been here, in all sorts of states. Now it was like diving into a pool, not necessarily a cold one, but certainly a deep one.

'When I last saw you, months ago it seems – in fact, it was at the beginning of August – I had been diagnosed with a recurrence, as you know. A serious recurrence. Breast cancer, with metastases in various places.' She never expected him to remember everything about her, he had so many patients and she wasn't a proper one; she was someone who flew in and out of this room a few times a year. But she always felt that he did remember the important things about her. 'So I booked a brief holiday away on my own, to France, as I think I told you.' She paused, and then continued, 'A sort of retreat, to be alone and see what I really wanted to do about further treatment.

'Oh dear, I don't necessarily want to give you a blow-by-blow account of the past month. Why did I need to see you? Not to decide about further treatment, because I've decided, after all sorts of doubts and definite "no's", to now say "*yes*, at whatever cost". I surprise myself in a way. But my decision is to do with two, or maybe three, major events in the past few weeks. You'll need to know what they are – but I'm not sure about the order.' Jane paused briefly to take in a deep breath.

'An... affair – don't like the word, it's so trivialising, so sort of fickle sounding – a brief... liaison with a young man, a very young man, in France.' Glancing at Adrian, she thought he did not look in the least surprised and wondered what that meant about him or about her. 'And then, the discovery, *my* discovery, of a... body, a corpse, in a shrine.' She felt like giggling: a childhood feeling of irrepressible laughter that used to overcome her at the most unsuitable moments. 'You'll think I'm crazy. I'd need ten sessions on that alone, but strangely that's not why I'm here – I don't think. And then the third event was the birth of my... our first granddaughter, Daisy.'

Adrian nodded benignly.

'I think what I'm struggling to find, through all this.... By the way, the three "events", all in their different ways, helped me to decide resoundingly to opt for further treatment, no matter what the odds, even if there's a recent spread of the disease – as long as they'll give it to me – the treatment, I mean. What I'm struggling to find out is what I do, what I do now, with the… discoveries I made in that fling, that encounter, with Pierre – that's his name. The feelings in my body' – she felt herself blushing and looked down '– the different kind of sexuality, that I've hardly known, or allowed, for most of my life. By the way, I'm old enough to be his mother.' She looked up at Adrian and thought she discerned the slight rise of an eyebrow.

'Yes, I know, powerful stuff,' she said. 'But there was something precious and – what's the word I'm looking for – affirming, and fresh, and invigorating. More than that. I realised that I did not have to mourn the loss of life, of sexuality; I could make a comeback – if I may use that phrase – with a vengeance.' She blushed again, feeling a mixture of shyness and pleasure at letting Adrian, who she found attractive, know how sexual she was.

She wished he would say something. So she said, 'I'm talking too much.'

Now Adrian spoke as if to himself, in some kind of reverie. 'It's not surprising, what you have discovered. Well, the way you've talked before, about you and your husband.'

Jane was surprised at this response and questioned it in her embarrassment. 'What do you mean? I never thought I'd have an affair, a physical affair, so how could you?'

'Well, it showed.' He smiled and seemed to blush too, slightly.

Jane took a deep breath. Now it was her turn to raise her eyebrows. She felt annoyed with him for his omniscience.

'Well,' she continued, 'now that he, Pierre, is miles away and he – it – is completely out of the question, what am I to do with my newfound vitality – sexuality? Especially as I only have about nine months to live if I'm lucky. Lucky,' she repeated in a serious tone.

There was a silence.

She tensed. And looked at the fine little glazed pots on the mantelpiece and the mediocre painting of boats on a beach somewhere, a disappointing picture for Adrian to have.

She was about to talk about knowing she idealised Pierre, when he spoke, 'Well, from what you say, you have discovered something, something like a gift in you, a richness in yourself, and of course, as you know, wealth is always more rewarding when it's shared rather than kept to oneself, but you don't know how your discovery, or rediscovery of... your vitality will be used for....' he gave a little cough, before continuing, '... for however long you have. To live.'

There was another silence. She found his capacity for reflective silence remarkable. But even he avoided naming 'death'. She hardly dared feel disappointed in him, now, when she needed him so much. Then he continued, 'Of course, what you've hardly touched on is the life sentence. Well, not directly. And what you're making of that. What it's really like.'

He looked at her kindly with his unblinking sapphire eyes. Jane glanced at her watch. Only about ten minutes left. She remembered Alice telling her that when time had flown in her therapy session she had said to her therapist, 'Cor, if I only had an hour to live, I wouldn't come here!'

Jane said she was not sure that there was enough time to really go into that, to risk such a big subject.

When he calmly offered the possibility of another time next week, she felt as if much-needed air was allowed to rush into her lungs. Tears of gratitude seeped from her eyes. The room felt warm, almost too warm.

'I don't know really – not yet – about the 'nine months", she said. 'But now's a good time to start. Amazing irony of that span – don't know what to call it, a "gift" or death sentence. Or a life sentence. That's what you just called it.

'Haven't had any memorable dreams recently to bring, unfortunately,' she went on. 'Had lots when I was away in France, but I think I worked on them – well, up to a point. Recently, since I've been back, there's only one I can remember, which I guess is obvious: of a white moth disintegrating into dust, and the specks or motes catching the sunlight quite beautifully, floating slowly downwards, but in other directions as well – you know, the way snowflakes can do. The slowness of their movement was mesmerising. I suppose the sudden transformation from a moth that was flying to an explosion of dust is quite shocking when I think about it now, but not in the dream. It seemed inevitable.'

Both were briefly silent.

Knowing there was so little time left today, even with the possibility of another appointment, Jane did not want to leave with such a suspended, albeit evocative, image.

'I think I can accept the inevitability and finality of death, my death – with part of me anyway – but, you know, even nine months isn't long.' Her words felt so inadequate, even clichéd, but she had to struggle in the confusion to make something of the few minutes left. She knew the race against time in this session was parallel to the big question that she was trying to talk about now. 'I could rail at that, but no, you know, I think I want to find a way that some of the deep alive feelings I found in France, within me... I want them to be part of my marriage. I may be asking for the moon, but... after all, in the dream I'm not some great peacock butterfly, I'm just an ordinary white moth, and I want to be an alive fluttering moth that brushes up against the light, sometimes gently and sometimes passionately, until I fall apart and become part of the cosmos. How's that for a note to end on?'

'I thought you said "mote",' said Adrian with a twinkle.

She knew they had to stop. She thought of her use of the word 'cosmos', and how she loved cosmos daisies. But she was not going to challenge the necessary time boundary of this meeting by mentioning that now.

Jane reached for her diary, asking Adrian what times he could offer the following week. She said she had treatment starting on Tuesday and did not know if she would feel well enough, but from previous experience, she thought that it was only impossible to do anything the day after chemo.

On her way home, she stopped at a corner shop to buy milk and *The Guardian*. The latest issue of *Homes and Gardens* mentioned an article on growing sweet peas on the cover, so she bought that too.

SEPTEMBER 2ND, 2003

On Monday 1st September, the MRI Department of St Catherine's had telephoned Jane to offer her a scan the next day. She did not know whether to be pleased or alarmed at this quick response. She knew it was to discern any brain metastases in order to plan for treatment that could encompass that.

She chose to go on her own, by train, to manage while she could, even to enjoy some time alone. In a detached and somewhat nonchalant mood, she reminded herself of the thousands who must have had the same experience. Dr Greenberg had asked her if she suffered from claustrophobia. When she said no, he seemed to think an MRI would be easy.

She felt weary and slightly sick by the time she arrived at her station.

Walking to the hospital, she thought how the death of Giselle was like a mirror image of her own plight: a sense of the cancer being an underground malignant network that ruthlessly strives to achieve its own ends, and how the doctors and the treatment were like the police, or the law, attempting to bring it to light and redress it – but that there was damage beyond repair in her own body. And in the death of Giselle. Exhaling heavily, she wished to share her thoughts with Harriet. *How to get the balance between time alone, to reflect, and time with Harriet.*

It was a relief to be in a pristine space, like the engine room of a ship: all interior spaces, whites and creams and steel, with a plump radiographer who looked as if she would be more at home baking bread than manning this scanner, *Maestro Symphony* emblazoned on its prow.

She explained the procedure to Jane and asked her to lie on the narrow bench leading into a tunnel. Jane wondered what they did with obese patients who would be too wide for it. A loud regular beat sounding like a garden sprinkler was already chugging along from somewhere high up in the room. Although Jane remembered the machine with its ominous tunnel from her first time around, six years ago, she felt detached, almost as if there must be a mistake, that someone else should be having this scan.

As if on a classy flight, she was invited to choose from a menu of music.

'Had to leave my glasses in the locker. Can't read. Anything classical?'

'Yes, a compilation. Or opera.'

'What opera?' hoping it wasn't Gilbert and Sullivan, or Puccini.

'Mozart?'

'Oh fine, great. Yes please.'

The woman explained that Jane probably would not be able to hear it well as she had to have pads on the sides of her head, and not the earphones they normally provided.

Lying there, she was quite comfortable, with a wedge under her legs, a buzzer in case she wanted anything, and a mirror above her head that reflected the technician in a glass booth. Jane was not sure if she was moving slowly or the machine was moving over her, but it didn't matter. She was determined not to feel anxious. One of her favourite arias: – *Là ci darem la mano* – the near-successful seduction scene from *Don Giovanni* – burst forth. It made her think of Pierre, but then he had not exactly seduced her. She could even enjoy this way of spending a Tuesday morning. The radiographer parted from her with a gentle touch on her leg. The human touch. Kindness. Jane sensed that the woman knew that for some patients this would be an ordeal.

With an eruption of sound in her head that was nothing short of a pneumatic drill – *Damn right I won't be able to hear the music!* – she wondered if she could bear it for half an hour. When the noise stopped briefly, the Don was in his manic drinking song. It did not help her state of mind. She wanted to scratch an itch on her forehead but knew she must not. Trying to relax, she looked at the radiographer in the mirror. She looked bored, stretching her arms above her head. Jane felt imprisoned in her straightjacket. More drilling. Having had a moment of music and then to have it drowned out was like being offered a feast, only to be told sorry, you can't have any, you can't even look at it from afar. The back of Jane's throat itched and seemed to be closing up; she was choking, felt that she had to cough. She knew she was having difficulty swallowing these days. What would happen if she moved, coughed, had to have a break? Would they have to start all over again? What if she *was* claustrophobic? Don't they anaesthetise some patients for this? She was too good at being good, too good at complying. She visualised numbers, did sums in her head, and the choking feeling went away. Everything vibrated now, including the bench beneath her. Between the bouts of 'drilling', there seemed to be more snatches of the music with the Don in a frenzy. Not the most suitable opera, after all. Perhaps the safe compilation of wallpaper Classic FM-type music would have been better.

The whole procedure took three-quarters of an hour. The woman thought they had the necessary images. Jane would find out the results when she next saw her consultant. That would be in three days' time, to finalise plans for treatment.

In a corridor in the hospital, Jane passed a vase of orange lilies mixed with purple flowers, and checked that they were real. They were. They looked gaudy, almost ugly. She wanted a soft image of something that would connect with baby Daisy.

The ordinary sounds of the street outside, the daylight, sunshine even, seemed pure and sweet. Well, soon she wouldn't know it, wouldn't even miss it. No ghastly cacophonies of noise, nor soft pure sounds. Unbelievable, but true. 'Probably', she added, when coming up against the full stop. For a moment, Jane wished she had kept some of those 'Miracle Recovery For Cancer Patient' stories she had read over the years in magazines. But no, that might make this more difficult. She preferred to think of this as an 'end phase', like when her father's body slowly wound down, a great engine spluttering to a final halt. And then… nothingness. She too would return to the non-existence that had preceded her conception. Yet she knew that her father was so alive in her mind that he did live on in a way.

Jane remembered that grassy mound in Istanbul where a tree grew directly on a grave, out of the corpse she was sure. It seemed perfect. She wondered why everyone was not buried in a cardboard or easily biodegradable coffin, and with a sapling directly over the body, so that as the body rotted the tree would grow.

She was sure she wanted to be buried, not cremated.

September 2003 – January 2004

During the five months of chemotherapy, every three weeks Jane had to go to the hospital for an infusion, which was over so quickly. She never wanted to bring anyone with her, for she needed to concentrate on the procedure, wanted to think positively about the cancer cells being killed. When she did not do this, when she tried listening to music or reading, she felt panicked and out of control.

Some of the other 'victims' waiting for their treatment looked so dreadful in the true meaning of the word, and so close to death. Jane did not want to think of herself as one of them. If she brought someone with her she would worry about their reactions to these walking skeletons. Bald heads, eyes hollowed out with fear, like concentration camp inmates.

The nurses were all pleasant, some too jocular for Jane, well-versed in upbeat banter. Jane no longer thought she had to join them if she did not want to.

The sickness after the first treatment was far worse than she could have anticipated. She felt as if she was being run over when already knocked down. She almost bottled out of the whole thing. But then, in the intervening weeks, her body rallied and her mind did what minds deceptively do with extremes of pain or trauma: she almost forgot the horrors of it. The subsequent treatments were not as bad.

When she embarked on the prescribed radiotherapy that followed, it was a relief to have something so quick and painless. She almost skipped into the radiotherapy room and leapt onto the couch.

Yet, she felt that despite it being 2003, it was all so primitive: last time around, with the operation, they had cut her; this time, they poisoned her. And then they burnt her with something that could damage vital organs if they misfired. But she told herself that if this was the state of the art, she was up for it.

MAY 2004

Music floated through the trees to the time of a polka, a tenor voice, like a strong branch, holding it together. The *Wiener Bürger* waltz was lilting and resonant in air so clear that the sound seemed to echo, to fall tumbling from on high.

Down by the lake, the little row of soft-coloured lanterns – mauve, lemon-yellow, pink – shivered in the breeze, and bright red, purple and acid green triangles of flags brightened and defined the wooden stage. All, it seemed, flickering in time to the music.

The French, thought Jane, were so good at making music to express emotion, to give ambience to every public occasion. The motley collection of instruments – a piano-accordion, a flute, and a drum – lent a medieval air.

Lennie and Jane lay head to head, their bodies forming a straight line. He lay on his front, his head facing sideways, resting on a bent arm. Jane lay similarly, her head resting on his strong forearm, their faces toward each other. Armagnac added to their relaxed euphoria.

Lennie had flopped down on a patch of grass beyond the small crowd and the trees after they had danced together; danced more fluidly and fluently than they had ever danced before, danced like sped-up puppets, or the teenagers they had been, danced on the worn grey wooden planks of the jetty, unseen by anyone who knew them, until their bodies refused to obey the commands of their spirits. Jane's illness did not impede her; aches in her body were ignored, she knew that most of the pains went away if she did not focus on them. Her weaker leg gave her dancing a lopsided gait, but she went with it, so that it became part of the rocking movements.

Jane did not know why she had chosen to lie head-to-head at that moment. She did it humorously, waiting to see Lennie's response, as her head appeared silently, bodiless and upside down right next to his.

He pulled out his other arm to gently stroke her neck and shoulders. The beat of the music syncopated with her heart; when it sped up, hers did too. When it became silent, she could feel her own heart's vigour.

Lennie, still supporting Jane's head on his arm, turned half on his side to shuffle around and lie at her side, facing her. She turned to face him. He moved his arm under her head to wrap it around her shoulders. Soon their bodies were pressed together with a strong seriousness. Jane felt as she had that time on Hampstead Heath, with Lennie, thirty-three years ago.

He kissed her cheek softly, then her neck, then her closed eyes, as gently as a butterfly's wing brushing a petal. Her steroidal swollen face felt beautiful. Tingles ran through her body and her palette thrummed as it did occasionally, as if some errant nerve was being stimulated.

The music continued to throb assertively.

Lennie seemed to take his cue from that, for his delicate kisses became urgent, passionate and almost biting. Jane awoke as if from a slumber, opened her eyes, and looked into his brown eyes. She felt her blood warming, and a need to swallow his kisses, to absorb them into her body.

'Yes, yes, yes,' she said, almost amused, and added, 'What, here?' But soon nothing seemed to matter except his passion, which flowed into her. So she lightly whispered, 'Yes, yes,' again, kissing him too, in a lilting waltzing way that went with the music and the warm weather and the blood coursing through her veins.

She could feel Lennie through her thin skirt, taut and hard, but neither had to attend to that – well, not in the way they used to, as if it was a master who could never be frustrated.

The singing beyond the trees changed to the deepest baritone. Jane felt a knot of tears in her throat, but crying would have dissipated the power of the moment, so she squeezed her eyelids tight. Despite herself, tears trickled out of her closed lids.

'Darling,' was all she said.

And what of Lennie? His deepest resources, like an underground spring, dark caverns of rich oil, oozed into the whole of his being, and like oil, it captured a rainbow, but a darkened rainbow of colours. From beyond the lake, a flute soared high, and Lennie felt like crying too, but words and tears would be too mortal, too finite.

He wanted to ascend to the clouds and the swallows and the flute at that moment, to fly with the highest leaves on the tallest trees, the bluest of skies above, the most airborne of larks dancing with each other, he and Jane, as light as spirits. Nothing could ever equal this moment. His sex was a part of his baritone self, but to bring it more into focus would have disturbed her ethereal soaring self. In a hoarse voice, he replied, 'Darling,' minutes after her utterance, but a perfect coda.

Both were aware of the something that had brought them together decades before. The fit, the perfect fit at times, his bigness and her smallness, his hardness to her softness, his rock to her water, his water to her rock at times.

'Darling' both said at the same time. And they laughed, and the laughter became a cascade, his louder and more tumultuous, hers echoing his and then finding its own impetus, and for a moment leading him back into laughter. No one else could possibly have understood that laughter. Laughter of relief, of joy, of escape, of love.

'My sweetheart,' said Lennie, but it could have been Jane who spoke.

'Umnn,' was all she needed to utter.

They were quiet and the quietness was as perfect as the laughter or the words.

'I don't mind dying, now.'

'I do. Mind you dying. Oh, my love. I couldn't love you more. My sweet. Life is so cruel. How can we… you…? No, my love. I won't be able to live without you, it's as simple as that. No… my love,' he spoke, into her sparse hair.

247

DOROTHY JUDD

She kissed his eyelids now, licked away the salt tears, told him that this would stay with him, that she was not dying in spirit, only in body. 'Darling love, I'm sorry. If I could stay I would.'

'I know. I mustn't burden you with what I'm thinking.'

'But I want you to.'

Briefly, he returned to his melancholy, to the beauty of the moment that was not to have a future, and together they felt the tragedy, but also the splendour of what they had. The music now returned to a quick waltz and they twirled together, not knowing that they were both having a similar fantasy, she wearing a long white muslin dress with a full skirt, a magenta silk cummerbund that emphasised her tiny waist, a white flower in her long dark hair, he in slim corduroy beige trousers, leading her in their revolutions around the dance floor, like that ball at Strawberry Hill when she had been only twenty and he twenty-four.

Jane did not know when their ways would have to part, but part they must, no matter how hard he tried to run to catch up with her, or she to dig in her heels. She sensed she would soon have to go on her own lonely journey, but that she would be looking over her shoulder for most of it, maybe for all of it. Like the story of Euridice. After all, not only Lennie would make her want to look back, but Daisy, Will and Tom. And, of course, Alice and Max and Eddie.

Now it was just the two of them, and they had earthly pleasures. Jane felt she was falling from a height, gently coming down to earth, to think about what had been a hard pressure on her abdomen, what had been an essential part of her marriage, that feeling of being wanted. The feeling of completeness it gave her, and how much she had missed it over the past – she did not know – how many years. Now too, on this late afternoon, it had faded.

She kissed him gently, and then licked his neck. The hardness returned. She smiled inwardly.

Not feeling perfectly safe, for there may have been a passer-by, she edged her more hidden hand down his trousers, and felt the freshness and warmth, as if it was the first time, and yet enriched by echoes of so many times when they were young.

'Darling, what are you doing!' Lennie said, purporting shock. Usually, it was Jane who worried about what was socially acceptable; she sometimes wondered how far he would go if she were to truly kick over the traces. She smiled a mischievous smile and undid his zip. And continued furtively, wanting to transport him, wanting him to have that rapture here, where it would have to be muted, and then in a way, all the more intense. She took her time though, and the rhythm changed from waltz to adagio to lullaby, until his body seemed to beg for release from the prolonged pleasure, and she quickened her pace and he soared as high as the topmost wisp of cloud, the sky a clear insistent blue, of an intensity that was also an inevitability. A brief gust of wind cooled their brows, and then he gripped her so tightly she thought her ribs would crack. Never before had he held her so forcefully.

Slowly, his heart rate returned to normal and gradually he released his pressure on her. She floated free.

He wanted to bring her back, 'Now you, Jane, now you.'

'No, I'm fine.'

'No, I insist. Come on.'

She did mean 'no', did feel perfectly happy, although her body had travelled with him.

His hand crept under her skirt. Up and down and beyond clothing until he found her. Both remembered the times before, like that time on the Heath.

She felt tired, and blocked in her body by the steroids, as if a muddy weir stopped the flow. But Lennie's hand gently teased and pressed and stroked her back into life, fully allowing the river to flow.

Through her current, she muttered that it was a miracle, that life was a miracle, that she daren't think too much about all that. 'Oh my love, I love you.' He smiled and kissed her.

She knew that rapture was in each of them, but how much stronger it was when someone shared it. She found herself thinking of Pierre, and of his way of just being, without imposing. Here Lennie was being insistent, directive, strong, and it was what she needed. So we are not clear templates, but can be capable of many formations, she realised.

She became soft and hard at the same time and allowed the orchestra to build up rapidly into the finale.

'Stop or I'll go mad,' she begged. He continued, extracting every ounce of pleasure, and a little more. When she really seemed to mean it, he stopped.

'So what if I die! Don't want to be callous, but anything more would be greedy.'

He stroked her arms and her back under her blouse in all the ways and places he knew she loved, like playing a mellow instrument he had played many times, knowing where and how to maximise its performance. He did not allow his sorrow at the counterpart to what she was saying to surface.

'Stop, darling. What if someone was to come by,' Jane whispered.

'Bit late now to worry about that!'

They both laughed.

'Better make ourselves look normal. At *our* age.'

They straightened their garments, and lay still, wanting this moment to go on forever.

As if in inverse ratio to the degree of intimacy between them, Jane began to feel that she could not stay with Lennie throughout each of the next three days of their short holiday.

For to be so close and yet to die were in opposition. She could imagine dying now with her love for Lennie reconceived, alive and warm inside her – in a way that freed her to go on her lonely journey.

How could dying ever be anything other than lonely, a final separation? Even if two people entered a suicide pact, she thought, their exits from the world would be individual and, in a way, lonely.

She thought of baby Daisy, and Tom and Will, and her three children. And Lennie. She saw them continuing their lives, busy, in the future without her. Of course, they would miss her. But what did that mean – to miss someone? They would find a way of living without her. She knew so much about the mourning process, had worked with so many patients who were experiencing it, in all its permutations. She had lived it first-hand when her mother died, and then Timmy, and then her father. If they really 'worked through' it, she knew her family would discover that what they valued about her lived on. Eventually. That was all very well – that was their task. She could not ease it for them.

But she was now deeply alone in her job of relinquishing and mourning life, this bitter-sweet life. The beauty and the pain, the gold and the shit. The love and the hate. The strange patchwork that men and women had spent millennia trying to make sense of. She did not know if global warming and other threats to the world as she knew it would put a stop to, or alter, those machinations. She hoped that baby Daisy, with her fresh limpid existence, would have a chance to live her life, to love and grow and be loved.

Increasingly, these days she could step out of all her musings and anguish and awareness of her plight and that of her loved ones, and think: *So what! What difference does it make? We all go to such lengths to live, but why? Isn't it more instinct than intellect?* She knew that philosophising made her task more difficult. Why didn't she just go with the flow, and exist without longing, without sadness, without regret?

Thinking about death and dying could make her feel nauseous. She did not know if the nausea was her illness, or if it was psychological. The various sensations in her body could be the cancer, or the chemo, or something else, or nothing.

She felt weepy in unexpected bursts on most days; she sensed that the tears were an overflow from a reservoir that she had hardly accessed.

After supper, Jane wandered out the front door, crossed the side road, and stood to look at the sky. She hoped Lennie would not come to find her.

The sun had dropped below the horizon, leaving orange and purple streaks that faded into transparent pale turquoise. The chapel, now semi-restored, stood before this very display. How still the air, and the chapel: more still than they had ever been when she was here before. A large hare that looked black in the fading light lolloped across a field. The two cypresses seemed much larger than she remembered, more perfect – not ragged as she had thought they were. How perfectly placed they were, to one side of the chapel, balancing the squat tower. She held her breath and listened to the distant cicadas, the occasional croak of a crow, the *tsk-tsk* of a huge agricultural sprinkler.

If she were to die tonight, she would have truly lived. She smiled at this thought, for she knew that she had had it before, in recent months, and that she would have it again.

Back at *La Retraite,* as they sat reading, Jane looked up and said, 'Darling, I'd like to spend some time alone tomorrow.'

Lennie was used to her clarity nowadays, her ability to say what she wanted, without consulting or considering his needs. Her words – 'If it's better for me, it may be better for you too' – came to his mind now.

'Sure, that's fine,' he said, as straightforwardly as possible. Nevertheless, she knew he found it hard, especially after their closeness in the woods. His response was slightly forced. She did not know if she should ignore it or try to help him with it.

She was familiar by now with this impossible dilemma. Should she follow her own need to withdraw from life and from Lennie, to ease her own exit, or should she try and please him, and his need to cling to her, to fuse, to pull her back into life as he had in the woods? Would that even redress the cancer, she dared to think for a second.

'Darling,' she said softly, reaching across for his hand. 'I can see how hard this is for you. I *will* try and stay with you, close, like this afternoon by the lake. But, but, I can't help having to also sort of move away, away from life to....' She took a deep breath, 'to withdraw a bit... to make it more... bearable for... myself. I don't expect you to fully understand.' She stood up so that she could bend and kiss his closed eyelids, 'Darling.'

In that moment, Jane knew that she would have to, indeed wanted to, give Lennie some of the satisfaction that he craved, the satisfaction of 'helping' her, even if it went contrary to her own instinct.

'I'm sorry. I don't want to hurt you, any more than you are already suffering. I won't have to be alone tomorrow. That's self-indulgent and may have been born of some struggles you and I had in the past.'

Lennie opened his eyes and looked at Jane as if from afar. Perhaps he had travelled away in that short exchange, to protect himself. Now he looked at her lovingly and somewhat dubiously.

'Darling, I don't know what to think now,' he replied. 'Perhaps you were right – perhaps you do need to withdraw or whatever you said. Perhaps I have to let go. Perhaps I'm being selfish.' He sipped from his glass of claret as if it was life-saving. 'But my instinct is to protect you, to help you as much as possible, to wrap you in my arms, to ease the way, so you won't feel all alone....' He looked down. Jane was sure he would cry. She held her breath, waiting. She knew that even in her dying, she was braver than he was.

He gave a wan smile, which she met with a questioning smile.

They looked into each other's eyes.

After a silence, Jane said, 'Neither of us are very good at this. We've not done it before. We don't know how, do we?'

He smiled with an expression of pain across his face, and his brown eyes became tinged with ochre as he looked at her with a great fire of love.

'Jane, I think I have an idea. An idea of what we do. You know how we joke that between us our minds make a whole mind – when you can't think something through, or remember something, and I can, or vice versa. Well, now, this is your journey, your plight, your time to be leading the dance. And I will try and follow. Just like you can be so wonderful when one of the children has a problem, and you mull it over and respond so admirably. I know I can be helpful too, in different ways. But right now, you have no choice but to lead. What was that song the children used to sing when they were in Infants' School – *Lord of the Dance*. And I will follow, as best I can. I may be clumsy at times, and not know the steps, but I'll do my best.'

This echoed how Lennie had said, 'I've done my best' in the past, and how it used to irritate her, for it usually meant he was being defensive and not owning some mistake or shortfall. But now she heard it as a sincere wish to try to enter this phase of their lives, as best he could.

But she felt frightened, frightened at this image of leading the dance. She remembered the sequence in *The Seventh Seal* – that line of dancers following Death against a lowering sky along the crest of a hill. 'But what if I don't know the steps, Lennie? What if I'm scared?'

Jane crawled into his chest as he sat on the sofa and he wrapped a big arm around her. The same arms and chest in a navy blue woollen jumper, enfolding her like a nutshell when her father died, years ago. How unquestioningly present he had been.

They stayed like this for a long time, until he had to move his arm, and the familiar pain in her side reared up. Reality would not allow them to escape for long.

'Darling,' she muttered. 'We have no choice then, but to play it by ear. To see what each stage throws up. Hmm, I'm not surprised that I'm reminded of being sick! But we'll do what we have always tried to do with the children: our best. I know it's often been far from that – but now let's try and do our best with each other, which may break down at times, but I know we can be quite forgiving too these days.' Jane felt she was being too mundane, yet she did not know another way of expressing herself. 'It's all we can do, isn't it.'

She came out from under his protection in her own time, grateful for the shelter, and for his quiet acquiescence, saying 'I don't quite know what that all adds up to – but perhaps you do.'

As she spoke, she worried that she was relinquishing too much, that the important steps of the exchange were lost. She struggled to say, 'No, I do know what we've said. We both know. We're a bit like babes in the wood, aren't we? But I'll try and find the beans or whatever the clues are in the Hansel and Gretel story – oh dear, doesn't that lead to the witch? Oh no, they're supposed to lead back home! What is "home" for me now?' She mumbled the last sentence more to herself, and then continued, 'I'll try and share some of these dilemmas with you, but... some of the time I'll be in the dark, and inarticulate. And please try and be patient when I can't explain adequately.' She knew he could nag her to explain or repeat herself when she felt that she did not want to. 'Sorry, love,' she added, shaking her head.

'We've both done pretty well, for one day!' he said.

Again this echoed his readiness to be self-congratulatory, but now Jane nodded and chose to agree with him.

'What about some supper? That restaurant – what was it called, Mon Plaisir? – we looked at yesterday in Ceneyrac, in that little lane? Do you feel up to it?' he asked. 'I know it's late, but I could ring them to see what time they close. I feel like trying some of the things on the menu that I noticed.'

She laughed at his healthy appetite and love of good food and wine. She could still share it some of the time and knew how to enjoy it vicariously.

They parked in the square and walked towards Mon Plaisir, his arm around her shoulder. She was glad that he was not maintaining the close sexual contact they had found earlier, by holding her waist or her hips in a way that would have led her to feel too connected to him, too open to her own and his bodily needs and the complicated exchanges that would mean. For now, to be soulmates felt better.

Jane thought, but did not say, that life was one big compromise, but when she truly managed to compromise, she did not always know the difference between that and something which felt wholehearted.

JULY 2004

Jane bought a book for each of her three grandchildren now, while she could still write and think with clarity. She agonised over whether the inscriptions were suitable, especially the reference to her death. She tried various drafts, but then decided that as there was no anaesthetic, no inoculation against the pain of loss, she might as well confront it even here. Perhaps one day, when they were older, they would each know what she meant.

So she inscribed each with:

To darling...
With lots and lots of love from Granny,
who could not have loved you more than she did.
Thank you for bringing such joy to my life.
I can't be sure that I can truthfully say,
'I will remember you always,'
although I would love nothing more.
But you may, hopefully, remember me always with love.
If I could stay here longer to see you
grow up I <u>would</u>, believe me!
All you can do is live, this thing called 'life'.
In part, you will be doing it for me.
You make it easier, but also more painful,
for me to say goodbye.
Big hugs and kisses,
Granny XX

It had not been too difficult to decide what book to give each grandchild. She gave a special edition of *The Velveteen Rabbit* to Tom, *The Bunyip of Berkeley Creek* to Will, and an old copy that she managed to track down on the internet of *The Runaway Bunny* to Daisy, though the parable about the mother always finding the baby further broke her heart.

She entrusted the books to Lennie to keep until they were needed. She was grateful that he did not read the inscriptions in front of her, as she knew that she would have had to deal with him getting upset once again over his loss when she could barely manage her own.

SEPTEMBER 2004

After one hospital visit, Lennie did not ask Jane how she had got on – she had been for a consultation with Dr Greenberg, and for a further round of radiotherapy for the pain in her bones.

On borrowed time now, she had attended the meeting armed with a list of questions for the doctor. She wanted to know how long a gap they might leave before she was offered more chemotherapy, and how that would impact upon how long she might have to live. Impossible questions, she knew. Jane was left feeling that a great deal of gambling took place at this stage. She could not make sense of the fact that her recent scans showed she had responded quite well to the chemo, and yet they did not seem to think she had much more of a chance now.

Jane felt there was still so much to discuss with Lennie, and yet she did not want to rush into it when Michelle – who cleaned and ironed – was there in the kitchen, and Max was going to pop in to borrow a spirit level. She laughed at the symbolism of this, for Max's spirits were indeed rather low nowadays.

That evening, over supper, Lennie did not ask her. Jane could have told him, but she decided that he was returning to his more self-centred self, that it took such effort on his part to really attend to her. She sensed that when he did really listen to her, he felt depleted somehow, and not enriched. She did not know if he was simply responding to her increasing need to withdraw, or was avoiding her, either through his neediness or because her situation was unbearable. But then was she becoming too self-centred, like so many ill people?

She decided to discuss the treatment options with Harriet instead.

Jane went upstairs slowly to the little room at the top of the house to sleep. She had to rest on the landing: dragging her weak leg pained her hip almost unbearably. She had been told that the muscle weakness was probably a result of the steroids. She wondered if she should ask for a stronger painkiller, like Oramorph. But worried that it would increase her exhaustion.

Jane chose to have all the curtains in the house dry-cleaned. She also arranged for a company to clean all the carpets and another to spring clean the whole place so that every trace of cobweb and dust was eradicated, and the windows sparkled. She bought red little sacks of pinecones impregnated with clove and orange that infused the house with a warm, engaging smell. She asked Michelle to spray verbena water on the linen when she ironed.

Jane was no longer seeing patients, except for two couples who came fortnightly. They had been coming for years and knew that Jane was ill. When she partially lost her hair and wore a scarf, they worried they were too much for her. Jane replied, however, that if she was seeing them, it was because she could manage it.

Later, discussing them in supervision, she decided – as had been the case with other patients – that it was better to have a planned ending than to curtail work in progress if she became too ill. She realised that she had been avoiding losing them, and the struggles they were engaged in.

In the final session with one couple, she told them truthfully how much she had valued working with them.

They had brought a gift of a large basket lined with a French checked cloth, filled with mangoes, pineapples, papaya, grapes and *marrons glacés*. She was grateful that they only produced the cornucopia from the lobby outside the room after the end of the session, for she would have found it difficult to work with it in the room. She was reminded of the ancient Egyptians burying their loved ones with food for the journey to the afterlife.

Jane painted almost every day, for a few hours every morning, before she tired. This was the first time she had painted for two years – since a holiday in Wales. At last, she had time to incorporate the driftwood she had collected for years into her work. She had always loved the way that the ocean eroded wood; how each piece had a history – partially revealed and partially hidden – and how they could look like the bones of creatures that never existed. How man might emulate these shapes, but never fully produce the same results. Then there were the aluminium drink cans that had rusted and squashed to the thickness of cardboard, which she had picked up on dusty roads in Tunisia and Morocco. And the peelings of posters she had stolen from walls in France, Italy and Greece. Ironically, a batch of the poster fragments from Italy were announcements of deaths, which had always intrigued her, long before she knew her own life would be so curtailed.

She could now assemble these oddities and stick them on board in whatever way she chose, unifying everything with washes, areas of wax relief, thin overlays and the crackled underlays of emulsion in chalky blue-greens and umber that reminded her of the colours of the sugar paper she had painted on as a child.

'It's ridiculous,' she said to Harriet, 'that I have to be dying before I make time to do this! I'm sure there's a lesson to be learnt.'

"Better late than never" has never rung truer,' Harriet replied.

Jane felt disappointed by this reply: her friend was not engaging in an exploration of 'why'.

Jane was making patchworks, she knew: her instinct to collect, salvage and save, to recycle and never to waste, now had a rightful place in her art. She had always loved to see artists' rough sketches, notebooks, marginal notes, their ways of making *aide-mémoires* with coloured blotches, and had always admired the work of Schwitters: his use of bus tickets, postcards and cuttings that were elevated to painterly collages. Jane's pictures and montages were bolder, more three-dimensional. She loved the paradox of ephemera or junk becoming *trouvés,* pinned down, kept and valued. She sensed that it had a much deeper meaning for her about the poignancy of transience and an attempt to arrest it, yet an awareness of the futility, for ultimately her art would disappear too.

Jane included the fine nature drawings she had made over the years, of flowers and twigs and insects. She was not wasting the old drawings, not confining them to sketchbooks that few would look at. These, with photographs she had taken over the years – black and white photographs of babies, of dilapidated doors and peeling walls – and small cuttings from magazines or newspapers, as well as a few swatches of fabric and antique braid and French ribbon, all added detail and the look of a noticeboard or scrapbook. At last, treasures that had accumulated in drawers, in her sewing box, and on her pinboards, had a purpose.

In one of her sketchbooks, she came across Pierre's drawing. She was not sure what to make of it now, thirteen months after the event. She almost laughed at the idealisation, the voluptuous youthfulness of the image, the naïveté, and yet it still looked like her: aspects of herself she liked, even now. Her wild and wavy hair, the shape of her face, the rather delicate hands, the sympathetic expression, all warmed her. She worried that Lennie would come across it after she died. It clearly was not one of her own drawings. And yet she did not want to throw it away.

She stared right into it to find Pierre and the way he had begun to give her something she had lost. Even now, she felt a deep tremor that was different from the warm feelings she and Lennie had re-established. Pierre was still a route to her young self that bypassed decades of patchwork. She would have to preserve the drawing somehow.

She took it to her local printer and made eight photocopies in varying sizes.

In the safety of her study at the top of the house, where she had created a work table by covering the desk with an oilcloth, she made an assemblage of torn fragments of the various prints, and after an hour of playing with them, she was satisfied with the arrangement. She stuck them down, some as delicate as onion skin, some overlapping, some half covered by thin tissue paper, a few coloured by Jane in watercolour or drawn over in wax crayon. The breasts, so firm in the original drawing, were now torn open in one fragment and intact in another, covered with dark grey in yet another, as if telling the history of Jane's illness and surgery, but also her revival. An observer would not necessarily see a picture of Jane, but a work that explored facets of sexuality and beauty and womanhood and the shadow of illness. Despite the shattered images, the whole was a woman with a statuesque splendour. The ambiguity of the place of the disease was how it was. Jane knew she would tell no one – except Harriet – about the drawing's origins, but say that she came across a sketch in a junk shop which had reminded her of her younger self, so she had bought it. She laughed at her own lie. Perhaps Pierre was a 'junk shop' to Lennie, but a treasure trove for her.

She destroyed the original, by tearing it into many small pieces, and stuffing them in an envelope, which she threw away. As she did so, she felt a deep pain in her left breast, which she had not had for a long time.

Although reasonably satisfied with the final work, she was aware once again that she could not altogether escape from her life of patch work, patchwork as a way of masking something like a tear underneath, or as a way of piecing together remnants rather than creating a new whole. It was too late to render something more singular in its conception and its execution.

She was unsure who to give this work to, if anyone. And whether to give Harriet one of her other assemblages.

Jane had often wondered if she should make a picture for each of the children, beginning with Alice, or Max, or Eddie. Jane knew she could be too directive, too much the leader of the dance, and perhaps it would be better to allow each child to choose the piece they liked best from what was a growing collection of about a dozen new pictures. Of course, they knew that after she died they could share everything of hers, other than things she bequeathed to friends or to Lennie or Ruth. But perhaps she could find a way of allowing them to choose something now. That might help her to bear to part with life.

She arranged an evening when all three children could visit after supper, without their partners. Lennie would be in South Africa on a brief trip to his parents, who were too old to travel to London. He had decided to go now in case it became much harder to go in the months ahead. Jane was glad that he would be away. That was one set of feelings less to take into account.

Her hair had regrown thickly, in a post-chemo curl, and now could be shaped. She had been lucky that the ice cap worked quite well for her, for she had never fully lost her hair. She had her curls specially trimmed by an expensive hairdresser and was pleased with the shape.

For this significant evening, she wore a long black taffeta skirt which she had found in a charity shop, and a new slim jade velvet jacket. She felt it was a waste to buy new things nowadays, but felt sure that someone would make use of the jacket after her. Around her shoulders, she pinned with a jet brooch an old Russian scarf patterned in black, white, and carmine, with touches of bright green. The black tasselled fringe formed a 'v' at the back. Her lack of appetite had at least granted her a slimmer frame, even if she did look haggard and yet strangely bloated from the steroids. She liked the rustle of her skirts as she walked, and felt quite matriarchal as she welcomed the children whose healthy glow she could absorb.

They drank, unusually for them, good champagne, and ate asparagus wrapped in smoked salmon, along with tiny blinis spread with cream cheese, surmounted by glassy orange sturgeon that looked like piles of rare pearls.

Max, looking particularly bright and neat with a very short haircut, said, 'What's the celebration, Mum? I haven't forgotten someone's birthday, have I?' The other two children looked embarrassed. Jane knew it was up to her to rescue the situation.

'Come on! You know what this is all about! Either we all cry together tonight, or we can try and celebrate life, your lives, Dad's life, the grandchildren's lives. And my life. There's plenty to celebrate – even if one of us won't be here forever.' She knew she was fudging the issue in her phraseology, but that felt alright.

Alice looked particularly troubled, biting her bottom lip. Jane worried – not for the first time – that she was, in particular, letting her daughter down by dying, and that now she was preventing them from crying if they wanted to, with her emphasis on 'celebration'. She decided that she would make time to be with each child on their own, soon, before she became too ill.

No one proposed a toast after Jane's general introduction.

She drank her glass of champagne rather hurriedly and poured herself another. The bubbles almost stung her drug-sensitive tongue.

'And you know I want you to each choose one of my *oeuvres* to take home with you.'

'Doesn't that mean "eggs", Mum?' Max interrupted, fuelled by the drink. 'But we are eating eggs, eggs of the caviar! *Hors d'oeuvres*!'

'Shut up, you great oaf!' exclaimed Alice. 'You know that "*oeuvre*" is French for "work", surely. Honestly, Max! And you don't think there's a fish called a "caviar", do you? *La caviare, une grande poisson rouge.'* All three children laughed.

Jane watched, not quite from afar, but familiar now with the sense of others' going-on-being. Relieved at their banter, she continued, '*If* you like the pictures enough, that is. Embarrassing if you don't. You'll just have to put it somewhere at home, and then one day you can burn it!' Jane felt she was becoming too garrulous, even macabre.

She told herself to shut up forcefully, a decisive pause between the two words.

'No, Mum, that will be good. I mean, yes. Really,' said Eddie. He looked at her with what she privately called his little foal look. 'Where are the pictures?'

'In my study. Studio, I should call it nowadays. Top of the house.'

Alice smiled softly, 'Yes, I've seen some of them along the way, when I've popped in. I'd really like to choose one. But how are we going to proceed?'

Jane remembered how she and Ruth had shared their father's possessions by taking strict turns in choosing. But she thought she should let them resolve this.

Max suggested they all go up now and choose, and then still have some time together downstairs afterwards. She was relieved to see Max in good form; he could be so withdrawn and troubled these days.

'Good idea – before I'm too drunk!' said Jane.

She led the way slowly to the top of the house, her knuckles white as she gripped the bannisters tightly, attempting to hide her limp.

In her study, she closed the curtains and switched on two lamps. Now the room with its attic slopes was bathed in a warm light; the buttermilk walls forming the perfect backdrop for the pictures, which she took out, one at a time, from a pile in the corner. With Eddie's help, she propped them in a row on the couch, and against the desk, and on the windowsill. Some looked too rough and ready now to Jane, too unworked. She was seeing them through different eyes and wanted to apologise. Again, she told herself to be quiet.

She knew that in the making of all art it was hard to know when to stop with a particular piece, and when to labour on. But then, she knew why the pictures looked hurried and was sure that they would realise too.

Alice and Eddie sat on the floor. Jane admired the way young people could sit on the floor with such ease, their legs crossed. Max perched on the arm of a big armchair, while Jane sat in the other armchair.

There was a moment's silence.

'Well, how about we draw lots as to who will go first, and second, and then each choose?' suggested Max.

'Okay, but let me think first and decide,' said Alice, getting up to peer closely at some of the pictures. She stared hard at the collage of Pierre's drawing, and then frowned at her mother briefly, before moving onto another picture. She returned to the first one. Searchingly she asked, 'Did you do that?'

Jane trotted out her rehearsed reply about finding it in a junk shop. 'But don't you think it looks a bit like me, when I was younger?'

Alice did not seem that bothered, for she was now looking at the other works. 'My goodness, you've certainly been busy, Mum! I'll have trouble choosing.'

There was a heaviness in the room at the implications for each child. Alice was putting the brakes on the process.

'What if we were to have two each, Mum?' she finally said.

Jane felt immense relief. Her eldest child had embraced the plan, and shown a hunger for the gift, in her own quiet way.

'Fine by me!' said Jane. 'There are so many anyway. That would leave at least five, and I'm still churning them out. You see, I need… it would be good, good to know, to see them taken away, by each of you. I'm sure you know what I mean,' she said, looking down tremulously. She wanted her children to have whatever they wanted of all her possessions. She did not know how to offer that degree of generosity and selflessness, and whether it could make her departure easier.

'Good', said Alice, trying to rescue her mother's distress. 'Won't be quite so hard now, if I can have two. One that is... no, I won't tell you, because the brothers may want the ones I think I want!' glancing at them with a smile.

Eddie wrote '1', '2' and '3' on three pieces of paper. They agreed that they would each choose a paper for round one, and then reselect for round two, rather than remain in the original order for their second selection.

The order that evolved was: Max, Eddie, Alice; then Alice, Max, Eddie. Eddie wrote this down, and the process began

Jane, as if from afar, watched her beautiful big children. Alice with her generous figure for she was still breastfeeding, Max with his tall frame and honest face, Eddie with his softer looks and long hair, watched how they moved about the room, her room, her private space, where she had often shut the door on the family in order to be alone. Eddie sipped his champagne. Alice had brought one of the plates of food, nibbled some asparagus appreciatively and then licked her fingers. Jane felt herself shrinking as they were growing, filling the room with their vigorous health and personalities.

Max said he should have brought his video camera: the evening would have made an interesting film. Alice said she wondered what Tom and Will would make of Granny's pictures: she thought it would inspire them to be more adventurous in their approach to materials. She said she imagined them 'picking rubbish, I mean stuff, off the pavement'.

Jane laughed, and said she could say 'rubbish' if she wanted; Kurt Schwitters had called his pictures of ephemera 'shit'.

'Okay then, are you ready for the selection?' asked Max in a mock-formal tone. Jane tried to ignore her chilling association of the Gestapo to that phrase, to which the children mercifully appeared innocent. This was not the first time that Nazi associations to her plight popped up.

Each child stood up, and as planned, Max silently selected his first choice: a greenish picture that reminded him of the sea, he said, with driftwood structures on it which he thought were like a raft. He swallowed hard.

They had so often taken turns in this way, to play charades, watched by the others attentively. Each one hated the situation that led to this charade of sharing, but went along with the game as best they could.

Eddie chose a complex detailed picture in which Jane had incorporated her old nature drawings. Photographs of coloured glass beads formed a decorative frame. Washes of sandy and burnt umber colours swept it all together into a harmonious whole. Eddie could not say why he chose that one – he just knew he would love it forever.

As Alice had two turns in a row, she went straight for the collage that had been made from Pierre's drawing, and then a soft painting in dusty rose colours, quite abstract, using old tin cans which had become twisted shiny shapes. She loved this picture's depth and mellowness, and said that she thought Jack would like it too. She smiled, glancing at her mother, as she took her two pictures.

And so the boys completed the process, although Max hesitated lengthily before he made his next choice. He asked the others if he could change his mind later, if no one had chosen one of the ones he liked. 'Of course – why ever not,' said Alice, in her eldest-child slightly bossy voice.

Jane watched, absorbed. She was touched by their choices, everything was working out so well. The only element of discomfort was the Pierre picture that Alice had chosen. She could understand Alice choosing this, as a complex statement about her mother, but was uncomfortable about the infidelity behind it. She knew she could justify it, as she did often in her mind – but now, for one of her children to have a picture born in this way, felt wrong. Jane sat still, surveying, stroking one of the bumps beneath the skin on her skull.

'How're you feeling, Mum?' asked Eddie.

'Fine. Really. Well, never that fine, as you know. But relieved that you're all sorting this out so well. Are you okay with your choice, Maxie?'

'Yeah, I think so. Never been good at deciding things...
It's either this one or this – possibly – instead of my second
choice. Mum, if I change my mind when I get them home, can
I swap them another day?' He glanced at Eddie's choice. The
old rivalry between them never really went away, especially
that way round.

She assured him he could, and called this her picture
library.

As the children put the remaining pictures away and
switched off the lamps, she wondered if she should reclaim
the Pierre picture. But, she thought, perhaps it was good for
Alice to inherit something about her mother's rebirth and
illness, all in one. She almost asked Alice why she had chosen
that one, but did not want to draw attention to it.

Downstairs again, in the sitting room, the atmosphere was
different. Jane felt weary and could not find the impetus
to give attention to each child in her habitual way. She saw
that Eddie was withdrawing, and that Alice and Max were
discussing a film that she had not heard of nor wanted to
know more about. Her interests were narrowing, she was
conserving her energies.

She offered to make hot drinks, or would they like some
wine or cognac? Max was not driving, so he poured himself
a cognac. Eddie came with her to the kitchen. He too looked
tired. Now was not the time to have a proper talk with him.
She asked how his job was – repairing and troubleshooting
computers, which he was so good at. He shrugged and pulled
a slight face.

She knew that his passion lay in writing, that the short
story that he had recently had published in an anthology had
spurred him on, so she asked, 'Any writing these days?'

'Don't know if I should talk about it, but yes, Mum. I feel
sort of, almost superstitious, that if I tell you I'm writing a...
a novel, it won't come true. That I dare not, that I'll be struck
by lightning!' he laughed. His tiredness disappeared.

She put an arm around him, feeling small next to him,
her baby, and said she knew what he meant, that being

the youngest may make it even harder to do this, to risk something that the others may also wish they were doing, or wish they could do. 'But you know, there's nothing to stop them. I think it's wonderful. I sometimes wish I had made more time to paint when I was younger... But I don't want to get into all that now, about my regrets.'

'I don't think it's so much the others – Alice and Max – as Dad, you know. I find it difficult to tell Dad about my aspirations.'

Jane could see the depths of the problem from her own subjective angle, as well as from her experience as a psychotherapist. All she said was, 'Well, that's a big one. We'd better take Alice her tea. But I think it may be... more a feeling you have than the actual reality. I know Dad can be a bit competitive with you and Max, like when he plays golf, or tennis, and I know he writes – academic stuff – but I'm sure he would be...' she shrugged, 'encouraging.'

As they re-entered the sitting room she asked him quietly if he wanted her to tell Dad? Eddie shook his head decisively.

Soon Alice said she had to go back as the boys would be up in a few hours; Daisy was sleeping through the night now. Eddie and Max observed their mother's tired face and said they would go soon. Eddie was giving Max a lift home.

Jane wondered if it was inevitable that the evening closed down with more unspoken than spoken business. She meant it when she said it had been lovely to see them, and how pleased she was that they had chosen paintings that they seemed to like. Eddie said that perhaps he had not said enough about the pictures: he thought they were beautiful in their simplicity: the big brush strokes and colour washes, almost a Howard Hodgkin feel to some, and yet so much fine detail, if one looked for that too.

Jane interrupted him, 'You don't need to say all that, Ed... sorry, didn't mean to stop you,' leaning against the hall door frame. 'I just get sort of doubtful at times about their worth, because they don't live up to my ideas or fantasies when I'm painting. Such a struggle. So when you praise them, I worry that you're seeing something superficial that doesn't, in fact, connect with my vision or my realisation. Oh dear, too late for a seminar. Get your coats!'

'Mum, I didn't mean to say they're pretty. I can see the struggle too, you know.'

'Sorry, Eddie. Yes, I appreciate all you're saying. I know you do know how hard it is: I mean, how much to try and put in, and what to leave out, of a small space.'

They all looked at their mother – Eddie rather anxiously, Max detachedly, and Alice with great love as she hugged Jane goodbye. 'Give my love to Dad if you speak to him. I know he'll be back soon.'

There was always one of the children she was worried about. 'Part of the job,' Lennie would say. Jane felt she had hardly touched the surface with Max this evening. She hugged him hard as he left. Eddie and his mother exchanged meaningful warm looks and a gentle hug.

Jane wondered, while she locked up and turned off the lights, if she would manage to really resolve her relationship with Max before she died. Over the years, he often seemed irritated by her in ways that implied that her very being was wrong, was not what he required, no matter how hard she tried. She had often speculated that he had never recovered from the betrayal by the birth of Eddie, only a year after he was born – as if nothing could really put that right. This upset her more than most things these days.

She cleared away their glasses, and put the Armagnac away, then changed her mind and brought it out of the cupboard again. *Why not?* And poured herself half a tumblerful. *What if it clashes with my medication?* She sipped it. It burnt her throat but she felt animated by the immediate effect on her brain, how it suddenly gave her a different view of everything. Ah, no wonder they sometimes prescribe marijuana.

With the drink at her bedside, she undressed. The Dvořák quintet that she had grown to love recently gave shape to her slight dizziness. She lay in the dark in the centre of the big bed, wearing only her petticoat under the duvet. Her taffeta skirt stood like a termites' nest on the floor, the jade jacket flopped on a chair, her tights spread across the bed. How lovely to be alone. The drink pulsed through her veins, made them feel heavy and hot, and the music filled her with its power one moment and its gentleness the next. She knew she was finding those qualities in herself: strength and soft melting lyricism.

Why worry about dying? Maybe dying can be like this.

She would ask Harriet – not to help her die, but what the best cocktail would be. Not that Harrie would tell her. Perhaps she could find out on the internet. There wasn't much you couldn't find out these days on the net.

She turned back to the music now. Jane knew she always found surprises with music if she really went with it: like dreaming, it was a way of plumbing her unconscious.

She began to feel an abundant aloneness that filled her up: not lonely at all, but resplendently full. She paused, hearing the phone ringing downstairs. She had switched it off in the bedroom. It stopped. After a few seconds, it rang again. Jane worried that it might be Lennie ringing from South Africa, that something might be wrong. Or Alice – the little ones?

She turned the music down with the remote control and picked up the phone by her bed. There was a brief silence, and then, 'Jane? *C'est toi?*'

She heard a strange voice, someone speaking French.

'Yes?' warily. She immediately checked in her mind that she had double-locked the doors downstairs.

'Jane, it's me, Charles. Pierre,' speaking French with a southern accent. 'Sorry to disturb you. Is it okay to talk? You can always put the phone down if it's not. Not okay.'

She sat up to put on the lamp. 'No, it's fine. Really.' But her heart was racing.

'How are you? I've been thinking of you. Just wanted to say that I really appreciate the help you gave me last summer, and above all, *how are you*? Your illness?'

She didn't know if she wanted this conversation. She had managed to pull herself back into her position in the family and in her marriage, and was now gently steering or being steered to her final exit. Pierre's reappearance felt disruptive.

And yet, and yet, she thought, perhaps she wanted this? This chance to say goodbye to him, and maybe thank him.

'Where are you?' she asked. 'Not in England?'

He gave a deep chuckle, 'No! No such luck!' His spirit, his youthful callousness, seeing the world through his eyes, flashed back to her mind. Not much had changed. She felt like telling him that the last thing she wanted was for him to be in London.

Perhaps he sensed her silence, her ambivalence. 'No, I'm in Avignon. Nice place. Going to College here, studying... landscape gardening. It's two years, maybe three if I go on to... But,' he halted, giving a little cough. Jane thought that he had been cut off in the silence. Then, 'Been in the clink, prison, for a few months. Released early for good behaviour. Felt I had to tell you. For stealing... you know... But it was important in a way. Had a chance to think, to really see how low, how bad I had got.' She could hear him sighing. 'Terrible people in there, the warders as bad as the criminals. Are you there?'

'Yes, go on.'

'At first, I was angry, thought I didn't deserve all that, saw myself as superior to them. Called myself a 'resident', which didn't seem so bad. But then, one day, when the sun was finding its way into my cell, I thought about Giselle, about her giving up, and her sort of... bitterness. And about you, how you seemed kind, and loving, in spite of everything. I knew I had a choice: to look at the damp dark corners of the cell, or at the bright windowsill, the way the bars' shadows angled out across the floor in a striped pattern. I stood in that squashed rectangle, felt some warmth, my face towards the sky, and thought there's no point in going on blaming others. I had to start doing something with my life. Are you listening? Should I go on?'

'Yes, Pierre, yes. Of course, I'm listening.'

'I even thought, then, that I had earned something better, that I had been punished enough for... my sister's ...'

There was a pause. 'Are you sure you want me to talk to you now?'

'Yes, Pierre. Yes, really.' She did not know if her racing heart was the alcohol or him, again.

It seemed easy for him to resume. 'What I really want to say is, somehow, the days I had with you were more important, they started me... I know I nicked, stole your car after that, but... oh God, sorry.'

'No point being sorry about that now, Pierre!' But as Jane said this she felt churlish and knew she was not allowing the real meaning of his story to reach her. It was as if some vestigial hurt, even humiliation, needed to be expunged first.

'No, I meant sorry to go on like this in the middle of the night,' he responded. 'But you're right... Only I've had this conversation with you so often in my mind. Can't believe I'm actually speaking to you now.'

Jane let his words flow. Returning to her more relaxed, almost drunken state, she easily slipped back into speaking French, interjecting with, 'Yes, yes,' once or twice. Yes, she too wanted this contact.

He managed to convey that her respecting him, seeing beyond his dishevelled state, had stayed with him and would never go away.

As she lay there and listened, what he said connected with something in her, how he had seen beyond her age and her illness, her class and her culture.

'Pierre, thank you. Thank you for telling me all this. I'm glad you're on track, seems you'll be okay. You have your health, and life ahead of you. And I hope you'll meet someone... or perhaps you have?'

'Yes, well, I have. A young Algerian woman. Cécile. But you know, she's special, and I don't think I'd... I don't know. But I hope you don't mind...'

'No, Pierre. Don't be ridiculous!' She made her voice sound hearty. 'I'm married – you know that – and my husband and I have got closer because of my illness, maybe. I'm not lonely at all. Really. More and more, I'm glad when others achieve good things in their lives, especially now. I've been busy having treatment and busy feeling ill!' She did not want to go into details with him. How strange that she and Pierre could still feel such intimacy and yet be so very far apart.

He asked her more about her illness.

'No, really. I'm too tired now. Sick of the whole subject. But I have gained a few extra months by having treatment.' She heard his sharp intake of breath. 'You know, chemotherapy and radiotherapy, and now I guess it's… downhill.'

Not wanting his long-distance commiseration, she rushed back to, 'Okay, then – I just want to say something to you, though, Pierre,' her voice soft and calm. She closed her eyes. 'I'm glad you phoned. I've thought of you often too.' She was unsure how to let him know how important he had been to her. He slid into seeing her as needy so easily that she had to be cautious. 'I too valued our time together – as I think you know. But it wasn't only the sex – it was something about you, can't easily explain… But believe me, something rare, that gave me great optimism.'

He replied, 'Yes, yes,' in a quiet way, as if to facilitate her. She suspected that he did not know what to make of what she said, that he would never know her side of the encounter.

'Let's just call it something of a mystery,' she said. 'Perhaps some things cannot be analysed.' She knew she was being intellectually and emotionally lazy – alcohol and tiredness and the illness sometimes left her like this – but that the circumstances could not be otherwise.

'Now, Pierre, I must get some sleep. My husband is coming back tomorrow,' she lied. 'But before we say goodbye, do you want to tell me more about your sister's… suicide? I mean, I read about some of it, but I don't think I ever really understood one of the most puzzling things: why she chose to die near your mother's grave?'

'Oh my goodness. Yes. Well.' Clearly, he was stalling. Jane did not know if he was too pained to talk about it.

'I've given it lots of thought, Jane. Felt so… guilty – still do. Even though she implied in her note that she was mixed up in something sinister, probably at work, I still feel that I may have played a part in her despair. It's hard, you know, when you row with your last remaining relative.'

'But Pierre, she left you her money, didn't she? So she couldn't have hated you.'

'That's true. That did make me feel better at the time. But not deep down. Oh yes, by the way, I never explained to you that I was so anxious about being discovered by the police because I had already lost my licence – for drunken driving, I must confess. And I really stole her car, without permission, because I was still of the mindset that it should have been mine. I feel so, so bad – words can't say what I feel – but that's useless now – and, yes...' He paused. 'I think she decided to top herself, got hold of the poison and all, and then wanted to die close to Maman. Strange. You know, dying is lonely, especially suicide. Don't know really. You still there, Jane?'

'Sure. Of course. Go on.' She realised he was not acknowledging Giselle's probable anger with her mother.

His voice sounded muffled. 'It seems too neat or, what's the word, "ironic"? to die near Maman. And to think I very nearly died too, down that precipice.'

Jane listened to Pierre's outpourings and thought that he needed to tell her all this. Perhaps she was the only person who knew him at that dreadful time of his life. 'But, sorry Jane. You didn't expect this long answer, did you?'

'No, but I'm glad you told me. I've had enough of... bad stuff. We both have. Must go now. Sorry, but I'm tired, very tired.' She felt a deep exhaustion that no amount of sleep would really restore.

'I wish you well, Pierre. I guess this is "*adieu,*" not "*au revoir*".' She was better at this than he was.

'But Jane, I want to pay you back, for the money you gave me, at least. What is your address? Or your bank details?'

A flash of anxiety crossed her mind. Her trust in him had been so damaged that she momentarily thought that he could be plotting another theft through her bank. But no, she couldn't go on thinking like that. 'No, Pierre, it wasn't a lot of money. Really, don't bother. You can look at it as something I wanted to do for you, a little gift. But hold on, where did you get my phone number from?' She wasn't even sure if he knew her surname.

'Ah ha! Not so difficult really. You know you asked me for your friend 'arriet's number? Well, I wrote that down before I handed myself and your phone over to the police. It's a miracle that with all I went through, I didn't lose the piece of paper I wrote it on. It was kept amongst my personal stuff by the prison authorities while I was "inside". Then, today, I phoned 'arriet and said I was a friend of yours from France, and asked for your number. She sounded surprised and a bit cautious. First, she checked if I knew whereabouts in France you'd stayed. Because I gave the right answer, she gave it to me!'

'Goodness, it's not only me who can be a bit of a detective.' She knew she and Harriet would have to have a conversation about this.

'Okay Pierre, thank you for ringing. And I'm really sorry indeed – that sounds so inadequate – about what happened to your sister. Terrible. I want you to know that – of course. I'll be thinking of you. Bye.'

She put the phone down gently, but still sensed that he found it abrupt. He had not said goodbye.

As with so much in her life now, there was little that seemed gradual. Jane also knew how much she took the initiative in saying goodbye, even ordinary goodbyes to people she would see again. Life was one big rehearsal for the final farewell.

The Armagnac seemed to have left her body. She turned on her side and was surprised by how sleepy and relaxed she could still feel.

Jane dreamed of a big house being renovated. It seemed to involve her and Lennie. A big interior wall had just had the doors plastered over, so that there were no longer openings. In the dream, she felt this was a mistake and was going to have a doorway put back in.

When she recalled the dream in the early hours, she felt that it was about her way of foreclosing things now, but with a sense of overdoing it: she needed to make sure that she and Lennie could still pass through that wall. Perhaps the conversation with Pierre had prompted this dream of keeping Lennie out.

She saw the intrinsic paradox in her instinct to withdraw from life now, and her wish for her and Lennie to be able to pass freely through the walls around her. She began to think that the dream was connected with the way Pierre had helped her to feel in touch with her own interior space, and how she wanted to put to rights the lack of access for Lennie.

She often puzzled over what indeed had developed between her and Lennie during the past year. She could not have explained it to anyone, not even Adrian. But somehow Lennie seemed less caught up in his own sexual world when they made love: as if he saw her more for who she was. Perhaps her withdrawal had shocked him. Or was it her illness? She knew that we only really appreciate someone when we do not take them for granted.

It really was a now or never chance, a way of expressing gratitude. She sensed that Lennie was grateful too.

Jane looked forward to Lennie's return. She hoped that when she withdrew nowadays, he understood that it was not like the summer of last year when she had fiercely kept him out to preserve her identity, but it was because she had no choice but to go with what was happening to her body and her mind.

Oh, she had railed against it, had cried and wailed when alone. She sometimes chose to sleep apart, and in the mornings she or Lennie would creep into the other's bed. But Jane needed some night times of being quite alone, to feel the fear, and the absurdity of life, the cruelty of something so precious being snatched from her. There was something about the *dead* of night – no wonder more people died at night than in the day – that freed her from earthly constraints and allowed her to plummet terrifyingly but essentially to her depths. All her rational perspective would desert her and Jane would find herself right back to how she felt when her mother died when she was only twenty. Standing at the graveside, watching shovelfuls of clay thudding like lead onto the coffin. The outrageousness of it. She had wanted to leap in there and join her, *Mummy must be all cold! How could they?* And her father, standing there too, a drop of clear mucous as bright as glass suspended below his nose, so pitiful, and no one to comfort him. Or her.

She saw her father's death following in quick succession, even though there were twenty-nine years between the two. Deaths have a way of concertinaing time, like the carriages of a train crashing into the buffers. For Jane, the word 'loss' was a collective noun. And inevitably, little Timmy's death was a part of the multitudinous loss, coming as it did so soon after her mother died. Why did she ever bother when life was so cruel?

But in those night-time lamentations, she knew that there was such beauty and joy, such mellow goodness in the world, and that was why she minded, why it did matter, why death was so painful. She used to think that it was always worse for those left behind because they had to suffer over a long period. But now, facing what felt as sudden and as shocking as a firing squad, she realised that it was worse for her. The words of a young woman she had worked with, who was dying of leukaemia, came back to her: that it was worse for her because she lost everyone – others lost only one person.

Most of Jane's adult life she had explained and accepted death as the other side of life. Now she was sick of that fact. No amount of philosophising could help her with what felt cruel. Gaining months had been at considerable cost: extremes of illness from the treatment. At times, the treatment itself almost killed her, when her immune system plummeted, and she was a prey to every bug around, when she shivered and suffered with utter weakness.

Dr Greenberg had said she had responded quite well to the treatment, and mentioned the possibility of another drug, Taxol, after she had given herself a rest. Jane discussed this with Harriet, but decided to call it a day. Further gains were likely to be one step forward and two back. She tried to stay with a perspective that saw a season in everything, and how impossible it was to fundamentally alter that pattern.

In one of her despairing night times, she thought of storing up a cocktail of drugs, to put an end to everything while she was still able-minded. The metastases in her brain scared her more than anything. The doctors said they had shrunk, but she knew it was a question of time – like saboteurs they lurked in the dark. *Why suffer any more?* Thoughts of at least discussing it with Harriet, and possibly having a consultation with Adrian, calmed her.

She got up to make herself Horlicks and when she returned to bed she ignored the pains in her body, the numbness in her leg and arm and tingling of her fingers. She had discovered that if she meditated on clouds high in a blue sky and tried to float with them, the pains lessened. But a new difficulty in swallowing and a slightly constricted feeling to her breathing frightened her, and made her more resolute to end it all. She did not want to call it 'suicide', for she was simply accelerating a process that was inevitable.

OCTOBER 2004

Harriet was doubtful, and said that those attempts often failed: people frequently vomited up the drugs, it was hard to get the right cocktail, and that no one knowingly could be with her at the end in this country where it was illegal. Indeed, anyone who helped Jane could go to prison for up to fourteen years. 'Of course, if this was Switzerland it would be different,' she said, holding Jane's hand.

The two women were sitting in a corner of the café in Regents Park, where they had been for a gentle walk to see the autumn colours. Few people were there on this wet weekday afternoon. Nearby was a bed of pink roses valiantly continuing to flaunt their petals, like women well past their prime who still wear bright short frocks, although many were straggly and beginning to fade. Within their line of vision, the trees, through their clarity and scale, defined near or far or mid-distance. Beyond the glass, they watched the squirrels attempting to salvage food from a bin.

Jane knew that Harriet, yes even conscientious Harriet, had bunked work to ride here on her bicycle.

'How do you know that your own death will be so dreadful, Jane?' Harriet talked softly, turning her back on the people in the café, enclosing Jane with her presence. 'You know that death in the normal course of events can be peaceful, and the pain controlled nowadays. Of course, you know all about good hospices or teams who come into people's homes, to help them and their families?'

'But what if my *brain* goes, Harrie! What if I become deranged! What if I no longer recognise my family. Imagine that for all of them. And then it will be too late to take it into my own hands.' She felt like crying but was too numb to what she was saying to fully enter into the horror of it.

'Jane, that is a risk, but not a very big one from what I understand. You said that Dr Greenberg said your brain mets have shrunk. Well, other things may pack up before they grow again.'

'What may 'pack up'?' She looked her friend in the eye. Harriet knew she should not have said that: like pointing out a monster being eclipsed by the present terror.

'Really, Jane, it's awful knowing so much about all this and being a friend, a close friend. I think I mix it all up, even though I try not to. Perhaps you shouldn't ask me anything. Sorry.'

For the first time in their relationship, Jane saw a cowardly side of Harriet. For a moment, Jane felt triumphant – so Harrie was not perfect – but soon realised that if Harriet faltered on this, it would be almost impossible for anyone to manage.

Jane took a deep breath, 'You're probably right, Harrie. I'm sorry.' She noticed tears in her friend's eyes. *Oh God, just when I need her so much.* 'Sorry, Harrie,' she repeated. 'It's me who should be sorry, expecting the impossible of you. No, I need you as a friend above all, you know that. Let's try to keep it that way.' She put an arm around Harriet's shoulders.

'Sorry, Jane. I shouldn't be snivelling.' She tried to laugh away her tears.

'Oh God, what a sorry conversation. So many "sorries". Let's just get on with the important things that we both have to manage and accept that we're both struggling. Okay? And I'll keep my medical worries for the doctors and nurses at the hospital. If I can.'

'Jane,' said Harriet in a small voice, 'if you're determined, you can look all that up on the internet, as you probably realised. About… 'assisted suicide'. And, a last bit of information before I take off my nurse's hat: if you end up in hospital – not a hospice – you never know – you can ask for "Do not resuscitate" status. They should ask you that anyway. That means that if you were to go into cardiac arrest, they won't call a crash team to revive you. I've seen that, even at end-stage of someone's life. It can be shocking, brutal even. You know you don't want that.'

Now Jane was moved to tears by her friend's courage and straightforwardness. She put a hand on Harriet's arm and squeezed it gently. 'Won't be able to thank you afterwards, will I? So I'm thanking you now.'

'Stop being so bloody poignant, Jane. I think I should get you one of those chocolate muffins,' diving into her rucksack for her purse.

'No, the coffee walnut cake, please!' Jane didn't particularly feel like eating anything, but knew that Harriet loved her erstwhile appetite for food and sweet things. 'And another cup of tea?'

One morning when Jane was alone with Tom for an hour while Alice took Will – with Daisy in her buggy – to his music group, Tom looked at his grandmother's swollen stomach.

'When will the baby be borned?' His eyes stared at her abdomen and then up to her face. She didn't know whether to laugh or cry. Kneeling down awkwardly, she placed her mug of tea on the floor, and put her arms around him, 'Granny isn't well, Tommy. I think you know that. The big tummy is from the medicines and the illness. Anyway, I'm much too old to have another baby! You probably know that too. That's what your Mummy can do instead now.' She tried to sound light-hearted.

He looked deep into her tired eyes, while she gazed into the brightest hazel eyes she had ever known, and with a profound hunger wanted to brush her lips over his downy cheek. She had felt such closeness with him ever since he was a baby.

'Is there anything you want to ask, Tommy?'

He was silent, and then, looking askance, 'Why do people die?'

She took a deep breath. 'That's a good question.' She wasn't sure if he meant 'why *people*?' or if he was questioning the dying itself. 'What do you think?'

'I know cats die, and dogs, and hamsters, and ants, and worms, and umn, leaves, and umn...' he glanced sideways at the fruit bowl, 'Do apples die?'

'Yes, all living things die, eventually.'

'But does an apple die if you eat it?'

Perhaps he was finding a useful side-track to avoid the real issue. She replied, smiling wryly, 'Yes, in a way. Or if you just left it on the grass, to... rot.'

But straight as an arrow, he zoomed into her with, 'Will you... rot?' his intense eyes blazing with a hint of anger.

'Yes, Tommy. When I die. Eventually.' Again she felt like laughing and crying at the same time, so her voice came out all bubbly, 'I won't know though, will I, because my brain will be dead too. And that way... you know... everything sort of goes back to the earth.' She could answer him so well because she adored him, because he was intelligent and deserved her most honest answer, even if it hurt both of them almost unbearably. But she knew she was only describing a physical process and not everything else that mattered.

'I don't think dying's a good idea,' he said. And then he looked away. She realised she needn't have worried about leaving out that side of things.

'I know. I don't either, most of the time. But there's not much we can do about it.' Her arm reached further around the small shoulders, which felt frail and bony.

He nudged the mug of tea with his chunky shoe and knocked it over.

'Does tea die when it spills on the floor?' he asked in a defiant tone.

'Don't know. Sort of. Let's get a cloth.'

Tom seemed to have had enough of this conversation, and so had Jane.

November 2004

Jane began to see beauty all around her, of such raw intensity that it was as if layers had been stripped from her eyes and her soul.

Dead tulips as thin as tissue paper, transparent even, petals clawed round to enclose their stamens. How fecund the stamens were, so full of pollen when the tulip itself had died. Tulips in November, imported from some hothouse in Holland.

People were always bringing her gifts these days – exotic fruits, rare flowers, poetry, music – a silent acknowledgement of so many 'lasts' for her, to capture the sumptuousness of the world. As if she had to shore herself up for the lonely journey ahead. They did not realise that ordinary things were remarkably beautiful, that she did not need further stimuli. Perhaps it was mainly their need to feel they could influence the inevitable. No, she countered. It's their love for me, of course it is. She felt pained and humbled.

White ranunculi bowed their pom-pom heads devoutly, even the fine hairs on their pale stems looked purposeful. A cup of hot chocolate, topped with a spiral of milk. A pigeon with its white collar like a plump prelate sitting still in a streak of sunlight on the lawn. The grain in the wood of a chair; the worn edge of an old table – how many hands had eroded the sharpness? Soap bubbles capturing a rainbow of colours. Sun warming her through the glass. The wind in the chimney, like a distant ship's siren. Shadows of leaded window panes casting curved dark lines that no artist could have devised. Branches pregnant with rowan berries swaying weightily in the wind. Life was everywhere and nothing was ever truly still or meaningless. At night, the sky was not really dark, the moon and the clouds gifted each other an ethereal beauty. She relished the little pictures framed by the window panes, moving her head to improve the compositions: a perfect small cloud in a pink sky; a magpie like a Christmas fairy atop a fir tree.

Leaves chased each other round the garden, then lay still gathering strength before the next gust of wind when, in a frenzy of circular patterns, they danced and played, cavorted, gambolled, frolicked, whirled and shuffled, frisked and waltzed, then rested, now next to different bedfellows, only to start up again. Sometimes, it was just one, sometimes others followed.

The shadows on the green grass made an endless moving pattern that Jane never tired of. She loved the two-dimensionality of shadows on a flat surface, two-dimensions denoting three. She knew it evoked more than ever the patterns and shadows of branches dancing when she was a baby, bundled warm under the hood of her pram, looking out from her dark cavern at the play of trees and winter sunshine – her earliest memory.

Jane was not surprised that her relationship with time altered. She could feel it racing, or going very slowly. She could count the days, tick off the months of the doctors' prediction – although it had been vague – and think of each day beyond as a gift. Or she could ignore the pulse of clocks and dates as best she could. She tended to do some of all those things, although she found herself adopting the way she handled time when on long holidays: she tried not to register the date or count how many more days, but to bathe luxuriantly in a sense of time's soft elasticity and rhythm, and yet accept its mischievous or even tricky games of playing with pace.

And so with the relief of not thinking about too many imperatives upon which time insisted, time drifted and floated, gentle as a bubble on water. Time became the spaces between dreams some days, days punctuated by sleep at odd hours. On other days, time's proclamation was as loud as the clash of metal on metal, sending shudders up Jane's spine, making her heart pound.

Paradoxically, the less time Jane had, the more she managed to do. She sorted out old boxes in the loft one weekend with Lennie and Max, made lists and sketches of her special jewellery and who she wanted each piece to go to, even updated the family photograph albums, sorting through photos that had not been catalogued for years.

She read, with a measure of detachment, through a few precious, old letters – only a shoebox full that she had kept over the years – exceptional letters and cards from friends, a few from her first analyst when he had been ill decades ago, notes from Ruth. The children's notes and letters were in a separate box, which Lennie would keep now. In the box were amusing rhymes and poems from Lennie – she destroyed the more sexual ones. But she left some and a few other letters in a bundle tied in lavender ribbon, with a label which read:

> To Lennie, Alice, Max and Eddie.
> One day you may like to read these. Not all are
> of interest, I think. But you never know.
> Couldn't bear to throw them away.

She tore up the letters and cards that were too personal or which only she would understand: tore them slowly, methodically, seeing it as a severing from the past. The thought, *But what if I live after all!* lay coiled in a corner of her mind.

Jane left a note about her books, giving her psychoanalytic journals and books to a needy and developing library in South Africa.

She wanted Harriet to have something special. This was more difficult to decide than many things. Perhaps it was

Harriet's selflessness that made it hard to think of something material that would be meaningful to her. She decided to give her all her poetry books, and her almost-new expensive walking boots (which she had bought in a wave of optimism soon after the recurrence) as they wore the same size, even though Harriet had a perfectly good pair. She put a note inside one of the boots:

> *Dear Harrie,*
> *You know how I hate waste, and how much*
> *I like recycling things.*
> *Climb some hills – or, knowing you, mountains – for me.*
> *Love, Jane x*

Finding time for this attention to detail was a luxury, and made her quite playful. She wondered if Harrie would look in the other boot and expect some note there, and where would their posthumous correspondence end?

She bequeathed to Harriet a cherished garnet brooch set in silver. She could not imagine her friend wearing it, though.

As an afterthought, Jane remembered a photograph she had taken of a beech forest in autumn that Harriet had admired – even though Harriet was a better photographer. The picture showed a glade through which the sun shafted onto leaves and moss. She had it framed in a broad walnut frame. On the back she wrote:

> *To dearest Harrie,*
> *You always gave me special space, like the*
> *clearing in this picture.*
> *Even when you may have felt overcrowded yourself.*
> *In fact, like the sun, you threw light on so many things for me.*
> *Thank you,*
> *With love, Jane*

She wondered if she should leave things specifically for Lennie? She imagined Lennie eating the food she had prepared in the freezer in the months to come, and wondered how he would feel about that. The freezer was well stocked with all the usual things, as well as Jane's carrot cake, chicken soup, and a lamb casserole.

Jane felt weaker by the day; her left arm was almost useless, and her left leg heavy and uncooperative. The vision in her right eye had deteriorated recently. Swallowing was increasingly hard, so she preferred liquid foods. A Macmillan nurse, Claire, acted as an intermediary between Jane and the hospital, paying attention to symptoms, providing medication, following up the results of scans. The ever-smiling specialist nurse at the hospital, Felicity, was still involved and made home visits, but it was a struggle for Jane to feel grateful for her input.

'Well, Jane, how're we today?' Felicity asked one morning, visiting Jane when Claire was away.

Why 'we'? What's that all about? Jane thought desultorily. 'Fine. Well, sort of. You know…' Forcing herself to continue, 'Nothing much to report. Constipation, as you know, but I think that Laxi – what's it called, is helping. Been swigging the Oramorph about every six hours.'

Jane turned away to look out of the window, to draw comfort from a pair of overlapping fir trees, like Siamese twins.

Felicity took Jane's temperature and felt her pulse while looking around the room at the cards and books.

Neither woman could find anything worthwhile to say. Jane knew she was saving her energy for a few people.

'Well, is it adequate? The Oromorph, I mean.'

And so their exchanges continued over the days.

Another day, Felicity asked hesitantly, 'Jane, I've been wondering, wondering if you are, *umn*, a bit low, you know, understandably?'

Jane almost laughed. 'Look, I can see why you ask, and what you're saying, but I'm sorry, I just don't have the energy to talk about any of that...' She silently completed her sentence, *'with you'*. 'I'm okay, really! I do talk to some friends. Thanks. And... thank you for trying.' Sinking further back into the pillows with a slight smile in the corners of her mouth, she thought that at last, she had the best reason on earth not to have to make others – well, some others – feel better.

She needed to have a few hours' sleep in the day, every day.

Her determination to pursue a few more errands increased.

In a large branch of Zwemmer's – which she visited by taxi – Jane searched for, and found, a magnificent book of photographs of landscaped gardens from all over the world. She marvelled at the way that nature left its mark, even when tamed and controlled: how the water irises in a formal pond expressed a vigour and flamboyant splendour while everything around them was clipped; how a well-placed Japanese acer danced like fire on a smooth rolling lawn. She intended to post the book to Charles Baudier at the University of Avignon, Department of Landscape Gardening. But later, she thought that she was being ridiculous. It may never reach him, and they had said their goodbyes. She did not need to reach him in this way.

Instead, she decided to give the book to Adrian, hoping that he would appreciate it. It was too late to work out with him how her gift to an ex-lover could be transferred to him. She wrote inside it:

Thank you for all your patience and understanding
over the past few years. I (probably) could not
have managed without it –
although you gave me the capacity to think that I might.
With gratitude and love,
Jane Samuels

She told Lennie that the pile of gifts to be delivered would need a lorry. He did not reply. So she said, 'Perhaps the hearse can do a round of deliveries when it's dropped me off.'

'Stop it, Jane!' But he grabbed her and hugged her. They knew they could never tell anyone some of the jokes they shared.

But she lay awake that night, thinking that she should have bought that book for Pierre after all, even if it never reached him. Of course. She ordered another copy from Zwemmer's.

Strange that she was giving the same book to Adrian and to Pierre. Both facilitators, of course.

Dear Pierre/Charles!
Thank you for your vital part in my life.
I wish you good health and happiness.
Love
Jane x

She managed to post it one afternoon.

Jane suffered another bout of hair loss from a short course of chemo – a trial drug which they hoped would further hold the cancer.

She hated her appearance now: the puffy steroidal face, the scrawny body, the swollen stomach, the loss of her waist, her hair so thin and fluffy. She joked to Lennie and Harriet that she looked like a baby orangutan. At least she had always been fond of baby orangutans. On another day, when looking in the mirror, she was reminded of a baby bird that did not yet have all its feathers. She hoped that most people would see her real self through all this.

She began to avoid seeing certain people – those who seemed to be visiting out of duty or because it made them feel better, or whose own upset loomed larger than her own. Lennie was her gatekeeper. She allowed family members and close friends to pop in more or less whenever they wanted to.

Jane felt increasingly fatigued, even though she was no longer on chemotherapy. A persistent headache lasted for days on end. When she felt unwell, everything she did was a struggle – like trying to build on soft sand. Back pain, nausea, other symptoms, scans, results, Macmillan nurses, telephone messages, medication, and side effects could fill her days.

But she decided not to allow them to. Now, more than ever, she needed to do what felt good *'for me'*, she said to herself. Those two little words, quite simple but relatively new to Jane, were now brought out and polished. She had tried to adopt them years ago, when she was in analysis, but had pushed them aside.

She still had to attend to some of the onerous tasks, but they were all cushioned or punctuated by reading a poem, or lying down and listening to Beethoven's string trios, or a short visit to a Vuillard exhibition, or poring over Bonnard's intimate interiors in a big book she had had for years, but had rarely really looked at. Or phoning Harriet, or being with Daisy or Will or Tom, or Alice or Max or Eddie. She gained succour from family and friends, watching their lives from a little distance. She was content with the balance. The good things seemed to lessen the physical pains and weakness.

And sometimes, being with Lennie was *'for me'*, though Jane could never predict the outcome with him.

As her body was clearly becoming more ill, Jane reached the point where she recognised that it was too infiltrated by cancer, too spoilt, for there ever to be a major turnaround. Like a machine that gradually slows down and operates haltingly, so Jane began to realise that she had no choice but to accept the appalling situation. Her physical state led the way for her mind, which had been far more resistant and protesting, but which now, in waves, allowed reality to register.

For years, Jane had earmarked favourite pieces of music to be played at her funeral. Now, this idea was becoming a momentous reality, like a play that was to be performed after years of sketchy rehearsals.

She found that there were far too many wonderful pieces to begin to select the definitive ones. She struggled with the power of some of them, and the knowledge that other people may not feel the same and may even find them too long or tedious. Just as she dreaded boring people in life, so she dreaded 'going on too long' after her death. She even wondered if it would be better to leave the choice to others. Some were far too poignant, and she could imagine her children or Lennie being overwhelmed if she arranged for them to be played.

One such piece was The Beatles' *She's Leaving Home*, which she loved because it evoked her mid-twenties with Lennie, her memories of parties and dancing, and the clear narrative that conveyed such an understanding of the main relationships in the story. Now she herself was 'leaving home' to the incomprehension, she felt, of Lennie, like the parents in the song. It seemed too raw a choice. She considered the duet from *Rigoletto* between father and daughter, about the death of Gilda's mother, but yet again it was probably too heart-rending.

She asked Harriet to make a tape of part of the slow movement of Schubert's Quintet. The overture of *Don Pasquale* was added as a gift to Lennie, one of their shared specials, which they grew to love on holidays in Umbria where it perfectly suited the landscape.

It now seemed obvious to Jane that she wanted to be buried in the vast Victorian cemetery near their home, among the chestnut trees and the tussocks of grass, the eroded statuary and grand tombs, the olive-green canal over which herons sometimes flew.

The different 'quarters', like areas in a city – Greek, Turkish, Afro-Caribbean – gave it an international feel that her family liked. Her parents were buried there. Above all, she wanted to be buried near Timmy, who lay there in his preposterously small grave. Whenever Jane visited the graves and stood by one of them, she could see across to the other two. Although there had not been room to place the family next to each other, she felt they kept each other company. She felt sure her mother had watched over Timmy when he was first buried.

Some of Lennie's family were buried in the Jewish cemetery in Golders Green. He wanted to break with tradition and choose this rambling, varied, and far greener resting place for himself too.

Jane said she wanted a non-denominational funeral, and left it to Lennie to arrange. Normally, she was so organised – 'so controlling' as Lennie used to say – this was her last chance to relinquish some of that. But Jane could not dispense with worrying, worrying that it was all too much for him, and she felt twinges of guilt at what he was going through, both now and in the future.

The difference between dying at home and dying in a hospice was like the difference between giving birth at home and giving birth in a good hospital, Jane realised. She would, on the one hand, have either her own familiar atmosphere which she could control to some extent, but carry the risk of frightening emergencies that might make her feel that she had made the wrong decision, or medical expertise and reassurance in a place that could feel impersonal.

'Well, where would you rather be?' Lennie asked, looking into her weary eyes, whose green-grey colour had faded.

She took a deep breath, anxious that on this point it would be too much for everyone if she spoke the truth. How much tidier it would be for the family to visit her and then return home. She and Lennie had touched on this many times, but now that she had a catheter, needed more nursing, and was in bed for much of the time, the question loomed large.

'I really would like to stay at home.' She looked down at the floor, at the oak herringbone parquet, concentrating on the neat pattern. She forced herself to state her wish and not betray herself. 'If you can manage, and if it's not too difficult,' she added. She felt a flicker of tearfulness in her nose, but remained calm. Jane wished that Lennie would state clearly that it was *his* wish, but that was not forthcoming. Nowadays, these things did not worry her in the way they used to.

Physical weakness, a floaty feeling, not unpleasant, enabled her to go with the flow. But months ago, when she was in France, she may have been clearer, may have said, 'Whose death is it anyway? Lennie, this is your last chance to man-up! '

Alice, Max and Eddie drew up a rota to come in for several hours every day and evening to help Lennie with domestic chores and to be with their mother. Harriet added her hours of help most days, as and when was appropriate.

Jane did not find it as difficult to ask for things as she had anticipated.

'Could I have a cup of camomile tea?'

'I'll just ring for the servant,' Lennie quipped.

Another time, the glass of water she had requested was not immediately forthcoming.

'What does a woman have to do to get a drink?' she said. Lennie laughed with her.

Jane found it increasingly difficult to swallow. Felicity was in frequent telephone contact with Lennie and visited every two days. She arranged for a doctor to put up a drip via a cannula to hydrate Jane with fluids. Jane was sleepy for much of the time from the Oramorph, which she administered herself from a pump. Her discomfort with Felicity was unabated, but as Lennie seemed to find the nurse helpful, Jane tried not to mind the visits.

One of Jane's pleasures was a nightly cup of Horlicks. When she could no longer manage this, she found it hard to believe that she could not swallow: one moment she could sip liquids, and the next it was impossible. It did not seem that the transition had been gradual.

'Surely, I have to be able to eat and drink, Harrie? It makes me a little panicky to think I can't.'

Later that day, Jane and Harriet were listening to a CD of *Ulysses* and the narrator had just got to the line: 'He ate off the crescent of water biscuit he had been eating...' when Jane interrupted. 'Harrie, do you think I'll never be able to eat again? Or do you think they can unblock something?'

Harriet tried to sound jocular, 'It's not like getting Dyno-Rod in, you know! This does happen... with what you've got. Not that unusual. Probably something pressing on the oesophagus.'

'But shouldn't I have it scanned?'

'Do you really want that? And if they see exactly what the cause is, what then?'

'You mean, it's only one thing when there are loads... like... mending one hole when the whole... I don't know... balloon is perished.'

'I never thought of you as a balloon, even on the steroids!'

Jane remained grave, 'No, I think I meant, like moving one boulder off the road when an avalanche will cause more and more.'

'Yes, Jane, it must be awful now to realise you can't eat or drink.'

'If I'd known, I'd have relished my Last Supper more. Can't even remember what or when that was.'

The two women smiled at each other with mirrored looks of poignant amusement, tinged with horror.

The CD had ended.

Jane lay back on her pillows. Harriet noticed a tear reach Jane's neck, yet her eyes looked dry. She remained quietly there.

Gazing through the window, Jane could see mostly bare trees sharply silhouetted against the steel-grey November sky. A few leaves moved in the breeze while all around seemed still: like the flicker of life in her, she thought, still going on, in an increasingly static environment. She avoided touching her distended abdomen, but knew it was becoming grotesque.

The next time she looked out the window, the trees and shrubs were undifferentiated black, the sky navy blue. Harriet was still there.

'I must have dropped off,' Jane said.

'Darling, I want certain people to visit me. Harriet, of course, and Ruth. Especially Harrie – unlimited access, please. The close family, of course, whenever they want. I know this may sound contradictory, but I want a time every afternoon – say, after lunch – of a few hours, alone.'

After a lifetime of negotiating and wondering about others' intentions, Jane now simply stated what she wanted and left it to others to take care of their side of things. Except when it came to the grandchildren.

'Don't know what the little ones will make of my state. Someone should be with them when they visit, of course, to explain and support them; especially Tom, he's so aware.' After a pause, '*Thank* you, Lennie. I know how hard all this is for you.' She could not fully encompass what that meant, nor unravel the legacy of any muddles between them.

By choice, she lay alone for hours in the afternoons, watching the winter sun stream through the windows to dapple the wooden wardrobe with lights like small glinting minnows.

She thought that a day might come when she understood things that she could not now understand. But then she remembered that she was dying and that nothing could be postponed. She felt the sun warming the scene without fully reaching her blood. She must simply accept that there was much she would never see now, never read, never come to know and understand.

That was how it was.

Forcefully, she breathed out her realisation of the coming end. She wondered if it was a fair exchange to become part of infinity, of the universe, of all that was unknowable. Drifting back into sleep, it felt that nothing could be more luxurious than infinity.

And when she half-woke again, she found that multitudinous questions remained with her, like the little golden fish swimming on the cupboard, spawning more and more, forever. *Was this the same afternoon or another one?* Perhaps she was already drifting into non-being, bobbing among the waves, already departing? But how could she go to something that was nothing, a void, a space? Then she thought of her excitement as a child when she first learned about osmosis – the experiments they had done with straws in school, the way the air pushed (or was it pulled?) sap up a stem in defiance of gravity. *Thank you, Miss Marsh, for explaining it so well.*

She felt her own essence moving in such a way, less clearly perhaps, with more fluttering, but propelled on a mighty journey out of life into eternity. The thought brought her solace. Happiness even.

She remembered the mighty contractions with which she had given birth to her four babies. Perhaps dying was like that, the body racked by forces beyond its control. How ironical that Greenberg had given her a death sentence of 'nine months'. Well, it had turned out to be fifteen and she no longer needed to count.

Now she saw herself as a small boat putting out to sea, leaving Lennie bereft on the shore, more careworn than ever, his face too pained to watch her go. When he looked her way, his mouth contorted into a smile, but his eyes said, 'Don't go! Please! I can't manage without you.'

Smiling to herself, Jane realised that in her fantasy he had not asked her how she was, but her smile was a smile of acceptance. She felt blessed to feel all that she could feel. Perhaps some of it would filter through to Lennie in the time that was left.

Later, awake in the middle of the night, she found herself wondering how strange it would be not to inhabit the world any longer, not to have wants. To know that she would never again watch a hyacinth break from waxy upthrust leaves, hard almost as plastic, into the heady scentedness of flower, before shrinking into the unkempt skeleton that carried the promise of next year's bloom in the bulb. Never again would the knowledge of the coming spring help her to endure winter, nor registering the year's shortest day, marking the turn towards the sun. How strange that she would no longer look forward to Daisy's next visit, with her brief shy smile and imperious gestures, and the softness of her hair, as fine as the fluff of a dandelion in seed.

> *Dear Life,*
> *Thank you for the plenty I have received.*
> *Amen.*
> *Amen.*

December 2nd, 2004

The end crept up upon them, one night at two a.m. Maybe it is never fully expected. Maybe death always steals from life. Or is it the other way round – as Jane had begun to believe – that our lives steal from infinity, before and after our brief sojourn?

Jane was drifting in and out of sleep, as if drunk; the world grew dizzyingly remote, and then swam back into focus. She quite liked the feeling, being in the arms of something far greater than her or any mortal. She gave herself morphine infusions through a syringe driver whenever the pains in her back or her abdomen began to register.

She was in her own bed, her and Lennie's bed, the bed in which they had conceived Alice and Max and Eddie – Timmy had been conceived in their old house, in another bed. The one in which Eddie had been born, the one that had been splattered with blood and semen and juices and breast milk over the years. How messy and basic human beings can be.

And now, this bed was like a ship carrying her forth into the unknown.

Lennie was at her side, holding her hand. Alice was sleeping in an armchair on her other side.

Once Jane had imagined candles and sumptuous scents of sandalwood and geranium, intimate and palatial at the same time. Instead, there was the powerful perfume of freesias – masses of them. Harriet must have known and bought what looked like at least eight bunches that she had delivered herself that day. They were amassed into a splendour of delicacy, white and ivory and virginal blooms erupting out of lime green calyxes, next to Jane's bed. Flowers that would outlive their recipient.

A small lamp lit the scene with a chiaroscuro glow: the walls amber, the white quilt blessed with cream where the light rescued it from violet-grey shadows.

Buffeted by waves, low waves on the shoreline, riding in and then dragging back the pebbles, as inexorable as the breaths that her lungs had taken for the past fifty-six years. Her mind wanted to say, 'Let go. Stop. Peace at last.' Her body, like a leaf skeleton without substance, craved quietude.

She did not know if she was thrashing around, or if it was the waves on the shoreline.

Nor if she, Lennie or Alice gave morphine from the pump, but sleep came, not thickly and heavily, but richly patterned with phantasmagorias.

Jane dreamed of a colourful burgundy place tinged with coral and pale ginger, where her focus was an image of a large penis, a wide penis that she wanted and found, with its strong shaft and exquisite dome, and which she incorporated fully. Lennie was in and out of her consciousness – or unconsciousness, for it was a dream – wholly there, giving her this prized possession, sharing it fully.

She half awoke in the pleasure and surprise that she felt, slightly embarrassed for Alice was there, wasn't she, somewhere in the shadows; but Jane glimpsed Lennie's benevolent face and now she knew she could float away.

She breathed deeply, and yet her breath was suspended as if she didn't need to breathe any longer, for she was becoming a different substance from flesh and bones and blood. Her head was full of air, intense cerulean air of such purity. Earthly breath was irrelevant. And yet she felt a heavy pull down towards the centre of the earth.

Jane emerged from her state of semi-consciousness,

'Verdi's *Requiem*, again.'

Amidst the elevating universality of the *Sanctus*, she squeezed Lennie's hand with her remaining strength and mumbled, 'I'm cold. Darling... warm my feet.... Isn't there something in...?'

'*Henry IV*?' he replied, as if scrabbling for the words, while he lifted the duvet to hold her cold foot in both his hands and massaged it.

A terrible rattling began in Jane's throat, issuing from her depths. It filled her head and Lennie's and Alice's – who awoke with a start – and like her father before her, Jane unwound from the skein of life. She spluttered haltingly, and then stopped. And restarted, as if this was a false alarm, but then stopped again, started, stopped, each breath after an interminable pause that the two witnesses, also holding their breaths, could hardly endure.

Jane was drifting on the swell of the ocean, on the bosom of waves far out at sea, until she sank, gradually – coming up for air which her body thought it still needed – and sank again. As she descended into the depths from which she had come, her whole being filled with white lightness even though, beneath the water, it was dark.

The Verdi continued. Lennie and Alice stayed with the music and did not want it to stop – father and daughter linked to each other through the hands they each held, linked through the woman who would always unite them, although her hands were becoming colder and harder.

By the time silence filled the room they could begin, falteringly, to believe what had finally happened.

ACKNOWLEDGEMENTS

Thank you to:

Denis Judd for encouraging my writing, both in principle and in practice, and for reading much of it.

Valerie Sinason, Anne Lanceley, Rebecca Mascull, Mary Adams, Felicity Weir, Sylvia Paskin, Eric Liknaitzky, Olive Somers, Anita Woolf, Gabi Maddocks and John Woods – all of whom, over the years, have read and encouraged this and other novels.

Tessa Dresser for post-writing encouragement.

Ron Britton, Dina Rosenbluth, Alex Tarnopolsky, and above all Margaret Rustin – the analysts and therapists – for their implicit encouragement, and for helping me to think over many years.

Lindsay Clarke for his inspiring workshops.

The Arvon Foundation.

Loic Germerie for his intelligent translations of English/ French.

Leila Green for detailed editorial attention and encouragement. And for rescuing another novel from the slush pile.